ALSO BY JULIA GREGSON

FICTION

Jasmine Nights

Band of Angels

East of the Sun

NONFICTION

Emigrating to Australia (with Caroline Sutton)

Crossing Borders (with Alex Pownall)

MONSOON SUMMER

JULIA GREGSON

TOUCHSTONE
New York   London   Toronto   Sydney   New Delhi

Touchstone
An Imprint of Simon & Schuster, Inc.
1230 Avenue of the Americas
New York, NY 10020

First Touchstone trade paperback edition August 2017

TOUCHSTONE and colophon are registered trademarks of Simon & Schuster, Inc.

For information about special discounts for bulk purchases, please contact Simon & Schuster Special Sales at 1-866-506-1949 or business@simonandschuster.com.

The Simon & Schuster Speakers Bureau can bring authors to your live event. For more information or to book an event, contact the Simon & Schuster Speakers Bureau at 1-866-248-3049 or visit our website at www.simonspeakers.com.

Interior design by Jill Putorti

Manufactured in the United States of America

10 9 8 7 6 5 4 3 2 1

Library of Congress Cataloging-in-Publication Data is available.

ISBN 978-1-4767-2526-0
ISBN 978-1-5011-3976-5 (pbk)
ISBN 978-1-4767-2530-7 (ebook)

For Sarah, Charlotte, Hugo, Natasha, and Poppy

- PART ONE -

Wickam Farm,
Oxfordshire

- CHAPTER 1 -

When I was young, and we were very alone, my mother tried her hardest to make the world seem a nicer, gentler place for me. Once during a terrifying thunderstorm she told me I was not to worry, it was only God moving his furniture in heaven, a thought that kept me rigidly awake all night.

Another time, in Norwich, where she was taking care of an elderly widower, I saw, on our way home from the cinema, what I now realize were two people having vigorous sex in an alleyway. They were playing trains, she said, and when I said it looked nothing like the trains we sometimes played, when we put the soles of our feet together and cycled them round and around, she laughed, or maybe she smacked me. You could never quite be sure with her.

But that time, driving to North Oxfordshire on a wet November night, she was fresh out of cheerful things to say. We were going to Wickam Farm, home of Daisy Barker, my godmother, my mother's friend and sometimes employer when all else failed. Daisy had invited us down "for reasons, we'll discuss when you get here," which was more than fine by me, not just because London, bombed out, boarded up, rationed, was so depressing but because I loved the farm. It was for me a place of refuge, but for my mother, for reasons I didn't understand, a place of shame.

Sheets of rain fell on our taxi's windscreen faster than the wipers could keep up; on either side of us, hedges as high as small houses narrowed the world down to wet lanes ahead, gray skies above. It was quiet there too—just the whoosh of water, the croak of a wet pheasant.

A herd of Jersey cows, steaming from the rain, stopped us at the Roman ruin crossroads. Our taxi driver, a dear old boy who'd earlier looked as if he might die happy under the weight of my mother's suitcases (she had that effect on men), burbled away, trying to catch her eye in the rearview mirror. Lately, he said, he'd driven all sorts to Miss Barker's: missionaries, school teachers, nurses, even some black people. "Doesn't she run some sort of Indian charity there?" he asked.

I felt my mother stiffen beside me. "No idea," she said in her most Home Counties discussion-closed voice. "Haven't seen her for absolutely ages."

Behind his head, she dug her nails into my hand and rolled her eyes. The impertinence of the common man was one of her themes since the war, even regarding conversations she'd started. But that was my mother all over, a medley of mixed messages.

We'd come to the iron fences that marked Wickam Farm's boundaries, and around the next corner, when I saw the long drive, the pollarded ash trees, the dark woods beyond, my heart stirred. We were here: Wickam Farm, the closest place to home I'd ever known. Daisy was here.

Daisy, with her large and generous teeth and her honking laugh, had become something of a mother figure to me, though she had no children of her own. It was Daisy who'd encouraged my nursing ambitions: "Something solid and useful to go back to when the war is over." And Daisy who when I was accepted at Thomas' took me up to Garrould's to buy dresses and aprons, the navy blue suit and little hat.

Daisy, who looked endearingly like an overgrown schoolgirl, had before the war run an orphanage in Bombay, written books and political pamphlets, and during the war, come home to manage the farm, which had been requisitioned by MI6 and become a boisterous dorm for a cast of artists, bohemians, and academics who'd lived there. I'd spent as much of my hospital leaves as I could down here, and when I'd listened to her debating with the clever men around the kitchen table, I'd seen their equal in intelligence and bravery. I couldn't wait to see her.

The porch light went on as we drove up the drive. Daisy, wearing a man's coat and galoshes, dashed down the drive shouting to the driver, "Ware! Ware!"—an old hunting cry—to warn us of a new and enormous pothole in the drive. She flung her arms around my mother.

"Glory, how wonderful to see you!" That made me happy. I wanted other people to love my mother even when I couldn't. I buried my face in the old tweed coat. "Daisy."

Daisy said the drive was so dangerous now, it was safer to walk the last hundred yards. "Would you mind frightfully carrying their cases to the house?" she asked the driver. "Oh, aren't you kind!" He trotted off happily. It was one of Daisy's many gifts to make everyone feel they were an essential part of whatever action they were involved in.

Wickam Farm was a handsome, three-story, late-Victorian building with low gabled roofs. Tonight rain had left a halo of mist around it, giving it a ghostly look. Its peeling windows wore a shaggy gown of Virginia creeper through which four faint lights peeped.

A horse cantered to the gate to greet Daisy.

"Bert was demobbed after the war." Daisy rubbed him between the ears. "His owner was killed, so we bought him for nothing, didn't we, Bert? At the world's largest horse auction, the Elephant and Castle sale. Half the poor loves go for horse meat now." She handed me a piece of bread to give him. I felt the soft velvet of his lips in my hand, and I saw his dark eyes gleaming in the half-light, and I took a deep breath.

"I'm so glad to be back, Daisy," I said with more emotion than I'd intended, aware that my mother was standing, shivery and taut, beside me.

"We're a job lot at the farm at the moment," Daisy said, as

we crunched up the drive. "I seem to be running a sort of ex-Raj boardinghouse—I say, do watch out." She flashed her torch down another large hole. "Ci Ci Mallinson's back from Bombay with her daughter, Flora, she's rented the upstairs bedroom, plus I have various doctors coming and going from Oxford, and of course Tudor, my half-brother."

My mother's grip tightened on my other arm. She'd told me in a deliberately casual way on the train down about Tudor, aged forty, old by my standards, unmarried. Owner of half the twenty-acre farm; Tudor whom we'd never met and who might, just might possibly . . . Well, I knew the rest, because as my mother, an incorrigible matchmaker, never failed to point out, men were a scarce commodity after the war and I was approaching the fatal abyss of thirty, when "a woman loses her bloom. Not you, darling—and don't you dare roll your eyes at me! I'm only thinking of you."

"Tudor was at boarding school most of the time I was in India," Daisy continued, "so we're getting to know each other again. We've delayed supper in your honor."

"Sorry if we've held you up," my mother said, on the defensive already. She went on about the cows, the rain, the shocking condition of the road.

"Glory,"—Daisy put a steadying hand on my mother's arm— "I'm just so happy you're here."

The shadowy hall was as I remembered it: The crunchy fur of a lion skin beneath our feet. The severed heads of foxes, deer, a tiger, staring coldly down. (Daisy's father, a civil servant in Mysore, had been a keen shot.) The sweet familiarity of dog smells, bacon, soups, and damp raincoats.

"We'll need the smallest room first," my mother told Daisy, whisking me into the downstairs cloakroom. "Won't be a sec." She locked the door, whipped off my hat, and got out a lipstick—a sample with no proper lid—and tried to dab a little surplus lipstick on my cheeks.

"Mummy, for God's sake," I said. "I can do it myself if I need to." I pulled away from her, washed my hands, and tried to control myself.

"Trust me, darling," she said, "you do. You're so pale, we must get you on a tonic soon."

"Not the tonic!" I said in my pantomime voice, knowing we mustn't fall out now. Her gorgeous black hair crackled like a forest fire as she brushed it and she was breathing hard. To calm her I put a slick of lipstick on.

"There." She straightened my dress, shot her big brown eyes up at me. "All done. What a fuss you make about nothing."

Conversation stopped as we walked into the dining room. Four pairs of eyes swiveled to look at us, not in a friendly way.

"So . . . introductions"—Daisy's amiable smile did not falter—"before we tuck in."

"Close the door first," said an impatient male voice. "There's a hell of a draft."

"Tudor, my love,"—Daisy closed the door with her heel—"this is Kit! The wonderful nurse I was telling you about." She twisted the knob on the oil lamp so I could see him, a thin man dressed in shooting clothes, plus fours, and a green waistcoat, with one of those very pink English skins that look as if they could peel off in damp weather, a high forehead, and gingerish hair that was already receding. He didn't look or seem like Daisy at all, but then he was only her half-brother.

"Tudor," Daisy said, "is frightfully interested in archaeology and knows all the Roman sites around here." When Tudor raised a languid arm in my direction, my mother gave me a little dig in the back. *Sparkle*, its message. *Go bendy.*

"Soup, please," he said to the figure on his right, "before it gets cold, butter when you're finished."

"And that is Ci Ci passing the butter," Daisy continued. "Or Mrs. Cecilia Mallinson if she prefers. Recently home from Bombay."

An old lady, late sixties I guessed, dressed in a lurid kimono,

waved vaguely in our direction. There was a King Charles spaniel
at her feet. "I hadn't quite finished with it, Tudor, but as you like it."

"Kit and Glory," Daisy continued, "have kindly agreed to help
me with the charity." My mother's eyes flickered in my direction.
Daisy, who'd bailed us out at intervals over the years, was always
good about explaining our presence here without denting our pride.
"But Kit's been nursing at Saint Thomas',"—she smiled at me—"so
she deserves a bit of a break first."

"Oh, well done, you, that must have been ghastly," said Ci Ci. "Is
the mother the Anglo-Indian one?" she added, making me think
Daisy had briefed them before we arrived to avoid any conversational pitfalls. "Looks awfully white to me."

I felt my mother flinch. Of all forms of introduction, this was
her least favorite. "And this is Ci Ci's daughter, Flora," Daisy continued smoothly.

A plump girl, early thirties, made her way crabwise to her place
and sat down.

"It's the pea and ham again," her mother said. "Did you wash
your hands?" She took a scrap of ham rind from her own plate and
put it in the dog's mouth.

"Flora was a land girl in Wiltshire during the war," Daisy
explained. "Fearfully hard work."

"Hello, both." Flora, who had a kind, sweet, hopeful face ("gormless," my mother described it later), held out her hand across the
table, her dirty knuckles visible for all to see. My mother, who had
a horror of germs, took it gingerly.

"Are you still nursing?" Flora said, handing me the soup. Same
old lovely Royal Worcester tureen and battered silver ladle with
grape vines on it.

"Yes and no," I said. "I'm studying again hoping to go back
to . . ." I could see my mother silently shaking her head. I'd promised, on the train, not to mention the midwifery course too soon.
"To London soon. And you?"

"Well . . . not actually sure." She crumbled her roll. "Now Mummy's back, I'll probably stay with her for a while, which is nice. You see, I was in school before the war, while Mummy was in India, so tons to catch up on." Her smile that of a mongoose being left with a snake.

"I like your shoes," the old lady said, looking at my mother, who was sitting very regally, her legs on a slant like a model's, displaying the exquisite, almost finicky table manners she'd tried to pass on to me.

"Thank you." My mother glanced at her snakeskin pumps. "They are rather fun, aren't they? I can't remember where I got them." I'd last seen the shoes on the high-arched feet of the wife of the solicitor she'd worked for in Norwich. She finished her jam roly-poly and custard in silence, and when everyone else had finished theirs, Daisy explained it was cook's night off. My mother and I rose automatically to help her.

"Stay where you are," Daisy commanded. "House rules: no work first night." She piled the tray with our dirty dishes.

"It's been impossible getting servants since the war," Ci Ci complained. "Everyone thinks they're too good for it."

Flora looked at her mother uncertainly and half rose. "Should I ?"

"Sit down, Flora," the old woman snapped in a we're-paying-for-this kind of voice. "My husband," she told Tudor after pouring herself another glass of damson wine, "had twenty years in the jute industry and loved his job. Flora only met him twice, which was sad. You never stop being a mother, you know." She pronounced it ironically, as *Muthah*, as if worried she might sound sentimental.

I saw the heat rise in Flora's cheek and thought, Poor creature. No father, no visible husband, no home, no job now that the war had ended: just a future of rooms in boardinghouses and cheap hotels with this strange old bird. But then we were all feeling the aftershocks and the strain, and hungry too, with rationing being worse than it had been even during the war.

After another glass of wine Ci Ci tried to lift her dog into the lamplight, and I saw how strangely she'd put her lipstick on. It extended far beyond the corners of her mouth and in the half-light looked like a wound.

"And where are all these people going to sleep?" she asked the dog, giving him a kiss.

"In Nannie's old room at the top of the house." Daisy had returned with the coffee. "You can see all the fields and the woods from there." She produced all her friendly teeth at once.

"Bless you, Daisy," my mother said, sounding every bit as regal as the old crone. "It's splendidly quiet too."

"I hope you don't mind the attic," Daisy said to me the next morning as we were walking across the farmyard. "I would have given you separate bedrooms, but I've had to rent out all the others since the war, and you've seen the drive!" This was said with an aristocratic lack of shame: Daisy was never furtive about money.

"How did you meet Ci Ci?" I said, circling round a large puddle.

"In Bombay, at a party. She had a splendid house then, servants, a husband. He died of a heart attack doing up his shoes, and then of course everything ended shockingly fast after Independence. She can barely boil an egg, poor love."

Four geese waddled across the yard, and in the distance, mile upon mile of fields lay bathed in pale sunshine. The rumor was that in the valley below us, seven Roman charioteers had burned to death. A headless man smelling of charcoal was said to haunt the house.

"I'm happy in the attic, Daisy," I said, and meant it. I didn't believe in the ghosts, and I liked my room's whitewashed plainness with its sloped ceiling, the washstand, the small, soft bed that had once belonged to Daisy's parents. But what I most liked was the expanse of open country outside, the silver flash of the river that ran through it. The quiet of the space (so quiet you could hear an apple drop from a tree at night) was a blissful luxury after four

years in nurses' dorms in London. My last dorm—spluttering gas
fire, clotheshorses crammed with other people's dripping underwear—was claustrophobically small. Nowhere quiet to cry there,
with about two feet between each bed and the next.

And I was crying, uncontrollably at times, and I needed to
think. It wasn't, I told myself irritably and often, as if I were going
through some special kind of interesting crisis. It was the war. It
was life, and nobody's fault that my year at Saint Thomas' had been
catapulted straight from the classroom into the Blitz. In my first
year on the wards, when London was bombed for fifty-seven con-
tinuous nights of horror and bedlam, the hospital, plum opposite
the Houses of Parliament, was a sitting duck. One night we'd seen
what looked like the whole of the Thames—houseboats, ware-
houses, park benches, trees—on fire.

And now the war was over, and this great quiet blank had opened
up. I wasn't the only nurse to still feel in the deep muscles of my legs,
in my brain, and my spirits, extraordinarily tired, as if I'd gone from
twenty to seventy in a few short years, or to wake suddenly in the night
to the nerve-shredding sound of screaming ambulances, or to find
there were times when it took all my mental strength not to give in
to the series of gruesome snapshots pooled at the bottom of my mind:
burns with a rotting meat smell, the young fireman injured by shrapnel
in the gullet, who gargled blood before he died, and of course the girl.

Everyone tells you, if you are a nurse or a doctor, that mistakes
happen, that we're only human, but the girl was the one who took
me to the edge, and I can't write about it, can't think about it now. All
I can say is I found it hard to forgive myself and probably never will.

Daisy beamed at me as she unlocked the door to the barn.

"I've been dying to show you this," she said. There was an immediate smell of dust and hay and I remembered feeding lambs here
during bad weather—the muscular suck of their tongues, the way

their eyes rolled when the milk entered their mouths. "It's been our greatest challenge so far."

The barn was freezing inside, almost colder than outside. She switched on a naked bulb festooned with cobwebs and the first thing I saw was a large blackboard with the words The Mother Moonstone Maternity Home Fort Cochin chalked on it in Daisy's slashing hand, with a column of figures beside it. Next to the blackboard were two battered school desks piled high with files, three boxes labeled Medical Supplies and Not Wanted on Voyage. Tacked to one of the walls behind was a large chart, one I recognized from R. W. Johnstone's textbook on the internal workings of the pregnant woman at term.

"I do prefer the office to be separate from the house, don't you?" said Daisy, seeing my dubious gaze. This office was arranged like a small stage set in the middle of a few bales of hay and stacks of old gates.

"It's essential to get the house out of your head, at least for part of the day." Daisy, I knew for a fact, was often up at five, feeding animals or cooking stews, in order to clear this time for herself. She knelt to light the stove in the corner, brushed a dozing farm cat off her desk.

"That's yours." She pointed to the chair opposite hers and handed me a rug to wrap myself in. "But Kit," she said, looking at me steadily and kindly, "before I bamboozle you, how are you, honestly?"

There was a time when this kind of invitation had led to some of the best and frankest talks of my life. Not now.

"So much better, Daisy," I said. "It's so good to be here." The vague idea I had had about confiding in Daisy already felt like self-indulgence. Sharing the house with dispossessed strangers was no piece of cake either, and I thought she looked tired and had lost weight since I'd last seen her a year or so ago.

"I wonder if it was a mistake," she offered, "for you to plunge so soon after the war into the midwife course. What does Glory think?"

"Not thrilled," I said. The truth was my mother hadn't spoken to me for a week after I told her. Her plans for me ran along the lines of something sanitary and secretarial, maybe a doctor's receptionist, in a place where you wore nice clothes and met men and flirted discreetly with them.

"Hm, I didn't think she would be." Daisy sucked in her lips.

"But I was enjoying the training." I faltered, "I really was," furious that my mouth was wobbling. "I want to finish it. It's not that. I got tired, I think," I added lamely. "And this awful winter . . . you know . . . normal things." I closed my eyes tight to blank out the memory that followed me everywhere: the girl. Her screaming mouth.

"Well, we don't have to do any of this today if you don't want to. And don't let me bombard you." The expression in her eyes was so kind, I had to take a deep breath.

"Honestly, Daisy," I stood up. "My brain's going to turn to dust if I don't work again soon, so spill the beans."

She laughed as if I'd made a splendid joke, opened the desk drawer, and said, "Let's get cracking."

In the next hour Daisy, intent and serious, sketched out what seemed to me a dangerous plan. "Do you remember me telling you about the orphanage I ran in Bombay in the late 'twenties?" she began.

"Of course!" I'd enjoyed her stories about Tamarind Street.

"Well, it was a marvelous time. I set it up with a group of egg-head women I'd met at Oxford, and we ran it with Indian volunteers. We all got on splendidly, and I was very happy there, and although it was a drop in the ocean, we did at least do something. Not nearly enough." Daisy, who never blew her own trumpet, looked sad at this.

"In August, after Indian Independence, I think we thought we would be kicked out, or worse—but something's cropped up." Her eyes flashed. "Something very exciting. I've been asked by my very good South Indian friend, Neeta Chacko, to continue to help a mother and baby clinic at a small hospital in Fort Cochin. The plan is to work alongside their Indian staff and develop a short course to share Western knowledge with the local village midwives, the vayattattis. So we're on the hunt for English midwives to go back to India. The right kind."

"The right kind?" I asked cautiously. "Meaning . . . ?"

"Well, not pigheaded know-it-alls. We can learn a lot from the local women."

"But who would go?" I asked. In the last few months, the papers had been full of lurid accounts of the mayhem that had followed Independence: the three hundred thousand Muslims hacked to death, the slaughtering of innocent passengers in burning trains, neighbor killing neighbor, and so on. "Don't Indians loathe us now?"

"Well, you see, that's rot," Daisy said. "Some do, with some justification, but the others, we worked with them for years, they were our friends, and besides they need all the help they can get."

"Don't they want to cut the apron strings?" That's what my mother had told me, a bitter note in her voice.

"Not entirely." Daisy put a kettle on top of the range. "God, it's cold in here. I'm going to make some tea. It's partly our fault that India still has an appallingly high infant mortality rate. Tackling it wasn't high on our government's list of priorities when we were there, and sensibly, their government wants foreign midwives from America and from Britain, to fill in the gaps."

I must have looked skeptical. Handing me a mug of tea, she said, "The situation, frankly, darling, is dire. The riots and killings have placed a tremendous strain on local hospitals. Neeta has begged us to come back, to bring equipment, books, money, anything we can."

She got up and put a piece of rotten gate on the fire.

"Are you going?" I felt my mouth grow dry.

"I can't." She looked stricken. "I have to run the farm, else it will collapse, and anyway it's important that the Moonstone have its own Indian administrator. It's midwives they need. Have a flapjack." Daisy's flapjacks were good: moist and chewy with just enough golden syrup in them to make them sweet.

"I'm not a proper midwife yet." I took a flapjack from the tin. "I have two more supervised deliveries to do before I sit my part twos." The rule was that pupil midwives who were qualified nurses had to take responsibility for twenty women during labor, ten of these in the patients' own homes, so a total of thirty deliveries over a year. I'd taken part in twenty-eight, and then, because of what happened, I'd dropped out.

"So, almost there." Daisy tucked the blanket around my knee. "I was trying to remember if you'd ever actually been to India with your mother," she said innocently, while I was chewing.

"Daisy," I said warningly. I had an inkling where this was heading and had already decided to say no. "I was never there, or if I was, I was too young to remember."

My mother's stories about India were so odd and variable, that I always felt, to use her own word, "eggshelly," when the subject cropped up, not wanting to casually blurt out what she had carefully concealed.

"I think Mummy went to school there."

"She did," Daisy said.

"Did she work for some governor there or something? A good job."

"Maybe." It was Daisy's turn to look wary. "You'd better ask her."

A gust of wind made the barn door fly open. Three ducks waddled across the mud, the wind flattening their feathers. Daisy bolted the door shut, put another log on the grate.

"So, back to the Moonstone." She stood up and wrapped a blanket mummy-fashion around herself. "What Neeta and I are working on is a simple training program that won't mystify the local midwives, some of whom are illiterate, and joy! I think we may have tracked down the proverbial needle in the haystack by finding a young doctor at Oxford who speaks Malayalam, the local language in Cochin. He's going to help me with the translations. It is a bit of a minefield out there at the moment, and we must avoid any hint of English women bossing their women. We want to train their best and brightest, but you know, it can be terribly tricky: some high-caste Hindu women have to go through complicated cleansing rituals if they so much as touch the bodily fluids of another person."

"Daisy," I said, "it sounds insanely difficult."

"That's what Tudor says." She smiled sadly. "He's completely mystified at my spending my time on this, and probably best we don't discuss it at mealtime. It can be an explosive subject."

"I think my mother would say amen to that, but I'm not mystified, Daisy," I said, looking at her: she was the best person I'd ever met, though she'd have hated me to say it.

She looked at her watch. "I'll get through this quickly—lunch in half an hour. Our most desperate need is coin," she said urgently, "to get the Home up and running and show what wonders we can achieve. If we can do this, I'm sure that in time, the new government will support us. I'm sending out begging letters to everyone I can think of. Can you help?"

"Of course, of course!" I felt shamefully relieved to hear that was all she wanted. "I can type one hundred and twenty words a minute," I boasted. My mother had insisted on it at the Balmoral typing school in Oxford Street. "When do we start?"

"Today." She moved a pile of files from the empty desk. "Let's start by making a list of supplies. Nothing too taxing."

- CHAPTER 2 -

And so it began. For the next month, every morning after breakfast, wearing three pairs of socks, every sweater we could lay our hands on, sleeveless gloves, and long johns, Daisy and I dashed off to the barn as quickly as we could. We read textbooks, wrote to student midwives, went methodically through the telephone directory for possible donors, and typed begging letters. We wrapped parcels that, when the lane cleared, the postman would take on the first leg of their trip to India.

We kept replies to our begging letters in two old Bath Oliver biscuit tins on Daisy's desk, one labeled YES! and the other NO. After three weeks the yes letters didn't even reach the ten-biscuit mark, but Daisy looked joyful as she showed them to me. A ten-bob note and a "Well done, Daisy," from an aunt. A hard-earned fiver from an ex–India nurse, now retired with stomach problems to Brighton. The promise of twenty packets of swabs from a local chemist, and some aspirin. That sort of thing.

The letters in the no tin, on my desk, all but burst with rage at our stupidity at continuing to help an ungrateful India.

"Here's a beauty," I said to Daisy.

"Dear Miss Barker," wrote Col. Dewsbury (retired) from Guildford. "(Am assuming you're a Miss.)

"In receipt of yrs 20/10/47, am frankly flabbergasted that you still consider India has the right to bleed us dry anymore. I don't know if you read the newspapers, but after enjoying the railways we built for them, the schools we set up, and a thousand and one other advantages we fought and died for, <u>THEY HAVE KICKED US OUT</u>." The colonel had underlined this so emphatically, he'd gone clean through a sheet of Basildon Bond. "Two generations of my own family have given their lives to the country (Father in Innis-killins), Great-Grandfather caught in the riots up North, where Indians holed us up for two days without water and food. So sorry. NO, from now on, charity begins at home."

His stabbing signature left another bullet hole in the paper.

"So, I think we can safely assume the colonel won't be putting us in his will." I shut him firmly in the no tin. "Colonel, I can hear you shouting,"—I put my ear to the lid—"but you can't come out."

"Oh, Kit," Daisy said, after series of schoolgirlish snorts, "don't leave too soon."

I didn't want to. I loved working with Daisy, and cocooned by the snow and immersed in this exciting project, I was secretly dreading that the roads would be cleared soon and I'd have no excuse for not going back to Saint Andrew's, the nursing home where I'd gone to study midwifery after my general nursing training at Thomas'. I wasn't frightened of the study, which I enjoyed, or the exams; I was resigned to the temporary claustrophobia of being back in an all-female dorm. The particular horse I had to get back on was the idea of delivering another child on my own, which made me feel sick and light-headed, not a good feeling for a pupil midwife.

"You can stay forever as far as I'm concerned." Daisy patted my arm. "Your mother's occupied. Tudor likes having you around."

"So not stinking fish?" I tried to avoid the hopeful glance that nowadays went with any mention of her Tudor's name. It was an awkward thing, but I'd really taken against him, his languid manner, his prissy way of eating as if the food were some sort of insult, when my mother was trying so hard, the way he treated Daisy like a skivvy.

Daisy tried to twang my heartstrings with excuses for his boor-ish behavior: Tudor wasn't used to so many women around after the army, and before that Oxford and an English boarding school. Tudor found it hard to talk at the table (at which my inner censor sagged and said, Oh, poor ickle bickle Tudor). He was fearsomely intelligent and didn't do small talk. He was half owner of this farm too.

"You could never be stinking fish," Daisy said stoutly. "You're family, not guests."

"It's been good for us," I said, and meant it. "Mummy and I were barely speaking on the way down, and being together every day means . . ." I was faltering as I said this because it already felt disloyal. "We're at least under the same roof and I'm not so worried about her."

"That's good." Daisy's look was steady and kind. "She loves you, you know."

"I just wish," I said eventually, "she could find something to do that she really liked."

"It's not ideal"—even Daisy couldn't deny this—"but she's saved my bacon with the housekeeping and she's a wonderful cook." I felt the old glow of reflected pride when she said this, and it was justified. Maud, Daisy's regular cook, was off with her recurring bronchitis, and when snow had threatened to cut off our food supplies, Ma had performed small miracles with sinister-looking bottles of peas and vegetables she found in the cellar, making them into creamy soups with a pinch of this and that, and delicious stews from unpromising scraps of lamb and muddy carrots, or the odd chicken retired from egg laying.

A shame then that my mother, a practiced hand at nipping the hand that fed her, complained ceaselessly about Daisy's hopelessly inadequate kitchen utensils, the Rayburn, the heating, the dreariness of the gray skies, but I was used to this. And at least she and I were talking again.

When I'd tried to tell her a little bit about the charity, she'd crumpled her forehead and said, "Not now, darling," maintaining she was too squeamish, but then I'd hear her from another room, boasting about my cleverness at school, delighting in the fact that I was typing again, triumphant vindication of her original plans for me.

If I wasn't too tired at nights I took the typewriter up to my room and, fingers flying over Daisy's battered Remington, wrote to Josie, my dearest friend at Saint Thomas', the straight-as-a-die farmer's daughter, with whom I'd shared so many laughs, confidences, and when we could afford it, nights out with during the war. It was Josie who had been with me on the night it happened and told me endlessly it was not my fault.

Sometimes I wrote in my diary too, and when I finished I'd cross the hall to my mother's room and kiss her good night. If she was sitting at the dressing table, I'd sometimes brush her beautiful black hair and she'd whimper in appreciation, which made me feel so sad.

She was so beautiful, my mother then, have I said this? The Indian blood she tried so hard to hide had given her wonderful, smooth, pale caramel-colored skin and glossy hair. And she was tremendously well-dressed considering how broke we were—the quintessential Englishwoman, from a distance, only much, much better-looking; my glamorous princess once, green satin dress, diamond necklace (paste). She was my cook, storyteller, exotic traveling companion too: funny and superstitious with sudden bursts of gaiety that reminded me of a cat dashing up a curtain. She had the sudden spitting furies of a cat too.

Some nights, when I went across the hall to say good night, she'd slide her tortoiseshell eyes up at me and say in a little-girl voice, "Read me a story." She carried with her always a small collection of romantic books; her then favorite was Georgette Heyer's *The Spanish Bride*. And so, huddled under the eiderdown together, just like in the old days, I did all the voices—Juana's, Lord Wellington's, Harry Smith's—and she was happy again.

Sometimes she'd try to persuade me to try on one of her pretty dresses (some of them donated by rich employers, others—how to put this?—self-donated), saying it would cheer everyone up downstairs, meaning Tudor, I suppose. She pleaded with me to let her polish my nails. "A lady is always judged by her hands."

(When I'd told Josie this, she'd said, "But what about this?" pointing at her wild red off-duty hair, "Or this?" holding herself erect so the world could admire her bosom.)

But Josie was working the night shift in London and not available for jokes about my mother, and knowing I'd be leaving soon, I sat patiently (a huge effort) while my mother frowned at my cuticles, and pushed dead skin away with a special little pointed dagger from her shagreen case, and finally held my hand.

The bigger things between us we brushed away under the carpet like so many unpleasant toenail clippings.

"Kit, you're awake," she said one night when she walked in and found me wide-eyed at three a.m.

I'd been thinking about the girl again—her red hair, her screaming—but said something vague about night shifts at the hospital, and how it was hard now to sleep normally again. Sensing distress, she cut me off with a strange fake laugh that was as bad as a slap and said, "Oh, Kitty, let's not be morbid. The war's over now."

On the day when things began to shift and change for me, there was a thaw outside. The cook, Maud, arrived midmorning, red-cheeked, puffing, and with a barking cough, saying it was still blooming cold out there but the snow was melting in the lanes, which made Daisy and me happy. We'd been wrapping parcels of maternity packs, books, and wall charts, which could now leave for India.

When I walked in for lunch, Tudor and Flora were framed like silhouettes against a bright window, Tudor behind the pages of *The Listener*, making important rustling sounds. Flora glanced nervously at him from time to time. Poor Flora, barred by her mother from the kitchen. ("We're *paying*, darling. There are people to do that.") Ci Ci had made it clear that Flora had one job and one job only at Wickam Farm. Earlier, I'd seen her, lipsticked and overdressed, with her mother in the hall, and overheard Ci Ci, who was as subtle as a megaphone, saying, "Oh, for God's sake, Flora, don't make a meal of it, go in there and talk. To. Him."

Over lunch, Ci Ci kept giving Flora prodding looks, because Flora, apart from a few timid observations about the thaw, and how nice it was to see green again, and the prettiness of raindrops against the window, hadn't exactly set the table aroar. My mother was in a foul mood: the Rayburn was playing up again—something to do with poor-quality coke—and the turnip and carrot soup was well below her usual standard. Ci Ci had pushed hers aside after a few spoonfuls.

Daisy came late, her pink face and bouncy walk bringing energy into the room. Melting snow, she said, had flooded one of the stables, and William, the cart horse, was absolutely soaked. She'd been drying him. "Our towels, I expect," Ci Ci complained.

The phone rang.

"Get that, would you?" Tudor's goldfishy eyes swam up from behind the paper. "Bound to be for you."

"Ramsden fifty-eight." Daisy's fluting tones came from the hallway. "How nice. Oh, my goodness me, yes! Of course, of course, of course, splendid!" and then after a pause, "Lovely. Lovely! No, no, no, not at all. That's absolutely perfect."

"Sounds like we've won the pools," Tudor said to me, "but probably just another guest." He gave a ghastly mock-happy grimace.

"Let me get a pen. You can spell it out. No, no, no, no, no. It's gone straight into the book."

My mother sighed and sagged, walked wearily to the kitchen for the shepherd's pie. Tudor threw aside his paper and left the room. He stomped upstairs; a far door slammed.

"I don't blame him for being cross," Ci Ci broke the silence that followed. "Not one little bit. She never says no." She took a nip of the crème de menthe she drank after every meal for her indigestion and carried on eavesdropping.

"And you're from Travancore?" Daisy's delighted voice drifted back from the hall. "Yes, yes, I know it of course, a wonderful part of the world. How many nights can you manage?"

Ci Ci was listening avidly, an oily green mark on her lipstick.

"Oh Lord in heaven," she said. "She's asking Indians to stay now." She stroked her dog, breathing deeply. "Your aunt Ruth's in Eastbourne," she said to Flora. "We can always join her there." A look of pure panic crossed the girl's face.

"Tudor's promised the house will be quieter soon, Mummy. Can't we wait?" Flora turned her pleading eyes to me. "And Kit's going back to London soon, aren't you?"

"Soon," I said, with no clear idea of when.

"Splendid news." Daisy had returned with the dish of shepherd's pie in her hand.

"My Indian friend Neeta Chacko has found a doctor for us. He trained at Barts, postgrad work at Exeter College, sounds absolutely charming. Speaks good English and Malayalam and is happy to stay with us for a few weeks, work on his thesis, and help with the translations. Isn't that marvelous?" She couldn't stop smiling.

"Whoopee." Ci Ci's voice was slurred. "More cold baths."

"Mummy," murmured Flora.

"Thekkeden." Daisy spooned a bit of shepherd's pie onto Ci Ci's plate. "That's his surname. Neeta says they're a Nasrani family, well educated, possibly communists. A lot of people from South India are."

Ci Ci's lip furled. "Indians. Communists. Better and better."

"Mummy!"

"It will be nice for Tudor to have some male company in the house," Daisy said, "and critical for us." She had her scheming face on. "Right, Kit?"

"Right, Daisy." I smiled back at her, hoping that my mother could cope.

"He'll be here next week," she said, "if the snow has cleared."

- CHAPTER 3 -

Daisy decided we should welcome the young doctor with a curry. She had the wheels put back on the Austin and went to Oxford in search of mango chutney. I offered to help my mother in the kitchen because Maud on the previous day had, on doctor's orders, given in her notice.

Growing up, I'd seen my mother make the usual ration stodge—rissoles, boiled cabbage, suet puddings—but making curry had a whiff of something secret and special about it, because it only ever happened when we were on our own. Then my mother would get out a battered green tin, uncork the small bottles inside it, and with a finicky, witchy kind of precision that thrilled me, measure out the five or six spices she used. I was under strict instructions never to touch the tin, which she kept in one of the side pockets of her suitcase, or the spices inside them, or to talk about them. When the curry was cooked, she would eat it in a kind of trance, her eyes half-closed, very quiet.

But this morning, the old magic wasn't working. Her spine looked rigid as she lashed herself into her apron, a frown line like a sharpened blade between her eyebrows.

"I'll do that, Mummy," I said, seeing a pile of onions and muddy carrots on the draining board. I took an onion and started to chop it, but she snatched the knife from my hand.

"Not like that, like this." Her hand flew down the onion in a blur. "There." She scooped up the tiny pieces, hurled them into the large frying pan, made them sizzle, the air turned blue and for a second, there she was again: my sorceress, my magician.

Daisy had brought her own spice box home from India, a carved wooden box with rows of tiny cupboards inside, each one filled with a different spice. My mother opened it now and sniffed.

"Musty," she said with an exasperated sigh.

"Tell me what they are," I said, still hoping for a bit of fun with her.

"This is chili powder, very hot. Fennel seeds, chili, dried coriander. I won't put that in, Ci Ci will complain of indigestion. I'll use Daisy's for the chicken curry, and mine for the vegetable. So . . ." She was lost for a moment, her voice lilting, leaning over the onions that had started to turn brown at the edges. "I put spices first, warm them nicely, now lentils."

"Get out! Go away!" Her sudden shout made me jump. It was Sid, Daisy's old black Labrador; he was circling and about to flop in his usual place in front of the Rayburn when she kicked him.

"No dogs in the kitchen!" she shouted.

"Keep your hair on, Mummy." I was softhearted about animals. "He's not the Loch Ness monster."

"Dogs are full of germs and fleas," she told me after I'd shut him in the freezing hall.

"Now here, come close." She added a teaspoon of coriander to the lentils. "These first," she whispered, "now the other vegetables."

And soon it was all lovely in there, with the kitchen filled with smells piquant and strange, the fat hissing, windows steaming, and us absorbed and getting on again. I was accustomed to watching my mother as anxiously as a farmer observes the sky for signs of storms approaching, but now, almost in spite of herself, I saw her whole body soften and relax.

"Stir it clockwise," she told me, stroking my hand. "Counterclockwise is bad luck."

My mother had a number of strange beliefs like this: don't wash your hair on a Thursday, never shave your armpits on a Monday—things that when she was in a good mood, I could tease her about.

"Um." I closed my eyes, glad to feel the touch of her hand. "I love these smells."

"Does Tudor like curry?" she asked out of the blue and with a sly look I recoiled from.

"How should I know?"

"You should make it your business to know." She dropped my hand. "Because men appreciate these things, and you should wear a dress at night and stop wearing those awful gloves, like some farm laborer, and have you told him about your job?" I had the sense these reproaches had been dangerously backing up, and now they burst out like steam from a geyser.

"My job!" I put down the spoon and sat down. "Why would I talk to him about it?"

"Well, Daisy has, because he's mentioned it to me, and by the way, he thinks her charity is madness when the farm is so run-down, but anyway . . ." She'd said what she'd been building up to and now she continued in her wheedly voice, "Let's not have a row about it." She lifted a scrawny chicken from the saucepan. "Let it cool, take the flesh off it, chop it small."

But my blood was up. "Why are you so ashamed of it?" Meaning the midwifery training. "Why do you hate it so much?"

"Because . . ." Her hand was on the steaming carcass, water streaming from its bottom. "Most men hate that sort of thing, they find it squelchy." In another, better mood, I might have laughed. However infuriating she could be, I loved my mother's odd turns of phrase: "she's gone all bendy," for a friend who was trying to be feminine and seductive; "I'm forky today," for when she was cross. Today, I wanted to crown her.

"And I'm just so happy," my mother went on in her crooning-mummy voice, stirring and sniffing, "to see my lovely daughter looking healthier. That's all. I was terribly worried about you before. God knows what would have happened if the matron hadn't phoned."

I chopped the chicken and tried to smile. My night sweats, the insomnia, the bouts of weeping I'd tried to pass off as the after-effects of the flu that had swept through our dormitory, but Matron Smythe, my no-nonsense superior at Saint Andrew's, had described my inability to get out of bed one morning as "a perfectly ordinary case of nervous exhaustion brought on by overwork and the war." Fourteen-hour shifts and sleepless nights had clobbered quite a few of her girls, she said.

A dash of rain fell against the window. Ma's dark eyes filled with tears. "Please, darling," she said, "let's not talk about this anymore, it only makes us both unhappy. Soak the rice, and we'll sit down with a cup of tea, and I'll try and think what on earth we're going to do next. We can't stay here indefinitely, and honestly," in a fresh spurt of indignation, "is it really such a crime to want to see you settled and happy?"

We drank the tea, and when she was breathing normally again she pulled a copy of *Horse and Hound* from her knitting bag and began the obsessive routine I remembered from childhood. The varnished nail skidded over the results for jumping competitions and advertisements for country homes, which, she observed with relish, no one could afford to heat now, stopping at the classified sections at the back that were her employment exchange.

"Hampshire landowner needs housekeeper to run home and do errands, walk dogs, et cetera," she read aloud.

"No good," I said. "Woofers." She had a deep conviction that dogs were filthy and full of disease. She was frightened of them too, even ones she knew.

"Elderly widower, Derbyshire, desperately seeks all-round fac-totum to help run house and do accounts for small farm, and help with entertaining. No pets, small self-contained flat. Time wasters need not apply."

She made a small mark with her pencil. In her glory days, she'd worked as the assistant to some big cheese in Indian royalty, the nabob of somewhere or other. And oh! the balls, the polo, the fun.

Poor Mummy. My bad mood collapsed at the sight of her hunched over her magazine, her expression both hopeful and cynical. She was circling a couple of advertisements when Ci Ci's face appeared around the door, her expression stagily dramatic.

"Oh, the bliss of curry." She closed her eyes. "It does takes one back."

"Keep the dog out," my mother said curtly. "Nosy bloody woman," she added when the door closed. My spirits sank. Nothing seemed to work anymore, not cooking curry, not being with me, and it felt in that bleak moment that we were trapped in a duet that had once been sweet but now played nothing but duff notes. The spice tin went back in her handbag; I cleaned the countertops. So, no magic wand and maybe she was thinking the same thing. When I looked up, her mouth was struggling.

"Don't say anything," she said fiercely.

"Is it the onions?"

"Yes, it's the onions."

She wiped her eyes on her apron and went to the sink.

"You hate this, don't you?" I said at last.

"Don't talk for a bit." She kept her head down. "And don't feel sorry for me."

I watched her dabbing her eyes and patches of white forming on her cheeks, a sure sign of her strongest emotions, and I disliked myself intensely.

"Would you want this?" She was splashing her eyes with water. "Doing this?"

"I like watching you cook," I said, but only to soothe her, because I knew in a moment of absolute certainty that I must not end up like this: angry and unsatisfied, dependent on the kindness of strangers.

"Oh, fruit pie" (one of her swear words), "the flipping Rayburn is low again." My mother sank to her knees. "It will take ages to boil the rice when he comes, and take those awful gloves off."

"Oh, for God's sake, Mummy. It's cold in here."

"Then don't hang around in the kitchen if you're cold."

"I thought it would be fun to cook with you." I was more upset than the occasion warranted but I couldn't stop myself.

"Well, it's not fun," she said, a wild look in her eye. "And for your information I hate making it." She was back at the sink, washing her hands like Lady Macbeth. "I hate the smell of it, the fiddle of it, and now, with the nig-nog coming, I'm going to have to make it all the time."

The ugly phrase echoed in my mind all afternoon. It mingled with the smell of spices that spread so tantalizingly throughout the house and over tea, taken as usual in the threadbare sitting room.

Ci Ci, hunched on a sagging sofa near the fire, sneered at the Indian doctor's qualifications. "Some of them make it up, you know."

Through a mouthful of jam sandwich, she told Tudor and Flora that she, personally, would rather die than set foot in an Indian hospital. Her beady eyes, glaring at us over the rim of her "special teacup," were those of a disheveled old parrot forced to share its perch. "Does anyone even know which lavatory he'll use?" Ci Ci said, as if there were dozens of WCs throughout the house. There were actually two, one on her floor, one on ours. "Some of them don't even know how to use the lav, you know. They squat over the bowl like campers."

Flora closed her eyes. "Mummy."

"Flora, you haven't lived there. I have. Twenty-two years."

"Twenty-two years what?" Daisy appeared, showing no sign of having overheard this unpleasant exchange. "Any more tea in that pot?"

"In India. Some of our servants were quite wonderful," Ci Ci improvised quickly. Daisy had reminded us firmly at breakfast that

Anto Thekkeden was a clever young man from a distinguished family. He would be a huge asset to the charity and she would appreciate it if we would all make him very welcome.

"Pandit ran our house like clockwork," Ci Ci continued with a sneaky smile to Flora.

"Tell them about the Daimler, Mummy," said Flora, who was a useful prompt when the occasion demanded it.

"Oh yes, our lovely, lovely car," Ci Ci told Tudor, who was looking blankly at her. "Pandit worshipped the thing. Couldn't stop polishing it, put lovely fresh mints in the glove box. I—" A knock at the door interrupted her.

Maud's husband, Dave, stood there, breathless and important.

"Miss Barker, sorry to trouble you, but a young colored gentleman has fallen in the ditch. He come on a motorbike, skidded, and fell there. Do you want him at the house? He's approaching it now."

"Did you leave him in the ditch?" Daisy sprang from her seat.

"No, ma'am, I—"

"In the snow!" Daisy was appalled.

"No, I just didn't know if you'd want him up at the house like."

"Oh for heaven's sake, of course we want him in the house," Daisy snapped. "Get a torch, and I'll come with you."

"Glory," she said, "go upstairs quickly and check the bathroom is presentable. He'll be sopping wet and need a bath before supper. Honestly."

She sent me to the barn to finish sending invitations to a talk she was giving the following week titled "Infant Mortality in India." I was licking envelopes when I heard the throaty roar of a motorbike coming up the drive, the skid of brakes, and then the front door open and close as the new arrival walked in.

It was dark by the time I'd finished up the letters. I took a hay net down to Bert the demob horse, then walked back up the drive. When I got back to my room, I saw that my mother had put a blue dress on the bed for me, a pair of pearl earrings beside it. I was struggling with their clips when the lights went out. Melting snow down in the valley, Daisy had warned us; happened every year. As I felt my way downstairs, step by step, I could hear the splash of the Indian doctor having his bath upstairs. Daisy was on her hands and knees downstairs, getting oil lamps from the cupboard in the hall.

We lit about ten of them and placed them at strategic points around the house. Golden light pooled around the portraits of the frock-coated ancestors in the hall and gave them a startling intimacy. It bounced off the glass eyes of the stuffed foxes, the eagle bagged near Pondicherry. Glory was frightened of the dark, so I went into the kitchen to help her. She was standing motionless beside the battery of small dishes she'd prepared to go with the curry.

"Oh, Mater," I said, "this smells nose-toddlingly good."

It had been our joke once to speak like this when the lights failed and pretend we were toffs in a Georgette Heyer novel, not tweenies (between-stairs people). Tonight she wouldn't play.

"It's all gone wrong." The whites of her eyes showed through the gloom. "No grated coconut, no fresh mango, no fresh tomatoes: I'm fed up with rationing."

She plonked a dish of dried-up raisins on the plate, and the WI green apple chutney, which Daisy had found in a cupboard under the sink, having drawn a blank in Oxford.

"Is he here?" she said. "Have you seen him?"

"He's having a bath," I said.

"In Ci Ci's bathroom?"

"Yes."

"Oh my God." She closed her eyes. "This is going to be awful."

We'd set the table with white linen napkins, the good plates, and what was left of the Waterford crystal. Did I say that Daisy had bought a beautiful cedar table in India and shipped it home? Terribly impractical, but it looked lovely that night polished to a high conker-colored shine. I think it was Daisy who told me once that you never regret your extravagancies, and this had been one of hers, and it always raised my spirits to see it.

When we walked in with the trays, Ci Ci, Flora, Daisy, and Tudor were blurred figures in the candlelight. My first sighting of him was as a vague silhouette against a dark door, and when I got closer, a slim man in a too-large jacket that looked peculiar on him, like a boy wearing his father's clothes. His face was in shadow. Daisy leapt towards him.

"Everybody." She looked down the table towards us. "I have the greatest pleasure in introducing you all." She pointed to us each in turn and said our names. "And this," she concluded with a drumroll inflection to her voice, "is Dr. Anto Thekkeden, from South India."

"And more recently, from a ditch near Whitney," he said. His voice was cultivated, Home Counties clipped, with just a faintly buttery undertone, a purring of the *r*s that sounded foreign. I was surprised by it, expecting the Indian singsong that Tudor had done as a turn before he arrived.

We laughed politely.

"That corner is a brute," said Daisy. "What kind of motorbike do you drive?"

"It's a Norton, twin cylinder. Very old, and the tires are bald."

"But frightfully economical on petrol, I expect." Flora was determined to be kind, or maybe to head off Ci Ci, who'd been muttering about hotels again.

Anto sat between Tudor and Flora. I was opposite him. The fuzzy light from the candles meant I couldn't see him clearly at first, but when the light suddenly bloomed, oh Lord, he was handsome: high, dignified cheekbones, a wide and tender-looking mouth, and pale cinnamon-colored skin that made him look more like a Spanish grandee than an Indian. The other striking thing was his eyes: wide-set and almond-shaped and green, and at this moment, expressing a polite, faintly quizzical, watchful interest in the proceedings.

Daisy had asked me earlier to get the conversational ball rolling.

"I'm Kit," I said, flustered enough to forget we'd been introduced.

"I'm Anto," he said, as if we hadn't. He stretched his hand across the table and I shook it.

"And you know Mrs. Mallinson," I said to show I wasn't a complete idiot.

"Delighted to meet you," Ci Ci drawled at her most patrician. She'd put on lots of eye makeup, and her silk jacket had a small cigarette burn on the lapel.

"It's a pleasure to meet you all," he said softly.

Yes, a Spanish grandee, I thought, without the faintest idea really of what a grandee looked like, except from the pages of *The Spanish Bride*. And off-puttingly good-looking, my thoughts ran on: unfair and unnecessary for a man to have cheekbones like that and those eyes. Josie and I had a theory about all good-looking men, based on one or two God's-gift-to-women doctors we'd met at the hospital: they were shallow and unreliable, and vain, and usually not very bright. To be handsome was like earning interest on money you hadn't earned in the first place.

"Glory has made this in your honor." Daisy put a steaming plate of chicken and vegetable curry in front of him. "No luck, sadly, with the mango chutney, but this is rather good."

"Thank you." He took the plate, closed his eyes, and breathed in deeply. "I haven't had this for years." For a moment he looked so troubled I wondered if we'd got it wrong and he was a strict vegetarian like some of the other Indians I'd read about.

My mother appeared, dressed for defiance in a green satin shift with jade earrings. *Family friend*, her outfit signaled, *not servant*. She spooned rice and the lentil dish onto her plate with her usual slightly finicky delicacy and then looked around the table, where there was a sudden uneasy pause.

"So, Dr. Thekkeden," Ci Ci said at last, her head at an ironical angle. "What brings you to our shores?"

He put down his knife and fork and looked at her. "I've been here for ages," he said in his soft, posh voice. "I was educated here."

"Ah! So that's why you speak good English." Ci Ci was quite the Bombay hostess again. "Do have some more of this rather peculiar chutney."

"What school?" Tudor looked up.

"Downside." His reply was clipped. "My parents are Catholic."

"Oh." Tudor sounded surprised. "Is that unusual?"

"The school or the religion?"

"Well, both." Tudor was sounding prickly.

"It is most unusual," the young doctor confirmed. "But my father loves all things English." There was a dry note in his voice as he said this, something a little mocking and public schooly. "He would wear plus fours if it wasn't so hot in South India."

"And what profession does he follow?" asked Ci Ci.

"He is a lawyer. He was called to the bar at Lincoln's Inn."

"Am I correct in thinking Gandhi practiced law in England too?" Tudor asked. "Before he took up spinning and good works?"

Stop peppering the poor man with questions, I thought.

"Gandhi was called to the bar at Grey's Inn," Daisy jumped in. "But he never practiced here. I met him once, you know, in Bombay, where we ran a children's home. He was a great man."

"A great man," the Indian doctor confirmed quietly. "I've been reading about him in the papers." I noticed the cuffs on his jacket were frayed.

"Would you like some more rice?" I asked.

"I would." He looked at me across the table. "Thank you."

I walked to the sideboard, where the food was kept warm on a small steel tray with three candles underneath it.

"Sit down." My mother spoke for the first time. "I'll do it. Our maid has the flu," she explained briefly to Anto. "It's a real bore."

"The food is very good," he told her. "Thank you."

I saw her considering whether to tell him about her job in India now or later. The governor, the picnics, the polo games.

But Flora said, "So did you get stuck here during the war?"

"Sort of," he replied.

"Stuck here!" Ci Ci's voice held a note of muted outrage. It was all right for her to hate England, but it was cheek for an Indian.

"My father was keen for me to do my medical training at Bart's Hospital, and then the war came. I haven't been home for nine years."

"So you're practically one of us," said Daisy.

He didn't answer, just a little smile.

"Did you mind?" Flora asked. She was wide-eyed like a child.

He put down his fork and stopped eating. "That's a big question," he said. "None of us expected the war."

"Will you go home soon?" Daisy asked.

"That is the plan." He looked at her directly with his long-lashed green eyes and gave an almost smile. "I'm worried they won't recognize me. And may I ask about you?" He addressed the table generally.

"Oh, us." Ci Ci's lip furled backwards, showing her sharp little teeth. "Oh, we're Empire flotsam and jetsam." She laughed to show this was a charming and self-deprecating joke. "We're renting here while we catch our breath." After a sip of Daisy's surprisingly potent elderflower wine, she rambled on at length about the Daimler and Godfrey's factory. How India had taken years off Godfrey's life, and how Gandhi had spoiled things by stirring people up.

"Sorry about this,"—she flung a defiant look around the table—"but I personally thought he was a ghastly little man, sitting there spinning in his nappy."

Daisy was shaking her head as if to say, Stop stop, stop! but said nothing, not wanting, I imagine, to stir up any storm clouds on his first day.

"Just a tiny bit more, dear." When Ci Ci held her glass towards Tudor, I stood up.

"Would you like me to show you your room?" I said to the doctor. "It's on the first floor."

My mother shot me a look of pure venom.

"What a splendid idea." Daisy looked relieved. "There was only time for a bath before dinner."

"Thank you," he said, "I'd like that." And to Daisy, and my mother: "A delicious meal. I can't thank you enough. I look forward to seeing you all tomorrow."

As we left the room, the door releasing an icy draft, Ci Ci Mallinson said quite audibly, "Well, he's got quite good table manners: that's something, I suppose."

- CHAPTER 4 -

The girl, whose name was Kit, stood up with a forwardness that startled him. She must have thought he needed rescue. He didn't. He filed all such conversations in his mind under *Indya*: press button one and you got reams of stuff from the ex-colonials about the railways and the ungratefulness; or the rhapsodies about the sunsets! the spirituality! the smells! and not forgetting, ah! the cow dust and the fires, the spices! Add in the rifle dust and you had Parfum de Partition.

In the hallway, she picked up his briefcase. "I can take this," she said, leaving the heavier ones for him. He almost blushed, conscious of the packet of French letters scattered amongst the few shirts, his cigarettes, the Catholic missal his mother had packed with the note inside saying, "Don't forget your prayers."

The condoms were standard issue for red-blooded medical students, but for him an invitation to a dance full of complications.

Walking upstairs in the glow of the lamplight, he did his best to ignore the slim ankles, the straight line of her stocking, the silk sway of her dark hair: women were off limits now that he was going home. To make this absolutely clear to himself, he'd gone back to Downside the week before and spoken in great confusion to his moral tutor, Father Damian: a dear, fat old man with a great sense of humor, who had made his life so much better during his four years there.

Over a glass of port in the book-lined study, he'd started with the smaller sin first: he was too addicted to going to the cinema, and it was time spent away from his PhD. "Well." Father Damian had taken a sip, bunched his eyebrows judiciously. "Exactly how many hours a week do you donate to this pastime?"

"Sometimes a whole afternoon."

"And what proportion of the week do you devote to your studies?" Anto thought about this. "It depends if I have lectures or tutorials."

"Include both in the sum."

"Maybe sixty hours. I have to get my doctorate before I go home."

"I think God may forgive you for a little time off." Father Damian's smile was dry and fond. "And working too hard is another sin, you know. But I hope," the monk added with a sly look, "you have the intellectual rigor to watch Eisenstein, and not a lot of old tosh. I do worry about your cultural bearings; remember our night at the opera?"

Anto had never been allowed to forget it: the excruciating performance of *Madame Butterfly* during his first term at the school. His eardrums so punctured by the foreign screeching, he'd sat, hands over his ears, wanting to howl like a dog.

But films were different. A drug, a way of forgetting and finding yourself inside the big faces on the screen. He'd sat in the dark avidly noticing the details: the manners of the handsome men up there, their ways of smoking, of greeting women, of leaving rooms, and later, this close attention had led to him becoming a clever mimic who could make other boys laugh.

Towards the end of this pleasant meeting, Father Damian wondered if there was something else troubling him, and if there was, he might take advantage of his time here and go to confession. Half an hour later, he'd knelt in the old school chapel and, breathing in the smells of incense and old velvet, blurted out his confusion and pain.

During the past two years, he'd slept with two women, out of lust, not love. One of them, a student nurse at Barts, a nice girl, fair-haired, ethereal-looking, had fallen in love with him and been badly hurt when he couldn't return the feeling.

The other, a worldly WAAF, boyfriend in France, had hurt him by saying afterwards, "I've always wanted to sleep with a foreign man," making him feel like an exotic pet allowed for one moment into the sitting room.

With his lips close to the grille, he gave an abridged version of these events and, in the silence that followed, felt the familiar cold breath of the chapel floor.

The priest coughed behind the curtain. He said that while God understood war made many men lustful in ways they didn't understand, Anto must now, given the particular circumstances of his life, make an extra effort to control himself.

Was he mistaken, the priest asked, in thinking there was a bride waiting for him in South India? Not a bride, he'd replied, a young girl, the daughter of a family friend. He'd never met her, he said, or if he had, he couldn't remember her: he'd come to England when he was sixteen. Well, God would forgive him, the priest had said more robustly, but only if he now made a solemn commitment to change. The war had bent everyone out of shape, he said; it was time now to return to the old certainties.

The old certainties, he thought later, back in his Oxford digs, eating the cold macaroni and cheese his landlady had left on a tray, what a luxury it would be to know what they were. For years, the idea of a God, loving or otherwise, had been slipping away from him, like a small boat unmoored and disappearing in a dark sea.

"So, this is it." She opened a carved door at the end of the corridor and lifted her candle. "Your room."

When the lights pulsed and flickered into life, both of them jumped.

"Thank God for that," she said. Her smile was very pretty. "We have a dreadful time with the electrics here. If you like I could give you a torch?"

"Thank you," he said. He'd smashed his own when he'd fallen off the Norton.

He looked around him. He liked his new room. With its tilted floor and cracked ceiling it was shabby for sure, but far more homely-looking than his digs in Woodstock Road. Its walls were covered in a lovely old blue Chinese wallpaper, its vines and birds a little watermarked here and there but giving it a kind of faded grandeur. The brass bed with its comfortable-looking blue eiderdown faced the window, from which he could see the dark shapes of the valley beyond.

"Is it all right?" She was watching him.

"It's lovely."

"Bedside light." When she leaned and switched it on, the room became a cozy cave.

"Washstand." She pointed at a large jug. "Basin, towel. You must be tired."

"No," he said, "I'm not." He hesitated. "Actually, I spent the afternoon in the Odeon in Oxford." He didn't tell her about the five a.m. start to study the pediatrics bible. One of the many disguises learned by his second term at Downside was to saunter into exams saying he didn't know a bloody thing but what the hell?

"What did you see?"

He handed her his ticket. When she peered at it under the lamp, he saw she'd rolled her hair around a scarf.

"Celia Johnson. *Brief Encounter.*"

"Damn it! I missed it! We've been snowed in." She handed the ticket back. "Never mind, I've seen it twice."

"'I shall never, *ever* tell anyone else about us,'" he said, with Trevor Howard's look of crushed nobility.

"'Because all I want is to know that you are safe,'" she said.

Her laughter was velvety and deep. It showed her white teeth. "What a lot of tosh," she said.

"Complete pap," he agreed, although he'd sat there, heart worn, entranced. "But it passed a pleasant few hours, and I didn't want to arrive too early."

"The last picture I saw," she said, "was a real stinker: *The Steam Railways of Mid-Wales*. I thought I would die of boredom. Do you go to the cinema a lot?"

She was standing with her hand on the door, looking at him with her direct gaze, and part of him was shocked. Why did her mother allow her to go unescorted to a man's room? Where was everyone?

"When work allows it," he said in a discouraging way. "You see I'm—"

"Kit!" A sharp voice interrupted him. "Kit, come down here at once!" The screeching voice rose. "*Where on earth are you?*"

"I am twenty-eight years old," she said, with a conspirator's grin. "My mother thinks I'm two."

"You must go at once." His face was stern in the lamplight, his expression sincere. "Your mother is calling you."

- CHAPTER 5 -

"Ma, stop it!" I said, as she practically arm-wrestled me downstairs. "What on earth are you doing?"

"Taking you outside, so I can talk to you," she replied grimly.

"Fine with me," I said, and meant it. She was a shouter when riled, and I had no intention of being a floor show for the other guests. She marched me across the yard and into the barn.

"How could you?" she shouted when the door closed behind us, her face witchy and mean in the storm light.

"How could I what, Glory?" I used her name to remind her I was a grown-up.

"Take that man up to his room and stay with him so long. Everybody was waiting for you to come down."

Everyone of course meant Tudor.

"You were in the kitchen. Daisy was busy, I did it to help."

"To *help*. By being with a man alone."

I would have laughed had I not been so angry myself.

"Glory," I said, as patiently as I could. "I was a nurse during the war." I could have told her then about wiping the lips of wounded men, holding their legs in my hands, emptying their chamber pots, feeding them, changing their pajamas, and yes, seeing, sometimes, their most secret parts—what my mother would have called their nooks and crannies—but even in the heat of battle, I needed to protect her.

"And look where nursing got you." Her eyes glittered with spite.

"Right back here again." She looked around at the barn's cobwebby bridles and molding hayricks, and shuddered theatrically as her eyes settled on a two-foot-high technical drawing, "The Anatomy of the Genital Tract."

"Look at that revolting thing. Have you any explanation for your behavior?" she said when she had recovered.

"That foul old bag was attacking him," I said. "You know how nasty she gets."

"Oh, so a world savior now, like Daisy," my mother said sarcastically. "And look where it got her."

I disliked it when my mother sneered at Daisy, showing a deep mistrust of intellectual "bluestockings" that came from her own insecurities.

"Get this into your head, Kit." She held up a finger. "Number one: you are not a skivvy here, your job is in the office. You're a volunteer, you're Daisy's friend."

"Can't you see any good in this?" I asked her. I'd tried, at least once, to tell her about the charity but she'd turned a deaf ear.

She looked down for a second. "Oh, blast it!" Our walk across the yard had rimmed her suede shoes with mud. She set about scrubbing them frantically with a sheet of discarded writing paper from the wastepaper basket.

"Second." With a dainty gesture she dropped the dirty paper back in the bin. "Never, ever go unattended into the bedroom of an Indian man. You don't know them. I do. They are absolute predators, and they see all European women as sluts. Don't look so shocked. I'm only telling you what is true."

I rubbed my arm where she had pinched it hard, and pulled away from her. She'd once thrown a lamp at my head in a fury when I wouldn't wear the dress she'd laid out, and now she had the same wild look in her eyes. She'd bathed the cut later and given me a doll as "a sorry present" and had said she loved her little girl more than anything else in the world, but it was just so hard sometimes being all on our own together. And I'd hugged her back, flooded with sweet relief at our being friends again, and kept the doll, seeing loneliness forever after in its glass-button eyes.

"I'm a grown-up now," I said.

"That's exactly the point," she said. "I want you to find someone nice, to settle down, have babies, a proper home."

I had a sinking feeling as she said this that the doll with the glass eyes was back in my arms.

"And the thing is," I replied, "quite soon I want, I have to go back to London and finish the midwifery." (I had to say the word every now and then as if to inoculate her.) "It won't take long, I—"

"Oh, that." She squeezed her eyes shut. "Please, for God's sake, don't talk about that now."

A sudden wind rattled the barn doors and swayed the flame in the oil lamp. My mother, who was terrified of ghosts, clutched me in genuine terror.

"It's all right." I put my arms around her. "There's nothing here." And then, oh, how quickly her moods could change: she gave me a real hug and I smelled her perfume (Shalimar) and a whiff of cardamom from the curry cooking.

"I'm sorry," she said in a muffled voice. "There are too many people here, and it's driving me a little doolally. And I can't stand that old bat either. She never has a nice word to say about anyone."

She gave a little croaking laugh, which I could not return, and then looked around the barn with big black-and-white eyes.

"It's stopped raining. Let's go back. I hate it out here."

"Give me a moment to lock up," I said, her nails digging into my arm.

"I know you're a big help to Daisy," she continued. She glanced again at the midwife training poster. "It's just such a strange job to choose: I don't know how you can do it." She shuddered and clutched me more tightly.

"I know," I said, feeling fraudulent. I was so scared of it myself.

- CHAPTER 6 -

He woke up very early and stood at the window, looking out at misty gray fields, some ghostly cows, a church spire on the horizon. He remade the view into bright blue skies above the silent green backwaters of the Periyar. He would be there soon and needed to compass his mind there and not get lost.

It was cold in the room. With an overcoat over his pajamas, he sat at a desk in the window, working on the last fifty pages of his PhD thesis on sleeping sickness—"The Care and Treatment of Encephalitis Lethargica"—that had quietly obsessed him for two years. He was paying particular attention to a major outbreak between 1896 and 1906 in Uganda and Congo, where close to a quarter of a million people died and foreign aid had been patchy and poorly coordinated and had led to unedifying squabbling among the richer nations.

It was a sobering subject to live with day in and day out, and he, desperate to finish now, secretly hoped the work with Miss Barker would not take up too much time, even though it would pay for his rent and food.

Deep in his studies, he skipped breakfast, until the knock on the door reminded him they were to meet at ten thirty.

"I must apologize in advance"—Daisy bounced beside him as they walked towards the barn—"for making you, temporarily, the lone male in what Shakespeare called a monstrous regiment of women. We didn't plan it that way at all. In fact, we absolutely welcome the masculine point of view, but you know Indian doctors who speak Malayalam aren't thick on the ground around here, and we're up to our eyebrows at the moment with fund-raising and speeches and so forth and, well, this is it."

She unlocked the huge door and together they stared into the cavernous space.

"HQ Moonstone. We've cleared a desk for you near the fire; make yourself at home there. There's rugs in the corner for when we're really freezing," she'd added. He liked her already, her big friendly teeth, her air of purpose.

"Miss Barker." He sat down, keeping his coat on. "I hope I'm not here under false pretenses: my circumstances mean that my Malayalam might be rusty."

She stopped moving papers and gazed at him sympathetically. "What a rotten thing, being caught out by the war like that."

"I was one of the luckier ones." He had fought against the role of poor Indian boy for years, particularly at school where chinks in your armor were ruthlessly exposed. "But my main goal now is to finish my thesis before I go home."

"May I ask what it's on?"

"The human African trypanosomiasis. Sleeping sickness," he added helpfully. "Have you heard of the particularly bad epidemic in the 'twenties?"

"I have, and it was appalling. How very worthwhile." She peered at him in frank admiration. "I vaguely remember a number of foreign powers tried to combine aid, and it led to the usual complications."

"I'd be happy to show it to you." He felt a tug of eagerness; it was rare now for people to even know about the disease.

"And when you finish it, you'll be a double doctor. What an achievement! Tell me, are you very swotty or just naturally clever?"

"Is there a good answer to that?" he asked with a quizzical smile.

"That doesn't make you sound like a fascinating big head?" They smiled at each other. "You're probably both, but anyway, onwards.

Here's the plan: weeks. If you can spare an hour or two for translation in the afternoon, you're free to do your own work in the morning. Does that suit?"

"Perfectly," he said. "My passage is booked for November, so good practice for me to speak my own language again."

He spoke lightly of the thing most dreaded: forgetting his mother tongue. A few months ago he'd woken in a sweat after a vivid nightmare in which he stood, dazzled, excited, on the quay at Fort Cochin. His mother had run towards him: soft white clothes, soft brown skin, the thick gold hoops in her ears glinting, but when he tried to speak to her, he found his mouth stitched up in crude cross stitches and woke sweating and afraid.

Inside the barn, three battered desks were arranged in a semicircle around the fire. A poster of a gruesomely naked woman was propped against the wall. Not the kind of naked woman sniggered at after lights out at school or the kind of anatomical drawings seen at Barts, but the inside of a woman, with all her pipework, her veins, her arteries, her secret caves shockingly exposed.

"Those are a work in progress. Do you find them a bit lurid? Do be honest."

"From whose point of view? Don't forget I'm a doctor."

"Well . . ." He sensed her struggling not to patronize him. "Yes, of course, I don't mean you, but this is part of our dilemma. Some of the Indian midwives we'll be instructing may be very experienced, very technically skilled, but will have absolutely no idea of what a woman looks like inside."

"Miss Barker," he said after a desperate pause, "I am at sea here. I left India when I was sixteen." *Deliver me from evil, from temptation, from embarrassment* ran in a silly conga line through his head.

"So any instruction about childbirth at all?"

"Remarkably little," he said. The truth was the war had disrupted and reduced quite a bit of their training: at one point Barts had become a casualty receiving center. Later they'd been moved to

Cambridge, where accompanied by much raucous laughter, they'd raced through reproduction and birth in a week.

"Before I start," she said, "would you be kind enough to call me Daisy? 'Miss Barker' makes me feel like a maiden aunt. Kit, who occupies that desk,"—she pointed to the one beside him—"has a delightful but rather highly strung mother. She doesn't approve of her daughter doing this kind of work, so we try not to talk about it in the house. Does that sound very silly to you?"

"Not at all." He was amazed she would ever imagine he would discuss such things in mixed company. "I shan't say a word."

"So," she began again delicately, "I'm to start from the assumption you know nothing about midwifery in India."

"Not a thing," he replied promptly. "Absolutely nothing. The only thing I know is that the midwives are, in some parts of India, called *dais*."

"Correct."

"And that when a baby was being born in our house, the men kept out of the way."

"In some respects it's a great shame," she said, her clever eyes on him. "Sad to say, India has a truly lamentable rate of infant mortality—one of the worst in the world. The British should have done far more to tackle it while they were there. They didn't, and that's a permanent blot on our record."

She briefed him concisely about the hospital in Cochin and their aims to combine the best of West and East in its practices.

"Some of your village midwives have more knowledge in their little fingers than our Western-trained midwives will acquire in a lifetime. They come from centuries and centuries of midwives, who have done thousands and thousands of deliveries. Alienate them and we lose a vast sea of knowledge we can use.

"But some of these women,"—Daisy pulled a mournful face—"are shockers: they cut umbilical cords with rusty knives, jump on bellies to speed births, drag placentas out. We have to teach them that small things like basic hygiene and medical kits will make a vast difference. Our aim is to become an extended family in which we all learn. What do you think?" She gazed at him hopefully.

"It sounds very impressive," he said politely, when all kinds of alarm bells were clanging in his mind. He'd read the papers about the tidal wave of fury unleashed after the British had left.

Daisy's glasses flashed at him as she showed him an account book. "To date we've managed to raise the sum of two hundred pounds for teaching equipment and medicine, which we plan to take to India in three months' time to help maintain the Home. Kit's been a marvelous support with our begging letters, and with your help we can get the training manuals right. Is there anything else you'd like to know?"

"I don't think so," he said. The barn door rattled as the girl walked in. She wore a woolen dress and gum boots and an unflattering head scarf. Her cheeks shone with rain. "God, it's hideous out there." She wrestled the door closed against the wind. "Sorry I'm late." As she swept off her head scarf, her dark hair fell in a cloud around her shoulders. She sat down on a stool near the fire and performed an unintentionally erotic striptease, as one gum boot was inched off with the heel of the other, revealing slim lower legs.

"Have I missed the sales pitch, Daisy?"

"Nothing you haven't heard. How's your mother's headache? Did she make breakfast in the end?"

"Not good. I should probably leave early. So, Dr. Thekkeden," she said, and turned towards him with a professional smile, "how was your night in the Bird Room? Good, I hope."

"We're going to call him Anto," said Daisy.

"Anto," she said.

"And Kit," he said shyly.

"Is Anto an unusual name in India?" She unbuttoned her raincoat and set it on a pitchfork near the fire to dry, then tugged at her dress to straighten it.

"Not for a Catholic boy," he said. "Most of us are called by Christian names. My family calls me *An*to," he said, putting the stress on the first syllable.

"*An*to." Her plump lips cupped the sound.

He took a deep breath and said, to distance her, "Does that sound more Indian?"

She gave him a straight, unembarrassed look. "I don't know, but I shall definitely call you that."

"Whatever you like." He gave her a brief smile and opened the files he had brought with him.

"Well, Anto, don't let me interrupt you," she said. If she'd registered the slight, she showed no sign of it. "I have a ton of letters to write."

They worked in silence until the lunchtime bell came across the yard. The silence was soothing, giving him time to restore himself amongst his books. Being in the company of women was pleasant too, he reflected, after being alone now for months, in libraries or in his digs, often working between damp-smelling sheets in bed to keep warm. This was the reason for the unusual slightly electric glow he was feeling.

Towards lunchtime, she stood up. "I've replied to most of the letters in the yes tin, Daisy," she said. "There's a very angry nurse in the other pile. I'll sort her out after lunch, if that's all right." Her blue Fair Isle sweater rose as she yawned—a slim waist, a glimpse of liberty bodice. "I'm starving," she said. She turned to him. "How about you?"

- CHAPTER 7 -

In early March, I got a letter from Saint Andrew's saying my course had to be postponed until the next academic year. The roof of the nurses' home had been deemed unsafe, and with much of London still in ruins, it was impossible to find builders to fix it before the new term began.

When I read this to my mother, she said, "So, together again like old times." She dabbed her eyes and gave me her loving look, and from long habit I smiled back and returned her quick hug. But my feelings were complicated, and since our row, I had become more and more secretive with her.

The truth was that as much as I loved the peace of Wickam Farm, without the Moonstone work and the challenge of helping Daisy, I would have been climbing walls by now, and there was something else far more troubling to me, which was the Indian doctor.

For the first few weeks, he'd expressed a preference, in the politest way possible, for working on his own in the Bird Room during the mornings and skipping breakfast. I was never sure whether this was due to my mother's chilly treatment of him or his way of avoiding Tudor and Ci Ci at breakfast, but it had definitely helped with my mother's worries about having this potentially wild beast housed under the same roof as her daughter.

Daisy tried to talk him out of it, saying, rather shamefacedly, they could only afford now to light two fires: one in the dining room, the other the ancient solid fuel range in the barn. But he'd insisted, until in February during one particularly bitter week, the rotten wood surrounding his window had fallen away with a chunk of Virginia creeper, and he'd been forced to move back into the barn.

For the first few days, we sat several feet from each other at the old school desks that had been brought down from the nursery. I was making sketches and notes from Comyns Berkeley's *Pictorial Midwifery* and sending out letters. His glossy head was bent over piles of academic textbooks.

Whenever I sneaked glances at him, I was amazed by his industry and his concentration, because for years I'd heard my mother say that Indians were lazy and stupid and this was why they'd let the British lord it over them. Ci Ci often sang the same song, recalling servants straining soup through their turbans or needing a good boot up the "you know what" to get them going at all.

I felt a spurt of jealousy too sometimes. Men were lucky that way, I thought, remembering how my mother had dragged me away from my matric books saying if I worked too hard, I would ruin my looks. Men, she warned me, were put off by bluestockings, whereas a man's industry was applauded, fed with meals and cups of tea, and not interrupted by countless scurrying tasks.

But anyway, it was I who started making him cups of tea, at first because I felt sorry for him missing breakfast, and later because it gave me a queer happy feeling putting on the kettle for him, pouring water in the teapot, adding his spoonful of sugar from the jam jar, and carrying it to him.

When I handed him the mug, he would look up and smile at me—the sweetest most sudden smile lit up his face—before going back to his books again. Working together like this felt domestic, contented, even though I was sometimes aware of a deep reserve about him, not exactly shyness but something deliberate, and I could never be sure which version of him I would be presented with.

One day, as I was measuring out two spoonfuls of tea, he told me his uncle grew tea in the hills above Travancore. He had vague memories of his first visit there as a child, and of how grown up he had felt when an aunt had found him a special cup and poured him his first taste of tea. When he mimed a child's solemn face, I saw what a dear little boy he must have been with those long-lashed green eyes. But when I looked at him again, I found him intimidating with his high, jutting cheekbones, that serious, remote, Spanish Grandee look.

Shadow and sunshine, I thought when, on the following day, he put the tea cozy on his head and said in the plummy tones of an elderly vicar, "Thank you, my dear good woman, six lumps will suffice," and I laughed too much and felt light-headed.

He was a very good mimic—one of the reasons, I suspect, that he never complained of any bullying or name calling at Downside, where, he said, apart from a few twits, he'd made good friends. Daisy told me he had been in the first eleven cricket team too, which must have helped.

Our laughter felt shockingly indiscreet, like the piercing of something formal, and afterwards I found I was shaking and was relieved when Daisy appeared.

I'd started to eavesdrop when he was working with Daisy; I liked hearing him speak in his own tongue. It turned his voice into something buttery and strange which I felt as a pulse in my own stomach. I felt it hurt him too: when he stumbled on simple words, he winced like a man setting out on a familiar walk and finding glass strewn under his feet.

Daisy agreed it must be peculiar to speak your own language again after so many years, and particularly to be discussing childbirth, sexual intercourse, ovulation, periods.

She said she'd let him off translating words like *vagina* and *nipples*. "The poor boy left home so young, I doubt he even knows them." These omissions could easily be filled in by Neeta, she said, who would add her own additions to the notes when they arrived in South India.

So far, so purposeful. After a few weeks of this, we started to feel like a good team at the barn. We had something separate from the house, something new to rescue us from the dreariness of ration- ing and February gales and the strange silence and even stranger memories the war had left.

Thanks to Daisy's talks, a jumble sale, and our begging letters, a slow trickle of money was coming in. The refurbishing of the Moonstone Home, scheduled for autumn that year, was beginning to look entirely possible.

And then Tudor began to drop in to the barn at inconvenient intervals, in what I can only describe as a claiming way.

He sprawled on the edge of my desk and monologued, in a self- conscious showing-off way, about his jazz collection or his socialist principles or some archaeological paper he was about to publish.

If he spoke to Anto at all, it was antler-clashing stuff about old schools and cricket scores and university results, or he was noisily sympathetic to Anto at having to put up with "the girls."

As the days wore on, the sight of his bony tweed bottom on the corner of my desk made me want to scream or stick a pin in it, but I tried not to show it, both for Daisy's sake and my mother's.

It was my mother, I was sure of it, who was encouraging these visits, her mind leaping ahead to weddings in Saint Peter's Church, which was part of the farm, to food for the reception, the naming of our children, to manicures, hats, canapés. And why not? Or so she would reason. In the deliberately classless world of Wickam Farm, anything could happen.

But another fly in the custard was Ci Ci, who, noticing Tudor's visits to the barn, began to unsheathe her claws. Poor Flora, poor me: reluctant gladiators, for a prize neither wanted. Or maybe Flora did; she'd become so wary of her mother it was almost impossible to tell.

The storm finally broke on a night when Ci Ci was in bed with a hot water bottle and a tray, because she had a bad cold. Anto was working in his room, Daisy in Cheltenham giving a speech.

On that freezing wet day, Tudor had laid aside his socialist principles to swagger off in plus fours to shoot at the Blenheim estate, which was close to us. He'd come back garlanded with dead birds that he wore on a string around his neck. At dinner, when my mother brought in the partridge, nestled in bacon and with a sage and onion sauce on the side, he regarded them with the complacent pride of a man who has just slapped a bison on the cave floor.

"I took them 'em down just behind the Shakenoak Wood," he said, in his usual careless drawl. "Lord Clyde was there too, but his dog had a bad day, so they both retired. Here, have some of this. I found it in the cellar—it's Pomerol 'thirty-five—very good." He looked at me. "Part of your education."

The wine was a surprise. Usually if we drank it at all, it was Daisy's carrot, damson wine, or elderflower, combustible and variable brews that might have a thin layer of green mold on the surface and occasionally went off like bomb blasts in the larder.

Tudor got out the dwindling set of Waterford glasses, poured a full one for himself, one for me, a thimbleful for Flora, who was profuse in her thanks.

I had no idea what the significance of Pomerol '35 was, but the taste was good and I liked the warm burr it gave to my bones.

"When you drink a good wine," Tudor instructed me, "you should hold your glass like this." He put one hand daintily around the stem of the glass. "Never by the bulb, then hold it in your mouth for a moment." His eyes were moistly intently on mine. "Now roll it around." His thin lips rotated. "And swallow." His Adam's apple bobbed.

"Don't you love learning new things?" a suitably entranced Flora was saying when Daisy appeared in a wet mackintosh.

"What are we celebrating?"

"Birds," Tudor said shortly. "Partridge. Got 'em today."

"Golly, I'm famished." She unbuttoned her mac. "This smells wonderful." She lifted the silver salver on the sideboard. There was a small amount of partridge left, a few tablespoonfuls of bread sauce, bacon, three shriveled carrots.

"Has Anto been fed?" She stopped helping herself. "He's still in the barn. I saw the lights on."

"I thought he went with you," I said.

"No, too busy. The poor boy must be ravenous. I'll take him some food."

"I'll go, Daisy," I said. "You stay and eat."

We put a few morsels of meat and some potatoes on a plate, and what remained of the vegetables. I put a steel cover over the plate to keep it warm. When Daisy left the room to hang up her coat, I saw there was about half an inch of Pomerol left.

"May I take some for Anto?" I asked.

"Don't bother," he said. "It'll be against Inky's religion."

He'd taken to calling him Inky behind his back. When I heard Flora chortling dutifully, I felt a surge of pure rage.

"Don't call him that," I said.

"It's a joke," he explained patiently. Some of the wine had stained his chin like a birthmark. "It's what Billy Bunter called our tinted brethren."

"It's not funny," I said, "and he does drink wine, you know that."

"Well, let him bring his own—or take him the other." He gestured towards a carafe of damson at the end of the sideboard. "I don't give a damn."

The glass trembled in my hand. I wanted to see wine drip down that smug, taunting face.

"You're pretty when you're angry," he said.

Daisy walked in, which was lucky.

"Oh, you angel," she said. I had the tray in my hand. "Would you mind terribly taking it to him?"

It was misty outside and very cold, with the moon hanging behind a skein of clouds. I had the keys to the barn in my pocket. We'd had a minor break-in recently: nothing serious, an old typewriter and eight pounds in petty cash. When I unlocked the door, I saw Anto asleep at his desk in a pool of yellow lamplight, his head resting on his hands like a child's, dark hair flopping over his hands. Under his right hand was a sheet of paper on which he'd written in his small, neat handwriting: "Oxygen Exchange System." A tiny sandstone elephant sat cross-legged on top of a pile of textbooks.

The fire had gone out; it was cold enough to see your breath. In the stable next door, I could hear Bert munching hay.

As quietly as I could, I crept across the room and relit the stove, and when it was crackling and glowing, I put the tray on the side of the desk, trying to decide whether or not to wake him, he was so deeply asleep. Lord, he was beautiful. I'd never thought of a man being so before. The sharp curve of his cheekbones, the softness of his mouth.

The collar of the tweed overcoat he was wearing was up. I turned it down, and then I touched his hair. A puff of air came from his mouth like smoke.

"Thank you," he said, quietly.

I leapt back, managing to catch the plate of food in my hands, but the tray fell with a noisy clatter onto the floor, scattering knives and forks, and wine which spilled like blood over the hearth.

"Blast." I was furious and embarrassed. "I didn't mean to do that."

I set the plate back on his desk and we got down on our hands and knees to pick up the fallen cutlery and mop up the wine. And it was then he put his hands on either side of my face and kissed me.

"I know," he said. He kissed me again.

We were kneeling, staring at each other like two people about to be executed, when we both heard the clatter of boots outside the door, the horse stamping in his stable.

"Let me in." A slurred angry voice.

"Hang on," I called through the door.

It was Tudor, red-faced, half plastered, proprietorial.

"Why did you lock it?"

"There was a break-in recently."

"Silly me. I thought the purpose of a key was to keep robbers out." He smiled at Anto unpleasantly, showing his yellow teeth.

"Boom boom boom boom!" he suddenly shouted, making his umbrella into a gun and pointing it at the sky. "Did you enjoy my birds?"

He stood close to Anto, less than a foot away.

"I haven't tasted them yet," Anto said. His voice was very quiet; I could see a muscle twitching in his jaw.

"Well, I can tell you, they're damned good," Tudor said, and then to me, "It's raining, Kit. You can share my umbrella back to the house. Your mother told me to get you."

"Thank you," I said with as much dignity as I could muster; I felt weak-kneed and uncomfortably aware that my hair was mussed.

I looked at the now cold plate of partridge and potatoes on the desk. And then I turned to Tudor and gave him the tray.

"Could you hold this for me?" I loaded the tray with the dirty cups and cutlery Anto had used earlier in the day.

Bull's-eye, I thought. You wait on him, you horrible man—he's worth two of you.

A small, sweet victory, which I feared could not last.

- CHAPTER 8 -

One day he would struggle to even remember the name of the pretty girl at Wickam Farm, or the Bird Room, or the barn. He would shut down this part of his life just as he had shut down India on the ship coming here, or at least managed to cram it into some back room in his mind.

But right now: the crunch of loose floorboards above him, Kit's faint tread on the stairs, the clink of her bottles in the bathroom, the rustle of her dress coming off. To corral his mind, he got out the box from under his bed and laid out letters and photographs of his family on the eiderdown and switched on the lamp.

His long-ago family: Appan, his father; Amma, his mother; Mariamma, his sister; and his grandmother, Ponnamma. The women who pinched his cheeks, fed him delicious meals, tucked him in bed at night, loved him up until they suddenly sent him away. He tried never to be melodramatic about this, tried to believe Father Damian's suggestion that it might have been the making of him.

And underneath, more photographs, splayed like a deck of cards, the extended family groups: hundreds of vaguely remembered ghosts from Christmases, christenings, Onam festivals, weddings. He studied them with the expression of a man studying for an exam he was bound to fail. He picked up a faded snapshot of his father. Studious, bespectacled, grave, Appan stood a few feet away to the right of a group of young Englishmen. A photo taken, as his father had told him many times, on the greatest day of his life:

his graduation from Lincoln's Inn, where he was called to the bar. Appan, wearing the dark Savile Row he still wears, stood skinny, scared-looking on some grand-looking steps, holding a piece of rolled-up cardboard.

Anto's face clouded as he remembered his father: the handsome, authoritative face at the end of the table. The family ringmaster who could change the emotional temperature of a room simply by walking in. His father's car, a Bullnose Morris, one of the few in the district. Appan leaving for an important court case in Pondicherry, conker-colored briefcase bulging with grown-up mysteries, shaking his hand in the hall as he went to an overseas conference. "Look after your mother."

His hungry desire to keep his father's love with good results, good cricket innings, good behavior felt like a source of weakness now. When he fell below Appan's high standards, he saw disgust on his father's face. "You're on the seventh stair, my friend," before the cane came out of the top drawer of his desk.

When Anto first arrived in England, it was a freezing September. No sun for days on end, gray skies, gray streets, and he'd wondered if this was the eighth stair: a place where you could die from unhappiness. This abandonment from home felt so unexpected, so complete that it almost destroyed the balance of his mind. Being happy, being loved, he now saw, had been the worst preparation possible for a life in which nobody knew him. Not a single soul in England.

His mother sent letters to Downside. Ordinary things: Pathrose cooking prawns and okra in the kitchen, the cricket match with the whole of the Thekkeden family on the lawn with, she'd written, "an Anto-sized hole in the fieldings."

The letters, in her impeccable handwriting, faint tang of jasmine oil on the envelopes, had in his first term almost destroyed him.

Before the other boys came, he'd snatched them from the basket in the refectory, where milk and biscuits were served, taken them to his room braced for the exquisite misery of remembering. It was only later that their lurid envelopes had become an embarrassment.

Now, in the lamplight, he squinted at a picture of her when young. Both of them were in the garden at Mangalath, near the small wooden summerhouse, where she tended her orchids. She was dressed simply in the plain white cotton chatta and mundu she wore at home. Her dark eyes were staring at the camera with a look that was both distant and scrutinizing. He was sitting on a tricycle at her feet, his expression pure and trusting as he looked up at her. She was his entire world.

Any moment now she would give up her camera face (she'd always loathed having her picture taken), she'd scoop him up murmuring, "My little pot of gold." Her only son, after years of trying. He can hear her in the kitchen now, barking orders to the servants, clinking the battered saucepans. The spices prickling his nostrils.

Did she truly love Appan? He wondered now. It wasn't the kind of question the sixteen-year-old he left behind would ask. He turned the photo over. Mangalath. Anto. Three years old.

Now, with a sigh, he picked up his mother's latest letter. It was dated February, 1948, postmarked Fort Cochin.

My dearest boy,

I'm sending the pictures taken with my new box Brownie. Sorry to have sliced the head off your father several times. He was the one who gave me the camera for Christmas—not too grateful of me. We had fifty-four family at Mangalath on Christmas Eve but, as usual, missed you badly. I don't know what I did in a previous life to have suffered without you for so many years, but now I hope it will make sense to me.

Appan is so proud of you, says the new India needs people like you to show people we can strive and thrive without the British. So I'm proud of you too and the sacrifices you've made. One day, I hope you will be a great man in our community.

I wish I could send you the fresh pineapple we had for breakfast; I know there is still very severe rationing there for you. All I can send is a mother's love and prayers. Your father, up to his neck in a new case, will write separately and send money for your fare. My love to you,

Amma

P.S. Today, Vidya came with her mother; she asked to see a photo of you, sends hers to you. She says you are handsome!

The sly aside saying the big thing was typical of his mother. The girl in the carefully tinted photograph is slender and shy in what looks like a new sari. She is the daughter of his mother's best friend, beautiful, as his mother has not failed to point out in three of her previous letters. Did Anto remember meeting her when he was a little boy? Answer—not really, or if he did, only vaguely as a shy pair of big brown eyes behind her mother's skirts. It was Anu, her mother, he remembered: the head patter, and bringer of homemade sweets enticingly wrapped in tissue papers, and once a new cricket bat.

This letter, that he'd read anxiously several times, gave Anto a tightness in his scalp, as if parts of his brain were shutting down. He was being netted and hauled in, and yet, during the long lonely years of exile, he'd ached for them, wept for them, looked forward to the security of being married to a nice girl, back safely in the bosom of his family again.

Now he lay facedown on the pillow as if to smother his confusion and panic. He didn't feel Indian anymore, that was the nub of it. During the long years of his exile, he'd got used to freedoms that his family would disapprove of. Going off to the cinema on your own when you felt like it. Having conversations with women who weren't discreetly chaperoned. The one-night stand with the WAAF, a huge and daring adventure before the shame set in; wearing Western clothes—he had no intention of wearing a mundi again, for him it would feel like fancy dress.

But his most pressing problem now was Kit, sleeping above him in what felt like almost indecent proximity. Up there now, sleeping, breathing, so close it felt like agony, for more than anything else, he wanted to kiss her again.

A rattle from upstairs—her curtains being pulled. Earlier she'd worn her hair up in a messy bun, stuck a pencil through it while she was working, but now he imagined it tumbling down.

He tried to joke himself out of it. "My God, Miss Smith, you're beautiful," because nothing about her had escaped his attention: the curve of her jawline, her dark eyes, her long neck bent over her work, the dark waterfall of her hair, her flashing smile when he made her laugh.

She was brushing her hair now. She was cleaning her teeth.

"Oh, for God's sake." He looked up frozen and afraid. "Stop it, you stupid bastard. Go to sleep."

- CHAPTER 9 -

Clearly alarmed at what had passed between us, Anto went back to working in the Bird Room in the early mornings. When we met in the dining room, I saw that he looked exhausted, and he would not meet my eye. I kept on working, talking, pretending not to care, but I couldn't stop thinking about him: the satin feel of his cheek, the softness of his lips on mine.

The memory kept me awake, and sometimes, when I crept out of the house at night to see if he was awake too, the light was still on in his window, and hearing my own breath, I felt myself in the position of a suicide trying to talk myself down from the edge.

I wanted him. My body was racing ahead of my brain like a naughty child, frightening me because everything about it was wrong. He was due to return to India in a matter of months. He would marry a girl there, or so Daisy had said, chosen by his parents, and it went without saying that my mother would be horrified.

But when in early April I got a letter from Saint Andrew's saying my course had to be further postponed until the next academic year—more problems with the roof—I was not disappointed.

My mother hugged me when she read the letter. "It's just like old times," she said, and from long habit I returned her fond look, but my feelings were far more complicated and secretive than I let on. What I wanted most was to speak properly to Anto again and not get caught.

Was it odd to have fallen for him so quickly? Not to me, it

wasn't. Not really. I was dangerously ready for love after the war, and he was terribly handsome and impressively clever and he already made me laugh, and he called up a maternal feeling in me because he seemed both brave and lost. There was something else too: I wanted to be properly loved, in the high old way, by a man, a young man who would exorcise a nasty memory, because there was a time, before I was eighteen years old, when I was so wet behind the ears that I honestly thought you could get pregnant if you kissed a man.

One of my mother's employers, Mr. Frank Jolly, a Yorkshire optician, a widower, had put an end to that by gently sliding a hand down my school uniform in the car one day. I know it's usual for young girls to say they are appalled by such advances. I wasn't.

What I felt, at least initially with Frank Jolly, was experimental. He was not bad-looking, and fairly young. He started to pick me up from school, and at first his advances were mild enough to be called caresses. But then, one afternoon when my mother was at the pictures, I was shocked when a thing like a landed fish leapt out of his trousers.

We were in the sitting room, the curtains drawn, when he touched me, his face all jumbled and mottled, like a jigsaw gone wrong. He said I'd led him on to this and, as he laid me down on a towel on the sofa, said I must now go through with it else my mother would lose her job and there would be a scandal. And I believed him and went through with it and afterwards shouted and cried in the bath trying to wash him away.

When I tried to tell my mother later, she blamed me, or maybe she didn't but it felt like it. She said that it was not a bad thing to marry an older man who would do things for you, and that Mr. Jolly was an attractive man anyway, so what about settling down with him? I said, "What about my exams, my matric? My life?"

"Oh, don't be so serious," she said. I didn't speak to her for three days after that, I felt so empty and pointless: a paper cup tumbling down a stream towards a future entirely out of my hands.

*   *   *

Anto had been waiting for ten days to hear whether his fifty-thousand-word PhD thesis had been passed when a letter with an Exeter College monogram on the envelope arrived. Daisy, who'd once played hockey for the county, snatched the envelope from the postman, raced across the yard with it, and pinged it on his desk.

He went so pale, she said, "Do you want me to open it?"

"No," he said. He stared at it, his lips moving silently.

"Prepare for the worst and expect the best," Daisy said.

He took the letter, touched the sandstone elephant, gave me a strange look, then closed his eyes. A few seconds later he said, "Damn it, damn it, damn it!" Over his head, which was in his hands, Daisy and I exchanged a look. This was heartbreaking, horrible—all those hours and hours of burning the midnight oil.

"Anto, I'm so sorry," I said. "You worked so hard."

I wanted to stroke his hair, to find words of comfort that wouldn't sound too maddening.

He looked up at me out of his right eye, grinned, and said: "Doctor Doctor Anto Thekkeden, please, from now on. They liked my thesis."

"You absolute fiend!" Daisy whacked his head with a roll of cardboard, and without thinking I hugged him, and if Daisy noticed the quick kiss Anto gave me, nothing was said.

"Now, Anto," Daisy said, when we had quieted down, "we must definitely have a party; if we dig around the cellar, there might even be some champagne. We could invite some people from the village over too, to make it more fun."

Anto was sitting at his desk again, staring ahead, in shock, I imagined, at the good news. His normal Indian way was to be very polite and to hate saying no to anything, but now he looked up and said, "What I'd most like is to go to the cinema in Oxford."

"That sounds fun," Daisy said. "We can have dinner afterwards at the Cardamom. I'm going to suck up to him now," she said to me with no attempt to quiet her tone. "He'll be a great asset to the Moonstone when we get him home."

"Maybe." He sounded guarded. I knew by now that Daisy's "Notes for Indian Midwives" worried him. We'd had a careful conversation about it the week before.

"She knows that Indians aren't exactly in love with the British at the moment," I'd said.

"Well and good then," he'd said softly. "I know she is a kind lady and that her intentions are good, but my fear is she is stepping into a snake pit. So much has changed since she was there."

The Ritz on George Street had once been a church but was now a warm, smoky, exciting dungeon with a flaking plaster angel on the roof and the cinema organist hidden behind a faded red velvet curtain.

And later that night we followed the usherette's torch towards the middle rows, and I sat down in the middle with Tudor on one side and Anto on the other. Flora, wearing a dress of stiff purple satin that crackled like fire, sat down on Tudor's other side.

The film, *To Each His Own,* was about a girl who falls for a handsome pilot, has his baby, and then spends the rest of her life in mourning for him. Watching it in the dark, with Anto beside me, I felt almost unbearably excited, as if this shabby little cinema was charged with life and some promise of excitement that I felt in the pit of my stomach.

Halfway through the film, I dropped the box of Black Magic chocolates Daisy had given us. He and I sank to the floor to retrieve them, and when I looked at him and saw a flash of reflected light in his eyes, it was hard not to take his beautiful face between my hands and plead with him, for what I was not sure: I was so aroused, and so unhappy too, because earlier, when Tudor had asked him, "When are you going home?" he'd said one word: "Soon."

"I hope you're not going to eat any of those." Tudor frowned as Anto put one of the chocolates from the box into my mouth. When we sat down again, breathless and inclined to laugh, Anto held my hand, and I felt a high kind of joy that I'd never felt before.

When the film reached its tear-jerking conclusion, Flora and I dabbed at our eyes with handkerchiefs, and I found I was sweating, from my palms, my armpits, my forehead, as if I'd been through some intense ordeal.

Looking back, it was lucky that Wickam Farm had as many digestive groans and gurgles as an old person. The tepid radiators clicked like arthritic bones; the boiler in the basement occasionally roared as if in agony. We were lucky too that Ci Ci often drank herself to sleep, and it was my mother's habit to always make a fortress of whatever bedroom she happened to be in by bolting the door and sometimes stacking furniture against it.

Because he came to me that night. It was a beautiful night with the moon high and the stars bright outside my window. I still have no words to describe how inevitable it felt. He stood looking down, and when he took off his shirt, I saw what a perfect young specimen he was. Years of cricket at boarding school had hardened him, slatted moonlight fell in bars over his sloped shoulders and strong muscled legs, and I can honestly say I felt not one scintilla of shame about what happened next. As I reached out for him in the dark, what I felt was a kind of singing in my veins. I had no choice.

I was perfectly aware of what a mistake this would be, how disastrous the timing, and so on, but my body bounded towards his, and once we'd started to touch each other, we could not stop, and I was glad I wasn't a virgin, because I didn't want fear or pain to spoil anything.

I lay in the crook of his arm afterwards feeling both wicked and victorious. It felt so right and he smelled so good: sweet and cinnamony. His skin was soft. He stroked my hair. The moon fell very brightly on the Indian quilt. It was only when he reached over me to draw the curtain that I saw that he was crying.

"Anto, what?" I felt my scalp prickle with alarm. I wanted him to feel the same high joy that I felt.

He didn't answer, just turned and put his head in the pillow.

I was going to say something else when, across the corridor, I could hear the scrape of my mother's door opening, the creak of her foot on the floorboards. The whoosh of the lavatory chain a few seconds later, and then Ci Ci's rusty cough.

I froze until I heard the click of the door closing and took my hand away from his mouth. We laughed silently, a scared laugh.

"Don't be sad, Anto," I whispered when I could breathe normally again. "It's been a perfect day," meaning his triumph, the cinema, and now this.

"I know." He gave a jagged sigh and said after a while, "I don't think I will ever feel this happy again."

"Don't say that." Now it was his turn to clap a hand over my mouth.

"Be careful," he mouthed, and pointed towards my mother's room. Before he crept out the door, he got up on his elbow and studied me. He smoothed my hair back from my temples and kissed my forehead.

"I should never have done this," he said a few seconds later. "It was wrong."

"No," I said. I was like a child not being allowed to eat a favorite sweet or pet a dangerous beast. "Don't say that."

He sat up and turned his back to me.

"Stop," he said as I reached out for him. "Please."

"Why not?" I hardly heard him. What I felt most lying there in the half-light was fantastically, thrillingly alive. I kept my hand on his back and ignored his sigh. My mind was racing ahead. I could get a job in India. I could go alone if I wanted to.

God, how stupid I was.

- CHAPTER 10 -

We didn't stop. For the next few months we lived by day like dutiful workers and by night like pagans. He'd creep into my room after lights out, and in the dark we made love with a sweetness and abandon I'd never felt before, or we'd talk in low whispers for hours about our lives so far and our families, almost anything but our future, because everything seemed heightened and either impossibly happy or desperately sad.

Our time was running out; he was going home. The actual date set was November 16. His mother was disappointed because he'd miss the festival of Onam. He'd showed me her letter, as if to make it real for both of us. When I asked what the festival was like, he said, "It's something to look forward to, like bonfire night, or Christmas. We play games, have big feasts." And again, I noticed how his voice sounded warmer and slightly buttery when he spoke of India, how the word *fire* became a soft purr. It frightened me.

"I thought your family were Catholics," I said, wanting to make them sound more normal.

"They're Catholics but they're Indian too," he said. "They are Nasranis, who got their faith from Saint Thomas the Apostle in the first century." When I asked what most did for a living, he said now most of the men were lawyers or bankers or doctors; before that they'd had coconut plantations or traded rice or tea.

These snippets of information, delivered in his public school voice, thrilled me, of course. My Indian with green eyes. My Spanish Grandee. My exotic lover. Oh God!

"What does Travancore look like?" I asked one night. I liked saying its exotic name, and I was feeling fuzzy and contented after making love.

"That I remember? Lie still, voman. I am giving you a geography lesson," he said in the mock Indian voice he'd amused the boys at school with.

"My country has three mighty rivers." He drew his hand down my breast and rested in on my ribs.

"Beside them are lush paddy fields and palm groves." His finger traveled down slowly from under my chin to my belly and made me shiver."

"You're making this up."

"I'm not. I'm not. Lie still. No talking in class."

"The dark shadows here are the Southern ghats."

"What's a ghat when it's at home?"

"Hush. I'll tell you later. Don't laugh, you'll be tested on this."

"The Western ghats." He circled my right breast.

"Anto, Lord, you're the corniest creature on earth."

"And here," in a Pathé News voice, "is the source." He ran his hands down my belly, and I was pulling his hair and stifling a laugh when the door opened and my mother burst in, so angry she'd forgotten she had her hairnet on. She stood in the doorway, breathing heavily, eyes going like searchlights across our naked bodies, the rumpled bed, the candle we'd lit in the saucer the better to admire our flickering bodies in.

I pressed my face into the pillow, my heart thumping like a generator, and then turned to look at her.

"May I ask," she said after a deathly pause and in her smallest and most terrible voice, "what you're doing in my daughter's bed?"

She remembered her hair net and shot me a look of pure rage as she snatched it off.

Anto sat up and pulled the blanket around him. "Mrs. Small-wood." His voice, subdued and low, seemed to come from a great distance. "I am so terribly sorry for this, and it is not how I planned to say it, but I love your daughter, I have prospects now and was hoping to ask, with your permission, to marry her."

If he could have clicked his heels under the sheets, he would have. The air went very still around us, we were waxworks in a tableau. I closed my eyes, not sure whether to be aghast or delighted. It was such a strange way to hear your proposal but, in the ticktocking moments that followed, I found, to my surprise, I was smiling inside.

And even stupid enough to think she might be pleased, Anto being a proper doctor now, her being half Indian. The silence lengthened.

"You stupid bastard," she said at last, the first time I had ever heard her swear in public. "I could have you arrested for this."

"Don't you dare talk to him like that," I said. "He's done nothing wrong, and I love him too."

"Oh, love." She snatched at her hair in frustration. "That's a joke?"

"Maybe for you." I sat up ready for a fight. "What do you know about that? I don't even know my father." My mouth was so stiff with rage I could barely speak.

"Well, that's just as well," she said. "Because if he knew about this, he'd get a gun and shoot him."

"Oh, so he's risen from the dead, has he?" I said, coldly sarcastic. "Last thing I heard was he'd succumbed to a fever in Hyderabad."

"I don't know what you're talking about," she said vaguely, which made me even angrier.

"So where is he?" My voice rose. "*Where is he?*"

It wasn't even a conscious effort to knock her off track, just the way my mind worked, like a blindly flying bird, when it was most disoriented.

Somehow, during all this, and the exchange of words that followed, Anto managed to get dressed. He stepped out of the shadows, wearing his shirt and trousers again.

"Kit," he said in a stern voice, "stop it. This is not a discussion for now, and your mother is right to be worried for you. We've all had a shock. We should all go to bed, unless"—he turned to my mother—"you would like me to go to Miss Barker and explain all this to her now."

This, I realized later, was a brilliant move, handing back to her authority and humiliation in one swoop. It worked in a way that apologies never did with my mother.

My mother pulled her satin dressing gown tightly around her.

"I feel quite sick. I will go to bed and think about it. And you, miss," she said, "I'll see in the morning."

"Say it quickly," I said to him before he left, "I won't blame you. Say it quickly if you don't mean it." Meaning marriage, meaning me for the rest of his life.

"I mean it," he said, very quietly. "I love you."

But he looked exhausted and pale, as if there were other things he should say but couldn't find right now. In the end, we kissed like two sleepwalkers, and during the sleepless night that followed, I seemed to run through the full catalog of human emotions: confusion, and a kind of crazed delight at Anto's unexpected proposal, embarrassment that my mother had caught us red-handed, fury at her for exhuming my father so unexpectedly and then pretending it didn't matter.

Out of this tangle I could only pluck one clear idea: that in the morning, I must tell Daisy before my mother did. Daisy loved Anto; she would understand.

Daisy was in the office the next morning, when I, foolishly happy, dropped the news at her feet, like a cat bringing a dead mouse into the house. She was in her overalls, gloves on because her chilblains were bad, wrapping up kidney dishes in brown paper. She straightened up, the expression in her eyes moving from their usual look of quiet pleasure at seeing me, to bewilderment, then horror.

"Oh, Kit, oh Lord," she said, when I had finished. She clapped her hand over her mouth and stared at me. "Don't worry," she said. "You can still get out of it. Have you spoken to him this morning?"

"He meant it," I repeated. "I know he did."

I was still feeling a kind of victorious expansion and babbled on for a bit about how we loved each other and how, in India, I could work at the Home, which was what Daisy had suggested all along.

"It won't happen." Her head was shaking even before I'd finished. She looked ashy white. "It can't. His family won't allow it."

"But Daisy, they're not *Indian* Indians." I tried to explain to her. "They're educated. They're Anglophiles. His father lived in England. He trained to be a lawyer here."

She sat down and put her head in her hands and groaned. "I know that. Oh, my dear girl," she said, looking up, "you're stepping into a bear pit."

"I thought you'd be pleased." I sounded like a child even to myself.

"It's true I'd hoped you might consider being a worker there, on a very temporary basis of course, you know, a month or two months, part of a team, with a small salary, not as a wife, not as an Indian wife. And of course Tudor will be desperately disappointed too. He's such a dear." She put on her glasses and stared at me, looking very sad. No, he's not, I thought. Tudor was definitely Daisy's blind spot. *Not in a million years*, my mind clanged, only I loved her too much to say it.

"And it will kill your mother," she added. Unusual for Daisy to try emotional blackmail; it made me realize how desperately she minded.

"She'll come round, Daisy."

"No, she won't." Daisy was shaking her head, looking sadder than ever.

"You don't know that."

"I do."

"How?"

There was an extra intensity in her gaze, which linked with other things I felt I didn't understand: my mother's half-truths, the occasional sly dig from Tudor and Ci Ci.

And I was sick of it suddenly: this unspoken thing that seemed to follow me round like a whiff from a drain.

"Daisy," I said, "what are you talking about? If you know something about my mother that I don't, why won't you just say it?"

"You must ask her yourself." She got very busy rustling papers and putting her pens away in the old Stilton jar she kept on her desk. "It's nothing to do with me."

"So there is something?"

"I don't know . . . I don't know."

I'd never seen Daisy look more furtive or trapped.

I ran to the kitchen, where my mother was chopping spinach with her usual economy of movement. Two dead pheasants lay on the table, their necks flopped over, their little eyes all blank now. From the door I surveyed her quickly: the neat waist, the trim ankles, the beautiful black hair, caught this morning with a marquisette comb. The apron was the jarring note: an actress cast in the wrong play.

"Mother, I need to speak to you."

"Well, I don't want to speak to you."

She may as well have added "you revolting slut," her look was so shuddery and thoroughly disgusted. She carried on chopping.

"Mother," I announced grandly, "I'm terribly sorry about last night, but we are in love and I'm leaving soon. I really am, you know." Did I really believe it then, the grandiose words, the concrete travel plans? I don't think so, but it felt important to make a stand. She stopped chopping and laid the knife down.

"Shut up, Kit," she said. "I refuse to talk about it here with all those blasted nosy parkers listening in."

She was almost levitating with rage as she took off her apron, put on her coat and a head scarf, and we walked out together into a raw autumn morning to have it out with each other.

"Oh, don't you bloody well come," she said when the poor old Labrador tried to squeeze through the door with us. There was a yelp as she slammed the door shut and caught his front paw.

We took the track that led through the avenue of elms and into Shakenoak Wood. Autumn leaves lay in brilliant soggy piles under our feet, and when two fallow deer did grand jetés across our path and disappeared into the woods, neither of us remarked on them.

At the end of the track, I undid the hunter's gate, and when we stepped into the wood, I was close enough to hear her breathing, which was hoarse and labored.

"I am going to marry him," I said. "Try not to mind too much."

"Well, I do mind," she said. Her eyes were very black, her skin very pale. "Because if you marry him, you will be dead to me." Those were her exact words.

"Are you serious? Is it so bad to marry the man you love?" I said.

"Oh, love," she said, as if it were some dog mess she'd stepped in. "It will be an absolute disaster. You know nothing about it."

My mother always refused to wear galoshes or Wellingtons, saying they made her feel "elephanty," and now, walking blindly ahead of me, she stepped into a puddle, splashing her good shoes and stockings with mud.

"Don't touch me." She flinched as I tried to lead her to drier land. "I'm so ashamed of what you've done." A tear rolled down her face.

"Mummy," I said, as she dashed it away with the corner of her head scarf. I felt cold and determined to keep myself separate from her in a way I'd never felt before. "There's something else I must ask you because I keep thinking people know something about me that I don't know."

"People will say what they want to say." She spat; her complexion had gone the sort of khaki-green color it went when she was really upset. "They're spiteful."

"But what is it they're not saying?" I was the tearful one now.

She shook her head violently. "About what?"

"You? My father? Why is it always so bloody mysterious?"

"Why do you go on like this, *on and on and on* at me." She made a stabbing gesture with her hand as if I were eviscerating her.

"Because I'm leaving and I have to know."

"You won't like it."

"Why not?"

"Because it's not nice."

A mizzling rain started to fall as we stepped into a deeper part of the wood. I stared at the silk head scarf my mother had retied under her chin. It was a hideous but posh thing, patterned with brown and gold horseshoes and very distinctive. I was almost certain it had once belonged to Laura McCrum, the wife of a businessman she'd worked for near Bromley. These items had a worrying way of turning up in her wardrobe after we'd left, a small gesture of revenge maybe, but it shamed me on her behalf.

"Let me tell you one or two things about India," she said. "It's the most complicated, class-bound country on earth. Any European putting one toe in the country and thinking they can understand it is a complete clot."

"I know that," I said. "I've talked to Daisy about it."

She poufed at this nonsense, and when I protested I was one-quarter Indian myself anyway, she snapped, "Why do you bang on about that? Your skin is so pale you could pass for English anywhere." Her face was all squeezed under the head scarf, her teeth bared, and then another thought brought dismay. "Do you go on about it to Tudor? Because if you—"

"I can't remember," I interrupted her furiously, "and I couldn't give a damn. He's got nothing to do with what we're talking about." She groaned as if I were the thickest person on earth.

"Tell me about my father." It came out louder than I intended, and a pheasant scuttled out of the tangled undergrowth, clucking and complaining.

She started sighing and pacing around. I looked through the wet autumn leaves at a darkening sky with huge clouds roiling in the west.

"Kit." She closed her eyes like someone locking herself into a cell, and when she came out her eyes were very black. "I'm only ever going to tell you this story once, because it makes me feel like the worst bloody twit in the world, and if you are rude to me, I will stop."

"I'm sorry, Mummy, please don't."

I waited in terrible suspense. The rain was coming down more heavily and any moment now I expected her to run for the house.

"God, I hate this climate." She tied the knot on her scarf again.

"When Tudor marries," she said, "he'll own all this wood, plus almost one hundred acres of prime Oxfordshire land. Daisy told me that, she spoke to me this morning before you got up. She's as upset as I am."

"Really." I could not resist the sarcasm. "Well, always nice to have company in your opinions. And just to make things perfectly clear, I wouldn't marry him if he was the last man on earth. I don't even *like* him."

"She knows Indian men as well as I do," she went on, as if I hadn't said a word. After a breath, she spoke again. "First, I was not born in Wrexham." This hardly came as a great shock to me. I'd forgotten, or discarded, the Wrexham version of her story.

"I was born in Pondicherry on the southeast coast of India," she said, taking on the queenly drawl I thought of as her telephone voice. "My father, your grandfather, was an Englishman, a high-up engineer on the railways there. I don't have any pictures of him, so don't ask." A flash of anger there. "My mother was an Indian woman."

I knew that already but didn't want to stop her.

"My mother died giving birth to what would have been my sister. I don't remember ever meeting my father. I was sent to an orphanage in Orissa, an English convent. I don't know who by, I was just sent. Is this the kind of information you're after?"

She gave me a look of muted fury, as if I were an impertinent journalist, not her child.

"Mummy, I'm sorry."

"It was a home for half-caste children."

Half-caste. I'd certainly never heard her say that before, and the word fell in an ugly way—like a dead bird or a turd between us in the woods, and for the first time I wanted her to stop because I hated hearing it applied to her, and in a way, it interfered with my dream of her because when I'd thought of my mother in India, I'd thought of cocktail parties, and tiger shoots, and pink and peach skies. Now I thought of a girl I hadn't thought about for years: Dymphna Parry, a miserable little thing who'd arrived midterm at my Derbyshire school. She'd been adopted by the vicar and his wife from somewhere in Africa.

I saw Dymphna's face again: gray-green with cold, the terrible tweeds she'd been togged out in, the woolly hair pulled into plaits that looked like unshorn sheep.

She wasn't exactly bullied, but she was one of the never chosen: not for rounders, not for special seats on the school bus. I'd discussed her frequently in pitying, condescending tones with my mother.

"Why didn't you say this before?" I felt sick because my mother's eyes looked wild now and somehow unhinged, as if I'd cut the rope that kept her safe.

"It was nobody's business but my own."

Yes, it was, I shouted inwardly.

"Our school was a convent." My mother's tone was frigid; she had not forgiven me. "The English nuns encouraged the English side of me, just as I have with you." She flung me a look of great bitterness. "Or tried to. We learned grammar and Shakespeare and manners. We ate shepherd's pie, toad in the hole. They were right to do so. The Indian towns around us were filthy places." My mother shuddered. "The people so poor and full of disease. There was a smallpox epidemic there."

"How did you meet my father?"

"I was clever, ambitious. I had good punctuation, so I secured a job with the British government. I was personal assistant to a resident, a delightful man." My mother's voice took on a certain swagger here. "I've forgotten his name. He was cultivated, kind, good to me. My pale skin, my English name meant my background was never discussed. I went to their parties as the spare girl, the decorative girl. I was pretty."

"And my father?"

"We met at an elephant hunt. Look at me, Kit, I'm soaked, I'm cold. Do you want me to get pneumonia telling you this?"

"Five more minutes, please."

"All right, an elephant hunt. A horrible affair. They built a cage for this beautiful creature and they smoked him out and then they stabbed him to death." She looked at me as if I had personally driven a stake through the elephant's heart. "That's your Indian. He is two steps away from being a savage."

"Your father was an army officer, good regiment." Again, the showy drawl. "Good job—aide de camp to General Smythe. I thought he was the bee's knees. Why should I talk about him? He behaved so appallingly."

"Please, Ma, I hate feeling other people know and I don't."

"Only Daisy knows," my mother said. "And Daisy won't say either, so don't bother asking her."

"Did you love him?"

"It doesn't matter. I'm freezing. I'm not going on." She was like a horse scampering on the spot in agitation.

We had come to a bench in the woods, its seat shiny with rain and old bits of moss. There was a clear view of the hills beyond: the heap of stones that had once been a Roman fort, a peaceful farmhouse in the arm of a placid field, a farmer on his tractor followed by a sheepdog.

When my mother almost collapsed on the bench, I wanted to put my arm around her and make her better. She was so upset, and I'd always had this haunting sense of her: of something fragile that I, her only child, could break. The idea of her as an orphan explained so much: her defensive hauteur, her longing for nice clothes and the outward trappings of respectability, her angry admiration for Englishness, even her mild case of kleptomania.

I'd planned to ask more about my father: specifically, Is he dead dead? Or dead to you? But instead I said, "You're cold, Mummy," because she was shaking. I wished she could have a bath when she got in but knew she couldn't. We'd been having trouble with the thirty-year-old boiler again, but Daisy hadn't wanted to call out a workman in case of a huge bill.

As we limped back to the house together, I hated suddenly this feeling of female powerlessness. I wanted action, change, the competence, the money to fix things, a new life, even if it was risky.

"Look at my shoes," my mother said, taking my arm at last. "Completely ruined, raking all this up." We'd stopped on the grass verge near the drive. Daisy drove past us in the Austin. I saw the dim outline of Anto—hat, dark overcoat—sitting in the front with her. We looked at each other, but none of us waved.

"Where do you think they're going?" I watched the car disappear.

"To the railway station, I hope," said my mother. She tightened her grip on my arm. "It will hurt for a while but not for long. I've been through it myself."

"They're probably only going to the post office," I said. I was frozen to the bone with cold by now and not sure what I felt myself as the glint of the rear mudguard disappeared around the corner. "They'll be back for lunch."

She turned on me.

"You don't believe me, do you?" she said. "You'll be dead to me if you do this. It's everything I didn't want."

I made myself look at her.

"You don't know the first thing about him," I said, feeling removed from myself and heroic and not a million miles away from Olivia de Havilland in *They Died with Their Boots On*. "He's clever, he's kind . . ." I might have added "and besides, I love him," when she interrupted me with a jabbing gesture of her hand.

"Mixed blood is like oil and water," she said, her face very pale. "Everything bad that has happened to me in my life comes from it. It's a taint." Her eyes were wild.

"Mother," I said, "how many dead people can you afford to have in your life?"

"As many as I need to get by," she said.

– CHAPTER 11 –

"I know about my father," I lied to Daisy that afternoon. We were sorting clothes for the jumble sale. "My mother told me pretty much everything this morning." Daisy's head shot up like a startled horse. She was sitting in a sea of moldy riding clothes, tennis racquets, pith helmets, and several rotting canvases: her father had been a successful artist before the war, and we often joked about the undiscovered Matisse we'd find in the attic that would change all our fortunes.

"Golly," she said. She put down the cardigan she was folding and looked at me. "What a time you're having."

"She's furious about Anto," I said. "Absolutely spitting mad. She's cut me off." I was trying to sound jaunty and not cry. Her look was steady and kind, the same old safe shore.

"Come on, Kit," she said, "you know what she's like. She won't keep it up for long."

"I think she means it this time, but I am going to marry him, you know." I was trying to hang on to the Olivia de Havilland feeling—heroic, dignified, quietly determined—but it was slipping like an actor's greasepaint in heat, though I was too proud to say so, and confused. Somehow my father and Anto had become jumbled in my mind, if only as places of escape.

"Did you know him?" I'd never asked her before.

"Briefly." A child's Fair Isle pullover fell to pieces in her hand. She put it in the bin.

"Is he . . . was he . . . a good man?"

"I honestly hardly knew him." Daisy's eyes stared into mine, terrified of causing me pain. "I think he tried to make amends."

"For what? How?"

"Kit, if I could tell you I would, but it's not my story to tell."

"I'd like to write him a letter. Do you know his address?"

"I'm sorry, Kit." She put a hand on my arm. "But why now after all these years?"

"Because she told me I was dead to her this morning, not once, but twice . . ." I was having trouble breathing. "And because I am going to marry Anto."

Daisy shook her head and sighed. "Kit, are you sure this is what you want? It's a hell of a thing to take on."

"Yes . . . if it's still what Anto wants."

"It is. I spoke to him this morning." She gave me an anguished look, and I could hear her groan as she tried to stuff a bell tent into a canvas bag.

"Forgive me for overstepping the mark here, Kit, but I do understand how addictive a physical attraction can be . . ." She was pink suddenly and daring-looking and starry-eyed and stuttering and I was mortified and wanted her to stop. "It's the most wonderful thing, like being plugged into the universe or something. But it has to be more than that. So are you quite sure?" Her eyes were gleaming and moist behind her glasses.

"Yes, Daisy," I said, frozen with embarrassment at the thought of those sensible square hands touching a man. "You know the other things about him," I said in a steadying voice. We seemed somehow temporarily to have swapped roles. "How clever he is and hardworking."

"Well, there is that," she said uneasily.

And the thought came like a flash of sunlight inside me, *Bugger the lot of them, I love him, I don't have to explain.*

Daisy sighed again as she wound the guy ropes into a neat

figure-of-eight. "Well, if his parents are liberal," she said after a long and thoughtful silence, "and if you can work for the Home, I suppose you could do worse . . ." Her voice tailed off. "And who knows? The new India is terra incognita for all of us, and it's not much fun here, is it?" I could see her struggling and leapt in eagerly.

"Oh, Daisy, thank you. You're the first person to sound even slightly pleased. Did he seem happy when he told you?"

Daisy hesitated. "No, Kit. Not really. He hardly said a word all the way to Oxford. I think he's terribly worried. He wanted to go on his motorbike but the roads were too slippery. He said he'd take a taxi back." And then I wondered if he was on the train already, running while he could; some part of me would not have blamed him.

"I love him," I insisted stubbornly, and then, "Didn't you ever want that, Daisy—a husband? Children?"

"Only once," she said. She hugged the bundle of clothes she was carrying. "He died young . . . a fine person." She looked through me at some dusty ghost beyond. "He was twenty-five. One day when I've had a few glasses of whisky, I'll tell you about it."

"Oh, Daisy." I took the clothes from her and said foolishly because I didn't know what to say, "I don't drink whisky."

"Nor will you ever again," she said, recovering her old teasing self quickly. "Not if you are to be an Indian wife."

Anto tried to have one sensible conversation with me before we married, in which he warned me how different our life might be in Travancore, and how I mustn't mind if his mother took a while to warm to me, and how Daisy might be embarking on a dangerous enterprise with her Moonstone Maternity Home, but we were lying in each other's arms at the time, him stroking my hair, my hand on his flat stomach. Somehow that dreamy post-lovemaking daze seemed to short-circuit the worry centers in both our brains.

*   *   *

And so we married, more in the spirit of two cars dashing through a green light before it turned red than in the spirit of, well, what? Thoughtfulness maybe, or a long and considered courtship, in which we carefully weighed up each other's assets in the way you might if you were buying a car or a house: value for money, enduring qualities, good workmanship, suitability for the job, and so forth. We seemed to be running on our own unstoppable electricity supply, one we could neither explain nor deny. And he did make me laugh too, have I mentioned that? A great aphrodisiac always, so it was more than youthful impetuosity, and it was true what I'd said to Daisy, I respected him: the dogged way he worked, the gentle way he'd deflected Ci Ci's and Tudor's barbs.

But now, since this is a confession of sorts, I'll admit that part of me opened like a flower at the thought of sunshine and blue skies and new experiences, an escape from rationing and bomb sites and the thought of going back to London and into digs with nurses again. I was longing for new things to happen. I wrote that night to Josie, asking if there was any chance she could be my maid of honor. "Dear Dark Horse," she wrote by return of post, "I'm going to miss you so much. As soon as you have a date, let me know. I'll twist Matron's arm and get the day off."

But Matron's arm was not for twisting, and Daisy was, in the end, our only guest. The wedding took place on a cold Thursday afternoon at the Oxford Registry Office. It cost us one and sixpence to hire it, two shillings extra for the use of a vase of yellow dahlias the last wedding party had left behind.

And I did drink wine at my wedding: Elderflower '47, as Daisy joked, bringing two bottles from the cellar to wash down some sausage rolls and a fruitcake. She was our only guest: my mother had stayed in bed, claiming she had a tight chest, possibly pneumonia coming on. Ci Ci, who'd been noisily sympathetic to my mother, declined to come and forbade Flora to come too, all of which was a relief. Tudor, who when he heard had suggested to Daisy that both of us be asked to leave the house, went shooting for the day. My last image of him was him standing in the hall, looking like a Victorian rent boy in his plus fours and peaked cap, his father's dead animals all around him. He could hardly speak he was so angry.

"Good luck," he said stiffly, picking up his gun and making a rattling sound with the cartridges on his belt. "I think you'll need quite a bit of it."

"Thanks, Tudor." I pretended he'd been nice. "I absolutely can't wait." In spite of the guns and the shooting paraphernalia, there was something oddly prissy and flouncy about the way he walked out to the waiting car; it made me think that maybe all the match-making females in the house had been barking up the wrong tree anyway.

After the wedding, Anto and I, strangely quiet and shy in the car, went to a guesthouse, the Culford, where they also bred budgies. It was on the edge of a soggy plowed field near Burford. Nothing special: we were saving all our pennies now.

I was worried immediately that our landlady, a stout farmer's wife, would notice that Anto was Indian and make a fuss, but he looked very distinguished in his one good suit and gray hat, and was even paler than usual due to the tension of the day. In an upstairs bedroom with a swirly carpet and sagging bed, we stood, side by side in front of the wardrobe mirror. He took my hand and turned my wedding ring around my finger.

"I love you, Kit," he said gravely. "I'm going to take care of you forever."

"Yes," I said, but perversely, I couldn't stop thinking about my mother in bed now and alone and almost certainly sobbing her heart out. "Thank you." I couldn't think of anything else to say. It was cold in that room. It smelled of mothballs, and I could hear rain lashing against the window.

"Your ticket came yesterday," he said. "My mother sent it to me with a letter."

"Oh, good." But it felt peculiar being sent a ticket by someone I didn't know, and I foolishly hoped he'd say something else: that she was happy, that she was looking forward to meeting me.

"Did you say I'd pay her back when I was working again?" The Home's trustees had agreed a working wage of sixteen pounds a month when I started in India, but I hadn't had enough in my bank account to cover the seventy-pound ticket to get there on the *Kampala*.

"Not yet." His face in the mirror looked guarded, his voice distracted. "It's not the right time now."

"November sixteenth," he said, as if the date of departure wasn't blazed on my mind.

"Yes. I love you, Anto."

"I love you too."

"You're frightened," I said, as his face swam out of view. He'd grown quieter and quieter over the past few hours. "I don't blame you. It's all happened so quickly." I felt a great big blank as I said this, as if we were in a play and acting very badly. He didn't say anything, just held me tight, our two shadows meeting and closing in the mirrored door.

"We've crossed the Rubicon," he said in his Pathé News voice.

"What exactly is the Rubicon, clever clogs?" I asked him later, trying to keep things light. We'd gone to bed early and were lying in each other's arms.

"A river in Italy," he said. "A place of no return. When Julius Caesar crossed it, he said to his troops '*Alea iacta est.*' 'The die is cast.' He knew if he didn't triumph, he'd be executed."

"A cheery tale," I murmured half-asleep, and then, "Were you always an egghead?"

"I'm not clever," I remember him saying sadly. "Not clever at all."

We went to sleep and woke to the tiny cheeps of hundreds of colored budgies singing inside their cages.

- PART TWO -

Cochin,
South India

- CHAPTER 12 -

New husband, new country, new climate, new mother-in-law, and whoopee! one hundred and seven new relatives all speaking a new language. When I opened my eyes in room four of the Malabar Hotel in Fort Cochin, I closed them again quickly. I lay in an elaborately carved rosewood bed, a dazzling light stabbing my eyes. The fan above me shifted air that smelled of the sea and old drains, and still feeling the sway and tilt of the sea in my blood, I longed to go back to that dreamy indeterminate place where it was just Anto and me on the ship together.

I could hear Anto splashing around in the vast antiquated bathroom next to our room. The concentrated energy with which he washed every part of his beautiful honey-colored body was a source of silent fascination to me. Ears, teeth, armpits, toes, nothing was missed, then the fierce scrubbing of the nails, the startling garglings when his tonsils got sluiced.

Once, during our early days on the ship, I'd called through the bathroom door, "You're worse than a girl." The door had opened and he'd given me an odd, intimidating look, and I'd made a mental note not to joke about this again.

I looked at my watch. Nine o'clock and I was already slippery with sweat. A slender lizard dashed up the wall. From the bathroom: splash, gargle, throat clearing, the slap of a towel. We'd made love twice during the night, but now my brain was waking, fear was releasing like a drug in my veins.

We'd come alive on the ship. Released from home, from war, rationing, people, we'd made our tiny cabin a secret cave where, on some nights, we'd gone to a level of wildness and freedom with each other that left us both gasping, laughing, speechless, and a little afraid. And knowing in some secret cell of myself that we might never be this free again, I'd stored it all inside me: the hours lying in deck chairs on the top deck, dreaming between sea and sky; the flaming sunsets; the new cities; our small cabin on F deck with the salt-smelling sea racing by. Long, whispered conversations; fresh fruit, the new taste of mangos, bananas, melons; moonlit walks with the night skies so close and bursting with stars; cocktails in the Sunshine Bar.

We lived like kings and made no new friends on the ship. We only wanted us; now the thought of sharing Anto with dozens of inquisitive strangers made me pant with alarm.

It's an adventure, I tried to tell myself, but my insides were swirling. Now that we were back to some sort of reality, I found myself worrying about my mother again. After staying in a more or less permanent sulk since our wedding, she'd promised, in a special cracked voice, to come to Tilbury to see us off. On the day we left, she'd worn her tweed traveling suit and a beautiful silk scarf. The paleness of her makeup, the scarlet lipstick gave her face a startling, almost Oriental look—like a Kabuki actress in a play. She'd toyed with her food over breakfast and later, in the freezing hall, announced, "I'm not coming to the station with you. I'm too busy here."

She'd flung me a look of wild accusation. "Thank you for ruining my life," she might as well have added, and then she gathered herself up, pecked my cheek, and said in a stagy drawl, "So, the very best of British, darling," possibly for the benefit of that old bat Ci Ci, who was peeping around the door, her eyes full of a kind of malicious glee at the horrors ahead for both of us.

"Don't forget to let me know how it goes," my mother had continued in the same vein, as if I'd planned nothing more than a trip to the dentist. "There's a pet."

God, I was furious. "I will. Thank you, Mummy," I said.

I knew my mother well enough to know she became more English than the English when she was scared, but this was more than I could stand. She ignored Anto altogether, didn't even shake his hand, and at the moment when I needed her most, I hated her for playing to the gallery.

Ci Ci contrived an equally stagy farewell: "Darling honeybun, farewell," she'd cried with more warmth that she'd ever showed me before. The clawlike hands she wrapped around my shoulders smelled of nicotine and her large ring nicked my cheek. She'd kissed me for the first time ever. "Give 'em hell," she'd added, a remnant maybe from some cowboy film she'd watched.

Daisy stood apart and watched us, warily and sadly. She knew the limits of her own embracing hospitality. And it was Daisy who drove us to the railway station, the back seat of the Morris stacked high with our luggage, and the boot jammed with medical supplies for the charity, labeled Not Wanted on Voyage. Two large tea chests had gone ahead of us.

The fields were frozen on either side of us, and the sky without color. Daisy broke the silence. "She'll miss you, Kit, I know she will."

"Do you think she'll write?" I was too shaken to say much.

"I don't know, but I'll keep you informed, I promise."

For that moment, I wished Anto wasn't with us in the car, because I'd kept the silly idea in my mind that my mother would crack before she left, and hug me, or give me some kind of blessing, maybe even some more information about my father, because although this trip wasn't like dying, it felt like a point where you wanted to get things straight in your mind. But he was there, looking pensively out of the window, thinking his own thoughts.

During our brief courtship, I was aware that although we'd

thought each other soul mates and talked about many things both small and large—books we liked, films, the war, the life we wanted to live—he'd asked me very little about my background. When I'd raised the subject, knowing he must want to know something, I told him my father had died during the Great War, but I wasn't absolutely sure because my mother didn't like talking about it. He hadn't pressed me for details, and the death of loved ones was such a commonplace since the war, I'd accepted his reticence as tact and been grateful for it.

And later, when I'd tried to take another run at it and be more open, something had always stopped me: a cringe of shame, a sense of guilt, a feeling that my admission might lessen me in Anto's eyes by making him feel he'd been sold a pup, a half-breed at that.

It felt like a long trip to the station. I wiped away a line of condensation from the car window, Anto still silent, and I stared at frozen fields, at ponies with breath like plumes of smoke being fed hay. I thought, Now you're a married woman, you must stop thinking about your parents, because your mind could whirl on this particular hamster wheel forever and it's quite possible you will never know the truth. I took my glove off and put my hand down on the leather seat hoping Anto would hold it, but he was not a natural hand holder.

Three waiters leapt forward with bowls of fruit and offers of tea or coffee as we walked into the Malabar's cavernous dining room for breakfast. A strange embarrassment came over us because neither of us had stayed in a hotel before, and in between the clinking of our cutlery, I could hear myself making stilted conversation about the furniture (massive, ugly), the fruit (tiny, delicious bananas), and the heat, which was, even this early in the morning, a startling ninety-two degrees.

I was hungry but didn't want to eat too much. Between us we

now had a grand total of one hundred and twenty-three pounds. He'd counted the notes out on our mattress that morning, and I was aware that if I hadn't been there, he would have already been enfolded in the bosom of an ecstatic family and spared the expense of this.

He ordered eggs and bacon for me and something called an appam, a kind of thin, flat pancake, for himself. He wrote the words carefully on a napkin as if for a child.

"Is it lovely to eat that thing again?" I watched him tear it into bite-sized pieces with practiced hands and dip it into what he told me was coconut chutney.

"Yes," he said. In the awkward silence that followed, I looked around the dining room. Four other Indian couples sat, half-secreted behind the palms or wooden posts. They were absolutely silent; all I could hear was the scrapings of their spoons, their gulps as they drank chai, and the bleak thought came: I wonder if he'll stop talking to me now.

After breakfast, he said we should stroll down to Cochin Harbor and make sure the tea chests had been taken off the ship. After that, we would find a bank, open an account, and change our one hundred and twenty-three pounds into rupees, and I could feel my spirits lightening, as if this anxious in-between day needed a proper job to do to give it shape.

"I'll show you around the old town too." He smiled the sudden, thrilled smile that made me fall in love with him in the first place, the smile that made his eyes light up, a seam of green and tortoise-shell, and the dimples that made him look about ten again. "And then shall we have lunch, and go back to bed . . ."

He did his Groucho Marx suggestive eyebrows, and I laughed and longed to kiss him but remembered, in the nick of time, not to: on the ship coming out, he'd warned me that in India it wasn't done for a man and a woman to hold hands in public. Not even married people.

*   *   *

The sun was eye-piercingly bright as we walked, an hour later, towards the Fort Cochin seafront. An old beggar lay half-naked under a tree, his eyes covered in flies, and the smell of old fish rose periodically from the rubbish-strewn drains.

Anto had the look of an eager boy as he picked up speed and rushed towards the dazzling sea, where more ships were coming in, and when we reached the water's edge, I heard him groan and saw him pass his hand over his face.

"Beautiful," I heard him murmur in a dazed voice. I didn't know what to say. The palm trees, the aquamarine sea, the cloudless blue sky, all looked to me like stage scenery to which the smell of fish and bad drains had been added.

"It hasn't changed a bit," he said softly, sadly.

"I always think a place will change if I'm not there." I could hear myself babbling nervously as we walked further down the seafront, when what I really wanted to do was to hug him, to say, "How wonderful—you're home," or some such, but I felt uncomfortably surplus to requirements. Not Wanted on Voyage, because there was nothing here that spoke to me, not yet.

"My father had his law offices over there," he said, when we'd got to the end of a stretch of cracked concrete. "Just behind the English Club, there." He pointed towards an elegant building set back from the seafront and surrounded by lawns. I looked over the hedge at the well-ordered building, with its potted plants and fine shrubs. Now the green, orange, and white flags of the new India fluttered from the veranda.

"Look at it." Anto seemed stunned. "We thought it the height of elegance when we were children. My brother and I sat in the car while my father had fierce games of chess with his old pal, Hugo Bateman, his English barrister hero. My father usually won. We were proud of that."

"A nice place to come and play," was all I could think of.

"Not really." Anto was squinting at one of the placards, arranged on the veranda, "My father couldn't even enter the club without Mr. Bateman's permission. That was always made clear to us." He gave a curious lopsided grin.

"What do they say. The signs?"

"Um . . . let me see . . . Malayalam may not come instantly," he said, a playful mimic again, "Ur . . . well, sorry for this, madam, but 'Quit India' . . . and 'India is ours again,' but you, my beautiful Lady Sahib are not to take it personally please. You're my wife," he added softly, "you are most welcome. Do you like it so far?"

"Yes," I said, my smile quick and insincere. "Of course I do." We were passing a group of very old women squatting on their haunches in front of piles of fish laid out on burlap sacking. They stared at me.

"Those," he told me. "These are the famous Chinese fishing nets." He pointed towards two skinny old men performing what looked like a lithe and practiced dance as they hauled up large stones and pulleys, followed by a net full of gleaming, jumping fish.

"Our physics master from Ignatius College once brought us here to watch them," Anto told me. "He said that these nets were 'a little miracle of design.' A brilliant use of energy and counterbalancing weights. When the stone goes down, the nets go up. No stony, no fishy."

I smiled at him. I liked the way he knew how things worked, his good memory for certain facts and solid things. It felt masculine to me, another kind of counterbalancing weight.

Next, while we were walking around a drain that oozed what looked like oily manure, he told me that India had once led the world in modern sanitation, that its drains, chutes, cesspits, and clever devices for moving rubbish out of town would be the envy of the modern world today.

He was warming to his theme when he glanced at me and, seeing my expression, said, "Good pillow talk, hey?" and we burst out laughing, and I was relieved, even for one brief moment, to have my old, clever, funny Anto back again.

On our way back to the hotel, we passed a large Indian family, eight or ten people, padding slowly and companionably down the seafront. The two men, dressed in Western suits, and their wives in violently colored saris of the brightest apricots and pinks and lime greens, their arms covered in bangles.

"Most women here don't wear the sari," Anto explained to me, pointing to another woman in a plain white long skirt and blouse. "They wear that: the chatta and mundu—quite boring by comparison."

The gaggle of children who followed them walked backwards to stare at me: the white woman in the white dress with the white hat on.

When one of children—a cheeky-looking boy—muttered something that made the men laugh, a strange little line of poetry (one of my mother's favorites) wafted into my mind.

Oh why do you walk through the fields in gloves,
Missing so much and so much?
O fat white woman whom nobody loves.

I kept it to myself (knowing he would instantly assure me of my own slimness, lovedness, and so forth), and also because he'd strode a little ahead of me, pleased to remember a shortcut, through a gap in the fence and down a path, that took us past the English Club.

Close to the club, I could see part of the veranda had been damaged and several windows boarded up. A skinny cat dashed from under the house with something in its mouth. When I asked Anto if the riots had been bad here, he stared at the building and said, "Nothing like as bad as the riots and massacres up north. But my family were sparing with information, so I don't really know yet."

He picked up some empty firework shell from the veranda that must have been part of the victory celebrations. "I only really know what I read in the *London Times*."

We threaded our way down a bustling street: rickshaws and stray goats, street merchants selling buckets and bright sweets, lurid papier-mâché gods, a whole head of lamb buzzing with flies. It felt exciting, and I wanted to explore, but he was intent on showing me the Church of Saint Francis, where, he said, Vasco da Gama had been buried before they moved his body back to Portugal. I trailed dutifully behind him into a large building with curved sides like ship sails.

He dipped his hand in the holy water near the door and made a sign of the cross—a surprise for me; he'd told me he was a lapsed Catholic.

I felt he wanted to be alone, and a few moments later, I watched him from a distance: this handsome stranger—my husband—sitting in soft candlelight, eyes tightly shut, face gleaming with sweat, surrounded by stained glass and stone effigies, and the thought came to me: I hope he's not regretting this already.

- CHAPTER 13 -

"Do you have an aspirin in your handbag?" he asked me on the following day. We were speeding in a battered taxi towards Mangalath, his family home, one hour's drive from Fort Cochin.

"Sorry, no," I said. "Headache?" He looked so pale and distant.

"Not really."

I'd heard him, in the middle of the night, groaning as though in the grips of some kind of nerve storm.

"All right, darling?" I said when he came to bed, hoping he would confide in me.

"I'm fine." And then, after a long and expectant pause, there was a sucking sound as he turned his back on me. "Thank you," he said politely, before he went to sleep.

He'd expected the family car to be sent for us with a driver, but a note left for us at the hotel that we were to take a taxi had clearly perplexed and hurt him. I wondered if this was a concealed snub but kept the thought to myself.

It was so hot in the taxi that my dress stuck to the seat, and I felt sick as our driver, a juicy sniffer, drove hectically, one hand on the wheel, through ramshackle villages and potholed roads. And then, on the edge of town, quite suddenly, we were in the most spectacularly beautiful country I had ever seen: a dream of water and earth and sky, where bright-green fields and gorgeously colored trees seemed to float on a series of lakes and waterways, lagoons and backwaters, connected by fragile bridges. Anto stared stonily out the window, hardly moving.

We were crossing a bridge, approaching the village of Aroor, when he turned to me as if remembering I was there.

"Are you nervous?" he asked, at last acknowledging the momentous day ahead. "You will shortly disappear under a mountain of relatives, and I'm afraid they will be very, very curious about you."

"Not nervous," I lied. "Excited." And then, "Is it all very changed?"

"I've changed," he said softly. He was looking at a small boat adrift in a dazzling stretch of water, sailing towards the horizon.

"It looks like a giant picture postcard," I said, feeling like a hearty aunt in my startling unoriginality. "It's nice to see it with you."

When we stopped on the road at a tea shop selling cigarettes and sweets, Anto arranged for us and our luggage to be transferred to a horse and cart. The horse stood in the fierce sunlight, its eyes obliterated by flies. Its barefoot owner cut the top off a coconut with a machete and offered Anto a glass of its milk, which he downed with an ecstatic look. He told me not to drink it until my stomach got stronger; we'd be home soon. I said nothing. I was too hot, and too anxious to talk because we were nearly there. After ten minutes or so, down a dusty road lined with palm trees, Anto gripped my hand tightly.

"We're less than a mile away," he said when we'd reached a fork in the road. "Half a mile, one hundred yards." Figures seemed all he could manage now.

And suddenly, there it was: a small stone gatehouse against a lush backdrop of trees, and a wooden sign with *Mangalath* written on it.

Anto exhaled slowly. "This is it." He let go of my hand. The horse clip-clopped through an avenue of wonderful trees: as bold and showy as cancan dancers, with their waxy blossoms and strangely shaped leaves.

In a gap between the trees, there was half an acre or so of neatly planted vegetables and a chicken run, all very orderly, and then, through another gap, sapphire-colored water, blindingly bright in the sun and with the bluest of blue skies above.

Three women weeding the vegetable patch straightened as we passed and gave us a hard, bright stare.

"Do they recognize you, Anto?"

"I doubt it," he said, after another stunned pause. "I was hardly shaving when I left."

"Anto," burst from me, "how could you bear it?" Meaning Oxford, grayness, exile. "It's so, so beautiful."

"It is," he said woodenly, still staring.

At the end of the drive, two large gold lions glowered from gateposts, their paws resting on shields. Through the gate was an immaculate graveled courtyard, its low walls covered in geranium, hibiscus, and orchids planted in split coconut husks. Beyond the courtyard, a flight of stairs led up to a large, attractive house—far bigger and grander than I'd imagined—with a bright-red pagoda-shaped roof and deep, cool-looking verandas. The whole house was framed by exuberant tropical trees, and above it, that dazzlingly blue sky, so bright it hurt your eyes to look at it.

The horse stopped. I could hardly breathe I was so nervous. A woman in a soft white garment was standing on the veranda, looking down at us. Her hand was over her mouth as if to stop herself screaming.

"Amma," Anto murmured. "Amma."

She walked down the steps and broke into a stumbling run. I heard the muffled sob as she stretched out her arms, a long string of words that Anto answered in the same unknown language. I badly wanted Anto to kiss his mother to match her outpouring of emotion. But he stood there, stiff as a post, while she hugged him. And I wished, for his sake, I was invisible.

When Anto at last put his arms around her, I saw her shudder. He patted her back awkwardly. He glanced at me, his worried look conveying shock, not pleasure.

"Amma," he said, releasing her, "I'd like you to meet my wife, Kit. She thinks this place is lovely."

"I do." I smiled and put my hand out. "It's good to meet you at last, and then, absurdly, I said, "Thank you for having us," and thought, Oh no! Not *us*. This is his home.

Mrs. Thekkeden, who was tall for an Indian woman, seemed to grow then. I watched her shoulders go down, her neck lengthen. She tidied the tears away with a quick, deft gesture. Now I could see she had the same fine cinnamon-colored skin as Anto, the same aristocratic nose. She held out a gracious hand.

"Welcome to Mangalath." Her smile was tense, automatic. "Are you very tired?"

"Oh, no, no, no." I felt the need to reassure her. "Not at all."

"My husband can't be here today to meet you," she said to me. "He is involved in a big court case in Trivandrum. You don't mind?" A quick anxious look at Anto.

"Of course not," he said. "Work is work."

"To him, yes," she said with a quick hostessy smile. "So, Kit, I must show you our house." She turned to Anto. "I've decided to put you in the guest room. The others are coming later. We don't want to bury Kit under a mountain of relatives."

The exact same words Anto had used earlier. She smiled at me again, but her eyes feasted hungrily on Anto as we followed her through the veranda and into an elegant reception room. Inside this room, with its high white ceilings and dark, heavily carved rosewood furniture, photographs of elaborately framed Thekkedens glowered down at us from the walls: serious-looking people with dark eyes and thick hair in dark suits and wing collars, and occasionally in their own costumes. We were walking through them when I heard Anto make a sucking sound and then breathe heavily as if he needed to sob or shout.

"What a beautiful house," I said, to cover this raw moment.

"Thank you," said Mrs. Thekkeden in a disembodied voice. Her whole body was angled towards Anto, and then she hugged him hard, and said more words in Malayalam that I didn't understand.

"Tell Kit about the house." Anto disentangled himself. "She probably imagined us living in a mud hut."

"Anto! No!" I protested, although I was surprised at how posh the house was.

"What does she want to know?" she asked Anto, and then continued like a polite tour guide. "So, the house and the farm have been in our family for many generations. We have our own granary, where we store rice; our own tennis court; a cricket pitch; a schoolroom where the children were educated . . . I'll tell her more later," she finished, a faint note of impatience in her voice. "I can't think . . ."

An old man, wiry and short on teeth, burst through the door carrying our luggage. When he saw Anto, he put his palms together and bowed low and babbled.

"His name is Pathrose," Mrs. Thekkeden explained, with tears in her eyes too. "He is saying, '*Kochu muthalay vannallo*,' the young master has come. He's worked for us since Anto was a little boy; now he thanks God that he has seen him again before he dies."

A slender barefoot boy came next, staggering under the weight of my suitcase. "Kuttan is Pathrose's grandson. He will show you to your bedroom," she added.

"Thank you," I said demurely: the mention of the bedroom made me feel oddly shy, as if my new mother-in-law had somehow managed to see us in all our nakedness and abandon.

"May I ask what you would like me to call you?" I asked. "Is there a special name?"

"Actually, you must call me Amma too. It means *Mother*," Mrs. Thekkeden said evenly. It sounded more like an order than an invitation to intimacy. "That's what I am to you now."

We looked at each other. "Yes. Good," I said, feeling my smile as a shy grimace. "Thank you."

*   *   *

"When we were little, we called this the bridal suite."

Anto stood at the door of our bedroom, still sounding in a mild state of shock. It was a large, whitewashed room, sparsely furnished except for a superb wooden bed carved with fruit and birds, placed center stage and made up with a white sheet and thin-looking pillows. There was an old-fashioned wooden fan clanking overhead, but the air felt moist and heavy. The wooden shutters were closed, which gave me a feeling of claustrophobia.

"I've never slept here before," he added.

"Obviously," I said, and squeezed his arm, but he was in no mood for joking. "Where was your room?"

"Over there." He opened the shutter across the courtyard. "Next to Amma's." He stared at it.

"She's so happy to see you," I said.

"Yes."

"Do you mind about your father—not being here, I mean?"

"No." And then, "It was always like that. He was either in court or away on cases. I don't mind."

Sunlight fell in dazzling strips through the shutter. We sat side by side on the bed. "So," Anto said, "I'm home. Prodigal son returns." He put his hand under my hair and turned my face towards him. "With prodigal wife," he said, gazing at me. "And a cast of thousands coming soon," he went on. His voice—or was I imagining this?—had become more Indian already, that buttery thread running through it.

"I'm looking forward to meeting them." A complete lie. I was tired and overwhelmed and felt childishly close to tears. I saw the family as a test I was bound to fail. I said, "Anto, when they come, go down on your own first. I'm sure they'd prefer that."

"Do you mind?" His whole expression brightened.

"Not a bit. Honestly."

"Sure you don't?" He hugged me properly for the first time that day.

"No, really, just don't leave me for hours like the princess in the tower."

"I won't," he said. I hoped he'd kiss me.

Instead, he showed me the bathroom so I could wash while he was away. This odd-looking room had a large copper cauldron of cool water in the corner for the bath. Above the bath there was a shelf holding a bundle of twigs, and what Anto said were ayurvedic oils for hair and skin. Thin towels that didn't look like towels, just strips of cotton, hung on hooks on the wall.

"Be careful with water here—we're often short in summer—and don't drink it. I'll bring boiled water up later." The lavatory, he said, was a short walk outside the house, next to the chicken run. He could show me now if I liked. Later, I said, paralyzed with shyness at the thought of going downstairs.

He went to the bathroom to wash his face, and when he came out, his hair still damp, I lay on the bed and watched him change. He took off his shirt, dusty brogues, dark London trousers, and folded them neatly. When he laid them in a pile on the chair, the empty garments fluttered like ghosts under the fan. Naked apart from his underwear, he went to the rosewood wardrobe and took out a white shirt and a strip of white cloth with a gold border.

"Home clothes." He glanced at me shyly. "This is the Cochin version of the dhoti . . . Well, this feels strange," he murmured. He wrapped the white cotton around his waist like a sarong. "Most peculiar."

I couldn't tell if he was embarrassed or moved to be wearing again the clothes he'd grown up in. All I knew was that Anto, bare-legged, half-naked, had in one startling moment become an Indian husband.

"How do I look?" he said.

"Strange," I said. I didn't know what to think. I ran my hand down his spine, wrapped my arms around him. His back made a drum of my voice. "You smell different. What is it?"

"Coconut oil, from our own trees. There's some in the bathroom. You can use it too on your skin and on your hair."

"Um." I clung to him: my anchor in a shifting world.

"That's enough of that, woman," he said, disentangling me. "They're waiting for me downstairs. I'll come up and get you before lunch."

I'd expected him to say in half an hour, an hour at the most.

When he was gone, I put on my nightdress, and with nothing to do, lay down on the bed and slept, wishing in a way I could sleep forever, astounded at my own naivety at not thinking this through.

A few hours later, at the sound of a car horn, I leapt to my feet and, through a slit in the bamboo blinds, watched my new family arrive. A group of women stepped out of the car. They were dressed in dazzling clothes in every color of the rainbow: cerise, emerald, ocher, gold. They were chattering like jays, jiggling up and down on the spot as if they could barely contain themselves. They love him, I thought with a childish kink in my heart: *my Anto.* I'm not the only one.

I watched him walk his easy athletic walk towards them and stand between the two gold lions at the entrance. The sight of my husband in a mundu would take some adjusting to, but Anto at least had good legs: long and well muscled, not spindly like Gandhi's, but I decided not to tell him that. The old jokes wouldn't work here.

A youngish woman in a peach-colored sari detached herself from the crowd and ran towards him. She put her head on his shoulder and then sobbed, wiping her eyes with the corner of her stole.

Mariamma, I thought. The clever older sister.

Next, a plump old lady—the grandma?—waddled through the courtyard: mouth half-open, gait eager, a little off-center.

Ponnamma, Anto had warned me, was Amma's mother—a little doolally, spoke her mind. He'd warned me in the same breath that some members of the family abbreviated her name to Ponnae but until I knew her better, this would be disrespectful.

Three children exploded from the car next, skipping across the courtyard, followed by a young woman in a pale-lilac sari who hung back and looked uncertain.

I've no idea who any of you are, I thought; there were only so many family members you could keep in your head at once. The old lady stood in front of Anto. She patted his face like a blind person reading braille, and when her face crumpled, Amma gave her a handkerchief. And watching these tender scenes, my stomach began to knot and coil. In England, Anto had reduced his family to a few colorful or touching anecdotes—his grandma's startling outspokenness, Mariamma's bossiness when young. Sometimes, when I was slow to eat, he'd assumed a high falsetto mimicking Amma's admonitions to take a hanky or finish rice. Now that they were real and about to inspect me, I shrank behind the half-opened blind, my heart thumping as I listened to their voices rise and fall, swell into gunshot exclamations. And over this happy commotion came, suddenly, the clear sound of Anto laughing uninhibitedly too. I'd heard him laugh before, at silly films, at jokes, but this had a new clear and childish note to it.

The gargling sound of their conversation grew louder as they moved towards the veranda. And then, like a shoal of fish, they all stopped, turned, and looked up together, towards our window. I dropped the blind and blushed a fiery red.

Anto was mouthing indistinct words; he waved at me in an encouraging way. "Come on down, come on," he shouted up, and I wanted to kill him.

Come and get me, I thought. *Don't make me do this on my own.*

I've had years of this with my mother, I thought fuming, my cheeks still scarlet. Standing on the outside, marveling at families you would never be part of. I'd hoped that marriage would mean never feeling like this again, which was obviously absurd. And then I disliked myself intensely.

"Shut up, Kit," I told myself brutally. "You wanted this."

In the bathroom, I looked at myself in the mirror and Matron Smythe, the most feared matron at Saint Andrew's, came back to me. Brush your hair, girl. Straighten that dress. Smile!

"Grow up." I said it out loud. I was ready for my inspection.

As I walked into the dining room trying to smile, twenty-four pairs of Thekkeden eyes swiveled towards me. En masse, they were an exceptionally handsome family: fine dark eyes, soft brown skins, their high-cheekboned faces a fine blending of East and West, well dressed, cultivated. All of them examining me now with a frank but not unfriendly curiosity.

They were sitting comfortably around a fourteen-foot-long rosewood table. I had been told (in bed, in Oxfordshire) about this table by Anto. He said it had been made from wood salvaged from the deck of a splendid ship that the family had owned when their great-great-grandfather was one of the principal spice traders on the Malabar Coast, taking coriander and green and red peppers to Africa, to Northern India, to China. The table was set with copper cups, jugs of water, and no visible plates; in front of each chair there was a green banana leaf.

Anto saw me hovering at the door. He jumped up. "Kit," he said, "sorry I've been—everybody . . . . *Shush, shush shush shush,*" for the old woman had just boomed, "Is that her?"

"This is Kit. My new wife."

The family greeted me with beaming smiles and perfect polite-ness. When the fuss had died down, his mother, waiting tensely by the kitchen door, raised her hand and two servants arrived carrying dishes filled to the brim with chicken curries and ginger-scented prawns, elegantly spiced rice, fish molee, the creamy, coconutty curry, and lentil dishes, each one giving off its own tantalizing aroma.

"All Anto's favorites," said his mother. Anto was seated at the head of the table. My place beside him was the only one set with a bone china plate edged in gold, a crystal glass, and a knife, fork, and spoon.

"You must say grace, Anto," Amma said, a deep emotional throb to her voice. "You're the head of the family today."

When the old woman said loudly, "Where is Mathu?" Amma put a reproving finger against her mouth. "Say it, Anto," she insisted. "Go on."

Anto glanced at me. "Well . . ." He blinked and closed his eyes. "For these and all thy gifts, may the Lord make us truly thankful. Amen," he mumbled.

"And bless you, God, for bringing back Anto," Amma said. "Kit too," she added politely. She pronounced my name *Keet* to rhyme with *meat*. "And now,"—she looked at me, smile wobbling only slightly—"it's time to introduce you properly to your new family. Not everyone of course: Anto has one hundred and ten cousins," she said with evident pride. "So we had to tell some people to stay home today, which was a bit awkward. All my husband's family and mine grew up together. From childhood."

"Thresiamma is sulking badly," boomed the old girl, and everyone laughed. "Amma's in the doghouse."

"We couldn't have everyone," Amma snapped, throwing a dark look.

"It wasn't possible," Anto said consolingly. "We can stay with the others later, can't we, Kit? This looks wonderful, Amma."

He helped me to some of the food. "Try this, Kit, it's called meen molee. The best fish curry you will ever eat." He smelled it ecstatically. "It's all cream and coconut, and this is a roast pork dish, and vegetables, and pickles, and rice and buttermilk—I'll tell you all the different names later. All my favorite things," he told Amma, who was so overwhelmed with emotion she couldn't speak.

"She's been cooking for days," Ponnamma yelled. "Nothing better than feeding your children."

I must learn to cook for him too, I thought. I could barely boil an egg; we'd joked about it before, but now it didn't seem so funny.

When the pickles, the rice, and the appam—the lacy coconut pancakes—had been passed around, it surprised me to see these exquisitely dressed people eating with their hands.

"You must teach me to do that," I said in a low voice to Anto. I meant later, but he had already taken the fork out of my hand and put a thick green banana leaf in front of me.

"Here." He squeezed my right hand into a pouch.

"Your right hand is your eating hand, so put your elbow on the table. It will give you a firm plank," he instructed. "Now use your fingers to compact the rice, and use your thumb to push it into your mouth."

"I'm undoing twenty-eight years of her mother's teaching," he joked with Mariamma.

"She is twenty-eight! Old!" roared Ponnamma. "I was married at fourteen," she confided to me, and then, "Your left hand is to wipe botty with, so don't use."

I saw Amma flush with anger and wondered if it was Ponnamma or the spectacle of her son teaching his wife to eat that had made her cross.

"And make your rice into a neat tight pile like this," Anto closed his hand over mine. "And put it in your mouth. It tastes better like this. Add in a little of lentils, a piece of chicken, and there," he smiled at me. "Try it now for yourself."

I put my hand into the bright sauces and the sticky rice, and immediately thought of my three-year-old self holding out food-splattered hands to my fastidious mother and saying "dirty" in tones of deep disgust.

"Like this?" The whole table watched, fascinated, as I left a blob of bright sauce on my blouse, half a handful of rice on my new skirt. Halfway through this mortifying spectacle, Anto got up and washed his hands in a sink in the corner of the room. On his way back, he looked at me and said something in Malayalam which made the family rock with laughter.

"What did you say?" I asked.

"Nothing," he said. "We're not laughing at you," he added at last, breathlessly. "I promise."

I believed him. He was too kind to mock me in a situation like this, and besides, I liked seeing him laugh and dab his eyes, the sharp planes of his face relaxing.

"You'll get the hang of it soon." Mariamma, my new sister-in-law, had placed her plump, sweet-smelling body beside me. She picked some grains of rice from my lap and told me in faultless English that she was so happy to meet someone from England, she was a great fan of English literature: "George Eliot is my particular favorite, and Mr. George Orwell speaks to us particularly since Independence."

At the mention of the I-word, several heads were raised and looked in my direction. Over lunch no one had said a single sausage about Independence or the British or the war or the massacres up north, and though I'd been bracing myself for this conversational cliff, I'd been grateful for their tact. But when Amma came back from the kitchen, I took the plunge.

"Anto was sorry to miss Independence," I said. "It must have been a tremendous moment."

"It was," Amma said with a quelling look. "Let's talk about that later. Did he seem homesick in England?" she said, her eyes very bright, very hurt.

"He was brave," I said after a confusing pause. "He must have missed you so much, but he was never self-pitying about it. He simply put his head down and worked."

"He had no choice." Amma gave me a level look. "Did he?" She ate in silence for a while and then continued, "He broke many hearts while he was away."

I felt a surge of panic at these words. If I'd known her better, I might have asked, "Do you mean here or in England?" But I was dimly aware that these were the dangerous spaces between us, so I kept my mouth shut and she went back to the kitchen.

Later, over coffee on the veranda, twenty or so of us sat around a mother-of-pearl–inlaid table. Anto gave me sliced pineapple and then plucked a few leaves from the saucer beside them.

"These are betel leaves," he said, "good for digestion and palate cleansing." He opened the small brass pot beside them. "Take a bit of this lime, smear it on the leaves, put some chopped betel leaf on it, pop into your mouth, and chew—nicer than a Mars bar," he assured me. I chewed away dutifully (horrible taste) thinking, Wonderful! Thank you, Anto: bright-red teeth to add to the humiliation.

When everyone's cup was poured, the granny said, "So, what I am waiting to hear is how the two lovebirds met."

"Nosy." Mariamma gave her a reproving tap on the shoulder as the table fell expectantly silent, and one or two people were shushed. I saw Anto's head jerk up, and my mind leapt to the first night we'd made love. The speed with which we'd ripped off each other's clothes felt positively indecent in this setting, and because Anto had never once mentioned it again, not even to me, I'd sometimes worried that he'd found my behavior worryingly fast. I didn't understand it myself. My body had decided, and morals had lumbered on behind.

"Well . . ." Anto crossed his legs.

"It was very romantic, I'm thinking. Was it?" The old woman prompted, head on one side, her eyes twinkling coyly. "A love match maybe. Come on, young lady, how did you meet this themmadi?" The table notably sucked its breath in but nobody stopped her.

"Bad Granny." Mariamma smacked her hand softly, but her eyes gleamed with curiosity too. "*Themmadi* means rascal," she translated helpfully.

"Well, why else would he bring her all this way?" the old lady protested boisterously.

"Actually, it was not romantic at all," said Anto. "It was terrifying."

"Terrifying?" Amma's eyebrows rose.

"Yes, terrifying. I didn't tell you this before, but we were together in Saint Thomas' Hospital on the night it was bombed. Actually, it was bombed several times; the first time, fourteen people died."

"Oh, dear Lord." Amma crossed herself and her hand flew to her face.

"This time, not so bad," Anto said. "The roof fell in, there was a lot of shouting and running and I met Kit. We were both covered in soot, so she had no idea I was Indian."

No one laughed at his little joke.

"And why were you there?" Amma asked Kit. "Were you ill?" I took a deep breath. All of this was the truth, but a strange version of it: the fact was, he'd told me once he'd been seconded to Thomas' that night, but I had absolutely no memory of meeting him then, and we'd never discussed the coincidence, not even with Daisy. My memory seemed to have blanked out that awful time, and I hated talking about it, mainly because of what had happened next. Now when I looked at Anto, he shrugged and nodded as if to say, Go on.

"I was a nurse. I am a nurse."

"A nurse." A dribble of red betel juice ran out of the old woman's mouth. She grimaced at the others in an unguarded way.

Daisy had warned me in advance that it would be best to call myself "a medical researcher" or some such, until I got to know the family better. Nurses, she'd said, were considered a low form of female life in India. When I'd protested that Anto's family were well-educated Catholics, from the more progressive South India, she'd said simply, "Trust me, darling, no woman in their family will ever have been a nurse."

But now the point had come, and I wasn't going to lie about it.

"An English kind of nurse," said Anto in the incredulous silence that followed. "Kit did her three-year training at Saint Thomas'. She nursed during the war. She has a war medal to prove it." No mention of the midwife training, I noticed.

"Oh," Amma said doubtfully.

"So more like a doctor, or a missionary?" Mariamma supplied helpfully.

"Not really," I said. "In England, doctors are doctors; we look after their patients." When I saw Anto giving me his "stop now" frown, I frowned back. He'd led me into this particular land mine, and I found this level of surprise ridiculous.

"The Thames was on fire on the night we met," Anto continued doggedly. "The entire hospital had to be moved down to the basement."

I remembered that part, of course: the flames, the sirens, the meaty, coppery smell of blood in the wards. The girl screaming and yelling at me, her dead baby inside its mother's air raid helmet.

"And were you hurt badly?" Mariamma, the peacemaker, wanted to know. She placed a warm hand on my arm.

"Only a bump on the head."

I found I couldn't speak. When I looked at Anto, he looked back blankly, as if we'd just met.

"So . . . do you think of working here?" Amma's face was arranged in polite inquiry. "As a nurse, I mean?"

So Anto hadn't told them. Wonderful. I felt the shock of betrayal, and then the suspicion that I might have to lie about myself here, over and over again, and that made me suddenly furious with Anto, who was staring down at his plate.

I was about to tell them about the Moonstone when I looked up and saw Anto frowning and shaking his head.

"It is good you have a training," said Mariamma, filling the even more awkward silence that followed. "My years of study were the happiest of my life."

"First-class honors in English and history," said Uncle Yacob, "and she played the piano to a high standard.

"The family brain box," Grandma Ponnamma shouted.

"Before children," Mariamma reminded them, biting into her sweetmeat. And looking at this plump, complacently smiling woman, I thought, Is she my future?

- CHAPTER 14 -

"You were the one who brought up Saint Thomas'," Kit said to his bare back. "Why should I have to lie about it?"

The big old fan whirled arthritically above his head. Its sound would keep him awake for hours and he longed for sleep.

"Forget it." He stretched an arm behind himself but didn't turn. "It's your life, your work. I understand." Liar, he thought. He wanted to scream with frustration.

Because she was right—his fault for deliberately bringing up, and distorting, the bomb incident at Saint Thomas', thinking that the idea of his possible death would mitigate the sin of his bringing an English girl back. A cheap trick. And he should have warned her more about the status of nurses in India, not left it to Daisy to sugarcoat it.

But with that cat out of the bag, she could have helped him by sounding less determined. It was not the way things were done around here.

He'd also had the vague hope—one he wouldn't admit to himself, let alone her—that once in India she'd change her mind about working at the Moonstone or find the job too overwhelming, or that a baby of their own would change her priorities.

She thrashed around beside him for a bit, turning and bashing her pillow, and then, hearing her breath grow even, he covered her gently with a sheet, tucked the mosquito net around her, and sat by the window, trying to untangle his thoughts.

He was home. He was home. This day, so dreaded, so eagerly anticipated, had brought with it a rush of sensations: the joy of seeing Mariamma again, the relief of hugging Amma, the aunts, delight at seeing the new children, eating his own food, breathing that moist, warm, blossom-scented air. It was like slipping into a warm bath after the long, lonely years away. His father's absence had been the only disappointment of the day. Mariamma said he couldn't wait to see Anto too, but "you know"—humorous rolling of the eyes—"that man can't ever stop working. It's his drug. Don't know how Amma puts up with him."

Oh, Kit. He looked down on her as she slept. How will we do now? The risk suddenly felt enormous, like bringing home a large and unmanageable animal, thinking it would thrive here. Had he lured her into a trap?

He thought of the day when he'd drawn the map of South India on her belly with his finger. How full of love he'd felt drawing his child's picture with its promise of exploding sunsets, exotic fruits, and smiley faces—everything blitzed-out, worn-out Britain wasn't. He'd needed her so badly there: her warmth, her succor, the out-spoken fun of her. Now he tried to remember if they had even come close to one sensible conversation about how hard this would be.

It was dark outside their window now, a dense, perfumed dark-ness, occasionally pierced by the screech of an owl on the hunt, the chirping of crickets. Kit was asleep now, her hair in damp tendrils against her cheek, arms spread out. She's brave, he thought. I can't not love her now. She'd looked after him in England; he would do the same for her here. He crawled back into bed, tucked the mos-quito net around them, and put his arms around her.

He was drifting off when she rolled over, touched his arm, and said, "Anto, they're horrified, aren't they?"

"Um," he mumbled, feigning sleep.

"And you know, we didn't actually meet that night at the hospital."

"Well, we might have. It was chaos."

"I was much too blithe."

"About what?"

"Everything." A note of desperation in her voice. "What was the name of the other girl—the one they thought you'd marry?"

"Vidya," he said after a tense silence.

"What happened to her?"

"No idea. I was sixteen when I left, and then I met this crazy woman in Oxfordshire." He ran his hand around her stomach. "This wonderful crazy woman who stole my heart."

"Do they mind? Terribly, I mean." A plaintive note in her voice. "Amma, the others?"

He kissed her shoulder. "I love you," he whispered, "and they will too when they get to know you."

She accepted his embraces in silence.

"Were you sad not to see your father?"

"We'll meet him soon; you'll like him. We all look up to him."

"Amma was telling me about him; he sounds terrifyingly per- fect."

"He's . . ." Several possibilities ran through his mind. "He'll think you're swell," he said in his Humphrey Bogart voice. "Now go to sleep. I can't talk anymore." He smoothed her damp nightdress over her thighs.

"I'm trying, I'm trying, and don't you dare, Anto, it's too damn hot."

- CHAPTER 15 -

I was dying to start work, but an inexhaustible supply of relatives began to arrive in horse-drawn phaetons and in rickshaws to welcome Anto home and give me a discreet once-over. After days of smiling at people I didn't know, my mouth felt rigid, my reserves of small talk dangerously low, and I understood how a caged animal might feel claustrophobic and overstimulated all at once.

"Anto," I said, towards the end of the second week, "I've got to start work soon." I didn't add "or else I'll go mad" but my meaning was clear. Because the thought of delivering babies so frightened me now, I'd told Daisy before I left, that I could only be counted on to do administrative work or research at the Home. I'd dreaded her examining my reasons, but she hadn't, she'd simply looked at me and said quietly, "Give it time, then see how you feel," and we'd both tidied the conversation away quite quickly.

Now in the silence that followed I heard the scrabbling of the family of bats that lived in the attic above us, and heard Anto's sharp sigh.

"Kit, listen." His voice was stern. "I'm going to Fort Cochin tomorrow to see a Dr. Kunju, an old friend of my father's. He's a bigwig in the new Medical Directorate. Lots of new appointments since Independence, so the timing seems good. Do you mind, Kit?"

"Mind?" I could hear my voice rise. "Why on earth would I mind? That's what we're hoping for. It's exciting."

"Depending on what's available," he continued, "I may have to travel for a while."

"That's fine, I—"

He put his hand up to stop me. "I haven't finished." He turned my face towards him. "Listen . . . while I'm away, I'd like you to stay at Mangalath for a few more weeks at least and give my mother a chance to get to know you."

"What?" I sat bolt upright in bed. "No, Anto, I can't. We've already been here nearly two weeks. I promised Daisy I'd get cracking as soon as possible." He'd also promised we'd get a place of our own as soon as possible.

"I've been thinking about this." Anto sounded uneasy. "I think I should go to the Home first."

I stared at him. "Why?"

"Do I have to explain?"

"Oh, sorry, forgot. Me white woman nurse, you Indian man, that sort of thing." I was breaking my own rules now: Be nice. Be calm. Give it time.

"That's below the belt, Kit." He was smiling cautiously, hoping I was joking. "Kit." He stroked my shoulder. "We're part of a family now. Try to see it from their point of view."

"Anto, I have a job that I get paid for. I can't not do it."

When my voice rose, he put his hand over my mouth and glanced towards the walls, beyond which were dozens of sleeping Thekkedens.

"Anto." I pulled his hand away. "Tell the absolute, honest truth. Do your parents mind me working? I mean, will I have to lie about it more or less continuously?"

I saw him take a deep breath.

"No, no, no, no," he said, but with no conviction. "They know, through the church, some fine missionary women who help the poor women here, and they respect them. But here's the thing: we need to take it gently." Holding my hand, he stroked it. "If I start by telling them you are part of a British organization that trains our midwives, it gets tricky. The British are not the most popular people in the world right now . . . You know that, Kit."

"Anto . . . please stop." He was stroking my head now as if I were a feverish child, and it felt like the worst kind of blackmail. I got out of bed and put my dressing gown on.

"This isn't what we said it would be." I was determined not to cry. "We both promised Daisy I'd go quickly to the Home. I absolutely can't leave it for weeks."

"I'm only asking you to stay here for a few weeks more. That's all."

"Please, Anto . . . at least take me to the Home for one day." I heard a note in my voice I didn't like: a wheedling wifely voice.

It took a great effort of self-control not to add, "before I go into purdah." "Let me at least introduce myself to Neeta; I promised Daisy I'd unpack the boxes with her and tick them off the inventory."

"So, what should I tell Amma?" He sounded grumpy.

I don't give a damn! my rebellious heart shouted.

"I don't know. That we're having a sightseeing trip before your work begins, a few days off. Would that seem so unreasonable?"

His head was pressed between his hands. "If we're having a sightseeing trip, she'll want us to go and see our Travancore family. I know she will." He'd warned me of this in a jokey aside in London: that holidays meant family reunions. If you stayed for less than a week, the relatives took umbrage.

"So tell her straight that I am going to work at a home which trains midwives. That I get paid for it and that I am expected to turn up."

He looked at me incredulously, as if I had no idea of the intricacies involved in this simple explanation. He scratched his head and gave me a cold look that in another person I might have taken for hate.

Was he in a huff when he went downstairs? I couldn't tell anymore, only that the old sweet-tempered Anto had left the room with a firm click of the door, leaving me in a stew of heat and frustration in our room. I fell into a feverish sleep and when I woke, an hour later, found myself less than a foot away from a hideous monster. A bat caught in the mosquito net around our bed was staring down at me like an angry old man. It let out a horrible high-pitched squeal—purple gums, little yellow teeth—and I screamed into its open mouth and, shuddering with disgust, prized its claws from the fine gauze and flung it on the windowsill, where it stared at me with large, panicked eyes.

- CHAPTER 16 -

Amma heard the girl scream from her own room, watched him sprint upstairs to investigate, and heard the sobbing that followed. When he'd explained, somewhat shamefacedly, that it was only a bat, she'd expected him to laugh with her about it. But he'd looked at her sternly and said, "Amma, Kit needs a day out. This is all very strange for her. You have to understand that."

As if she were a heartless creature. So *Kit needs a day out,* she repeated to herself sarcastically, watching the family's car disappear in a cloud of dust. Didn't they all? Perhaps Kit should inform herself about the price of petrol now in Cochin since Independence. The cost of paying their driver extra. The great privilege of the car, since there were only ten or eleven of them privately owned in Travancore. She thought of Vidya, who would need more than a day out to recover from her change of plans.

She knew she was being unfair but couldn't help it. So far, the golden boy's return had proved a crushing disappointment. The girl was a handful—all the relatives, the servants were already talking about her behind her back—and Anto himself seemed permanently in flight, leaping upstairs at every opportunity to make sure she was all right.

The table she was sitting at was scattered with the remains of their breakfast. And suddenly, as she swept his crumbs into her palm, relief seeped into her bones, a shaft of sunlight, at the thought of having the house to herself again, and then she wanted to weep or shout: relieved to be away from Anto—could she ever have imagined such a thing when he'd lived in England and seemed closer to her than now?

And now the next big hurdle was Mathu's return. Prodigal husband, she thought, throwing the crumbs over the veranda rails and into the garden. He'd telegrammed that morning to say his case had concluded satisfactorily, he'd be home on Thursday to meet the happy couple. Calm as a cucumber, as if nothing had happened. He wouldn't be pleased about the car's being used in this way.

Drinking a cup of chai without tasting it, she had a brisk mental conversation with Mathu. This was all your fault—the thought came as vicious and unbidden as a dirty punch. You've destroyed the best thing in my life. After having Mariamma, she'd been slow to conceive and after five years of waiting had been told it was doubtful she'd have another child. But on the day she'd been sure the new baby was inside her, she'd come to the prayer room, carefully prostrated herself in front of the Virgin Mary, and prayed, "Make it a boy. Make it a boy!" and afterwards for some reason, sure it would be, taken a boat out on the water. She felt the sun on her shoulders and saw kingfishers skimming, the egrets, the green fields, the banana palms, and had known for absolute certain that this was the happiest day of her life. Her little pot of gold: this curious, infuriating child, with his almond-shaped green eyes that everyone commented on; his clever, inquisitive face; his way of listening hard, even when young, as if trying to discern the meaning behind what you said.

Aged two or three, he'd toddled around the grounds with her while she supervised the women threshing rice, and then on down the winding path that led to the backwaters beyond. When she'd shown him the birds and the trees, he'd screwed up his dear, solemn little face in concentration, repeating the names: first in English (flame tree, banana, coconut, tulsa) and then in Malayalam, or they'd sing songs, and sit on the swing and close their eyes, and dissolve in sunlight and sweet smells.

Before Anto, no child in their family had been sent away. Never, never, never. It was unthinkable, like throwing away the most precious gift of your life. It would never have happened if Mathu hadn't met Hugo Bateman, his English barrister hero: so flatteringly genial, so well read. Bateman had played chess twice a week with Mathu at the club, filled his head with posh dreams of a Thekkeden going to his old Oxford college. Bateman's easy charm had turned Mathu's head (*My dear chap! The one person I'm longing to see.*) At lunch, at their house, he hadn't bothered to hide his patronizing surprise at the extent of the farm, her orchids, the glistening stretch of water beyond. (*My God, this is paradise on earth.*) He'd recommended Mathu for a role in the fevered preparations for India's first budget. (*The shrewdest lawyer in Travancore.*) And a month after Independence, Bateman had packed up his house—a Tudor pagoda mess called The Larches—left his servants in the lurch, and scuttled back to a cottage in Dorset with Pru, his hearty tennis-playing wife, leaving poor old Mathu to find he'd been batting on the wrong team all along.

That was when an embarrassed Mathu had suggested they change the name of the home, where they'd lived for one hundred and twenty years, from The Anchorage back to Mangalath, which meant "happiness, auspiciousness." He also suggested Parappurath, a Malayalam word meaning "built solidly on the rocks"—another joke, now that they seemed to bog along in a dizzying whirlpool of events: new government, new flags, new leaders, new friends, and most bittersweet of all, this new son (or one who had lost his marbles) with this new wife.

She rubbed her forehead vigorously as if it were a blackboard on which unthinkable thoughts could be erased. This dislike of her husband was new and hateful to her.

They'd had another nasty row last month when she'd begged

Mathu not to be away when Anto came home. Mathu had asked her with a patient smile if she had any idea how much money it cost to run this place.

"So, go to Madras!" she'd shouted, meaning the opposite. Anto would be heartbroken not to see him. "And if your fancy woman is there, hope you'll see her too."

She referred to Jaya, who'd been his legal secretary once, an educated, unlikely love object she privately called "the mongoose" on account of her long face, short legs, and solitary, predatory ways. She'd found Jaya's love letter to him twelve years ago, while emptying his pockets for the wash. Mathu had confessed, bought her orchids, and sent her a long sweet letter of love and contrition, and knowing he was a good man at heart, she'd tried to forgive, but the memory was a thorn that worked its way to the surface, particularly when they were going through a bad patch.

Climbing the stairs towards Anto and Kit's room, Amma had turned detective again, with the same old feeling of dread and self-disgust. At the door of the bridal bedroom, she stood and looked in. It was too early for the servants to have tidied the room. The bed was crumpled, the pillow on the floor; the girl's peach silk night-dress flung over the chair.

In the bathroom, she panted softly as she ran her fingers through his shaving brush and held it against her cheek, with a feeling of anguish: he'd grown up without her. Now her fingers touched the girl's toothbrush, still damp, her Pond's cold cream, her lipstick.

Why couldn't you wait? she asked him. Was this our punishment after all these years? The girl's three dresses, one blue, one made of thin flowery stuff, a black cocktail dress that looked too old for her, hung in the cupboard, drab-looking things, she thought, not fair to judge after the war in England. The girl had no dowry; she'd already asked Anto.

Vidya's family was wealthy, and since they had no sons, she and her two sisters would one day inherit twenty acres of beautiful rice paddies, and grazing near Ernakulam. Vidya, who was studying at the Women's Christian College in Madras, was pleasingly traditional, no silly bobbed hair like some local girls who fancied themselves modern, hers in a thick plait down to her hips. She bought her saris from the new shop on Broadway in Ernakulam, and wore the exquisite jewelry her mother had been collecting for her since she was born. To put it crudely, Vidya was a catch.

Amma's hand had moved to Anto's tweed jacket when her eye was caught by a blue folder on the floor of the cupboard, just behind a row of shoes.

"Notes for Indian Midwives," the label read, and scrawled underneath it: "Refer Neeta Chacko—Mother Moonstone Maternity Home, Fort Cochin."

A page fluttered to the floor. She picked it up, turned it round and around, and when she saw what it was, hurriedly shut the door, her heart making a sick pounding in her ears.

The most disgusting thing she'd ever seen: a close-up picture of a woman's spread legs, her yoni, there for all to see, with a huge bulging extrusion the shape of a split pear. The text read

FIG. 76—EDEMA OF THE VULVA.

May precede labor, and may then be an indication of pregnancy toxemia, chronic Bright's disease, or gonorrhea. It may also occur during labor in those cases in which the head of the child is impacted in the pelvic cavity, because the head is too large or the pelvis is generally contracted.

Her hands trembled as she turned more pages of more naked women, one, legs apart, sitting on a bench, demonstrating something called Walcher's position. Women kneeling with their naked behinds in the air. Women with babies drawn inside them in colored pencils; beheaded women on their backs like insects, legs in the air, one with a terrible-looking condition called varicose veins of the vulva, which the notes said might rupture during the delivery of the child and cause fatal hemorrhage.

I am not a prude, she mentally told her new daughter-in-law furiously, putting the notes back in the cupboard. What woman is after having two children? She'd enjoyed the physical act of love with her husband, still did, in spite of all their disagreements over the years. But these disgusting things had no place in a bridal suite, where dreams and hopes, joy, purity should be celebrated. Had Anto been made to share these terrible images?

She tucked the folder back where she had found it, in the space on the wooden floor of the wardrobe behind Anto's London brogues. And now what? First she hears this girl is a medical researcher; next she hears she is a nurse, something no Thekkeden would ever stoop to; now the even more unbearable thought that she might be a midwife swooped into her mind like a black bat and flew around wildly and then out again, for in the next second, as she closed the cupboard with trembling hands, she decided she must never tell Mathu, or anyone else in the family, about the contents of the blue folder. Mathu, for all his alleged liberal views, was an old-fashioned man: he would be disgusted; he would express his distaste forcibly, and then Anto, so obviously besotted by this creature, might leave this home forever—more heartache for her. For a brief moment she considered confronting Anto or the girl, but the bat flew around again: if she did, she would have to admit to snooping or pretend and blame one of the servants, who would be dismissed. Ergo: she was caught in her own trap.

- CHAPTER 17 -

Anto sat beside me in a pool of sunlight, freshly shaved, smelling faintly of limes, ridiculously handsome in his smart linen interview suit.

We were colleagues again, that's how it felt: friends, with unfolding but richly connected adventures ahead of us. In a voice low enough to exclude our driver, Anto apologized for what he thought had been his overbearing manner in the last few days and said he was feeling his way here too. I said I was sorry too, for being a drip and for crying, when it wasn't just the bat-in-the-net incident that had so thrown me but the general strangeness of everything.

We laughed like young lovers again, silly and inclined to laugh at anything, as he made a bat face and we held hands surreptitiously in the back of the car.

"This place is paradise." I watched a flock of parakeets fly over soft green fields, towards the floating water, and up into the huge blue sky.

"I can't wait to show you everything," he said. He put his cheek close to mine and said in a low voice that Amma hadn't turned a hair at the thought of my visiting the Home.

"Visiting? Is that how she thinks of it? Does she know it's a job?"

"With Amma, the drip-drip approach is best," was his unsatisfactory answer. "She'll know when the time is ripe. Look, look!" He pointed towards a blurred green horizon. "That's where the tea plantations are. When I was eight my father took me there on my own for a special treat. We stayed at a beautiful rest house in the Cardamom Hills. Down there"—he pointed south—"is Trivandrum; that's where the monsoon arrives. You'll never see anything like it in your life: first this massive cloud, then this roar. It comes over the horizon like a wild animal. Makes you feel so small, makes English rain look like the dribble from a tap."

Oh Lord, he was sweet lit up like that: eager and boyish, longing to show me things, and his excitement was infectious. As we drove through the landscape of inlets and coves and bays and backwaters, we laughed like children at the adventures ahead.

On the outskirts of the city, birdsong and lapping water gave way to the mad jumbled music of streets. An old woman with a skeletal baby approached us at the traffic light and put one wrinkled palm through the window. The baby's face was covered in flies and dried snot. Anto felt my shudder as our car sped off.

"Those are the people you'll meet at the Moonstone," he said quietly. "No disgrace if you decide it's too much."

I forced myself to sound confident. "I'm actually sort of . . . really looking forward to it, I mean . . . obviously, well . . . I'm a bit on edge about it but—" Aware I wasn't making a good case for myself, I turned to him. "You must be nervous too?"

He gave an incredulous huff but didn't answer directly. "For you, there's no shame in giving up. It's different for me." He squeezed my hand. "And I'm only saying this because I love you."

The answers I could make to this odd declaration of love were to me so baffling and contradictory that I remained silent. It wasn't just Daisy who made me want to do this job, it was more twisted and deeper than that. My failure of nerve that night at Saint Thomas', my cack-handedness, haunted me. If I didn't have the motor skills and the kind of quick thinking it took to be a midwife, I still wanted to use some of my training to be useful again.

I knew too that much as I appreciated the peace and timeless

beauty of Mangalath—the long unhurried meals, the gently padding feet, the exploding sunsets, all of it—my motor (forward,
quick, now!) was set at a different speed, and it was clear to me
already that I could never be an Indian wife if that meant being
the kind of smiling, docile presence I saw in, say, Mariamma or
Amma.

"I can't go back on my promise to Daisy," was the easiest way of
explaining it. I had to shut up then or be sick, as our driver, Chandy,
swashbuckled his way through a mass of pedestrians, ancient trucks,
gharries, donkeys, and alongside us a hand-pulled rickshaw carrying a woman with three tiny children in her arms. I saw the hem of
her sari flirting with the wheels, sparks flying, babies wriggling, and
couldn't bear to look.

"It can't be!" were my first words when we arrived at the Moonstone
ten minutes later. We'd parked on the edge of a crumbling pavement. The Home, once the offices of a spice merchant, or so Daisy
had told me, was a tumbled-down pagoda-shaped slum. I saw a
dangerously sagging roof with missing tiles. The mess of electric wires that bulged from the roof and crossed the street looked
like a bad hernia. A skinny dog flopped in the bare front garden,
exhausted.

Anto looked at the piece of paper again and reeled off a question
in Malayalam to the driver, who shrugged and pointed at the house.

"This is it," he informed me curtly. "The Moonstone. Now listen, Kit. Please." Anto clutched my arm. "I can't come in—I'll miss
my appointment—but promise me you won't leave the Home until
I pick you up. I'm not sure yet when that will be—I'll come as
quickly as I can. Promise; you must promise."

"That's fine, Anto," I said. "I understand. I promise. Good luck."
And to show how perfectly all right I was, I gave him a cheery wave
as he drove away.

*   *   *

And truthfully, I didn't want him there as I walked towards the house. The shock felt easier to absorb alone. There were goats in the garden munching at overgrown weeds, a rusted bicycle, a sign *oonstone* hanging from a dusty palm tree.

To be fair to Daisy, she had described it as "modest but serviceable," but I'd foolishly imagined it pink-bricked and full of light (an image supplied by an old India print in the lav at Wickam), not a worn-looking shack. I was walking down the path when a slight figure on the veranda stood up and waved me towards her.

"I'm Kit Smallwood," I said when I reached her. I'd decided to use my maiden name to save the family embarrassment. "I'm from the Oxford charity."

"We've been waiting for you," she said in a shy whisper. She wore a medic's coat and had a broom in her hand. "I am receptionist." She led me through a beaded curtain into the dim recesses of the waiting room inside. Its cracked floor was painted in red oxide; walls covered in a selection of flyblown posters showing pictures of various bloodthirsty-looking gods and goddesses. Propped up on an artist's easel was a crudely drawn cardboard sign that read, in English, "Happy Birthday, Healthy Mother, Healthy Baby at the Matha Maria Moonstone Baby Clinic, Fort Cochin." Matha meant mother in Malayalam.

On low benches around the wall, ten or so local women in various stages of pregnancy sat with an air of weary resignation, surrounded by children, grandmothers, mothers. All talk ceased when I walked in, feeling large and conspicuous and white.

"I've come to speak to Neeta Chacko," I said to the girl. She stared at me for a moment, then shook her head vigorously and pointed towards a door with a cardboard sign on it: Dr. Annakutty.

"Neeta Chacko is not here," she said.

"Are you sure? I think she is waiting for me."

"No." Gently, firmly. "She's not here, definitely. She has another job now."

From behind a tatty door at the end of the room, two voices were clearly audible: one a hectoring machine gun, the other soft and sad and submissive, then the rat-tat-tat again. The thin girl, listening intently, tiptoed to the door, opened it an inch or two to say I'd arrived, listened to a hail of words, then shut the door quickly with the air of one crating a dangerous animal.

"Dr. Annakutty very, very busy today," the girl told me. "She says you must wait. Sorry, madam." She grimaced.

So much for Daisy's "Darling, they will welcome you with open arms." I waited for over an hour, cushioned on either side by pregnant women, whom I examined furtively. Looking down, I saw cheap leather sandals, one or two held together by string; one had garnished her careworn toes with a silver ring. I saw one woman unwrap a picnic for her child that consisted of minute quantities of rice and vegetables wrapped in a leaf.

But what struck me most after the war and the grayness of London was their colorful clothes, their beautifully kept hair. To use one of my mother's favorite (often furious) phrases, they'd made an effort.

The girl on my left wore a flame-colored sarong-type garment with a tight short blouse, her eyes carefully made up with kohl, a flower in her hair. Poor as poor but her own work of art. The girl beside her, who looked no more than thirteen, was heavily pregnant and had huge purple rings under her eyes. Her pallor suggested anemia, but her hair was plaited as carefully as a show pony's, and she displayed book-on-head posture that Mother (why did I keep thinking of her?) would have applauded.

It was hard not to compare these women with the slovenly, exhausted women we saw in London. Their gray aprons, the scuffed shoes, the threadbare underwear.

But, I mentally slapped myself, no romanticizing. Anto had

warned me of that and so had Daisy. To fall into the trap of pink-light thinking would be fatal for me now.

I sat, I listened (padding feet, low voices, the grizzled cry of a newborn in some distant room), and started to panic as a stained clock on the wall ticked to ten thirty, eleven, eleven thirty. My hours of precious freedom were being gobbled up and I was still not called.

Hearing my impatient sigh, the woman on my left turned and smiled at me, and if a smile could pat your arm and massage your neck and give you something soothing to eat, she'd smiled it.

I was a sweating heap of frustration when Dr. Annakutty finally appeared, wearing a white doctor's coat, a stethoscope around her neck. She was a heavy-shouldered mannish woman with a short neck. "I can see you now," she said.

She lowered her head and scowled—the first Indian woman to give me the evil eye. "Follow me," she said curtly.

I followed her large, wobbling bottom through the waiting room, down a curry-smelling corridor, and into a dim office cum storeroom.

"Hello," I said heartily, when she'd closed the door behind us. "I'm Kit Smallwood," and then, like a twit, "Daisy sends greetings." Very Dr. Livingstone.

"I can't shake your hand until I've washed mine," she said, making me feel like a contaminant when she was probably simply being hygienic. That was my problem already: trying to judge each situation on so many different levels and according to rules I didn't understand.

Her office was tiny: no fan, no outside window, and the floor blocked by the three large packing cases, the same ones Daisy and I had packed up so carefully in Wickam, what felt like a lifetime ago.

She switched on a naked bulb, then sat behind the desk looking at me and breathing deeply. A big woman, with a big pockmarked nose, a big frown, and a big presence. You wouldn't want to put her back up, and it seemed I already had.

At first she spoke so fast it was like being lashed with hailstones, and I could pick out only the odd phrase: C*losed down, too late, not happy.*

"I'm sorry," I said, overwhelmed by this avalanche. "I can't . . . could . . . would you slow down, please?" And then, rather ridiculously, "Has something gone wrong?" More pellets.

"I—am—sorry—too." She spaced her words now as if to a complete imbecile. "Because we have a catalog of woes.

"First,"—she held out a stout finger—"when Independence came we were given many prior promises from your Oxford ladies that they would not pull out as quickly as the British pulled out of India. Then we heard nothing, not for months, then this comes." She pointed towards the packing cases. "And I am given orders, from England, that I cannot open a single box until you come."

Her eyes bulged with fury. "So we are left like dogs with the food up on a shelf: we can see supplies, we cannot get them. And the new government is telling us to cut our ties with you, so what to do? Close this place down, which has taken us years of work to build? Tell the women to go home and to their village midwives and take their chances? You're here now, you tell me."

Daisy had warned me to "expect a few dicey moments," but being told a thing and feeling it are very different, and in that stuffy room (where this woman had clearly overestimated my importance), I was getting my first inkling that this woman saw our fund not as the Bank of Toy Town but as a necessary and compromising evil. I was its condescending representative: a white maharani, determined to keep hold of the purse strings in the new India.

"Why isn't Daisy Barker with you?" she asked suddenly. "She is the one I must speak to." I explained she had urgent business at home; it was impossible for her to come.

"Who are you?"

"I'm an English state-registered nurse, trained at Saint Thomas' Hospital in London."

"You have midwifery qualifications?" She sniffed and looked at me.

"Not quite. I've done my part ones and most of my part twos, barring a few deliveries at Saint Andrew's in London." Flunked one, my guilty heart added. "But I do plan to stay here, and I would like to work with you, Dr. Annakutty." (Was this even true now I'd met her?)

When I stumbled on her name, she snapped. "Call me Dr. A. I don't have time for the other."

Her chin made a bristly sound as she rubbed it. She tapped her fingers on the desk.

"What we need most is money to run this place. Do you understand that?"

"Yes, I do." Rude bitch. She was starting to put *my* back up.

"If we give you a job, it will be for creating funds and for writing reports." Dr. A.'s important nose quivered. "Nursing will come when I have assessed you. If you want to help now," she added, "open the boxes. We have almost nothing left."

"Of course," I said sweetly. "Happy to help, but first, may I ask if Neeta Chacko is here? I think Miss Barker thought—she said she—"

"Neeta is gone," she interrupted, eyes beady and cold. "She has another job, I don't know where."

When I said I didn't think anyone had told Miss Barker about this, she gave that most ambiguous of Indian gestures: the sideways head wag, the yes that could mean no—the one Anto confuses me with sometimes.

"So who?—forgive me—sorry, but have you taken over from Neeta Chacko?"

"I've told you," she snapped. "My name is Dr. Annakutty. I am the acting official head of the Home, put here by the new government." She reeled off a string of qualifications: a medical degree from Madras University, obstetrics, midwifery (Trivandrum Hospital) course, "six hundred and fifty-six deliveries"; the full deck of cards. "Plus, am now senior lecturer to the village courses we run with the vayattattis—the local midwives."

More muscle flexing followed from her side of the desk: she said she could be a full professor in Bombay at this point in her career were it not for political ideals, then she opened the door and yelled something in Malayalam into the darkness.

"I'm calling for a knife," she said. "Because you are here"—she gave me a quizzical look—"we can open the boxes."

I mumbled that the committee's rules were none of my doing, *big, fat, bully girl.* I was getting hot and bothered myself.

A boy arrived and removed the packing case lids with a knife and hammer. Dr. Annakutty lowered her considerable bulk to the floor. "I'll take things out," she said curtly. "You write," she added, handing me a pencil and a pad. "But only when everything is on the floor."

We worked in silence for a while, just the rustle of paper, a man crying *pani, pani, pani* in the street outside, while Dr. A. unwrapped the petri dishes, rubber enemas, one packet of thermometers, forceps, the swabs, sanitary pads, and cord clamps we'd wrapped in back issues of *The Spectator.*

At the end of an hour, my entire body prickled with sweat, but the job was done: the packing cases were empty, my inventory covered five pages, and Dr. A. and I sat inside a pile of nightdresses, baby clothes, medical supplies, and three copies of Comyns Berkeley's *Pictorial Midwifery.*

She signed each page of my inventory in a slashing hand, a big circle of sweat underneath her arm.

"Is this enough to last for a while?" I asked.

She gave a big sigh. "No. Not really. I was turning women away last week."

I made murmuring sympathetic noises.

"There was so much killing up north that medical funds have been diverted, and staff, plus it's hard to get women from good families to train with us. We had to send two away. Their families did not approve. One has promised to come back; the other I don't know." Dr. A.'s frown made a huge V in her forehead. "Her husband won't allow it."

"Is it dangerous to be short-staffed?"

"Of course, and I don't know yet if I can use you. I must check with our own government officials first," she said. "British people can't just walk in now and work."

She put some of the medical equipment back into the packing cases. "I'm taking this home tonight," she said. "There are bandits in the streets around here, and this building is not safe. Tell your Settlement ladies this. We need better locks on our doors."

"Look, I live here now," I said. "I need a job." I'd made up my mind.

"Why?" I could hear her thighs sucking as she heaved herself off the floor and sat behind the desk. "Are you married?" She was looking at me thoughtfully.

When I told her that I was married to an Indian, a Nasrani whose family lived at Mangalath, I swear it was like the sun coming out. "Thekkedens," she said, her face visibly brightening. "A well-known family here, though not personally known to me."

"I met my husband in England. He's a doctor. He did his training there."

This slight thaw between us encouraged me to add, "My husband did some translations with Daisy Barker in England. Both of them felt this home could do great work."

She gave me a hard look as if to say, What would Miss Barker know about the price of bread?

"Great work is our aim," she said after a considering pause. "But we have two big obstacles to progress. Number one." She stuck a large finger in the air. "In some people's minds, a nurse is like a prostitute—sorry for the word—and some doctors here do use them like that—not good information for you either, but if you are going to join us, better you know the facts." She adjusted her enormous bosom.

"Number two. If a girl becomes a nurse here, she has a very bad showing in the marriage market, even now after all our efforts. Even the married ones have difficulties; one of our best midwives was beaten badly by her husband last week. Even though she supports him," she added with a dark look.

"But I thought the Christian community here felt differently." I was anxious to prove I was not a complete tenderfoot. "And that women from South India are well educated and encouraged to work."

"Up to this point." Dr. A. made a small and not very encouraging mark on her desk. "And only to here."

"Our biggest obstacle in employing Hindu girls is they do not like to handle the bodily fluids of another, they think it pollutes them, so we do prefer Christians to work here. Some fathers will hand their oldest daughters over to us for training, but the families are not always happy about it.

"We're trying to start a revolution," she said tiredly, rubbing her eyes, "with not enough soldiers."

In that moment, I felt I could forgive the rattiness, the inability to give anything but the unadorned facts. Charm, jokes, emollient words take it out of you when you're working the long shift.

"So,"—she smiled at me for the first time—"you're a Thekkeden. Sorry for the confusion at first. Now I can show you the work we do. If you come back on Friday, we'll take a boat out from Alleppey, to the villages where we train some midwives. You can see it firsthand," she concluded, as if this had been decided all along.

Oh Lord, I thought, excited and startled. I had no idea what Anto would think about that, or Amma, who was now frigidly polite to me. It seemed one part of me was already thinking like an Indian wife, except the other part was promptly and eagerly replying, "Thank you: that sounds perfect. What time should I come?"

*   *   *

It was the tail end of dusk when we got home to Mangalath: cows munching hay on the edge of rose-colored backwaters, evening fires being lit on the edge of the village of Pookchakkal. As we turned the last corner in the road, the house rose out of the trees, a tangible welcoming presence with oil lamps glowing on the veranda.

It was then I saw a gray-haired man standing motionless on the steps as we drove up. He was staring at us. We got out of the car.

"Appan," Anto said, rooted to the spot. I saw his face twist as his father walked towards us. When he drew closer, I saw that Mathu Thekkeden looked eerily, disconcertingly like an older, wearier version of Anto. The same springing and abundant hair, though his was gray now; the same languid, slightly aristocratic bearing; the same jutting cheekbones; the same finely shaped green eyes, though his were wrinkled and deep set.

He walked straight up to Anto, put his arms around him, and hearing the father's muffled sobs, the half words in Malayalam, I hung back not wanting to spoil things. There were more anguished-sounding words, a keening sound from Anto, and then Mathu turned his wet face to me and, after a jagged pause, said in a kind but formal voice, "Forgive me, I am forgetting all my good manners. Welcome to Mangalath. You are Kit?"

"It's lovely to be here," I said, knowing I was an unwelcome surprise. "I've heard so much about you."

In fact, I knew surprisingly little, except the bare bones stuff about his being one of only a handful of Indian judges in South India, a clever man, an Anglophile with a tiresome predilection for cards. He had played bridge for his Cambridge college during his four years there and later had tried to teach Anto, aged ten: a disaster.

During the rare moments Anto had talked about his father, he'd adopted a lightly ironic tone, referring to his father as "the Pater," as if he were some spat-wearing character out of a Wodehouse novel—the kind of man who went on tiger hunts with English toffs, who ordered his cravats from Bond Street.

It was hard to connect these fragments with this anguished man who'd just hugged my husband as if he were the last person left alive on earth. Mathu was barefoot, he had a strip of cotton wound round his waist, and he had his back to me.

- CHAPTER 18 -

In the study after supper, Anto felt like someone surfacing from a long dream. It was all still there: his father's curved captain's chair, the magnificent cedar desk, the green lamp casting shadows on the teetering piles of books his mother was not allowed to touch, in French, Italian, Malayalam, English, Hindi, all languages his father was fluent in; the complete works of Shakespeare and Dickens, the ancient texts on agriculture that had been in the family for years.

And Appan: a little more stooped but still handsome, the usual cut-glass decanter of whisky beside him. Soon he'd pour his one drink per night in a special Waterford crystal glass given to him by Mr. Bateman, and smoke one of three cigarettes taken from the tin with Player's Number 3 on it. Anto used to be allowed to light them.

"Can I offer you one?" He pushed the tin towards Anto.

"No, thank you." He'd been beaten for less once.

Appan lit up, in the old methodical way: long brown fingers placing the cut-glass ashtray just so, click with the silver Dunhill lighter—another present from Bateman—the long slow drag that made his cheekbones pop out.

The bookshelves behind him were crammed with files on the thousands of court cases his father had taken part in. When they were young, he and Mariamma would hide, and Mariamma, in a thrillingly hoarse whisper, would tell him the lurid details of the serial killer from Bangalore, who chopped his victims in little pieces and threw them in the Ganges. The new bride strangled with her own hair. Rex versus Col. Thorn, the Hampshire-born Indian colonel who'd poisoned an Indian mistress.

The schoolroom they called the Torture Chamber was once in the next room. He and Mariamma were taught by the Scottish woman Ann McGrath; they'd privately called her Hoots Toots and imitated her. The place where Mariamma—whip thin, sarcastic in those days—effortlessly shone.

On his infrequent visits home, Appan would appear there, to check with thrilling gravity on their progress or sometimes to wind up his gramophone and play them his scratchy recordings of Shakespeare.

He was a many-headed god in those days: a pincher of cheeks, a flier of kites, but unpredictable: if you crossed the line, he'd appear with a face like thunder and a strap in his hand.

Anto was sixteen years old when his father had called him into the study and told him he was to be sent away to school. He still cringed at the memory of how he'd wept and pleaded to stay. Later he heard his mother sobbing and shouting in their bedroom, saw her red-rimmed eyes at the dinner table.

He'd stayed awake all night trying to make sense of this catastrophe: he loved the farm with its animals and tree house and warm sheds, the cricket hut where he and his friends smoked, the spangled lagoon outside, the shrine, the temple, the village where everyone knew him. The pattern of his life was fixed here, and he didn't mind.

Even at sixteen, the vague notion he might, one day, marry Vidya had not alarmed him. She was happily linked in his mind to her head-patting mother, Anu, who'd given him the cricket bat he treasured, and who brought him sweets wrapped in bright tissue paper—all things that mattered to the half-formed creature he was then.

*   *   *

"Sure you don't want one?" It was unusual to see his father light one cigarette from the stub of another. The second whisky was new too.

"No, thanks." In the glow of the lamp, he saw how his father had aged: the permanent mark on his nose from his spectacles; the slump of defeat in his demeanor, or maybe he's just bone-tired, he thought. Amma said he never stopped working.

"Is it funny being back, Anto?"

"Yes." Neither smile.

"So much to catch up on."

"Yes."

His father fiddled with the notebook on his desk. "How did your interview with old Kunju go?" he asked after a pause. "I haven't seen him properly for years, but I think he is quite a big nob now in the medical world."

"He is the chief medical officer: big desk, staff of eighty, or so he told me. He hopes he can find me something."

"Only hopes?" his father said sharply. "Did you not show him your qualifications?"

"Yes."

"Was he impressed?"

"I don't know." It felt too early to explain everything, so he took a cigarette instead, thinking, To hell with it, I'm a man now. His father passed him the Dunhill with trembling hands.

"We need all hands to the wheel at the moment. The estate has taken quite a dip in profits since the war."

"I'm aware of that, Appan. I want work too." Anto exhaled, took a piece of tobacco from his tongue. His father was looking anxiously at him through the smoke. "Dr. Kunju hasn't got a job for me. Not yet."

Doctor Professor Kunju, he'd thought privately, was a pompous prick of a man, with his walrus mustache and his office wallpapered with medical certificates and backslapping photos of him taking tea with Gandhi, and he'd caught the distinct whiff of old scores being settled.

"How long since you saw him?"

"Oh God." Appan plunged his fingertips under his glasses, rubbed his eyes. "Let me see, quite a while. We used to play squash at the English Club. I don't suppose he wanted to be reminded of that."

"No. He is a fully paid-up Indian now." They exchanged an awkward glance. "And when I told him where I'd been, he said preference must be given to those who had stayed behind and fought the good fight here."

"I see." His father rubbed his forehead rapidly. "So, nothing?"

"Nothing immediate," Anto said wearily. "A few things in this." He handed his father a copy of the *Hindu Times*.

Appan peered at the two ringed advertisements. The first announced, "Junior doctor wanted for TB Sanitarium."

"Look below."

The second read, "Urgently wanted, forty doctors for service in refugee camps in East Punjab. Pay 300-400 rupees per calendar month plus camp accommodation."

"Dr. Kunju peppered me with questions about Independence," Anto continued. "A kind of a test: Which politicians did I personally support? How many were slaughtered? He was horrified at my ignorance, and now you know, I feel I was in a dream while all this upheaval happened. I had no idea of the extent of it."

"It was a bloodbath," his father gasped. "Don't you read the papers?" His eyes, huge bruised plums, shone in the lamplight.

"The English papers were not so detailed." What did you expect? Anton thought bitterly.

Appan was holding his head in his hands like a balloon that might burst.

"Don't go away again, not now," he said urgently. "Surely he had local jobs for you."

"Nothing, Appan, not yet. You see, another awkward thing cropped up in our talk. Vidya. He knows her family well and told me what a wonderful girl she is: beautiful, clever, kind." The Doctor Professor had delivered this encomium in a voice dripping with regret.

Appan drew a hairless head on his pad. He blew his nose vigorously and took a sip of whisky. "Well, he is Vidya's auntie's cousin. Look, Anto, I can't lie about this to you, it's an awkward situation, you coming back . . . you know . . . not single."

"What did you expect, Appan?" Anto tried not to raise his voice. "After so long away."

"That was never our intention, Anto. It nearly broke your mother's heart. But we did hope . . . we did hope." Appan was trembling with emotion.

"Hoped what?"

"That you would have the self-discipline to wait for a wife. Would that have been so hard?"

"Kit is my wife." He knew he should say more: about her intelligence, her kindness to him in England, her bravery in coming here, but the words wouldn't come.

His father was holding back tears, teeth bared like a dead animal's, his eyes screwed tight. "Appan." The empty whisky bottle fell with a thud on the desk. "Is it really that bad?"

"Your mother was so excited, planned your wedding with Anu and Vidya, told all her friends, and then she became so upset and . . . it was too much."

Anto sat and tried to breathe. "Is this really so hard for you?"

"It will be if you can't work." His father took a deep breath. "I took out a big loan to finance your time overseas. Bateman promised to help with your fees. But you know, once he got back he had other priorities, and of course this family is top-heavy with women. That's why I'm working night and day."

"I'll find a job, I'll do whatever I can."

"Thank you, son." He'd never seen his father look so blank, so obedient. "Don't tell the others what I am telling you."

A tray rattled outside the door. Amma with their nightcap: chamomile tea for Appan, Vetiver for Anto, just as in the old days.

"Good night, Antokutty, good night, Mathukutty. I'm going to bed, son. Don't forget to say your prayers." When her cry woke a crow, which squawked from a tree outside, his father, who was superstitious, made the sign of the cross.

"And you, Ammakutty," Mathu replied. "Good night. God bless. Leave the tray outside the door, we're busy."

Anto took a deep breath. "Father, could you call her in for a moment? There's something I need to say to both of you. I've been putting it off."

Amma brought the tray in looking sleepy but pleased.

It was then he told them that Kit had to start work soon. It was work she was paid for.

"Where?" His father's voice was suddenly sharp—tears and sentiment tidied away.

"At a home for expectant women in Fort Cochin."

"How will she get there?" Appan's face was rigid with surprise.

"We'll have to use the car, until we get our own place in Fort Cochin."

His father's frown deepened. Amma was staring down at the tea, which lay untouched in the cups. "Who will pay for the car?" his father said after a lengthy pause.

"Kit will," Anto improvised. "She'll be paid sixteen pounds a month."

"Is she nursing?" A dark note had appeared in the old man's voice.

"No . . . I mean to say . . . I think her duties are mainly administrative. That was the work she was doing in Oxfordshire. They are doing an important survey on infant mortality here, and how it can be reduced." He noticed he had swerved around the words *midwife* or even *midwife training* and was not proud of the fact. "Look, I'm sorry, I know it's not what you want, but she has to do it."

"What do you mean, has to do it? She is your wife now. Do you let her dictate?"

"It's not a matter of dictating. I want her to do it too." Even to himself he sounded unconvinced.

Appan sighed deeply. He shot a quick look at his wife, who was trembling and shaking her head, but he did not ask for her thoughts.

"What will happen if I say no?" His father stared into the cold tea.

"Don't ask that question," Anto said grimly. "I've only just come home." He heard his mother give a small groan.

"Make sure she pays for the petrol," his father said at last. His face had taken on some of the greenish color of the lamp, and when he raised his exhausted eyes and looked at Anto, they were so full of frustration and foreboding, he might as well have added, This woman will ruin your life.

- CHAPTER 19 -

He came to our room that night, lifted my nightdress, and made love to me as if it were our last night on earth.

"I love you, Kit, I love you." He said it over and over again. My head was jammed against the headboard. "Never forget it."

"I won't." I was startled by his tone. "I love you too."

"This is hard for you," he said. "You're being brave. Do you trust me?"

"Of course I trust you. Now pass me a glass of water and let's get the mozzie net properly tucked." I was trying to make things sound normal because he sounded different in a way I couldn't put my finger on. When he didn't respond, I put out the oil lamp, squirted the deet, and tucked the net around us.

He said in a muffled voice and without turning over, "I'm going to sleep now."

He went off quickly, while I lay awake feeling the heat bear down on me like a soft, soggy cloak. I was getting more and more confused by him. When he woke in the middle of the night, I was still up. I put my hand on his shoulder. "Anto, something's wrong, isn't it?"

He didn't turn over. "Nothing's wrong." His back was a drum I could feel words through. "I just meant to tell you that Appan said you can start work whenever is right for you. He thinks it's good for women to work." He might have been reading from a report. I was even more confused. "Anto." I pulled on his shoulder. "Was it that easy? What did you say?"

"Nothing. It's just that I may have to travel soon. I must get a job."

"Of course, that's what we planned, and then we can get a house of our own."

"We'll try."

I felt my own life being organized behind my back and I hated it.

"Anto," I said, "something's wrong. I know it is. I can feel it." But he was gone, as quickly as if someone had stuck a chloroform mask over his face. I got up, knelt beside him, and in the slatted, silvered moonlight studied him: the curve of his cheekbones, his lips, his fine soft skin. Was it a simple case of lust that had led me here? Before him, I'd never known the matchless intoxication of sexual attraction, how it powered you with an energy you could neither predict or control. If another man had asked me to take this journey, would I have been more clear-sighted, less idealistic, less delusional?

For the next few days, I had the sense of him drifting away. He left early, going for every job he could find, and then one day there was a note, saying he'd had to leave suddenly: he had a job interview up north. He wasn't sure he would get it, but he had to try. He was sorry not to give me the message in person, but would I stick to our agreement of staying for another two weeks at Mangalath?

Mariamma handed the note to me at the breakfast table, with the possibly kind embellishment of "And he said we were to look after you, and have lots of fun."

"How far north?" I was trying not to look as shocked as I felt. We'd never once discussed the possibility of his working up north, plus it was so unlike him to leave without a word, a kiss, some reassurance.

She patted my hand, said, "Bombay, I think, but dinna fash yourself, the men in our family are always on the move. This morning I am going to show you how to tie a sari." She had

Anto's quick and irresistible smile. "A surprise for Anto when he gets back."

Threatened now by the shapeless days ahead, I was grateful for any kind of plan.

After breakfast, Mariamma's little girl Theresa, a sweetly solemn, plump child with huge brown eyes and the early beginnings of a mustache, sat on the veranda staring at me without a word until Mariamma came downstairs, her arms covered in stoles and saris.

The saris smelled delicious. Mariamma explained how depending on the time of year, she and Amma would take them out and refold them with different herbs: jasmine in spring; attar of roses, lemongrass in summer; mitti, or lavender, during the monsoon. She laid them out for me over the wicker chairs, explaining that the chatta and mundu, the simple white blouse and soft white skirt she and Amma wore every day, was "more or less the Nasrani woman's uniform." The more elaborate jeweled and colored saris were usually for weddings or for kitty parties, when all the women got together for fun and gossip. God save me from one of those yet, I thought in a panic.

"I hear you are starting official duties with a charity soon," she dropped in casually, giving me the feeling she had been part of a family discussion I hadn't been party to. "So this would be most suitable and cool." She held up the Nasrani outfit: the white draping skirt with the pleats at the back, the simple cotton blouse. Her smile was friendly, her hands busily folding, stroking, unfolding saris, tucking one or two in the tissue paper she explained was acid-free and protected them from termites, from sweat.

I liked Mariamma: she was was funny and affectionate, and proud of her Scottish sayings and her bookishness. If she felt any sibling protectiveness about Anto and me, she hid it well.

And as she wrapped the sari cloth around me with neat and

practiced hands, part of me was thinking, This must be what it's like to have a sister—getting fizzy about clothes, rolling our eyes about boys, confiding things—for when she told me about Anto earlier, she'd added, "As a boy, he was always sneaking off. He was quite a solitary soul."

"Really?" I'd said, thinking of our all-too-brief courtship at Wickam Farm and how we'd craved and plotted for more time together.

"We used to play tracking games." She wound the cloth tighter. "I would leave a trail of clues in the trees, the flower pots, on the jetty, once behind the donkey's ears. Anto and his friends would follow them, for miles sometimes, by canoe or by bike. They had wonderful fun. They were so free."

"I bet you loved that."

"I stayed home with Amma," she said serenely. "My job was to set the clues. I enjoyed that too," she added, a little defensive. "From an early age here, we're in training to be good wives."

It was tempting to ask how this fitted with her two years of intoxicating freedom at university. But she, focused, serious, was lifting a sari from tissue paper and putting one end of its length on my shoulder.

"So has he changed much since he was away?"

"Very much," she said.

"In what way?"

"He's more serious. He makes a lot of jokes but he's sadder."

I was quietly devastated to hear this, and she, glancing quickly at me, changed the subject, lifting up a sari of gossamer-fine, white silk gauze with a gold border that sparkled like sunlight on water.

"This was for my wedding," Mariamma said. "I was covered in gold jewelry too." Her eyes gleamed at the memory. "Such a wonderful day: feasts, fireworks, the wedding parties arriving by boat, and the jetty, the garden, all lit up with flaming torches—so beautiful you wanted to cry. The servants loved it too. I wish you'd been there," she added politely. "What did you wear for your English wedding?" The question I'd dreaded.

"Nothing fancy." Thinking of the freezing registry office, the curled sandwiches, my mother's expression, Daisy's frantic efforts to compensate. "A tweed suit, a hat." The look of pleasure in Mariamma's eyes turned to one of disappointment, even disapproval.

"Did Anto mind?"

"No." Thinking, Liar. I didn't know anymore. "Clothes are still in very short supply in England."

To cover the awkward pause, Mariamma, wafting rose water, made me try on a sari. Usually I hate the feeling of being dressed— I remembered Ma smacking me, spitting on her hanky, saying brooches out, belts in—but Mariamma's expression was gentle as she patted me, moved me around, and adjusted a fold here and there.

"What sort of clothes you are wearing in England as a very little girl?" She smiled over my shoulder at Theresa, who was watching us with rapt attention. "Our Scottie governess wore tweeds even in the heat."

"Anything Mother chose—usually in wool," I answered. "Yes, even woolen bathing suits. Mother knitted them, and they had buttons on the front, and when we went to the seaside and they filled up with water, I looked like a larva on legs."

"A larva!" Mariamma started laughing, and when she flapped her arms and translated this lam for Theresa, the little girl cackled and threw herself around, and we were all laughing. I was hungry and could smell spices and herbs coming from the kitchen. I was thinking I could be happy here.

"Yes," I continued, mainly now for Theresa's sake, "woolen hats, very prickly, woolen knickers, one woolen skirt in tweed."

"Woolen food also?" Theresa spoke in English at last. She beamed, showing her sharp little teeth.

"Definitely woolen food: woolen sausages, woolen potatoes." A stream of words followed from Theresa.

"She wants you to come to the ladies' party next week," Mariamma told me. "She says you're . . ." She stopped and drew in her lips. Amma had just entered the room, so quickly she may have been watching us all along.

"Of course, we must ask Amma first," Mariamma continued smoothly. "We start with a lot of prayers, which you may find boring, so maybe for later."

Amma didn't say a word, just took a long appraising look at me, half-draped in a pale-pink sari, another kind of larva about to shed, or add, a skin.

"Can you walk in it?" she asked at last, trying for a smile.

I tried, a sort of graceless hobble to begin with, and then remembering how Mariamma did it: smaller steps, greater awareness of posture. Theresa clapped her podgy little hands.

"How does it feel?" Amma's face was expressionless.

"Quite different," I said, which was true: I felt taller, more womanly, and, once I'd got the walk right, almost stately. I also felt bandaged, swaddled, held in, like someone in a three-legged race but thought it best not to mention this.

"She looks pretty?" Theresa closed one eye, screwed up her funny little face like a Paris seamstress. When I looked at her I imagined the children I would have with Anto—though, please God, not yet.

"Very pretty," said Amma faintly.

"We were thinking Kit could wear this for work." Mariamma held up the plain white outfit.

"For work, yes." Amma was sort of smiling and sort of frowning. "Anto says you start next week. Are you happy with that?"

"Yes." I tried to sound humble but clear, sure of myself but not obnoxious.

"Good," Amma said drily. "So you got your own way at last. You do know I'm not happy about it, don't you?"

"I sort of guessed," I said. "And I'm sorry." Her expression froze. Later, when I was walking back to my room, she stopped me in the corridor, pinched my arm, and glared at me, a hard, bright look full of intent.

"You must never discuss your work within the family," she said. "That's one thing I must insist on. Do you understand?" I told her I did, but I didn't, not properly, not yet.

- CHAPTER 20 -

Terrified that I would oversleep, or that Amma would forbid it at the last moment, I hardly slept a wink before my first official day at work. I got up at four a.m., read for a while, and arrived an hour early at Alleppey, where, at seven thirty in the morning, the wooden jetty buzzed with fish sellers, coconut juice vendors, and a sleepy child selling fried crisps and wooden snakes.

I found Dr. A. sitting in a wicker chair outside a wooden fisherman's hut looking very grand and impersonal, and not much friendlier than the first day I'd met her. The anxious-looking, bespectacled woman beside her, she introduced as Maya, "Our fully qualified midwife."

Maya gave a wincing smile, and when she looked at me, I saw, underneath an impressive pair of men's glasses, a fading green and purple bruise.

Our boat was a battered old rice boat with *Moonstone* written on its side in faded red lettering. It was a beautiful, romantic-looking thing with its gracefully curved lines and a bamboo roof which flung patterns of sunlight on the floor. Dr. A. explained to me, in a bored monotone, that its deck was tied together with rope coated with resin from cashew nuts and fish oil, and that the boat was both an urgent necessity—the only way they could visit some villagers—and "a serious drain on finances," since it needed "complete restoration."

While the boat was being loaded with boxes of medical supplies and cardboard signs for the midwife classes, Dr. A. settled back in her chair and withdrew into the magnificent citadel of her mind (either that, or she'd fallen asleep), and Maya, who had the sweet, shy smile of a child, became more and more animated as she hopped on and off the boat to show me around.

In a tiny squalid kitchen at the end of the boat, she pointed to a stove, "where you may cook your rice and chaya." And then, pointing to a duck innocently floating by, she mimed strangling him. "For our dinner."

When I asked what our plan for the day was, Maya beamed at me through her horn-rimmed glasses and produced a map from under the saucepans.

"Our first port of call," she said, "is Champakulam, where we will have a confab with some local midwives to try and persuade them to do our training. Next we'll go to see a postpartum mother who has had a big, *big* baby: twelve pounds, poor thing. The biggest ever in the village." Query diabetes, I thought, but said nothing.

"We'll also see a mother on the point of delivery."

I was getting used to the lackadaisical rhythms of India by now—the chai, the chat, the *hawa khana*, which Anto had told me was Hindi for chewing air—but this seemed an awful lot of work to get through in a day, and I'd promised, actually sworn, to Amma I'd definitely be home that night. I tried to disguise the panic I felt.

"How long will it take?"

When she replied, "Oh, two days definitely," my scalp prickled with alarm, and before the boat left, I had to jump ashore, yell for the driver (glares from Dr. A., whom I woke up), and scribble a groveling note to my mother-in-law, saying I might be delayed but no one was to worry about me. When our boat's bell rang, I was hauled aboard by Maya's surprisingly strong arms. Dr. A., frowning, watched me from the prow of the boat: a huge black shadow framed by the sun. But I soon forgot her and my other worries about Anto and Amma and all the rest of it, it was so wonderful being out on the river, and *I was here, I was working*. It ran like a song through my head all that morning. Plus, the first shy shoots of friendship had sprung up between me and Maya, whose general demeanor was sweet and friendly and whose English, like that of so many other locals, was excellent.

As the boat chugged through the narrow waterways, I felt a sense of relief: I was entering a wonderfully new and secret world, one that was separate from the Thekkedens with all their rules and expectations and disquiet about me. Around the first bend in the river I saw a whole family—parents, children, dogs, buffalos— washing in the water, and next, a row of rainbow-colored women walking in single files through rice paddies, with water pots on their heads—and there, colorful shacks and tiny, neatly planted gardens; hovels; a fierce old lady peeling her vegetables; a Hindu temple, so close its incense prickled my nose, with a temple priest waving at us from the bank. Around us were rice paddies and palm trees reflected in the water, and soft hills beyond that looked like clouds, and clouds that looked like hills, and families of ducks that virtually ignored the gentle splash of our boat. The flash of a kingfisher wing, the leap of a fish. I don't think I had ever been so spellbound or so happy.

A large canoe passed carrying a load of giggling schoolgirls, hair plaited and tied with white ribbons, long blue skirts, shirts white, smart enough to go to a posh girls' boarding school.

"I know them all." Maya returned their waves. "I delivered two of them. One took two days and nearly killed me."

On the opposite side of the river, a pathetic scrap of a girl—no more than six or seven—stopped washing clothes when she saw us pass. When she waved a skinny arm at us, her collarbone popped out like organ stops. Maya told me the poor people were poorer than ever around here, what with the war and the rice crop being bad last year. That girl was an orphan, but I was not to worry about her: "In India, the children belong to everyone, grandmas, aunties, friends."

So why had my mother fallen through this particular net, I wondered, and ended up in an orphanage? I felt the jagged pain, familiar as an old injury, of wondering if she missed me. On the ship coming over, I'd written two letters to her, half hoping to hear she still loved me, that she forgave me. I'd followed up with another letter and two postcards from Mangalath, but the silence from her end was deafening, and I was starting to believe her "dead to me" ultimatum.

To stop my gloomy thoughts, I asked Maya about her training and if she would mind my taking notes. She told me that after delivering babies for many years with no formal training, she'd been persuaded by Dr. A. to do three years of general nursing in Madras, followed by one year of midwifery.

"My family allowed me to do this because my husband is ill, he has a heart problem, but now he hates what I do," which was pretty obvious from the green and purple shiner. "Most nurses here," she added with a shrug, "are life dust: widows, orphans, or deserted wives. Until recently there was no formal training of midwives at all. We caused a very big stir." She added with a wide smile, "But now there is a very big government push towards it."

I marveled at her calm, cheerful presence; it made my blood boil too. Every bloody religion in the world pretends to care about mothers, children, the sick, and the lame—but they can't mean it, not really.

We were talking when Dr. A. rose like a large whale from the prow of the boat. She pointed towards a cluster of mud shacks on the riverbank, the spire of a white church.

"Champakulam," she said to me, adjusting her sari and picking up her large doctor bag. "Two local midwives will see us there."

Only two! Daisy had led me to believe there'd be a classroom crammed with them, but I followed the doctor meekly off the boat and down a dirt road—filthy drains, lots of stinky rubbish, an old woman with milky eyes selling fish—to a small whitewashed convent on the edge of the village, where an old French nun was waiting for us.

The nun led us to a windowless room at the back of the church where two women were waiting. The first midwife, Amba Kannan, was a small, wiry, aggrieved-looking woman, about thirty-five years old, arms covered in cheap gold bangles. The other covered her face when she saw us and said in a reluctant mumble that her name was Latika.

Amba greeted Dr. A. politely with a *namaste* but then let go a torrent of words. Dr. A. listened silently, sympathetically wagging her head, and then turned to me. "Her biggest problem is this: some of the people in this village have stopped paying the local midwives for their work because they hear that you are paying them now. She says—" She listened to another blast of invective. "They are being treated like criminals."

"Please tell them we only pay for training," I said to Dr. A.

"This I have explained to them, but they are angry and do not trust British peoples anymore." Dr. A. snorted noncommittally. "She would like some money now to make up for what she has lost."

"May I ask how much they charge for each delivery?" I asked.

"It's very meager; twelve to sixteen rupees is standard." In English money, between one and two pounds.

I made a note of it in my new notebook, as if I knew what I was doing. "How many deliveries does Amba do, on average, each month?" Another torrent of words.

"Last month five. In total, three thousand."

"Three thousand. Good God!"

"Yes, three thousand," came the firm reply. "Maybe more." Amba's s eyes darted towards me, a proud curve to her lip.

Now Maya translated for my benefit. "Dr. Annakutty is proud to announce that now Independence has come, Travancore will be the best country in the world to have a baby in, and that we have only come to show them simple things." Dr. A.'s head was waggling fit to fly off her shoulders.

"More hygienic methods." Maya rubbed her hands like Lady Macbeth. "Example: not moving from baby to baby without washing our hands, or leaving the—" She didn't finish the sentence. Dr. A. was shaking her head forbiddingly and looking at me.

"They are talking about the afterbirth," she mumbled at last. "I will explain this later."

"So." After another majestic snort, Dr. A. clapped her hands loudly. "Time to begin."

The two midwives sat cross-legged on the floor and Dr. A. rattled on at a tremendous pitch. She produced a plastic pelvis from her bag and a stained wooden doll and demonstrated various angles of delivery.

It was beastly hot, but it felt good to feel my brain engaged again. After a half-hour talk, Maya, like some obstetric Father Christmas, unpacked brown-paper parcels full of sterilized maternal pads, babies' milk bottles, a jar of lubricant, and three pairs of rubber gloves.

While these offerings from the wonderful world of modern medicine were laid out on the stone floor, I reminded myself to tell Daisy that Dr. A. had the rest of the supplies at her house. Maya was demonstrating how much lubricant she used on a rubber glove, when the door flew open and the old French nun appeared. She said there might be a baby on the way.

Dr. A. turned to me. "You must go with Maya; she knows this girl and will know what to do."

As we headed in searing heat down the dusty street, I was sweating with alarm. The memory of the redheaded girl was always there, lying behind some sopping black curtain in my mind, and I honestly didn't know if I could cope.

"Miz Kit," Maya said, "no rush." She steered me around an old man sitting on the pavement with his sewing machine and told me the girl we were going to see was sixteen years old. Her name was Prasanna and she was having her second baby. Five weeks before delivery, she'd moved into her mother-in-law's house.

"Her relatives sell fish like these people." She pointed to an ancient couple sitting on the other side of the lane. Beside them a bamboo mat was covered in shiny-looking fish and some bunches of chilies.

"When we get there"—Maya reached into the canvas bag she was carrying, handed me a stethoscope—"put this round your neck and I'll tell them you're an English doctor. They will think you bring good luck." When I shook my head, she put the stethoscope back into her bag, patted me reassuringly. "For later then," she said. "You may stay and watch."

We found the girl inside a dirt-floor hut, lying on what looked like a pile of packed sand with a few dirty rags scattered around. The sand, Maya told me, was a good way to soak up blood. Two women were cooking over a smoky wood-fire stove—one chopping onions, the other stirring a pot of rice gruel. There was no sense of panic here.

The girl was half-asleep when we arrived, beads of sweat gleaming on her forehead. She smiled when she opened her eyes and saw Maya. The pains she told her were coming, "*Vegan* and *adupichu.*" Thick and fast, Maya translated.

"I thought you said the village midwife would do this delivery," I said.

"Maybe." Maya shrugged. "We'll have to see."

The mother-in-law padded silently into the room, barefoot and holding a saucepan of unappetizing-looking lentils in her hand. Her hair was grizzled and gray; she looked tired. When I took out my recorder's notebook, I saw my hands were shaking.

When I asked her to confirm Prasanna's age, she looked blankly at me and scratched her head.

"She's not sure," Maya said, adding that wasn't particularly unusual around here. I carried on down my list: How many other babies did Prasanna have? One. Length of labor? Ten hours.

When half an hour later the girl's tummy started to tense and strain, Maya pulled the thin sheet back and told me to stand in a spot in the corner.

"This we call thinking with our fingers." She brushed her fingers over the pulsating dome of Prasana's belly, prodding here, listening intently, feeling the sides of her belly with questing hands. "The baby is in a good position," she said. "No need for fuss." A cockerel crowed through the open window; a bell tinged as a bicycle rattled through the lanes.

We both smiled when a small foot suddenly popped under the skin, as if the baby were saying, "Hear, hear!"

Maya put on her rubber gloves, lubricated her fingers, and did an internal exam. The quiet economy of her movements, her calmness, reminded me of old Jack, a horse breaker who came to Wickam Farm, and the sly, almost unconscious way he could slip a horse's head into its first bridle, almost before the animal knew it.

"Close now," she murmured, patting Prasanna's arm. "Now you will learn some new words," she told me. "Write them down. *Velum kondu vaa*, bring some water. *Choodu vellum*, hot water. *Tulle* means push. *Mukkeh*, bear down."

She told me to step outside the shack for a few minutes to give her more room to administer a massage. When I did, I realized I had almost stopped breathing. I knew of course that I would almost certainly have to watch deliveries again and was prepared for that, but that hut, with its fug so thick you could slice it, plus its other smells—sweat, smoke, human bodies, ancient meals—was making me sweat and almost heave a little.

When Maya joined me again, she was eating one of the dosas and smiling. The girl's cervix was well dilated. She had given the girl a light massage with coconut oil. Prasanna was happy. When, an hour later, the baby's head started to crown, I was ashamed to find myself almost on the point of fainting. It was as if my mind had blanked out the twenty-eight deliveries I had been part of and taken me back to being a knock-kneed novice. But when the hut had stopped wobbling, I saw from a distance that Maya was completely in command. One loud shriek, a full head of dark, damp hair suddenly visible, then Prasanna, puffing, blowing, shouting, gave one last almighty thrust and pushed a new person into the room. The mother-in-law yelled, "*Ente daivame aan kunju!* Oh, my God! It's a boy!" and Maya held it up so the girl, who was crying with happiness, could see it.

I was bundled out of the room for the cutting of the cord and disposal of the afterbirth. The baby was clean when I came back and Maya was kissing him, then looked at him slowly from his wriggling toes to his damp and tufted head. She said something which made all the women laugh.

"Why are they laughing?" I still felt sick.

"I said lovely hair, lovely fat legs, and a nice packet between his thighs." Maya wiggled her head, delighted with her own joke.

"I didn't expect that so early," I said, as I walked wobble-legged out of that hut and almost immediately experienced a nearly tearful rush of emotion I could not name. Today had shown me that possibly soon, if I could get over the faintness, I might at least work my way round to being a helpful pair of extra hands at the clinic. That was a start. Whether I could still be a midwife was debatable—the thought was enough to make my heart pound again—so to avoid having my mind go down the usual ratholes, I asked Maya if Prasanna would have been very disappointed had the baby been a girl. She gave me a sharp look.

"Of course," she said. "Girls cost too much: their dowries *ruin* families." After she'd had her second daughter, her mother-in-law refused to talk to her for weeks, but then, thank God, a son came.

"His name is Shiva," she told me proudly. "He is only eighteen but he rules the roost."

Proud grandparents stood at the door when we arrived at our next stop to see the whopper: the twelve-pound baby who had become a local celebrity. We found him sleeping serenely in a cloth cradle suspended from a rod which hung from the ceiling—a great, big, plump, smiling Buddha of a baby, coffee-colored and with deep creases around his wrists and neck.

The baby shone with coconut oil and had a faded marigold garland around his neck and what looked like a slightly infected umbilical cord.

"Did he get this in a hospital?" I asked Devika, his mother, when she lifted him up proudly. Maya had pleaded with me to put on the doctor coat for this examination, and since this was not a delivery, and seeing no great harm in it, I had put it on.

"No." Maya explained that Devika, who'd had her first baby at fifteen, didn't like hospitals. She went once and they were rude to her and jumped on her stomach to make the baby come.

"So her usual midwife came," Maya continued. "She trusts her. There was much bleeding and yelling," she translated, as the woman's voice rose dramatically, "but Devika is all right now."

Maya peered more closely at the baby's umbilical cord, which was red and weeping. "This one does it with a rusty knife," she told me in a mutter, while keeping a neutral expression on her face. "She is stubborn about that. Now put your stethoscope on, look at it, *frown*."

I peered at the cord, wondering why the baby wasn't screaming blue murder, it looked so sore. When Maya cleaned the wound, the baby kicked two legs the size of hams and just looked at me with its huge brown eyes. No squealing.

When I handed the mother a small bottle of potassium permanganate, she thanked me with a fervor that made me feel ashamed.

"What did you say about me?" I asked on our way back to the convent.

"That you were a fine English doctor."

"Oh God, you mustn't say that. I feel like the most awful fraud."

"It will help her, and her baby," Maya said simply. "The power of the mind is very strong."

I put it out of my mind. We were late for lunch and both hungry.

"That child was a baby elephant. Poor woman!" As we ran down the towpath together, I was laughing.

Fish curry for lunch, and after it Maya showed me my bedroom—a small whitewashed room above the church with an iron bed and a crucifix on the wall. The air smelled faintly of incense. When I crawled under the mosquito net, my head was reeling at all I'd seen. I heard birds singing as I drifted off to sleep, the lap of water from the river. I was too tired to worry much about whether Amma would mind my being here. As for Anto: what a wicked wife, I'd hardly given him a thought all day.

- CHAPTER 21 -

Before she took her breakfast, Amma went into the prayer room inside the house, determined to find some rest from the furious thoughts that kept her awake at night. Anto's new wife had been staying with them for close to two months now, and Amma had started to hate her. She blamed her for Anto's new reserve, when he was once so open and jolly with her; she blamed her for his frequent absences to find work. She was sure that by now he would have been deluged with job offers had he not come home with the impediment of an English wife.

Kneeling at the cedar altar made from the deck of an ancestor's spice ship, she breathed in the mingled smells of beeswax furniture polish and incense and wrestled her mind into a state of weary numbness. This is your favorite time of the day, she reminded herself: no relatives to talk to and placate, nothing to disturb you, only the discreet twitterings of birds, and from the kitchen the silky sounds of Pathrose pouring water through muslin and into the earthenware pots, the flash of spices hitting hot fat.

Soon the swish of Satya cleaning the steps with cow dung. Later, three other women in the yard would pick stones out of the rice stored in the granary on the left of the courtyard. They would fold at the waist like ballet dancers, murmuring as they worked; she might hear them giggle. If she heard the low drone of complaints, she'd go out to see what was wrong. That was her job: keeping the house running like a well-oiled machine. Mathu, at his most unreasonable, behaved as if any fool could do this. Let him try.

"Heavenly Father, make me an instrument of thy works. Don't let me be proud, or hard, or unkind. God, help me. Please!—"

Often nowadays, her formal prayers seemed to break down into a desperate pleading because, when he was home, Anto had almost stopped speaking to her and it was grinding her down. Ashamed of her weakness, she wiped her eyes, got up stiffly, and went into the kitchen, where Pathrose, standing in a pool of sunlight, was measuring out six cups of rice, then dhal and fenugreek seeds for breakfast dosas.

For dinner that night, she planned a beef ularthiyathu, a stir-fry, a spinach thoran, and a dish of the fiery red fish curry that the girl had praised extravagantly on the night they arrived, before she had a coughing fit. Anto had loved it, licking his fingers in sheer bliss. This much she could at least do for him.

"Don't make it too spicy for the English girl," she told Pathrose. They shared a brief look of malice and exasperation before she moderated hers into one of studied calm. Pathrose knew her too well, how she faked sunniness sometimes to keep this house on an even keel, just as she knew how he and Satya rolled their eyes behind the scenes and mimicked her sayings: *Aana karyam para-yumbol aano chena karyam,* "Must you talk about the yam when I'm dealing with the elephant?" or complained about her tongue-lashings. They shared her shame too, when on entering the young master's bedroom, they saw the blatant display of stockings, the silk slip on the rattan chair. They were simple people; to them, she was like an exotic harlot.

After breakfast she slipped on her sandals and walked into the garden.

Anyone watching her padding serenely towards the summer-house would think her a fortunate woman in full control of her little world, but today she felt she'd like to spit or smash or throw something. She was fed up to the back teeth with being the family's pet chameleon, cheerfully adapting to Mathu's moods and disappearances, or pretending she wasn't hurt by Anto's sudden disappearance or put out by the arrival of new wives, tiresome relatives, new babies, ill-timed illnesses, when the truth was that, like the weather, she had her own moods.

The path on either side of her was lined with orchids, planted in coconut husks. Mathu brought them to her, these beautiful, useless plants—the Singapore orchids, the painted ladies, the vandas—from all over India: his apology for his many absences, his pipes of peace. Each year she chose with finicky precision the exact spot to plant them, the right amount of cow dung to dilute with water for their flourishing.

Once these plants had seemed a poor substitute for him, but over the years she'd come to find something erotic and freeing in their pointless flapperish beauty: they did nothing but flower and dazzle and attract insects; they gave nothing back.

From the summerhouse she could see the lagoon, flushed pink in the dawn light, and hear the cry of the postman who came from Ottappuram every morning with packages and letters. Every morning for the past month, she'd watched the English girl walk down to the postbox at the end of the drive and walk back alone and empty-handed. And God forgive her, she did not feel one iota of sympathy for her. The girl was a pest, a nuisance, and her list of crimes was growing. Every morning since Anto had left, Kit was driven in the Morris to the women's home in Cochin. An unforgivable liberty. True, the arrangement was agreed on, in principle, by Mathu and Anto, but Amma had expected the girl to make occasional visits, in the same way she went to call on the poor children's school in the next village, as a representative of the Thekkeden clan.

When the girl offered to pay for petrol from her own funds, as per the arrangement, Amma, trained to demonstrate hospitality even when she didn't feel it, had from long force of habit smiled and waved away the suggestion as if it were a gnat. But Amma, in a ritual she hated, was the one who had to go to her husband's study once a month, and nod and smile as he got out the leather-bound ledger in which she had to write down every single rupee spent while he was away.

Other crimes: the girl added her opinion during meals when the men were talking about world affairs. She ate with her hands now, but badly, not using the fingertips as delicate prongs as they did but holding the food in a sticky mass in her palm. Amma had seen Anto wince at this, the last time he was home. Why didn't he correct her?

She wore lipstick, not a lot and not always, but some, and powder, and a few days ago, without permission, showed Theresa how to do it. Admittedly they practiced on a doll, but Theresa, soon to reach puberty, might get wrong ideas. When Amma reached puberty, a whole list of instructions had come with it from her mother. She wanted them passed on untainted.

Next Kit, responding to the frosty atmosphere, had turned to Amma and asked her about her own beauty routine. When Amma protested she didn't have one, Theresa interrupted, "Yes, you do, Ammamma." And Theresa had described to Kit how every day Amma's maid beat the bark of a soap nut tree until it was soft, so Amma could scrub herself with it and remove dead skin before she oiled herself. Personal things. Amma had stood by. Nodding, smiling, nodding, smiling, just like a good Indian woman. Tornado inside.

But the worst crime came last week when she'd seen Mariamma and Kit on the veranda talking in low voices and glancing furtively in her direction. She'd taken Mariamma aside and pinched her arm until Mariamma mumbled that Kit had asked questions about menstruation, childbirth, attitudes to marriage. Embarrassing questions.

"What a cheek," Amma had said, expecting Mariamma to agree, but Mariamma had said that Kit wasn't being nosy, she was writing a report, and besides would need to know local attitudes herself when she and Anto had children.

Children were another wound. Her son's would be half-breeds now; the ones he would have had with Vidya . . .

Stop! She pulled at a clump of weeds around her moth orchid so violently, she splattered her slippers in soil. She must try with all her strength to put an end to these horrible thoughts, but for now, let God tell her what she did in a previous life to deserve this?

It's your fault, she wanted to tell the girl. You should have controlled yourself; you should never have married him. Her last thought felt like the ultimate blasphemy: it would have been better for them all if Anto had stayed in England.

When Pathrose found her, he picked up her sodden handkerchief from the bench and made no mention of her red eyes. When she sent him off to see if the postman had come, he came back looking stricken. "Madam," he said, "sorry. No letter comes."

- CHAPTER 22 -

It was clear that the driver, Chandy, was sick of having to drop me at the Moonstone every weekday morning when he would rather spend leisurely days polishing the car and waiting for Appan's return. When we reached the first village, Karappuram, he threaded his way through it, hand on horn, swerving to avoid a fruit stall or a chicken or a man being shaved. He sighed a lot and occasionally glared at me through the rearview mirror. But I didn't care, because as we headed out into the immense skies, the green fields, the pearly water, I felt I could breathe again, because in spite of all my terrors, this was the first step. I was going to work again. *I was going to work.*

I'd never understood before what a salve it was in times of trouble. Work stopped me from minding about Amma, particularly at meals when she was so silent. It gave me less time to worry about Anto, who was still trying to find a job and away as much as he was home.

All of us, I suppose, have parts of us that are like foreign countries even to ourselves, but I kept remembering our first day at Mangalath and that strange new look, both embarrassed and challenging, he'd given me when he dropped his suit on the floor and wrapped the strip of cloth around his waist as if to say, This is who I am now, like it or lump it.

And then I would think of my mother and how much I'd hurt her. I'd try to remember the conversations we'd had before I left, but I couldn't exactly, only her tears and silences and my absolute determination to leave, and perhaps my cruelty to her.

My only other outlet during this time were letters home to my old friend Josie, married now to a childhood sweetheart, Archie, a newspaper journalist, and with her first child. Josie sent me a picture of her baby, Jack, and said he looked like a boiled egg but she loved him madly, though she hoped one day to go back and nurse at Thomas'. "I'd go potty if I thought I would never work again, though it won't be the same without good laughs with you."

And of course I wrote several times a month to Daisy, who, after my first three months in India, wrote to me asking for "a) an account sheet, and b) a full progress report—warts and all."

I'd headed my reply back "A Cure for Warts," to make her laugh but to warn her too that the Moonstone operated on a knife's edge. We needed money to patch the leaking roof and mend the rotting veranda (termites), parts of which were so soft you could crumble the wood between your fingers. We desperately needed more staff.

The official letters I wrote for the Moonstone were sent out via rickshaws, battered buses, barefooted boys, and bicycles, to everyone Dr. A. and I could think of: to Indian businessmen, maharajas, teaching hospitals, charitable funds. Our only significant response so far had come from a Mr. Namboothiri, a noisy, emotional paint manufacturer who supplied materials for the fabulously lurid lorries seen on the roads here. The day after we'd treated his maid at the Home for a late miscarriage, he'd arrived with what Dr. A. described as "a small cash donation" (she wouldn't say how much), designs for a new sign painted in gleaming yellows, reds, and purples announcing, Matha Maria Moonstone Home, First-class treatment for Expectant Females. He also brought a tub of hibiscus and geraniums to put beside the veranda steps.

Money worries and begging letters aside, safe in the knowledge that my role here was administrative, I was starting to relish the rigor and the challenges of the work, the sense, however misguided, that I was living under the skin of India.

After the shapeless days at Mangalath, I relished the routine. At eight thirty sharp, Maya would arrive in a rickshaw, chaperoned by her son, Shiva. Recently she'd confided in me that her husband and son had turned over a new leaf and were happy for her to support the family. That was her version. I hoped it was true. No more bruises that I could see, but huge, dark plum-colored circles under her eyes made her look permanently exhausted.

Her boy wore the same large, horn-rimmed glasses that Maya wore, but his face had none of her sweetness of expression, and he dropped her off with no more ceremony than a man delivering a parcel and left without a word or a backward glance.

This was painful to watch because Maya was a gem: highly intelligent, she loved the work and, best of all, was open-minded about the need to connect the best birth practices of East and West without letting the "pigheads," as she called them, get in the way. Her kindness and her quiet air of competence with patients, and all forms of living life, were wonderful to behold.

The first thing Maya did every morning was to peer at the new hibiscus and geranium through her huge specs, carefully measure out the water into an old petri dish, and give them all a careful dose.

At nine o'clock sharp, a bell rang, doors opened, and the straggling line of women that had formed in the garden surged forward. They came with every imaginable female problem possible: early and late miscarriage, pregnancy, incomplete abortion, gonorrhea, troubles breast-feeding. My job when they'd arrived was to move between the consulting rooms and take notes.

Their numbers were growing, Maya told me, because the Home, despite all our financial woes, had a reputation for cleanliness and kindness, and (great selling point) it was free. Some women were picked up by Moonstone volunteers in local slums and factories. We had to be extremely careful about the latter group, as men controlled the women there mostly, and some were very suspicious of the work we did.

Some of the women arrived holding hands or the tips of each others saris like terrified children.

"Women here aren't used to going to the doctor," Maya explained. "It makes them uncomfortable to show their private part." When she told me this, I thought of the erotic statues in Hindu temples—the bare breasts, the bristling penises—and thought I would never ever understand this country. I couldn't see a common thread here and probably never would. I longed to be able to discuss such inconsistencies with Mariamma, or Amma even, but I'd seen the lemony look on Amma's face when I asked any sort of personal question.

Sometimes, because we were so short-staffed, patients had to wait for hours to see us. Time moved at its own stately pace here, but no one complained and no one apologized.

The morning when my role changed without any warning began normally enough. "Chandramati Achari," barked Dr. A., standing at the door, list in hand, calling for our first patient.

A tiny, immaculately clean-looking woman stood up. Her sandals were held together by string, but she walked towards us with the kind of long-necked, straight-backed posture that would not disgrace a principal of the Royal Ballet School.

She lay on the consulting room couch, her eyes closed, dusty sandals on the floor. Dr. A. washed her hands at the sink. I sat by the side of the examining table, notebook at the ready. A dim electric light hung over the examining table. When the light failed, we were dependent on a wonky generator.

Dr. A. sighed, put on her glasses, and talked to me over the supine body. "This woman suffered from eclampsia last time and nearly died. Seizures were there, and a blood pressure of one eighty over one ten. It was frightening, wasn't it, Chandramati?" The girl nodded, eyes tightly closed. "But when she went to the hospital, they treated her very roughly, then left her on her own in a corridor until the baby was almost come. Correct, Chandramati?"

"Correct, ma'am."

"Now we'll take a look." The rubber gloves went on and were lubricated. I watched Dr. A. insert two fingers in the girl's vagina and feel around for several minutes. Her imperious face was calm.

"This baby," she announced at last, "feels very happy; it will be beautiful." The woman gasped, tears rolled out under her lids, a spurt of passionate words followed.

"She's telling me God is good," Dr. A. said. "That she likes coming here. That she's going to be brave about having this baby, and that she would like you to deliver it."

I felt the news as a swell of nausea in my stomach. When the room was empty again, I reminded Dr. A. that I didn't have my full midwifery certificate yet. She gave me a blank look and said with her usual humility, "I will watch you, and if I feel you're ready, you're ready. When that time is come, I will ask the gorement"—that was how she pronounced *government*—"for full accreditation."

In hindsight I would have saved myself a great deal of distress and humiliation had I said something then, or later insisted on seeing the relevant certificates, but instead I froze. If Anto had been home, I'm almost sure I would have discussed it with him, but he wasn't. The sense I had of being about to step off a cliff made me sleep badly that night. I was, if possible, even more frightened than before because every day the stream of patients was teaching me how little I knew about this country with its mind-boggling complexities of religion, of caste, its ideas of purity and pollution.

Anto had tried to warn me, Daisy too. She'd told me once that Indians were the sweetest and kindest people on earth, until they were the angriest. If I got it wrong this time, I had no doubt that revenge would be swift.

                        *   *   *

After morning clinic on the following day, Dr. A. pulled another alarming rabbit from the hat. She stomped off with me behind her to visit the inpatients, who were housed in a ramshackle brick building, once a barn, at the back of the main building. It had six emergency beds in it and a nest of rats in the roof.

To follow the ample buttocks of Dr. A. on her rounds was to feel like a queen's bridesmaid: even the sickest of patients attempted to smile or salute her. In one bed, an underweight child of fourteen showed the whites of her eyes at our approach. Dr. A. said she'd been admitted with a threatened miscarriage in the second trimester of her pregnancy. Her mother sat on the floor beside her bed with a small spirit stove to cook on.

In the next bed, separated by a small cloth screen, a woman, bleeding heavily from incomplete separation of her placenta, was being prepped for a transfusion by Maya.

After a very late lunch, some rice and lentils and the inevitable fried fish, delivered from a street stall across the road, I was changing to go home when Dr. A. appeared, her large nose quivering with importance.

"Come to my office, please," she said. "Don't look worried. Good news has come."

I was about to tell her that my driver was waiting—Amma got quietly furious when the car was late—but when I opened my mouth to speak, Dr. A. held her two palms up.

"Don't speak!" She opened the office door.

Maya was inside, plus two new nurses who smiled at us timidly. No one introduced us.

"Sit down." Dr. A. sat down at her desk and opened a letter. Her expression was one of rare joy.

"I have two special announcements," she said. "The first is that Nurse Kit Thekkeden can start delivering her first Indian babies." I heard Maya's little grunt of pleasure, hands clapping; I felt a rapid fluttering in my chest, but there was not time to absorb the full impact or to ask whether I'd been officially cleared, because Dr. A. had another announcement. "We've done it," she said, her eyes fixed on me. "A year's grant from the new Cochin Medical Foundation to support our work. I told you our own people would support us," she added in a same-to-you-with-knobs-on kind of way.

The new nurses beamed and clapped. Maya made a funny sound with her tongue. I felt sick.

"How much are they giving us?" I asked, to play for time.

Dr. A. gave me a dark look. "That information is between the minister and myself."

"But I'll need to tell Miss Barker," I said. Her letters requesting itemized accounts had so far been ignored.

"I have no time for this now." Dr. A.'s tone was chilly. Our priority, she said, was to enroll as many village midwives as we could and bring them to Moonstone for a ten-day training session. All the important national newspapers, the *Hindu*, and the locals, the *Malayala Manorama*, the *Mathrubhumi*, would come for their graduation ceremony and we could show them all the future of obstetrics for Indian women.

I saw Maya nodding her head, smiling serenely, a splendid idea, until Dr. A. added, "But there is one string attached. If we succeed, the gorement will extend our lease by a year. If we fail, we must hand our premises back for other gorement purposes." There was a combined gasp at this.

I put up my hand. "Forgive me. I think these premises were bought by the Settlement in Oxford." I'd seen the deeds at Wickam Farm.

"Not after Independence," Dr. A. replied. "It's gorement-owned now."

We looked at each other with deep distrust, and this would have been a good time to clarify my official position here, but Maya jumped into the tense silence. "So, Doctor, please may we know when courses start?" Dr. A. opened her diary, planted a finger on the page. "In one and a half month's time, I have already certified the date."

"Good Lord." I was aghast. This felt like an impossible deadline. Where in the Lord's name would these women sleep? What about a cook? Proper training equipment? Transport?

"Does that give us enough time?" I asked.

Dr. A. frowned and rubbed her bristly chin. "This is my decision now," she said. "Our gorement and God will provide." She clapped her diary shut and stood up. "Our first course will begin as stated on April third, for ten days. And important to note too, we have an official inspection coming up, so everything must be right. If it's not, they can close us down overnight. Now, no more questions please."

After the meeting, Maya stopped me in the corridor. "I am very worried," she whispered. "Why is she rushing, rushing, rushing?" This from Maya, who never said a word against Dr. A.

"I don't know," I whispered back. Maya pinched her nose in thought. "Maybe she is worrying about the monsoon. It comes at the beginning of June. The streets do flood round here."

"I don't know. "

"We must patch the holes in the roof to stop the drips."

"And kill the rats: they've just had babies."

"Beds for the vimmen?"

"Food and a cook."

"A blackboard, somewhere for them to sit."

We exchanged a look of terror. "But I think you're happy to be a proper midwife again?" Maya said, patting my arm, "Not a secretary."

There were no words to tell her how terrified I felt, because she assumed that I, being English, was better trained, more knowledgeable than she was. But even thinking about it brought that trapped-bird feeling in my chest again, as my mind tripped back to the baby inside the government-issue tin helmet, its lips turning blue as it gasped for breath. I knew I wanted to try again. I knew it would kill me to get it wrong again.

- CHAPTER 23 -

A fortnight later, Amma called me downstairs.

"Anto has written," she said tonelessly. She pulled a letter from the folds of her skirt and handed it to me.

"It's open," I said.

"Of course," my mother-in-law replied. "He wrote it to all of us." There was no mistaking the look of triumph in her eyes. The letter, postmarked Madras, was in a cheap brown envelope, the kind you buy in a bazaar with a red frill around its edges. I read it in front of her, trying to control my expression.

> Dear Appan, Amma, Kit, and Mariamma,
>
> My apologies for not letting you know sooner that I went for a few days to Madras to find out whether I could get immediate employment here. While here I was asked if I could volunteer to work at a refugee center (Chengalput) near Madras, where there was no functioning telephone line. I did not mean to be away for so long, or to stay here, and I hope I have not worried you all too much, but the need here was so great, it was hard to refuse. I shall come back on the Egmore-to-Quilon train and get a taxi to Trivandrum hopefully around Thursday the eighth. Will wire you exact times later. If convenient for Appan and Amma, perhaps Kit could come down with the driver to collect me at the station.
>
> Loving son,
> Anto

"Why has he had to go to Madras?" Amma asked me, her look turning spiteful. "What is he running away from?"

"I don't know," I said. I didn't want to cry in front of her, but I was so confused that Anto hadn't even managed a postscript for me.

"Were you getting scared he wouldn't come home at all?" she added. Of course I was bloody well scared, I felt like saying, weren't you? We looked at each other.

"Because you hid it very bravely." Amma smiled a strange, hard smile. Appan, she continued, had traveled for most of their married life, but when he was away, she'd stayed home, prayed, made sure the house was extra clean. I, on the other hand, rushed around like a mad thing caught up in my own work.

"Things have changed so much." Amma tucked the letter into her blouse. "In my day it was considered disrespectful to even say your husband's name in mixed company."

Upstairs, I closed the door, ripped off my dusty shirt, lay on the bed, and cried like a child. I was cut to the quick by Anto's curt letter and furious with him for writing to everyone and not to me. Fed up to the back teeth too with Amma and her wonderfully subtle talks about how a wife should behave.

When I heard the supper gong clang, I cleaned myself up, changed my blouse, and went downstairs. Outside, the night with its purple sky and brilliant stars was beautiful, but I was dark inside.

- CHAPTER 24 -

On the train that took him south, Anto was buttonholed by a Mr. Patel, a cotton manufacturer from Lahore. His new friend, in a shiny tight suit and plumply sprawled over two seats, had noticed English shipping labels on Anto's suitcase. He'd opened an array of greasy packages and offered to share his lunch, and before Anto could decline, Patel had spoken for twenty minutes without drawing breath: the market for cotton was diabolical. Independence, the famine up north, Gandhi's assassination had put a spanner in everyone's works. He personally thought . . . and on and on, while Anto tried to control a mounting distress.

He couldn't stop thinking about Habi, the two-year-old orphan in bed nine at the Madras Refugee Centre where he'd spent the last three weeks. Habi weighed nine pounds; he'd been found in a rubbish tip close to the track where the Bombay express flew. Someone had flung him from the train before or during the massacre. Now he lay in his narrow cot, blank-eyed and with the turkey-loose dry skin typical of malnutrition. Above his head hung a sign: "My name is Habi, please pick me up," because as the nurse had explained, when they'd first tried to hold him, "he didn't know how to put his arms around us. When he slept he used to clutch his own head." Anto had been assigned Habi, visiting him twice a day and sometimes leaving a sugar ball on his pillow. The first time he'd touched the child's shoulder, he'd felt him wince, but ten days ago for the first time Habi had squeezed his hand. The nurses had counted this as a great victory. "It's a big improvement," one of them had said. "He won't die now."

Habi had shown him in the starkest possible way what aloneness felt like, and by extension about Kit and how he'd been before he met her. Before her, it was normal for him to go to sleep hugging himself. He'd been so hidden, in spite of the superficial ease, and she'd coaxed him out, and now he seemed to be retreating again into some kind of emotional igloo, and it was desperately unfair to her. These thoughts were muddled up with a kind of anguish about Habi, who would be waiting for him that morning, for his touch, for his sugar ball, and he was on a train going south, once again whizzing between two worlds.

Guilty. He felt so guilty. The camp was run by one doctor, two nuns, and some volunteers; three doctors had died. At the height of the crisis they'd admitted seven hundred patients to fill three hundred beds, sometimes two or three to a bed.

"I'm telling you," Kanchana, the woman doctor said, "it was like Scutari before your Florence Nightingale moved in."

"Not my Florence Nightingale," he'd said. "I'm Indian."

"Oh, sorry," she'd teased. "A very posh one, I'm thinking."

In this place, the admission that he'd spent the whole of the war in England felt like something to hide. So did Kit. Everywhere he'd looked he'd seen glimpses of misery: a woman with a ravaged child at her breast, rags hanging out to dry, a dimly lit tent with four people staring out slack-jawed. Overnight, they'd lost everything.

At first he'd gone into a state of wary numbness that he recognized from the London wards, but once he'd adjusted, his time at the camp had passed in a dizzying round of examining, dosing, stitching, injecting, seeing patient after patient with stab wounds, dysentery, cholera, malnutrition, burns, pneumonia. The director of the camp had begged him to stay on, and he would have, but he had to get home, to a wife who couldn't possibly understand. Why should she? He wouldn't have believed it had he not seen such horrors with his own eyes.

The train was moving through a tangle of electrical wires and weary shacks on the outskirts of a town whose name he could not read. Out in the open again, the brown dirt horizon blurred and dissolved like a dream, and the world looked liquid and insubstantial. His feet squelched in his shoes, and he had developed a stinging prickly heat rash on his back. He'd forgotten how unbearable the weeks leading up to the monsoon could be: last week, the glass had reached 110 degrees for four days straight. His romantic account of the monsoon to Kit now struck him as another deceit. No mention of the suffocating nights before the rains came, the dying birds, the athlete's foot, the bad temper. What a tour guide he'd turned out to be.

As the train steamed into the station at Trivandrum, he saw her standing near the chai stall on platform one. Some part of him had hoped to see her in Indian clothes, as a mark of change, but instead, she wore the blue dress he'd once loved. He could see the curve of her patrician nose under the brim of her hat. Her hands clasped together tightly. When she first turned towards him, she squinted, whether to protect her eyes from the sun or in distress, he couldn't tell.

He'd booked a room at the Ambassador Hotel, a peeling, two-story edifice on the seafront.

"Kit." Aching, sweating, he sat beside her in the family car, close enough now to see the soft down on her cheek, the purple flashes in her brown eyes. He wanted to kiss her, but it was she who turned away, and said with a wary smile at the driver, "Chandy's come down to see his family."

And later, in their room on the third floor, they stood awkwardly opposite each other. She put her hand on his hair, and said, "You've lost weight." When she touched his hip bones, he pulled away involuntarily.

"What's the matter?" she said.

"I don't know," he said, bewildered by his flash of antagonism. Five minutes ago, he'd longed to take her to bed; now he felt anger at her easy assumption that she could touch him whenever she felt like it. He moved towards the window and lit a cigarette.

"It's very good of you to drive all this way," he said.

"Don't be silly, it's what we planned." She looked confused. "I haven't seen you for three and a half weeks. I was starting to think you would never come home."

"Well,"—he tried to smile back—"I'm here now."

"Yes," she said after a long silence. "You're here now." She shot him a look of pure exasperation. Her voice heated up. "And that's all, is it? No explanation needed about where you've been or, I don't know, a job, or where we're going next?"

He'd never seen her so angry.

"Oh, Kit." He sat down heavily on the bed. "Do you think I could possibly have a bath first and something to eat? Would that be too much?"

"No, Anto, naturally, it's whatever you want." She sat down on the opposite side of the bed and pinched her nose.

"Can I talk about it later?"

"Fine."

"Kit, give me a moment."

"Whatever you want." She breathed out noisily. "I'm sure it would be fine with you if I took off for weeks and didn't let you know."

"Please, Kit." He tried to take her hand. "I'm sorry. I'm so tired. Was it terribly hot on the way down?"

"Oh really, Anto." The ghost of a smile as she glanced at him. "'Was it terribly hot on the way down?' You sound like the King."

"Christ, I hope not," he said with sudden savagery. He stubbed out his cigarette and threw it out the window.

"Anto," her voice was tight and as airless as the day. "What in God's name is going on?"

Through the window he could see purplish clouds gathering at the edge of the horizon. The monsoon would be here in a matter of days, and he had a sudden wild wish that it would swamp them all.

"Do you want to stay?" he asked. "Here I mean."

"Of course I do." Her voice faltered. "Isn't this our holiday?"

He gazed at her, lost and miserable. Was it a trick of light or time, that the glow he'd once felt in her presence had gone? The Wickam Farm memories—the long whispered conversations, the childish jokes over whose turn it was to have their toes on the hot water bottle, the dream version of India he'd laid out—felt like pure self-indulgence.

He hated this room too: the sagging bed with its stained mosquito net, the uncarpeted tiles, had been all he could afford, a miserable place for what he'd once promised would be a proper honeymoon.

"Kit, I'm sorry but I want to go home," he said. "The monsoon won't come for a couple of days, we still have time."

"What home?" She lifted her chin and stared at him defiantly. "Mangalath? Oh, so that's our permanent home now, is it? Thanks for letting me know."

"I'll need money for our own house, Kit, a proper job."

"I thought getting a job was the point of your going away. Would it be too forward for me to ask about that?"

"I'm sorry, Kit, I'll explain later. It's complicated." He had a sudden irrational longing for Downside, the neat line of beds, the company of men, the suppression of violent emotion.

"And I'm sorry too." She pointed her finger at him without words for a moment. "Because the other thing—the other thing is . . ." Her eyes were flashing, her blue dress patched with sweat. "The other thing is, I have my own work to do, and this may be my only chance for a holiday for a long time, so if you want to go home, you carry on; I'll join you later under my own steam because I'm not going to simply, meekly,"—she was running out of words—"trot home after you . . . like a . . . like an Indian wife."

"What do you mean 'like an Indian wife,' Kit?"

As the air between them grew electric and thrilling; he felt a loosening inside him. If she wasn't prepared to hold back, neither was he.

"Well, the waiting, for one thing; the giving up any sense of yourself, the not taking decisions, the being told what to do, the boredom of it all." Her smile was bright, sarcastic.

He sat for a long time looking at the floor. "Kit, have I ever told you to give up your job? Have I? So bloody unfair . . . so . . ." He was too angry to form proper words. "You've been allowed to work," he burst out at last. "All I asked was for you to stay at Mangalath while I was away."

"'Allowed to work,'" she repeated. "Lucky old me!"

He put his head in his hands. He wanted to hit her. "What a lot of rot," he said eventually. "Really. Complete and utter poppycock." He shook his head. "But since we're talking about it now, how long do you intend to stay there?"

"As long as I can." Her voice was hard and defiant. "I promised Daisy, and I haven't told you this yet, but quite a few of the things that the Oxford ladies sent out have gone missing. I need to get to the bottom of it."

"You're heading into murky waters, Kit." He wiped his sweating face with a handkerchief. "I advise you to stay out of it."

"Really, thanks for the advice."

"These are violent times," he continued in a low voice. "The Home is a controversial place. If things are disappearing, men are almost certainly involved. They will definitely have weapons: guns, knives, lathes, boxes of matches, whatever they can lay their hands on."

"Anto," she repeated, "the Home's reopening, the midwives are coming."

He blew out air, chewed the inside of his lip. A gust of wind rattled the window. Black cumulus cloud was tumbling and turning in the sky. When he turned and looked at her again, he said, "So is Mangalath that bad? Is there absolutely nothing you like about being here, apart from your work?"

"Nothing." She put her face in her hands. "Actually, not a thing, now I come to think about it," she said in a muffled voice. Eventually, he heard her jagged sigh. She lifted her tear-stained face, went to the basin in the corner of the room, ran some rust-stained water, and splashed her face.

"Kit." He handed her a towel. "This is a terrible time to argue. Before the monsoon—everybody does it."

She dried her face and looked at him. There was a long silence. "You're right," she said in a small, expressionless voice. "Let's not." And after a considering pause, "But it's not just the monsoon. Mangalath is beautiful, the children so sweet, but I would have died of boredom in the last month if it hadn't been for work. The work you seem to want me to give up now."

"Unfair, Kit." He walked towards her and took her hand. "Definitely below the belt. All I'm asking is for you to make the family important."

"Compared to what?" She sounded very weary.

"To work, or to children, when we have them."

"Anto." Her voice softened. "We can do both, but not if you keep running away and writing your blasted communal letters."

"Come here." He stretched out his arms towards her. "Please."

"Anto," she said as she put her arms around him, "was it awful in the camp? I haven't asked you a thing."

"Not awful for me. I could get out."

She smoothed his hair and wiped his face. "Let's stay," she said gently. "Let's talk."

"Later," he said. "Not now." He hated the idea of crying in front of her.

There was a high, round window above her head shaped like a

ship's porthole. Outside he saw dark-purple clouds growing darker, a bird flying across the sky.

"We won't have much choice soon." He swallowed and hugged her tight. "Monsoon is coming, madam." His Indian voice. "Act of God now, and by the way," he added drily, "when you talked earlier about going home under your own steam, what steam were you planning: magic carpet, the jet stream? Who owns the car?"

"Don't make a joke of it, Anto. I still hate you."

"I know." He tightened his arms around her. "Poor me." He felt oddly revitalized by the purity of her anger, as if he were coming out of an anesthetic. "Kiss me." He held her hair in a bunch behind her head.

She took his face between her hands. "Why should I?"

"Because you love me, because you're beautiful, because you smell beautiful." He touched her hair. "Is it rose water?"

"Yes," she said in a muffled voice. "Don't try and get round me. So hot," she murmured. "Feel my dress." It had stuck to her back like glue. She took him by the hand and led him into the old-fashioned bathroom at the end of their room. It had a red oxide floor and a large pot of water in the corner. A pane of colored glass set in the ceiling flung jeweled patterns on the floor. Her dress made a sucking sound as he drew it over her head.

"Sit down." She guided him towards a small stool with a cork seat. She stood in her half slip and bare feet and washed his back and arms and kissed the nape of his neck.

"It's mad hot," he said. "No one should speak before the rains come. This is a very ancient monsoon custom," he said, lifting her slip and sponging between her breasts.

"Bloody liar." She leaned towards him and closed her eyes. The purple sky was humming when they went to bed, the light dappled, distorted. A line of sweat ran down his cheek as he kissed her, and afterwards, lying on his back and looking at the ceiling, he was dimly aware of the swelling sounds of a procession passing in the street outside. Drums, cymbals, a cracked trumpet, the gobble-gobble sound of human voices.

"Feast of Indra," he told her sleepily. "The god who makes the monsoon come." An hour or so later, rain rattled against the windowpanes.

"Is that it?" she asked. "Has it come?"

"Not yet." He was longing for its release. "The newspapers predict in two days' time."

"How will we know?"

"The sky will get even darker, the birds grow quiet, the air is electric."

"If only we were so predictable," she said.

He thought about this silently later. From certain angles, human beings were that predictable: the wild changes of adolescence, the longing for children, the nine months gestation period, the loss of hair and teeth in old age.

"When the rains come,"—he was falling asleep—"the beaches will be crammed with people dancing, shouting, celebrating . . . It is . . . it is . . ." His voice became a vague blur and then tailed off.

When he woke an hour or so later they made love again, with a violence and abandon he had never experienced before. When it was over, he got up, sat on the side of the bed, and smoked a cigarette.

He went to the window, where a thin muslin curtain was fluttering. From there he saw black skies, more wildly flying birds. He could feel the sea vibrate the floor under his feet. The monsoon was gathering force.

- CHAPTER 25 -

At breakfast the next morning, our waiter, with an air of barely suppressed excitement, brought a copy of the *Hindu* to our table, so we could keep up with news of the monsoon, which the front-page story confidently announced, would arrive, "in full power and glory," at around three ten that afternoon. The town, it said, was "full to bursting" with visitors: there was no more room at the government guesthouses. There would be parties tonight, and bonfires, great celebrations.

Anto looked up, his eyes gleaming. He looked film-star handsome that morning—his hair still wet from the bath, and a white shirt on, restored, or so I thought, by our lovemaking. I sat for a while enjoying the sight of him, my limbs heavy and sweet, but then, aware I knew so little of what he'd been up to in the last few weeks, I asked him again what the work was like at the refugee center and saw the light go out in his eyes and regretted it immediately. Bad timing. He played listlessly with the eggs and bacon he'd ordered, pushed his plate aside.

"Obviously, don't tell me yet unless you feel like it." I had my interview voice on, but there wasn't much I could do about that with his face so set. He rolled up his napkin, unrolled it again.

"It feels wrong to describe it, eating all this food," he said.

"Oh, come on, Anto." I felt anxious again and ready to be irritated. "It's me you're talking to; I think I should have some idea.

So he told me, at least some of it: as if he were reading a police report, looking but not looking at me as if there were a pane of glass between us.

"I had no idea how bad it was, and worse up north: thousands of homeless people crammed into tents. Gunshot wounds, cholera, TB, smallpox, women having babies. We did three clinics a day. Shit up to our knees."

"Why on earth didn't you tell me you were there?" I said. He looked so angry. "Do I really strike you as being that selfish?"

He ignored this. "Kit." He pushed his plate away and put his hands on the table between us. "We were living in a fool's paradise in England, all that guff about the happy end to the Empire. It was a shambles. These people have been left with nothing."

"Fool's maybe," I said, "but not a paradise. There was the small matter of the war on in England."

"I didn't ask enough questions."

"No one here asks us about the war in England: it's what people do to get by," I said to comfort him.

"Maybe." His hands were twisting; he was unconvinced.

"Will you go back?"

"I don't know, because here's the point," he said, still not looking at me. "There are jobs up there. I was hoping you might come with me."

And then he did look at me, so hopefully that I knew what I was supposed to say, that I would go with him to the ends of the earth, if necessary, but we were not in a film.

"When were you thinking that might be?"

"As soon as you could." He pushed his half-eaten breakfast away.

The waiter darted towards us with more chai and was waved off impatiently.

"I can't," I said. "We start our first midwife classes at the Moonstone next month. I've promised to be there."

"Ah." I could not read his deliberately blank stare, but I suddenly felt like Maya, a woman doing a distasteful and unpopular thing.

He heaved a big sigh, put his chin in his hand, and looked at me.

"Well, this is a nice holiday," he said. "Two hearts beating as one." I was shocked at his childishness.

"Anto, be fair," I burst out, to the considerable fascination of the waiter, ostentatiously dabbing a table nearby. "I promised Daisy to see this through. I told you that last night."

"I know," he said, and gave me a look of such bafflement and misery that I felt like the worst heel on earth.

We were so sad and ill at ease with each other again, it felt good later that day to join the crowd of mildly hysterical people on the seafront.

Clutching the railings, we moved down to the beach, where the wind was making a singing noise in the flagpoles, and the sky was dark and electric. At around three fifteen, there was a combined gasp, and Anto grabbed my arm as the drums started to pound. It was the most astonishing sight I had ever seen, this cone of black-ish cloud starting to mass and change shape and charging now like a live animal towards the shore. Birds were spiraling round and round like feathered tops; children were held tight lest they blow away. My dress was flapping like a sail, and my feet were moving to the sound of drums and cracked trumpets and crashing waves, and the louder and louder whine of the wind, and I was lifted out of myself. When I looked at Anto, his eyes were shut and his face twisted as if he was drinking it in.

Buckets of rain started to fall. "Do you mind getting wet?" Anto shouted. His hair was soaked, his face ecstatic, his shirt clung to his rib cage. I felt a great wave of desire for him.

"Not at all," I shouted back. "I love, love, love it, and I love you."

And there we stood, two dumbfounded savages, watching the rain pelt down and the wind roar, and the birds going backwards, and the great waves boom as they crashed on the beach. Soaking wet, we ran back to the hotel together, toweled each other off, and spent the rest of the afternoon in bed, with the wind still howling outside and the rain bashing down. I knew he was still upset, and so was I, so our lovemaking didn't feel like a truce or an escape, but something deeper, sweeter: an acknowledgment that human beings had their own weather and couldn't always control it. Something like that anyway.

Afterwards, when he lay back on the pillows with his arms above his head. I could almost see the thoughts traveling from his unblinking eyes to his mouth.

"Don't start thinking again, Anto," I pleaded, partly to make him smile. "I like it better like this."

"I have to." He squeezed my hand. "I wish I didn't."

"So try talking to me."

With his face partly concealed from me, he said, "Do you miss your mother?"

"Yes, " I said, surprised. I thought for a bit. "More than I thought I would."

He put his arm round me. "Write to her?"

"I've tried, she doesn't answer."

"Keep trying, it's only pride in the end."

"D'you really believe that?" I was on my elbow now, looking at him and feeling so sad.

"I do. You know, Kit, you can't escape it. I've tried with my own family, and now I know how deeply embedded in me they are."

He went on to say he would be away again for the next month. He would be working in the camp. It was work he would be paid for—not much, two hundred and fifty rupees a month—but he could save all of it and send some home for all of us. After that, he'd come back to Travancore and take any job he could find.

"There must be a job for you here." I was trying not to cry because I felt he was in flight and there was nothing I could do.

"And I know it's hard, but why have you stopped telling me things? In England, you told me things, and I liked that. Isn't that the point, or part of the point, of being in love: a sort of unveiling, someone to tell your secrets to?"

He looked at me and gave a small smile. "Do you keep secrets from me?" he said at last. "I think you do."

"I try not to," I hedged. But it wasn't entirely true.

The air had cleared, around us and inside us, and during the next sweet night, we made love, made promises, made up names for children we might have. It didn't last: over breakfast the next day, Anto told me we must go home on the following morning. When I looked surprised, he said, "Some roads will be flooded already. We can't get stuck." A peremptory Indian husband, firing out orders.

"Two days!" I said after a long and fuming silence. "For a holiday!" Anto looked up from his dosa. "Kit, I tried to explain this to you: Mangalath is losing money, and we must all save for it now."

The air between us sizzled with unsaid things and I hated his patient expression. I told him in a tight voice I was more than happy to contribute to the family coffers, but we deserved a break occasionally. He blew out air, looked out the window, chewed the inside of his lip. We went up to our room in silence.

It got worse. An hour later, while I was packing, he came out of the bathroom with my diaphragm in his hand. I'd washed it, powdered it, and in the excitement of the night before, left it in its plastic box on a high windowsill.

"Why didn't you tell me?" He put the box on the bedside table.

After a long silence I said, "I wanted to wait until you'd found a job closer to home. I didn't know how much of a Catholic you were. I was a coward. I'm sorry."

He barked with frustration and flew apart from me. *He's going to hit me* raced through my mind, he looked so angry. But he just blew out breath, put his head in his hands, and said, "And you say I keep secrets from you!"

It can't have been that much of a secret, I thought, sitting in the back of the car on our way home, feeling like a criminal—an angry criminal. When we'd made love during our first days at Mangalath, he'd sometimes withdrawn abruptly as if terrified of what might follow, and I'd understood, knowing how confused things were between us. Also, I raged inwardly, had he never wondered during the times he'd stayed inside me why I hadn't got pregnant? He was a doctor, after all: he must have known. While I seethed, the car skidded and sloshed down a broken road with waving wet palm trees on either side, trying to stay ahead of a monsoon that was moving northeast now. Chandy, angry, or so I imagined, at having his own holiday cut short, had his foot down.

The car stopped. Chandy got out to pee. Anto, who'd hardly spoken a word, turned to me and said, "So what are we going to do?" He rubbed his eyes and looked so weary and confused that my rage disappeared and I felt his sadness.

"Give me a month or two," I said. "That's all."

I told him in a rush what was true, that I loved him, that I longed for his babies. All I needed was a little more time. He took my hand and squeezed it tightly. "If you mean that, and I hope you do," he whispered urgently, "I am begging you not to stay beyond the point of safety at the Moonstone. You don't know the country well. Kill one baby and they'll kill you."

He stopped talking. Chandy had appeared from wet bushes and was jogging back towards the car. When he was close enough to see our faces, he stopped and stood waiting in the rain.

- CHAPTER 26 -

A letter was waiting for Anto when we got home, offering him a two-month locum at the TB clinic near the refugee center at Quilon and a proper working wage of four hundred rupees a month plus accommodation. He was to start in four days' time.

The offer of a job would normally have been a cause for celebration, but we took the news warily, both of us still badly shaken by the row in Trivandrum.

Two days after my husband left, Appan called me into his study at Mangalath, where we began with a cat-and-mouse conversation about Anto, Appan hoping I supported him, "because family is at the core of everything we do." He knew it was hard for a "young wife to be left alone so much." It had been for Amma, which was why she was so sensitive.

He lit a cigarette, looked at me through his hooded eyes, and said I was lucky that I had a career in South India which was advanced in its support of women's gaining professional qualifications. It was the future, but everyone had to be sensitive to the changes.

Finally, he grilled me about the Home, my work there, my training. "I'm assured it's a place the family can be proud of," he said, fixing me with the famous stare, "and that your work is mainly administrative there." In his next breath he told me I would be allowed to stay for two weeks in a family house near Fort Cochin Beach. The house, which belonged to Appan's cousin Josekutty, another lawyer, was used only as a holiday home. He showed me the location on his map, and I could hardly stop smiling when I noticed it was on Rose Street, two blocks away from the Moonstone and not far from the Chinese fishing nets—a lovely part of town. Two trusted family servants would look after me there.

When he saw me smiling, he became stern. Two conditions were not negotiable: number one (rigid finger in the air) that I come back to Mangalath without fail on both weekends I was away. Number two (finger pointing at me) that I never discuss my new freedoms outside the family.

"I don't want any gossip about you." The terrifying eagle-like glare reminded me of Anto's stories about the strap in the desk, the thunderous rages. As urbane and charming as he could be, you would never want to cross this man.

When I saw the house on Rose Street, I fell in love immediately. Here was the perfect place for Anto and me to live together and have the new start I longed for.

It wasn't a bit smart. It had the look of a tiny, slightly dilapidated Chinese temple, with its sloped tiled roof, and it had a deep veranda with a swing on it—a piece of wood fixed with thick coir to the roof. A cool corridor led straight through the house to a central courtyard scented with jasmine and mimosas.

The two servants—Mani, the odd-job man, and his wife, Kamalam, cook and maid, with their seven-year-old son, Uni— were all very sweet and proud of the house. They showed me a primitive but adequate kitchen and the four bedrooms, all of which had carved wooden beds, plain furniture, and tiled floors.

The timing, for once, was right too. On the day after I moved in, and after much consultation with astrological charts, Madhavan Thambi, the new Minister for Health and Family Welfare, came with the promised year's grant from the Cochin Medical Foundation (Dr. A. still wouldn't say for how much), which he handed over in an envelope after a short ceremony. He also gave us a shiny plaque for our waiting room, noting wryly that it hung next to a picture of the Goddess Bhadrakali of Kerala, a woman with three eyes, twelve hands, flames flowing from her head, and from her mouth a small tusk created to kill demons with the aid of a largely female army. "I won't cross her," he said roguishly, and we all laughed politely.

Thanks to our new funds, we now had a staff of twelve: Dr. Annakutty, Maya, myself, four nurses, four staff for general cleaning and cooking, and a part-time helper, Sister Patricia, a rawboned Irish nun of about forty who came twice a week from a local convent.

To prepare for the opening, Maya had mounted a fierce raid on the rats in the roof, now mostly dead; the Home's new purple, red, and yellow sign was hung and clearly visible from the road. And most importantly, Mr. Namboothiri, our local hero and tireless donator of paint, had driven off in the middle of the night in the smoking, paint-splattered bus we called Cyclops—one headlamp missing—to collect our first ten midwives, who arrived five hours later looking dusty and petrified. Most had never been in a bus before or left the network of small villages where they practiced. One tiny, pockmarked woman wrestled an enormous bedroll; several carried tiffin boxes, worried they might not get enough to eat here.

Some local musicians had been drafted to give the ceremony some oomph, and after drums and twiddly flutes, incense was lit, petals strewn. During Mr. Thambi's long and droning speech, the midwives sat at his feet, barefoot and on the new coir mats, staring at him in frank amazement.

Dr. A. jumped up next, her nose quivering importantly, and in her usual rat-tat delivery gave a stirring speech, which Maya translated for me.

"You women are the future of India. Some of you have more

knowledge in your little fingers than the male doctors at the hospital." Shy giggles at this; a tremendous frown from the Minister for Health. "But we have new things to teach you here: hygienic methods, greater understanding of physiology. Crisis alleviation."

When they'd finished the course, they would gain this certificate—she brandished a crackling sheet of cardboard—plus their very own sterile midwife kit. Maya opened a small tin box to show a tantalizing glimpse of its contents: small scissors, swabs, a small bottle of iodine, soap, and a clean towel.

Sister Patricia watched this with her head on one side and a fond smile on her face. "Look at their little faces," she whispered to me. "Trilled to bits, poor dears."

Shortly after this, Mr. Thambi, who'd been furtively checking his watch since the ceremony began, roared off in his government car. The midwives were given a small breakfast of steamed bananas with uppuma, a semolina-type dish, and the teaching part of the day began.

Each pupil was asked to give her name and age, the length of time she'd practiced, the number of babies delivered, and her marital status.

A few looked mulishly suspicious at this and refused. Then a small, stooped woman with dust on her elaborately tattooed bare feet, stood up and said in good English (what a relief) that her name was Subadra and that she came from Nilamperur, where she was a senior midwife. She had learned her English at a mission school there.

So far, she said, she had resisted the government's attempts to retrain her, because, she added, with considerable pride and a hint of challenge, she had "delivered hundreds and thousands of healthy babies."

"Hundreds and thousands?" Maya peered at her over her big specs. "For our study, how many exactly?"

"No idea," said the woman, "maybe four thousand." She sat down heavily and muttered something under her breath to the woman next to her, who immediately tried to hide her face.

"You?" Dr. A. pointed to her. "Stand up. No need for shyness."

The woman cast a fearful look towards the door and whispered something to Subadra, who translated for her.

"Her name is Bhaskari," Subadra said. "She is from a Dalit family. Her only job is to cut the cords and to dispose of afterbaby."

A low grumble broke out at this among one or two of the women. In some communities, I already knew, these women were regarded as the lowest of the low.

"You also have an important job, Bhaskari," Dr. A. said, bestowing one of her rare smiles. "We will teach you here how to do it sweetly and cleanly. We must all learn to work together." The one woman still muttering was given Dr. A.'s famous basilisk glare and visibly shrank.

"Sit down, Bhaskari," Dr. A. continued smoothly. "We're very glad to have you with us." One by one we took their histories, from the fat, the thin, young, old, bright, and stupid-looking. They were, as Sister Patricia whispered to me, "a bit of a job lot."

Each midwife was then given a piece of paper and a pencil.

"Your first task," Dr. A. announced, "is to draw what you think is inside a woman's body. Take your time. This is not a test, it's for knowledge sharing."

I saw Bhaskari take her pencil, take her paper, and strike off immediately in a series of confident slashing circles. One tucked her pencil inside the folds of her sari and gave me a truculent whyshould-I-tell-you? look.

After twenty minutes or so of pencil scratching, and sighing, and worried looks in our direction, Maya collected the sheets, adding names to the papers of the six women in the class who were illiterate.

Rosamma, who said she delivered up to thirty babies a month, piped up indignantly, "No one really knows what is inside the human body. You can only imagine it."

Sister Patricia whispered to me, "Well, I wouldn't want that one to intuit me baby out of me."

I left the Home exhausted and conscious of a mountain to climb.

Day 2.

The women returned to the classroom this morning looking far more relaxed. Rosamma, a fat lady with an exuberant smile, made everyone laugh when she said she would like to keep dancing all day because she was so happy to get away from her husband for a few days. Her good English and self-confidence had made her the group's leader and translator.

Today we asked the midwives to describe the work they did in their own village. It's possible that no one has ever asked them to do this before, because they listened to each other with open-mouthed fascination, and I thought, If we achieve nothing else here, they've been given the chance to talk to each other, because their lives, frankly, sound terrifying.

At first they were as furtive as criminals, but then Rosamma, settling in a comfortable cross-legged position and adjusting her large bosom, began.

There were two kinds of midwives in her village, she said, the visible midwives—the vayattattis—and the invisibles, who washed the mother after delivery and buried the afterbirth. Her voice dropped confidentially at this, and when one or two of the other midwives frowned, she said, with a note of defiance, "We are here to talk about these things."

It was the vayattattis, she went on, who were blamed for everything.

"Many things stop a woman from having a baby," she said, her voice warm with indignation. "Lack of good food for the mother to eat, and this year our rice crops failed," she said directly to Sister Patricia. "No proper place to have the baby. In my village some are sent out to cow sheds."

The gold bracelets jangled on Rosamma's right arm when she lifted it to cover her eyes. "Can you remember a time when you felt blamed or you were blamed?" Maya asked her softly.

I saw the expression on the women's faces change while they waited for her reply, and I wondered if Maya had made a mistake by asking for these intimacies too early.

"Last month," said Rosamma after a long silence, "a woman died in my arms. She was in labor for nearly eighteen hours; the baby got stuck. There was no bullock cart to take her to the hospital: it belongs to the head man in our village, he needed it that day. The family blame me now. They refused to pay me and avoid me in the street. This is not fair, and this is why I am here, to get more government protection."

The women murmured sympathetically. Rosamma said, "In my village, there is also much suspicion of me because I have the freedom to travel."

Another said, "Some will never forgive me if baby comes and it is a girl, or if it is crippled or dies; they think maybe I'm bad luck and they should have gone to another vayattatti."

"I am a poor woman," she added, breathing heavily. "I don't do this for money, I do it because God wants me to."

Anto wrote this morning to say his old tutor at Exeter College has recommended him for a yearlong research project at the Holy Family Hospital in Kacheripady. "It sounds," he wrote, "almost too good to be true, so only dare to be cautiously optimistic. But how wonderful it would be if it happened."

I burst into tears when I got the letter. At last, what sounded like the perfect job for him, and I was missing him badly: my days were crammed with activity, but nights at Rose Street got long and lonesome. I wrote straight back, happier than I'd felt in weeks, and with an edited version of events in our midwife classes.

We'd had such a funny morning when Maya announced, "Today, we're going to have our first Mother Moonstone baby. Who will be mother?"

Rosamma levered her considerable bulk on the floor, lay on her back, rolled her eyes, and groaned like an injured calf.

Maya chose Kartyani, a frowning, dark-skinned girl, to be midwife. So far she'd refused to join in with any group, and yesterday when I tried to persuade her, she'd said angrily, "My head is bursting with new information. It is not helping me." Maya thought she was simply homesick. Sister Patricia said she was dim.

Maya ignored Kartyani's scowl. "Our patient is having her first baby. She's been in labor now for fourteen hours, nothing is happening." From the floor Rosamma rolled her eyes convincingly and

clutched her belly. "*Owwwwwww*. Oh dear. No baby comes."
The class tittered.

"What will you do now to progress the baby?"

"I don't know," Kartyani said sulkily, and shook her head.

"Hurry up," Rosamma commanded from the floor. "I am paining badly."

In a mutinous drone, Kartyani began. "First, I would go to her house."

"Of course." Rosamma was irritated by this glimpse of the obvious.

"I would loosen her hair and her bangles," Kartyani said in the same unwilling monotone. "I would open all her cupboards and doors."

Maya peered up at me through her big specs. "This is psychologically helpful to a woman: it opens everything up."

"Then this." Kartyani sank to her knees and rubbed her hands expertly around the rim of Rosamma's belly.

"What is she saying?" I asked. Rosamma was rolling her eyes lasciviously, shimmying her shoulders.

"That I can't translate." Maya was blushing. "Too crude." Even Kartyani couldn't resist a faint smile at this.

Before the lesson ended, *pop!* Rosamma produced a plastic baby from the folds of her sari, and everybody cheered except Kartyani, who ran out of the room.

"She is not happy here," Maya whispered in the corridor later. "She says the teaching is too Western, and that she doesn't want to share her own secrets with us or with low-caste village people. I think she is a spy from the government." She laughed to show me she was joking, but it wouldn't have surprised me.

I wrote to Daisy about what happened next but left it out of my letter to Anto.

Kartyani refused to leave her room. She reiterated that her head was bursting with all this new information, that she wanted to go home.

"Stay there then, *mundi* stupid idiot," Dr. A. barked at her. "*Nee orikkalum nannavilla*, you will never improve."

"Write that down," Maya instructed me. "It's a good insult."

Kartyani missed that afternoon's lively debate on menstruation and contraception. Shanta, a sprightly young woman who had delivered umpteen babies, stood up and said, in her shy, piping voice, "I will share my knowledge with you. Monthly bleeding was originally given to the man, but God found it was too hard for the man, so he gave it to a woman."

"Do you all think this?" Maya asked the other women. They bobbed their heads in the yes-no Indian gesture.

"How you behave with your monthlies will depend on what caste you are in," said Subadra, noticing my confusion. "A Brahman woman must stay apart from her family during this time, wash many times, and not meet with her husband. She cannot take part in celebrations."

"A Dalit, an untouchable, will go about life as usual."

"In our family, we are very careful not to stop the period," Shanta piped up, unwilling to relinquish the floor. "If you do, you could become poisoned and lose your sight."

Maya listened patiently. "So now I am going to show you what really happens," she said. She opened the cupboard and took out a three-foot-high wall chart of the naked woman Daisy and I had christened Vera.

Vera's fallopian tubes, womb, and major arteries were clearly marked in red; stomach, heart, liver, and kidneys in blue. Her face was concentrated and thoughtful, as if it was hard work keeping all this complicated machinery going.

"Is this an Englishwoman?" Kartyani said at last, as if this might explain Vera's elaborate plumbing.

"No," Maya said. "This is what we are all like inside."

"No, we're not," Kartyani contradicted immediately. "I have seen other drawings done by ayurvedic doctors, and there are many, many more blood vessels."

One or two of the midwives looked defiantly towards me as if I were the snake oil salesman here. When Maya took off her glasses and polished them, I could see that her eyes still had dark-purple bags under them. She worked far too hard. She took a deep breath and began her menstruation talk. She was five miutes into it when I looked up and saw Dr. A. standing at the door. She was beckoning me towards her.

It was the wrong end of a hot, exhausting day. I was longing for home, a bath, an early supper, and to finish my letter to Anto. But Dr. A.'s gesture was insistent, excited.

In the corridor she whispered in a quick cinnamon-scented blast, "We have a patient, Laksmi, in labor. Maya is busy; Sister Patricia's gone home."

I assumed I was to assist her. Laksmi, with her slender child's body and her history of miscarriage, was anything but a straight-forward case. Admitted to the Home the week before, very anxious, she had had a show of blood. Her husband was a local policeman.

"She asked for you this morning," Dr. A. whispered as we sped down the corridor. "She said she wanted the English doctor lady to do the delivery."

I stopped aghast. "But I'm not a doctor."

"I am not the one saying it." Dr. A. handed me a starched white doctor coat with a bland stare. "And neither are you. But Laksmi needs a good delivery this time. With this we can make her confident." She put a stethoscope around my neck, patted me on the back. "Don't look so frightened."

I should have said no. Instead, I buttoned the coat with shaking hands and walked towards the delivery room on rubber legs. I could already hear Laksmi's weak cries coming from behind the door.

Anto once told me he believed everything we were was the result of what we had thought, so I knew that in one sense I had led myself down this corridor and towards this test. Half of me had wanted it all along. I knew too that if this was a normal vaginal delivery, I had the skills to do it. After all, firemen and panicked husbands had managed in the past. C sections were very rare here.

"Maya will be finished with the class soon," Dr. A. said, at the door. "She'll come and take over."

"So, I'll call if there are any complications," I said, in what I hoped was a calm voice. But she was already walking down the corridor.

"Yes," she said when she reached the end.

The first thing I saw was Laksmi's small feet sticking out from the sheet, clenching and unclenching in pain. When her head reared up, I remembered her better: a small, undernourished woman, a two-inch scar from a burn on her right cheek. I recalled that she suffered from anemia, which was not unusual amongst the local women. Please God, don't let her start bleeding again.

Her mother—a wizened woman dressed in a widow's white sari—sat beside her, fanning her with the neem leaves thought to keep the angry spirits at bay. Then Subadra walked in.

"Dr. A. sent for me," she said. "I know this girl and speak her dialect."

Subadra took a damp flannel from the table and wiped Laksmi's forehead, which was filmed with sweat. The girl's eyes fixed on mine, and with a desperate expression, she poured out words. "She is very afraid," one of the nurses said. "She thanks God you have come."

"Tell her I am glad to be here," I said, trying for a confident voice. "I'm going to have a look now, to see how her baby is."

When I rolled back the sheet, her taut belly was covered in gray ash.

"Don't touch it," Subadra said quickly. "Ash is put there for a boy." Another gush of words from the girl made the mother nod vigorously.

"She says she will kill herself this time if she doesn't have boy. She has conceived"—she shot an extra question at the girl, got a tearful confirmation—"six times in the past eight years, only two children survived. She says if she has another girl, her mother-in-law will take it away and harm it."

The girl moved her eyes from Subadra to me like someone watching a tennis match. Tears poured down her face; another fusillade of words.

Subadra murmured a string of the words Maya had taught me. "*Saramilla pottey ellam sheriyakum, njaan illay.* It's all right, let go, don't worry, everything will be OK." But the girl was crying again.

Subadra wrung out the flannel and sponged the girl's face and arms.

"She says she should have taken a drink of hot chilies, killed the fetus and herself before coming here. She knows it will be another girl."

The girl let out a groan like that of a tree before it loosens from the earth and crashes to the ground. The tight brown dome of her tummy strained, and I could see the clearly defined shape of a baby's foot kicking out.

"Can you stop her crying?" I was terrified of hurting her. "Get her to breathe evenly?"

After the internal exam, I estimated she was two fingers dilated. If all went well, the baby would be born in a matter of hours.

By five past six, a buzz of insects were whirling around the light, and beyond the barred window, the sky was growing dark. I could hear rickshaw wheels turning, a tea vendor yelling *chaya*, *chaya*, but the outside world felt distant and unimportant. What I most felt was the gathering of energy and concentration inside this small room, the glug, glug, glug of my own heart thumping.

Twenty minutes later when I examined Laksmi, my hand felt steadier, my head less swimmy. She was nearly three inches dilated, and her contractions, every eight minutes or so, lasted forty to sixty seconds. I mentally revised her delivery time to seven, seven thirty.

At eight fifteen, some rackety music struck up in the street outside. A dog barked somewhere. Subadra left the room and came back with food from a village stall: some pappadams and lime pickle, some spiced buttermilk, and a roll of banana leaves to use as plates. She washed her hands ostentatiously and, after a sneaky look at me, ate in the corner of the room near the sink. Maya, who'd spent yesterday morning on hygiene at the point of delivery, would have had kittens at this, but Maya had gone home, and I was so grateful for Subadra's presence, I said nothing.

I was aware of the vast stupidity of underestimating Subadra. Subadra knew how this girl talked and how she thought; the community she lived in, what she ate, who beat whom, who drank.

When darkness fell quickly outside, Laksmi's breathing between contractions became more relaxed and she seemed to sleep. Subadra put her fingers around the girl's birdlike ankle and, with her eyebrows waggling, said that this girl's mother-in-law was a very hard-hearted lady: she'd starved her of food.

"Why?" I was scandalized.

"She lost too many babies," Subadra replied. She waved an index finger from left to right. "They thought the evil spirits were there."

My old matron from St. Thomas' appeared in my mind again, wagging her finger. "Never ever gossip about patients in their presence." Here it seemed par for the course.

"She's slow," Subadra looked down at the girl, who was stirring again, and whose brow was now corrugated and sweaty. "I would like baby here soon. This will bring it on."

From her sari she produced a small bottle filled with an inky blue liquid.

"No! No, no." I leapt forward. "You can't do that."

In a brief flash I pictured the headlines: *Local Girl Poisoned by English Midwife*, and was wrestling the bottle out of her hand when Dr. A. stepped into the room so quickly I wondered if she'd been there all along. She looked shattered, and her normally neat gray plait was all mussed up.

She took the bottle from my hand. "This is good." She sniffed it with her voluminous nose. "It's castor oil, gherkin root, cumin, and other things. We use it." This surprised me: she'd told me earlier that the Brits had banned the use of local ayurvedic medicines and that she'd agreed with this.

She shuffled out, saying in a sleepy voice that she'd be in her office if we needed her. When she was gone, the girl's mother got down on her knees and began to pray.

"She's saying 'Mother Goddess, please give us a boy,'" Subadra said. "Not long now."

I knelt beside the girl, who was now having three or four contractions every ten minutes. At last she gave a hoarse cry, the muscles on her forehead corded; the baby's head started to crown.

"It's coming, Laksmi," I said. "Hooray!"

Subadra smoothed oil between her hands and rubbed the girl's tummy in deft, gentle strokes, first clockwise, then counterclockwise, and finally, more firmly, down the side of her waist.

When I examined Laksmi again, she was fully dilated and had the intense look of concentration I'd seen on other mothers at this stage of their labor.

"Push now," said Subadra. "*Tulleh pennay, nannayi tullekkay*, push, girl. Push hard now. Soon the baby will come."

The girl let out a guttural roar. Her legs started to tremble violently. The fluff of the baby's head appeared in the birth canal and the forehead, nose, mouth, chin, and the rest of a perfect little boy shot out in a rush of blood, so fast we almost dropped him. He started bawling.

The mother had torn her perineum on delivery, and I was good at stitching. Matron Smythe had once told me I would always have a job in upholstery if I got fed up with nursing. I threaded the needle and quickly put in two or three stitches with the mother barely noticing.

She was covering her son in kisses, sobbing with relief. His life would save hers. I was crying too as her mother put a smear of soot on the baby's cheek to ward off the evil eye, and then the baby began to suckle.

Afterwards, I sat on the step, all emptied out with happiness. I'd done it! I'd done it! The thing I never thought I'd ever be able to do again. The air was like warm milk and there were a million stars out. Subadra, beaming, happy, sat beside me, her hennaed feet on the step. When a servant bought us a cup of chai and some coco-nutty sweets, we ate them ravenously.

Relief kept flooding through my body and I was too tired to censor myself, so I told Subadra, in the next twenty minutes, more than I had ever told anyone about the last time I had delivered a child, how I felt I'd made a mess of it, and how it had taken me a long time to get over it.

She listened to me so quietly that I wasn't sure she'd understood, but then, when she took a sip of tea and patted my arm gently, I realized she was just doing what she did so well in the delivery room: listening, taking things in, not trying to hustle things along.

"Your stitches were beautiful," she said. "You are a very fine doctor. She didn't even know you were doing it."

Subadra continued after a long pause, "I couldn't say this in class, but I had a mother, only one month ago. She was too weak, she died. Nobody blamed me but I was not happy with myself."

Her worn hands pleated the skirt of her sari as she talked. "Don't tell this to the others," she said, and I promised I wouldn't.

I wasn't naive enough to feel that delivering this baby was the magic wand that would miraculously banish all fears. That red-headed girl lived with me and probably would all my life, but it did feel like a momentous night for me, and later that night, undressed for bed, longing to have someone to share it with, I wrote five pages to Daisy, telling her about Subadra and the Moonstone, knowing how pleased she would be. This was exactly the kind of collaboration she had dreamed of for a long, long time. While I was writing, a piece of paper fell from my lap to the floor. I picked it up and smoothed it out. It was Subadra's picture of what a woman looked like inside—a few random squiggles inside a child's body with pipe cleaner legs.

I'd planned to send it in a letter to Josie for a cheap laugh. I knew better now.

- CHAPTER 28 -

He was packing to go north again when Amma appeared carrying two ironed shirts. She looked down at the bed littered with his things—khaki trousers, spirit lamp, steel tray, scissors, antiseptics, painkillers—and she said, "When are you going to stop running away?"

He sighed and kept on packing. "Amma," he said, "I have three hours left in which to pack, go to Cochin, see Kit, and get the train." His nerves were so shredded it was hard to keep his voice steady. He'd been so sure he'd get news about the research job at Kacheripady, the job that was made for him, but no letter had come.

Amma shook her head. "So why bother coming back here at all?"

"To pick up my clothes."

"So, that's good." She tried another tack. "She gives you ten minutes at lunchtime. Lucky for you."

"Don't blame her, Ma." He hated her sour expression. "It's not easy for her either, and she knows it's not for long."

"I've been looking in the papers. They're still looking for people at Palluruthy; she could go with you, or you could talk to Dr. Kunju again. I can't believe there is nothing here." She put her head in her hands and gave a strange bark of frustration.

"Ma, please."

"If you wanted to leave her," she said softly, "we would under-stand."

"Leave her! What in God's name are you talking about?"

This was a blasphemy, particularly coming from her. No Thekkedens divorced. They knew marriage was hard work sometimes: that Josekutty drank too much, that Mathu, the family saint, neglected Amma for his work. But this was life, your karma. Accepting hurt was part of growing up.

"You do know that I'm properly married to her?" he said, thinking she might have imagined some counterfeit English arrangement, easily dissolved.

"You call it a proper marriage? A registry office, no relatives, no celebrations?" He saw in her face contempt, and also a kind of bitter enjoyment at finally being able to let fly.

"Look at yourself." She snatched a mirror from his shaving kit. "Skinny, sad—it's horrible seeing you like this." Their reflections shimmered and merged in the mirror—her huge brown eyes brimming with tears, his face all strain and bones.

"Work is all she wants to do," Amma spat out. "And that place where she works—I don't think you know the first thing about it."

"What are you talking about? I did some translations for them, for the charity, in Oxford."

"Oh, Oxford!" She flapped the place away with her hand. "Here, I'm talking about. It has a very, very bad reputation. People are gossiping about it."

"What people? What gossip?"

"I can't give you their names. What does that matter?"

This shrill, tale-telling voice was new to him, or perhaps it had always been there and before he'd had a wife, he'd never heard it, but it diminished her and saddened him.

"And you know,"—she shot a look at him—"there are already good government-trained midwives in Travancore. This charity is only interested in dirty, illiterate women full of disease."

"That's quite an assumption, Amma, and I thought you were a liberal." He made a great effort not to raise his voice. "All for progress, for new ways. Have I got that wrong?"

"Yes, you have." She was shaking with pent-up rage. "Because the new progress you are talking about sounds very like the old progress to me: foreign women coming here to teach us about something so private. How dare they insult us like this? What do they know of our ways? Maybe I should go to England now and tell your Daisy Barker how to have her baby."

He knew he should defend the Moonstone's aims, or at the very least Kit. But the moment passed: another plate spinning out of his hands, like his work, his life, his wife, the train that would shortly leave without him.

"There's another thing, Anto," she said. There was something bunched and venomous in her face. "Something I wasn't going to tell you about her."

"Go ahead, Ma," he said wearily. She'd already complained about Kit's untidiness, her lateness, unseemly conversations with Mariamma. "What crime now?" He sat down heavily on the bed and stared at his shoes.

"We had a ladies' party while you were away. Mariamma and I thought it would be a good opportunity for her to meet our friends." He knew this wasn't true: Mariamma had talked Amma into asking Kit.

"So, I asked Appan if the car could be sent for Kit," Amma continued.

He looked at his watch. He was desperate to see Kit before he left.

"We said prayers, as we always do." Amma was settling into this. "We laid out all the special food, nothing too spicy for her."

"Ma, you don't have to do that, she loves our food."

"Anyway, we waited, and waited, and waited. When she comes, she is one and a half hours late and as white as a sheet. There was blood on her sleeve." Amma's mouth was strangely twisted. "Mariamma says, 'She is delivering babies at the Home. She is not a report writer, she is not a social reformer. She pulls the babies out.'"

An expression of horror on her face. "This is the woman you have brought into our house."

He waited several moments before looking up.

"Amma, listen to me: she is part of a charity, and she is a midwife too. Try and understand that this is not a job to be ashamed of in England. We should be proud of her."

"Proud of her." His mother's look was one of angry incredulity. "That is too much. The situation grows worse and worse."

Driving back to Fort Cochin, he felt a dull anger settle inside him. He was angry with Amma for being so small-minded, angry at Kit for upsetting his mother, at Mariamma, who he suspected stirred things up, partly because she didn't have enough to do, and furiously disappointed at not hearing any more news about the possible job.

To shield himself from the piercing brightness of the day, he pulled the curtain in the back of the car and stewed in the darkness. He should have known no Thekkedens would happily accept a midwife as a daughter-in-law, not without a change of brain. However much they might give lip service to the new India and its shiny new ideas—the banishing of the caste system, better lives for women, including widows—privately they wanted things to stay as they always had been for this family: peaceful, privileged, content. Kit was an unexploded bomb in their midst, at least in Amma's mind. He'd brought Kit here, and now he would have to find ways of limiting the damage.

The row with Amma had left no time to go back to Rose Street. Instead, they sat opposite each other in the railway's restaurant.

"Anto." She looked pale and wary. "How long can you keep doing this?"

"Until I get a job here," he said.

"I'm sure you'll hear soon. It's tailor-made for you," she said. "How long will you be away this time?"

"Two more weeks, and then I'll come back and—" He was close to tears. "I'm sorry about this. It's just much harder than I thought." He didn't have the heart to tell her how many applications he'd made.

"Everything is changing here," she said. "It's not your fault."

He was grateful to her for saying this, because this clammy feeling of guilt had taken root in his mind.

"I love you, and I have a wicked plan. Let's ask your uncle if we can rent the house in Rose Street as soon as you get back. It's perfect for us. You'll get work in Cochin eventually, I know you will, and we can be a proper old married couple together."

"I like that idea," he said, knowing Amma would hate it. "A lot. I love you too. This has been a sort of fugue you know, all of this, coming back and feeling, I don't know, like a stranger, and then knowing how much I'd missed. I'm so sorry."

"I'm not sorry." She drew close to him and whispered, "I'd like to kiss you, but don't worry, I won't."

The other passengers were openly staring at them.

"So, how are things at the Moonstone now?" he asked in a neutral voice. She glanced at him and then at her cup.

"Good," she said. "Actually, more than good. We've got ten more midwives coming next month, and . . . and . . . drum roll announcement." She glanced at him quickly. "I helped deliver my first baby here. It felt like a big step."

"So I hear." He'd hoped to sound glad for her, but his voice was weary and flat.

"Who told you?" Her smile faded.

"Amma."

"Amma! God! What does she know about it?" She moved away from him.

"Did you really think they wouldn't find out?"

"No," she said, her voice tight, "I thought they would, which is why I wanted to be honest with them right from the start, remember?"

Kit heard him sigh. His glance traveled to the next table, where a plump man sat with his much younger wife and a clutch of long-lashed beautiful children. The family pored over a travel guide together.

"Poor Anto," she said, "I don't know why I expected you to be pleased. Nothing is easy now." They smiled unhappily at each other and in some treacherous corner of his heart he agreed with her.

"Not poor Anto," he said. "Both of us have a lot in common—we're rather fond of you."

She looked at him sharply. "That's not a good joke at a time like this."

"I'm sorry."

He watched the family leave, then looked at his watch. "I have ten more minutes, Kit, so I have to say this quickly." He drew a deep breath. "I'm happy, really happy, the work is going well, but I worry about you all the time. If something goes wrong, the consequences could be terrible for you."

"What consequences?" A bright look of accusation.

"Angry people, nationalists, those who think we should drop British charity now."

"I can't do anything about them, Anto, because I don't meet them. The women I meet mostly smother me in kindness."

"They will until something goes wrong." A train screamed through the station, rattling their saucers.

"So how long are you going to keep working?" he said, when they could hear each other again. "The last time we spoke of it, you said a month or two."

"I can't say exactly—as long as it takes to get things up and running. I'm loving it," she finished helplessly.

Another train drew in and disappeared in a shrieking mass of smoke. When he started to cough, she patted him on the back. He waved her hand away and kept on coughing until his eyes watered.

"How long?" he said when he'd stopped.

"I don't know!" She had to raise her voice against the babble of passengers swarming off the train. "Must I give you a date?"

"So, no children of our own?" He was suddenly furious again. "Is this your command also?"

"My command, Anto?" She looked shocked. "Don't be so bloody mean, you know that's not what I meant. I can do both."

"You know best," he said. "You're making all the rules now." That was the last thing he said before his train shrieked off in a cloud of smoke.

- CHAPTER 29 -

The row with him churned me up badly. I sat brooding about it on the veranda that night and thought about it all through the following day when we had a training session at the Moonstone. After the usual prayers, the midwives sat down on the coir mats, and Maya posed the question, "Who owns your body?"

"You start," Rosamma encouraged Kartyani, who had barely spoken for two days.

Kartyani glowered at her beautifully patterned feet. "I don't want to talk of such things in a public place."

"So I'll start." Rosamma beamed; she was impossible to offend and soaked up knowledge like a sponge. "I have plenty to say. In my village, men own our bodies. As girls we are given away young, often to older men, for sexual pleasure, or we are used as cooks, as beasts of burden."

"Why complain?" Kartyani picked sullenly at the folds of her skirt. "A man's life is no picnic either."

"No." Rosamma waited several moments before continuing. "But let me pose this: who eats first in your house, husband or yourself?"

"He does of course, but that is my choice."

"Really? And who gets the best food?"

No one bothered to answer.

"Who is the most educated? Sons or daughters?" Rosamma had her pouncing legal face on.

"Sons of course," Kartyani said. "They have to run the household. What is your point?"

"Here's my point." Rosamma brandished her finger. "I want a daughter of mine to be educated to live outside the cage, like this person." She pointed at me. "To be educated, not to pretend to be shy."

Oh God, I felt like a twenty-one-carat fraud. I did so much shyness pretending at Mangalath, and at the moment, I felt I did nothing but placate Anto.

"A woman should be shy." Kartyani's small fists bunched. "Shy and obedient, that is the way of the world."

"You are not shy and obedient. You contradict everything."

Kartyani joined in the laughter reluctantly.

"So, Miz Kit," Rosamma asked me, "who owns your body?" which set me back on my hocks.

"As a child," I said at last, "I think you could say my mother owned it." Colonized it, I thought, as her little fiefdom, to feed, smack, clean, dress.

"But you are a married woman now?"

"Yes." I showed them the cheap gold wedding ring Anto had bought in Oxford. "This is how we show we're married. It's like your bindi," I said, referring to the red spot married women here put between their eyes.

"Children are there?"

"No, but when I have them, my body will belong to them." My stumbling answer had confused some of the women.

"I think that a woman should—" I had another run at it. "That she—that there are . . . times in a woman's life when she should be brave. It's important to be brave."

"Otherwise, other people will use her up." Rosamma, who'd been examining my wedding ring, dropped my finger. "My own mother died at thirty-six years old, worn out with trying to please. Her last words: 'Thank God for the rest.'"

We all laughed at this, except for Kartyani, who was still look-ing sour and perplexed, but I found it painful too. I felt I'd lost the easy confidence that came from Anto's love and support, and I hated that. I missed the jokes, childish as they were, the sense of being lucky, lucky, lucky to have found each other, and I wanted him back.

Letter from Daisy Barker to Kit.

Wickam Farm, April 11th

Dear One,

Your letter gave me great joy. Your first Indian baby delivered! Golly, I'm impressed; so pleased for you too: there's nothing like being really scared of a thing and finding you can do it. Subadra sounds like a wonderful addition to things. We have so much to learn.

You don't give much news about the rest of your life in India. When I lived there, I knew my time would end, but you've traded a Western life for a life in India—much more difficult, and I hope rewarding too. Don't say if none of my beeswax, but I don't sup-pose anyone has ever solved it: the sense of never being exactly sure where one belongs; one's heart and mind seem a mix of such different things.

Nothing of great moment to report from this end. Tudor has found a local farmer to manage the land. He's moved to Lon-don and is doing sterling work on a treatise he is publishing on the archaeology of our Roman remains. House full of usual waifs and strays. Ci Ci, very much the grand dame, has moved into the Bird Room. Flora to London, living in digs and doing a typing course. Your sainted mother is back here, after work-ing for a family in Warminster, I'm happy to say, as we have two new residents. I'm sad to hear you no longer correspond. In great haste, blackberry and apple jam on stove and about to bubble, will write longer, later . . .

all love,
Daisyxxxxxxx

- CHAPTER 30 -

I'd stuck to my agreement with Appan and spent two weekends at Mangalath. One afternoon, while the servants were asleep, Mariamma took me into Amma's immaculate kitchen and showed me how to make karimeen mappas, Anto's favorite fish curry. We were chopping up garlic, ginger, and green chilies when she turned to me and said in her mocking singsong voice, "So, don't be a stuffed shirt, Kit, tell me some juicy stories from the Home. What are these women like? Salacious details, please."

She teased me like a sister now. I was no longer the polite foreigner, and when Amma got tricky, which she could even about something as innocent-seeming as our cooking together (in her book, servants were servants, and masters should keep a distance from menial tasks like cooking and cleaning), Mariamma would roll her eyes, lower her voice, wobble her head, and do Amma's voice to a tee: "You can stoop and pick up nothing."

"Come on." She brandished her knife in my direction. "Get on with it. More information, please."

"What are *they* like?" I teased her back. "I assume you're talking about the midwives . . . Well, here's a surprise. They're all different. Some are highly intelligent, very skilled, brilliant, in fact, and some are—how shall I put this?"

"Thick as bricks," Mariamma supplied.

"I didn't say that." I was trying not to laugh because I actually liked it so much more when she dropped the politeness veil, it was such a relief. "I would say, some are confused by what we're saying, and of course, we do have one or two awkward customers, who don't want to change at all."

I went on, "We had a funny discussion last week." I told her about Shanta's theory about men menstruating first, and God taking it away from them because they moaned so much. Mariamma laughed and said she was glad not to be a Brahman woman, confined to a dark room at the back of the house each month because you were considered impure. It had stopped one of her friends from going to university.

"Do you think you have made the women you teach happier?" The innocent mockery in her eyes had changed to something more challenging. "Or have you caused family problems?"

"No idea. It depends what you mean by happier." Now the conversation had veered into seriousness, I wondered if this was a not-so-subtle dig at me and my strangely absent husband. "Some have loved the teaching and the company so much, they dread going back to their villages, where they feel isolated. Others can't wait to see the back of us." I told her about Kartyani, her sighs, her sulks, her refusal to take part.

"How rude," she says in the Scottish voice she learned from her governess. "Very clarty behavior."

She finished chopping and put the garlic into a neat pile, then started peeling the ginger into parchment-thin slices. "So, have you learned anything from them?" She wiped the knife.

"Masses," I said. I peered at the long list of ingredients in Amma's handwritten recipe book, hoping to steer the conversation away from me. "So, we fry the garlic and ginger in oil, then what?"

"What have you learned?" she insisted.

I stopped and thought for a while, and then a new feeling bubbled up from nowhere, something like exhilaration or pride, or maybe it was just belonging, that loosened my tongue. "Oh, I don't know . . . so much: to think with my fingers, how to watch, how to wait. I'm still scared but nothing like as much as I was. How to shut up." I stopped suddenly. This was exactly what I should be doing. I liked Mariamma, but I didn't trust her not to tell the others.

"Show me something you've learned," Mariamma said with a glint in her eye. At moments like this I could see why Anto called her the family bossy boots. My mind raced through several possibilities. One that would emphasize my role as observer. Nothing to frighten the horses.

"Well, you know, last week, a girl came in whose labor was very slow, and Rosamma, one of the women, taught me the circular massage."

Mariamma slid the rest of the pearl fish into the bubbling liquid. She washed her hands and lay down on the floor. "No one will see us, servants asleep, Amma is out." I hesitated, then closed the door.

"The pressure is like this." I pressed gently on her abdomen. "You do it clockwise." I swept my hands to the right. "And then counterclockwise. It relaxes the mother and helps the midwife feel the baby. 'God is the doer,' Rosamma, the midwife, told me, 'the hands are mine.'"

It suddenly seemed a good idea to introduce a religious element into the discussion.

"God is the doer, the hands are mine," Mariamma murmured Her plump, round face was beaming but then thoughtful, as if another bit of the jigsaw had fallen into place.

"Your own midwife must have done something like this," I said, feeling stupid.

"Yes," she admitted, "but we've only ever used one midwife. She is properly trained, we all trust her, but good to know about these other things," she ended vaguely.

She stood up, washed her hands, and went to stir the curry, which had come to the boil.

"And you must have to touch them?" she asked, her back turned to me. "I mean . . . you know . . . in their private parts? It's so inti-mate." She added a sprinkle of salt. "So . . ." Her shoulders hunched as she searched for a word to describe the squalor of it. "So odd."

I felt a flash of impatience. This was life we were talking about. Why make the source of it such a taboo?

"It's thrilling to watch a child being born," I said.

"And even more thrilling to have one," she said pointedly.

Pathrose and Kuttan rescued me. If they noticed the strange atmosphere, they didn't show it as they smiled and sniffed appre-ciatively at the fish curry. Mariamma, after rapping out instructions about when it should be taken off and what served with it, put a protective arm around me. She led me into the garden, to a bench underneath a banana tree.

When we were seated she said, "I like listening to you talk about your work." She patted my arm reassuringly. "I think you're brave."

"No," I said, "not brave at all."

"Hm." There was still something watchful and guarded about Mariamma's expression. "I'm happy for you, but I must give you some serious advice." Her eyes flickered towards the house. "You've been married over a year. Don't wait too long to have your own babies; we're all very worried about you."

On the following Friday when I arrived at Mangalath, Amma came rushing towards me through the courtyard like a little steam train. I assumed she was angry, but when she stopped, I saw she was beaming.

"Kittykutty, Kittykutty," she said—the first time she'd ever added this endearment to my name—"we've had a telegram from Anto. He's coming home soon, God willing." Her voice trembled, her eyes were full of tears.

"It's for you too." She watched me while I read the dog-eared telegram, "Job offer from university. Home soonest, love Anto," and embraced me properly for the first time, murmuring, "Thank God, thank God." I cried too, feeling a flooding relief, as if some vital stability had been restored, not just to me but to the house. Now Amma would stop blaming me for his absence, he'd have a proper job, we'd get our first proper home together and be happy again. Life is never that simple, of course, but on that night it felt that way.

We feasted, and Appan, who was home, drank more whisky than usual before dinner, and the whole house floated on a cloud of relief and delight.

"We'll have a party to celebrate," Amma decided when we were drinking tea on the veranda. She patted my arm. The grumpy vertical line had gone between her eyes, and she looked a decade younger. "We'll ask Thresiamma, Ammamma, Sadji, Aby." Amma wrote the names down on a list. Appan mock-groaned. He'd been in Delhi—another conference on the shaping of India's new laws— and come home with a mountain of work to do.

After supper, when Father Christopher arrived to say a special mass of thanks, I knelt in the chapel and felt, for the first time in a long time, profoundly happy, a soft billowing rising inside me. It wasn't God who brought it to me—or if it was, I was not aware of it. It was Anto's coming back, and my having work to do that fulfilled me, and strangely, having Amma on one side of me, Mariamma on the other, Theresa beside her, and hearing Appan's sturdily male "Most grievous fault!" as he thumped his breast. My perspective changed as I looked around me at the samplers I'd watched Amma stitching, the altar made from the deck of an ancestor's spice boat, the smell of the incense, the lap of the lagoon outside, the melodious call of the koyal's *koo . . . ooo . . . oo* in the jackfruit tree outside. All this no longer felt like a foreign postcard to me. Tonight I felt anchored in a way I wasn't used to feeling, and it came to me that home was not, in the end, a place or a country, but something much deeper and more lasting.

- CHAPTER 31 -

And it seemed for a while that it was the old Anto who came home: the one who made me laugh, who confided in me, the one whose beautiful tortoiseshell green eyes would squeeze shut when he laughed and open in a gleam of mischief, not the Anto in flight, distracted and grumpy, who was beginning to make me feel like a dangerous pet. His new job paid a decent salary of four hundred and fifty rupees per month. His title: junior physician at the Holy Family Hospital at Kacheripady in Ernakulam. He was also to work with Assistant District Medical Officer Dr. Sastry on a newly funded research trial, the details to be supplied later.

Later that week, Uncle Josekutty, the distinguished-looking Thekkeden who owned our house, asked if he could call on us. Our arrangement with him had never been properly finalized, so we were both shockingly nervous, thinking our good luck had run out, but when, at the end of a leisurely conversation, Anto asked if we could possibly secure a year's lease, Uncle Josekutty, who was recently widowed and with no children of his own, said, "That's what I came to say. I think you should buy my house at a pepper-corn price."

When Anto politely protested, Uncle Josekutty patted him on the arm. "That's enough! I believe in giving gifts warm, not when I am cold in the ground."

We danced around the kitchen once he had gone. Couldn't believe it. Shortly after that, the deeds were handed over, the house blessed, and the entire family swung into action, not stinting with advice or help. Amma spent a day in the storage room behind the granary at Mangalath, a room crammed with rosewood and teak furniture, linen chests, mosquito nets, old mangles, Anto's first cricket set. She found a beautiful old rosewood table for our main room, and a carved four-poster bed for the guest room that would only need a few repairs before it was serviceable, a lamp to hang in the hall.

She was fantastically bossy about where to put everything, and so happy that it made me think about my own Ma, with her fierce high standards about carpet cleaning and the right hangers and mothballs and mattress turnings. Amma, rapping out orders about how much air to leave around the furniture, telling us our bed should face either south or west for health and luck, suddenly reminded me of her. Uncle Josekutty's workman came over to repair a couple of loose struts of wood on the veranda, where the men smoked their cigarettes. Thresiamma brought us a *kindy*, a brass utensil with a spout, filled with water, for cleaning the feet of those who enter the house. Pathrose came with fresh soil and cow dung and planted up the *ankanam*, the little courtyard, with hibiscus and jasmine and frangipani.

Exhausted by this whirlwind of advice and people, when they left, we sat on the swinging chair on the veranda. Anto put his arm around me. "Alone at last. Thank God."

When we got up, we walked slowly around the house together, admiring our bed, freshly made up with scented sheets; our whitewashed kitchen full of sparkling pots and saucepans from Amma's house; our own courtyard with its swinging chair, our guest room; our veranda with freshly watered plants plus a pot of cow manure from Mangalath. Anto turned to me with glowing eyes and said, "Can you believe this is ours?"

His salary plus my stipend from the Moonstone was easily enough to run the house and keep on Josekutty's two servants, so Anto was high as a kite when he got home from his second interview at the hospital. Dr. Sastry, he said, was young, progressive, and unblinkered. He took a great interest in ayurvedic as well as Western medicine and was about to undertake a funded three-year research project into the efficacy of both systems—right up Anto's street. He was to start work immediately. When I asked Dr. A. for a week off so I could unpack and settle in, she sighed mightily and made it clear it was at great cost and inconvenience to her.

On his way home from the interview, Anto tried to buy a bottle of champagne to celebrate but only managed to track down one dusty bottle of German wine at the Malabar Hotel; he told me it was playful without being impertinent. We gave the servants the night off, ate supper together, and drank all the wine. Afterwards, we wound up the gramophone and played the Louis Armstrong and Chic Chocolate records that Mariamma gave me. She had the best music taste in the family.

While we were dancing, he touched the salwar kameeze I was wearing. "I like you in that."

I joked that there were whole days now when I forgot I was English.

"Mostly English," he reminded me.

"Well, OK, three-quarters English, Mr. Pedant," I said. "But it's strange. Yesterday, I was in the market and about to buy myself a marigold-colored shawl, when I held it up to my face in the mirror and thought, Crikey, I'm white, this won't do. It was the oddest feeling."

"I used to feel like that when I was buying plus fours in Harrods," he said. "I'd see this impertinent brown face in the mirror and think, Um, maybe not."

"Liar!" I said. We were both a little drunk; we hadn't had wine in the longest time. "You never bought plus fours in your life."

When we got too sticky to dance, he said, "Let's go down to the waterfront. I want to see our house lit up from the road and think, What lucky brutes own that palace?"

It was lovely down there: a crescent moon, colored lights bouncing on the sea; some stalls still open, selling fruit and vegetables and fish. Two fishermen waved at us as we passed, their faces reflecting the glow of their paraffin lamps.

As we sat in a little café watching this, I was intensely, almost painfully aware of him: the sheen of his hair, his arm resting on the table, his hands around a glass.

He took a bath when we got home. Mani had come in to fill it while we were out. We were like children with many new toys as we admired the claw-foot bath—six feet long with beautiful brass taps, another gift from Uncle Josekutty. I washed his back and later we lay in our new, west-facing bed and enjoyed each other as never before.

"That has never left us has it, KK?" Anto said, in sleepy satisfaction afterwards. KK. Kittykutty, Kitty darling.

"Can't talk," I said, "too happy, no brain." I was lying in the crook of his arm, looking through the curtains at a sky bursting with stars.

"Not fishing, but do you mind it's just us here?" I asked him sleepily, "Will you miss Mangalath?"

He took so long to answer, I thought he'd gone back to sleep.

"I couldn't live like that again," he said eventually and a little sadly. He stroked the inside of my arm. "Anyway," he added as he stroked my breast, "with any luck, we'll have company soon, won't we?"

- CHAPTER 32 -

Breast: *sthanam* (singular) *sthanamgal* (plural). Womb: *udaram/ garba paatram*. Stomach: *vayar*.

My Malayalam notebook was beginning to fill up, and I was growing in confidence, but when I returned to work, on the following Monday, Dr. A. was in such a stinking mood that I felt back to square one. Ten deliveries had, she said, made the previous week their busiest ever. The emergency midwife they'd had to call in from the Victoria Gosha Hospital had been expensive, and with three more training classes on the cards, "The Home is in the red." I must write immediately to Daisy, she demanded, and see whether the Settlement ladies could tide us over. Without funds, the Home was, once again, on a knife edge.

This time I plucked up the courage to tell Dr. A. straight that I was sorry, but I didn't think that would be possible without turning over the Moonstone books. Daisy had asked three times for accounts of money spent and I had not been given them, so I doubted there would be more money without them.

Dr. A.'s right nostril widened into an incipient sneer when I said this, and when she bundled me into her study and locked the door, I wouldn't have been surprised if she'd slapped me as I'd seen her slap one or two of the nurses.

"You are forcing me to tell you a very unwelcome thing," she said, in full finger-jabbing flow. "Something I have been keeping back in respect of staff morale, and in respect of gorement funding."

"What is it?"

"Someone is taking money from the Home and I don't know who."

"That's horrifying," I said. "We must tell the police immediately. Why didn't you tell me before?"

"Because I don't want any gossip about this at the Home or to your family. It could ruin us, and we have so much good work to do."

"Does Maya know?"

"Maya knows, of course." She closed her dark eyes.

"I have to tell Daisy," I said.

She gave a great shrug. "It will be a shock, so tell her also what great work we're doing."

"It will be more than a shock." I found myself shaking with rage at the almost blasé look she was giving me. "She's put hours and hours of work into fund-raising. You may think of her as a rich white woman. She's not."

"Listen!" She was glaring now too. "I have two hours sleep a night, trying to run this place, and I am doing everything I can to find the miscreant; tell her that."

When I offered to help her find the thief and also the missing accounts, her scowl deepened. She told me to stop going on about the accounts, that she had far more important things on her mind. She would write to Daisy herself.

I didn't believe her, and I wrote to Daisy that night telling her about my strange conversation with Dr. A. and asking for advice. Several weeks later I was relieved to see, on a brass tray in the hall, Daisy's familiar slashing handwriting on pastel-blue Basildon Bond notepaper. Our letters must have crossed on the high seas, as hers answered none of my questions. Instead, it was uncharacteristically full of bad news. Without urgent and expensive repairs, Wickam Farm was on its last legs: high winds had blown most of the roof off the north barn, flooding the office;

a ceiling in the main house had collapsed, narrowly missing Ci Ci's bedroom.

"Also," she wrote, "I'd been hearing a strange munching sound for ages but had no idea it was the deathwatch beetle. Did you know they have fierce little jaws; you can actually hear them?"

I did sense a sort of panic beneath the jocular tone, but nothing prepared me for what came next.

"So, Kit, I am so sorry, but we've had to move all our boarders out for the duration, and I am in a quandary about your mother, who has had a very nasty bout of flu and who, I fear, can't go on working for much longer in this climate."

I almost stopped breathing when I read what came next.

"She is now planning a trip to India, with money she has been saving. I am not sure how you will feel about this, but the sun, to put it bluntly, may save her life. For God's sake, Kit, don't tell her I've warned you," Daisy concluded. "You know how proud she is."

Another letter, in a sealed envelope, lay inside Daisy's, my name written on it in a beautiful italic script that I recognized immediately. But now the writing, taught to my mother by the Pondicherry nuns, had a slight tremor, as though penned during a minor earthquake.

Wickam Farm, May 5th

Dear Kit,

This letter is to let you know that I have come into a little windfall—the details later. I plan to use some of it to come out and see you and maybe look up a few old chums at the same time, and get some SUN. The weather's vile here. I've been staying off and on at Wickam Farm, where we've had the usual dramas of burst pipes and, of course, the barn roof.

Daisy, who is getting more dotty by the year, tries to laugh at it all, but it's no joke, particularly with three guests staying—Ci Ci, plus Flora again after a broken engagement.

I hear from Daisy that you're doing well and are up to good works and tip my hat in your general direction. I've had flu but it was too cold to stay in bed as Daisy demanded. If she writes making a fuss about it—ignore. More news later when I hear from you.

Your mother,
Glory

I didn't know whether to scream or laugh or cry when I read this. Not a dickey bird from her since I left home: no reply to any of my letters, no messages via Daisy, no telegrams. A big fat nothing, and now this odd missive, so blasé and peculiar-sounding that I wondered if Ci Ci hadn't helped her write it, making her sound more like a person wanting to be asked to a cocktail party than a mother who had told her daughter she was dead to her.

But I knew too she was always at her most peculiar and unreal when she was ill, for the simple reason that she hated me to see her like that.

I stood in shock, the letter in my hand. She was coming and the timing felt cruel because in spite of my anxieties about the Moonstone, I was learning all the time, and things were finally settling down between Anto and myself. He was loving his job, very busy with a research paper, and it was wicked of me to confess this, but being dead to her had become, in itself, a kind of freedom.

My mind raced about for the rest of the day. How had she financed her trip to India? I wondered in sudden panic, knowing her predilection for helping herself to "treats" from other people's houses. Shoes and scarves, the odd pilfered belt were one thing, but a windfall big enough to blow you to India sounded unlikely. Dear God, I hoped it hadn't come from Daisy, who could least afford it. And what if this flu of hers was something more serious? And round and round it went.

*   *   *

"I'm terrified," I told Anto at dusk that night, when we'd joined the slow, peaceful crowd that strolled down the waterfront most evenings. The sun, melting like a fat peach, would soon flop over the horizon, and the evening breezes were soft and silky, except now I could imagine only too well my mother walking with us, paying attention to all the wrong things: the broken drain near the park with a few evil-smelling fish heads stuck in the grilles, the skinny dogs, the beggars. She'd be remembering why she hated India—its mess, its muddle, its Indianness—in the first place, and she'd be restless, wondering where all the amusing people were. Much as I'd resist it, I knew I'd feel her confusion too and feel responsible for her, because, damn it, I still wanted to make things right for her.

When we sat down on a bench to talk, Anto put his hand next to mine.

"This is the first chance we've had to be properly together," I moaned. "And I'm quite sure she'll hate it and make us miserable."

He didn't answer for a while.

"Make us miserable," I repeated, thinking he may not have heard.

"Come on, Kit." My husband looked at me almost in surprise. "She's your mother. You have the power to make her happy."

"Really?"

"Really."

I looked at him suspiciously in case he was teasing me, but he wasn't. His face, colored by the setting sun, looked weary after a long day at the hospital, weary and infinitely precious to me.

"Now I feel like a heel," I said, relieved he was taking it so well. "It's just such bad timing, and I've never heard her say a good word about India—*ghastly place*," I said in her voice.

"You're making her sound like Margaret Rutherford, who never said anything horrid about anyone," he said, doing his Madame Arcati.

The small boy who ran up and down the seafront every night with his arm full of bangles was delighted by our laughing and joined in with a loud cackle.

"Anto," I warned him when we'd stopped, "I'm not laughing inside. I'm terrified, and I wish I wasn't. There's just so much about her I don't know."

- CHAPTER 33 -

On the front of our calendar at home, there was a beaming lady in an orange sari floating down the Ganges and advertising Horlick's. And when I looked at her (*Horlick's is good for you!*) I went cold inside. Now there were only three weeks until my mother would heave into view aboard the *Strathdene* from Bombay. Our brief little idyll was over, and I felt like a selfish bitch for minding, but I did.

One of my new freedoms I particularly relished was my daily commute from Rose Street to the Moonstone. I liked the feeling of sun on my arms and saying good morning to the knife sharpener who sat outside the hardware shop on the corner, then to Murali on the next corner, the fruit seller who loved to instruct me on what to eat and how to cook it, and who sometimes chased me down the street with a ripe mango or a passion fruit, shouting, "Madam, your ladyship, stop! Special treat for you." The mangos tasted of roses, of honey and summer.

I liked the view from the seafront; the ships from China and Europe and Africa, laden with cedar and spices and oil; the sight of the Chinese nets rising and falling like prehistoric creatures against the sky. I liked saying hello to the old lady who cooked for the fishermen who now waved and beamed at me toothlessly when I passed.

Mind you, I was still sometimes an object of curiosity, and occasionally followed by overzealous traders who were irritating rather than frightening, so I didn't worry much that morning when I noticed three young men who seemed to be walking with deliberate casualness behind me. When I stepped from the curb into the road, I could hear the *flip, flap, flop* of their sandals.

When I stopped at a small kiosk on the corner of Fort Street to buy some of the sweets Anto likes, one of the boys stopped too. He was wearing a cheap shirt and had a thin mustache and an odd affectless stare as if he were looking straight through me.

"Take care of yourself, Mrs. Queen," was all he said, yet it sent a brief spasm of fear through me.

But one of the bonuses of working at the Moonstone was that the work was so intense, as soon as I'd stepped over the pile of dusty sandals in the doorway, I'd forgotten all about it.

We had five soon-to-be-delivered mothers on the wards, and eight new midwives in training. That morning, as I put on my overall, I could hear them singing with a fervor and a joy that was humbling.

Dr. A. had encouraged dancing in the group, and when I walked into the room, I saw our new group of trainees, their arms waving luxuriously above their heads, worn hennaed feet moving for nothing but pleasure. I knew by now that Achamma—eyes ecstatically closed, wheeling, stamping—usually slept on the floor of a cramped hut shared with ten other people in a nearby fishing village. When she wasn't delivering babies she did backbreaking work in paddy fields. Rama, from Quilon, now making beautiful sinuous movements with her wrists and fingers, had produced five children in rapid succession. Watching them dance was like seeing their secret selves come to life, and it always moved me.

This morning, after a tiffin of soft rice idlis and coconut chutney, the question posed was "What was your quickest delivery ever?"

"Two minutes from waters breaking," answered Rama, who had delivered hundreds of babies. "Slowest, three and a half days."

Low sympathetic moans at this.

"Did you take her to hospital?"

"No."

"Why not?"

"Doctors jump on you there."

Raucous laughter from some, timid shushings from Rama, who seems wary of upsetting me—the English memsahib taking notes.

"Be serious now." Maya gave them her stern look through the horn-rimmed glasses. "Mother has been in labor now for over twenty-four hours: what will you do?"

Rama said, "I would put ginger in her chai. I would get her up and walking. I would observe her vital signs, by taking pulses." (Some of the midwives follow the ayurvedic principle that the human being has seventy-seven pulse points, all of them vital to health.)

This worry about hospitals cropped up again and again and was probably why Dr. A. estimates ninety-nine percent of all births in India are home births.

A short but violent debate on contraception followed.

Madhavi, whose nose ring made her look like a stubborn old bull, listed some on her fingers: a stone placed in the vagina, sponges, and for many women, anal sex. Achamma pipes up that she thinks contraception is fine for some city people, but she doesn't feel country people need it.

A furious discussion then took place, lots of finger-pointing and flashing eyes. In the lunch break, Maya filled me in. Achamma was, she said, talking codswallop of course, but contraception is "a big blank" for many of these women.

"What was making them so angry earlier?" I asked.

"Abortions," she said. "In country areas, many midwives have to do them, and some are very primitive: sticks in the womb, stones, poisonous concoctions. We must stop them," she said simply. "Bad for their conscience, worse for the mothers."

After class, Maya and I flopped in the dispensary room and drank chai together. When she took off her glasses and polished them, I saw large blue circles under her eyes.

"You look tired, Maya," I said. "Is everything all right at home?"

"Yes, thank you, ma'am," she replied politely. She hardly ever called me ma'am nowadays.

"My son has not been well, but he is getting better."

"Does he still drop you off in the morning?"

"No, ma'am." She looked at the floor.

"How do you get to work?"

"Boat and bus and walk."

"But isn't it miles away?" I had only the foggiest memory of the village where Maya lived. "Couldn't we ask for some extra money from the kitty to get you here?"

"No." She was always nervous about rocking the boat. For her, being singled out for education, for training had already been a magic carpet ride powered by Dr. A. "Don't do that. If I lose this job, I have nothing."

She closed her eyes; she didn't want to talk anymore. I took our two cups to the sink. I was getting water from the old Ascot heater when I looked up and saw, from the corner of my eye, the backs of two young males scrambling over the wall that separates our land from the alleyway that leads to the street.

My shout was heard by Dr. A. She came rushing in with the night watchman, who bared his teeth convincingly.

"What happened?" Dr. A. had what looked like a hockey stick in her hand.

"I saw two men jumping the wall. I could only see their backs."

"Anyone hurt?"

"No, Doctor." Maya leapt to her feet; she was trembling.

"No crisis," Dr. A. told me, "just local boys."

"But shouldn't we call the police?" I asked.

"No!" she snapped with her position-closed face on. "Get on with your work. We'll put more barbed wire up later."

I understood Dr. A.'s reluctance better than I had a few months ago. Calling the police might mean a bribe we could ill afford or long negotiations with the new Ministry of Health officials, who already watched us like hawks. And for me there was a new fear— one which brought me out in a cold sweat when I thought about it. I was here, officially, to write reports, not to deliver babies. I was two deliveries shy of my full midwifery certificate. Dr. A. had assured me she would write to the relevant examining bodies in England to see if an Indian delivery would be accepted, but I had never asked if I could see the actual papers. Now I wondered if the letter had been sent at all or whether staff shortages, and her new respect for my fine stitching, meant she'd chosen to ignore it. If the rubber-stampers found out, I could lose my job and my reputation and close the Home down.

I seemed to be making a habit of secrecy. I didn't mention the intruders to Anto when I got home, even though the sight of their skinny backs, the speed with which they'd shimmied up that wall had replayed itself several times in my mind.

Walking up the path, through the mild peach-colored air of early evening, I saw Anto on the veranda playing chess with Uncle Josekutty, and the sight of them—whiskies, bare feet, dark heads bent together—was a comforting one. Later, after Uncle Josekutty had gone home, Anto and I sat in the courtyard at the back of the house and enjoyed the soft jasmine-scented breeze from the plant that now scrambled over our walls. I loved this time of day with him: the thrill, still, of our own house, the talk, him smoking a cigarette with the long fingers that would later touch me there and there.

"Do you mind being the new boy at work?" I asked him.

"No," he said. "I'm very much on probation still with some of the doctors. They think I chose to live in England, so with them, beta minus minus at the moment but trying hard."

Anto was strong like that: he'd learned how to be a survivor in a nonmean way; it was something I admired tremendously about him. He went on to talk eagerly about his work with his new boss, Dr. Sastry, whom he revered. "I can really work with him, and achieve," he told me. They'd had a long conversation that day about the African sleeping sickness, and Anto had promised to dig out his PhD thesis and show it to him.

When he asked about my day, I gave him selected highlights of the group discussions. He told me he was surprised at how open the women were with us. I took a puff of his cigarette and immediately put it down, it made me feel so sick.

"There are definite taboo subjects," I said, when I'd gone to get myself a glass of water. "Like today, when we talked about the imbalance of boys and girls in their villages, they were close as clams about it."

"I'm not surprised," Anto said. "Laws are changing all the time and these women will be useful scapegoats: some could even be had up for murder."

He put his hand on my hair. There was a long, considering silence. "It would never bother me to have a little girl." His voice was soft in the darkness. "Or a boy for that matter, if he came. It would be the greatest thing in the world."

And I felt like the worst sneaky wife in the world.

I was still using my diaphragm, but not every time. I longed for children too. But not yet, not now, with things so very interesting at the Home.

Four days after this conversation I was sick in the morning. Kamalam had brought in fresh bananas, a mango, some dosas. Instead of eating them, I felt sweat break out along my hairline, a mild state of panic. Five minutes later, I was panting beside the commode. I did a few sums in my head, and if I hadn't been feeling so lousy, I would have laughed, or cried. I was going to have a baby!

Deep in thought on my way to work, I decided I would tell

Anto in a day or two. I wanted time to collect myself, to feel as thrilled as he would, because now everything would change.

Amma had already warned me that Thekkeden women always spent the last six weeks of their confinement at Mangalath. This might drive me mad. Who owns your body? Not me. Not now. I was excited but fizzing with nervous tension that morning.

Later, calmer and at home again, I sat on the swing on the veranda and the cards seemed to change inside my head, and it came to me in a blaze of happiness that this dazzling spot of consciousness inside me would soon be my first child.

I was in this strange jumble of emotions when I arrived at the Moonstone. Before I had time to unlatch the gate, Maya ran out to meet me, sunlight bouncing off her specs.

"Quickly!" she said. "Come! Mrs. Saraswati Nair is here, her waters have broken, she's in a state. She is calling for you."

"For me?"

"She says she wants the Englishwoman."

"Are you sure?"

"Absolutely."

My heart sank. All of us were a little scared of Mrs. Saraswati Nair, who had already attended two antenatal clinics. Small, politically passionate, and of a peppery disposition, she was cut from a different cloth than most of our patients. Originally from a high-caste Brahman family, she had declared herself a feminist and a campaigner before Independence, and she had married, for love, a prominent local lawyer.

During an early examination, she had asked Dr. A. rather peevishly what I, an Englishwoman, was doing there. Dr. A. had, for once, inflated my importance.

"She is part of worldwide gorement initiative to improve standards for village women, a highly trained midwife."

"Are you quite sure she wants me?" I'd asked Dr. A. before she'd bustled off to another appointment.

Now as I changed into my white coat, I tried hard to control a wave of panic. Mrs. Saraswati Nair, with her clever, shrewd look and her legal training, had the power to raise my pulse without my even thinking about it. I knew she'd throw the rule book at me if anything went wrong.

I found her sitting in a chair beside the bed with a small suitcase beside her. Apart from a light sheen of perspiration on her forehead, she looked composed. Anu, a new nurse, came in and together we helped Mrs. Nair put on a hospital gown. While I was tying the straps behind her, we both laughed as her stomach bucked vigorously.

"So definitely a boy this time," Mrs. Nair joked.

She already had a much older girl who was away studying at university. Her husband, she said, wanted a boy.

She was only one and a half fingers dilated, so I told her she could either lie down or walk. While she was walking, her contractions came irregularly for the next hour, and when we could, we walked arm in arm around the room and talked.

"I had no wish at first to become a lawyer," she said. "It was my father who insisted on educating me. Now I like it."

She stopped, blew out air, smiled, talked again. "I approve of what you women are doing here,"—puff, groan, puff—"but you must be very careful." She sat down heavily, her face gleaming with sweat. "You can't just take the traditional form and put a hammer to it. That's a dangerous thing to do, particularly now."

"Are any of your family members coming in?" I asked when she was two fingers dilated.

"No." Her mouth turned down. "My family don't speak to me now."

"Why not?"

Mrs. Nair had begun to pant softly, like a marathon runner who knows there could be miles and miles ahead. I relaxed a little; she was a good patient.

"They are very traditional high-caste, so many rules . . ." She wiped her face with a towel. "Before my daughter was born, I had to stay with my mother-in-law for three months. Very boring, and I was not allowed out after dark. After the baby was born, I had to stay in for forty days. My parents-in-law wanted many grandchildren, so the whole thing would have taken up months and years of my life and made it impossible for me to work."

"My husband and I have both broken with the past," she continued after a pause. "We made our own wedding, and he supported all my law studies. Law is my language now," she added fiercely, and then after a wince, "and this is my last baby."

By eleven twenty-five Mrs. Nair, who at thirty-nine was an ancient mother by Indian standards, was still not in active labor. She lay on the bed, eyes wide open, looking pale and sweaty. After missing breakfast, I was starting to feel light-headed myself, and for one spiraling, panicky moment, my mind emptied as if I knew nothing, before I pulled myself together. I made myself breathe and wait.

"How is it going?" Maya poked her head around the door.

"Slow," I whispered. "Contractions every ten to twelve minutes, lasting about fifty seconds. When will Dr. A. will be back?"

"Don't know. Do you want food? Your face is pale."

"No, thanks, not hungry. A glass of water."

But Maya sent a nurse for a tiffin anyway. "I'll sit with her for ten minutes," she said, "if you need to rest."

It felt too early to tell Maya or anyone at the Home that I might be having a baby too, but she was looking anxiously at me.

"It's very hot in here. Nurse, a fan," Maya snapped at Anusha. Like Dr. A., Maya didn't waste her charm on underlings. "More towels too."

I took a short break. When I got back, Mrs. Nair was crouched beside the bed, head resting on her arms, howling like a dog.

"A word, please," Maya said curtly. We'd moved towards the end of the bed out of earshot. "The baby has turned. I have a mother and daughter in the class," she whispered. "Name of Charu and Ammini. They are very experienced in massage. I'm going to get them."

When the door closed, I turned to Mrs. Nair, held her damp hand, and heard my own heart beating.

"How are you feeling?"

"Horrible," she gasped. "Worse than last time."

"So, listen." My heart was flipping around in my chest. "Everything is going to be all right, but your baby's bottom will come out first, unless we try to turn it." I blew out a couple of puffs of air.

When Charu and Ammini came silently into the room, they put the palms of their hands together, bowed low, scrubbed up at the sink, and moved, without panic, towards Mrs. Nair, now rolling her eyes in agony. They poured coconut oil into the palms of their hands and I watched in awe as they performed their massage with the confidence of two pianists who had duetted together for years. It was a beautiful thing to see, but after a while, Mrs. Nair pushed their hands away.

"I must leave the bed." Her mouth was a rictus of pain.

When we'd helped her out, she got down on her knees and began to hug herself and howl.

"Try not to do that," I told her, peeling her arms away from her side. "Keep your tummy open." It was an instruction I'd learned from the Moonstone midwives. She gave me a look of ferocious dislike and was sick all over the floor.

"Check we have enough sterilized implements in the autoclave," I told Maya a few moments later.

When Mrs. Nair was half lying on the bed again, breathing in short, anguished gasps, I saw Charu give the baby one last beefy shove, and joy of joys, I could feel through her tummy the knobs of a spinal cord. The baby had turned itself like an eel in a basket.

Less than twenty minutes later, Mrs. Nair gave a guttural cry. Her legs began to tremble.

"You're doing wonderfully, Saraswati." I rubbed her legs.

"*Ippo varum*—you good girl, almost there," Maya assured her.

She closed her eyes; I thought she was going to give up, then came a string of words that sounded like desperate pleas to the gods she said she'd abandoned. It was the longest three or four moments of my life before she started to push again violently.

"Slow it down," Maya told her. "Hold for a moment and then push." A few seconds later: "*Tulleh umm! Tulleh onnum! Loodi ippo varum!* Push once more, about to come!"

After three more contractions, the baby's head appeared, then nose, shoulders, a tiny hand, a perfect baby boy with a shock of black hair.

I suctioned the baby's mouth, felt around his neck for the umbilical cord, and cut it, and then, because the baby wasn't crying, Maya held him up by both heels and slapped him briskly on the bottom and he bawled. It was a beautiful sound that made everybody laugh, and then he was anointed with gold and honey. Maya said if he'd been born in his Brahman home, a lemon would have been tossed out the window.

Mrs. Nair lay in an ecstasy of exhaustion on the bed, her baby's naked breast on hers. "My boy, my baby," she crooned.

It was late by the time I left the Moonstone. I was charged with energy: I had delivered a perfectly formed baby in difficult circumstances, and I was having a baby myself!

But my legs felt leaden and achy when I started to walk, so I took a shortcut home, through the iron gate that led into the English Club, and out onto Saint Francis Street. The guards who sat near the gate usually let me through with a quiet, "Good night, madam," but there was no one there tonight, and it looked deserted inside the gardens, the shadows lengthening.

In the tufty grass at the edge of the once-manicured lawn, I saw a pile of rusted croquet hoops, an old wooden tennis racquet press, and a faded cap. Some of the veranda's rails had been chopped down, presumably for firewood. A mournful sight, like a still life for summer's end, except I wasn't feeling mournful at all. I was in a semi-ecstatic mood, thinking of the new baby, feeling a part of the abundant trees springing from the earth around me, all manner of trees—the palms, the banyan, the Indian bean tree with its fat waxy flowers—thinking how beautiful this country was and how much had changed in my life.

When I reached the clubhouse, I sat down on a bench in front of it, wanting to savor the moment. It was then that I felt the light changing behind me, the sound of an opening door.

"Madam." The boy with the thin mustache who had called me Mrs. Queen when I'd bought sweets for Anto the other morning stood over me. I gazed up at skinny thighs in wrinkled trousers, a smiling face with cool calculating eyes.

"Don't be frightened," he said when he saw me jump. "I've been waiting for your return." He handed me the light muslin scarf I often wore to protect my head from the heat. "You dropped it this morning." He smiled as I took it. I wasn't too alarmed; I'd grown used to being tracked in India. Only the week before I'd been cashing a check at the bank when a voice behind me barked, "Wrong date, madam." A funny story saved for Daisy, but not now.

"How very kind," I said to the boy in what Anto calls my toff voice. "Thank you so much." I put the scarf in my handbag and got up to walk away.

"Do you walk here often, missus?" His sandals clattered down the steps behind me.

"No," I said walking a little faster. "My husband is an Indian man. He's very strict."

"That's good." He fell into step beside me, shot me a glance. "You are too pretty lady to walk on your own. Please don't run, I only want to talk to you."

"My husband is waiting for me."

"Lady, stop running!" His voice rose. "You're safe with me. There are bad men on the street who can hurt you."

"The guard on the gate knows me." I tried to sound calm. "He's there," I pretended. When he jerked his head towards the club, the line of angry pimples on his neck made him look younger than I'd thought at first: seventeen, maybe eighteen at the most.

"There's no one there," he crooned in a singsong voice.

"Look." I fumbled in my bag for my wallet. "You've been awfully kind to find my scarf, I'd like to—"

"Put it away, madam," he said, very offended. He smiled and looked down at the bulge in his trousers, which was growing. He grabbed my arm and pulled me towards a large banyan tree. Its thick leaves and impenetrable roots formed a small, dark room where I sat sometimes on the bench, to read a book or to get shelter from the sun.

"This is what I like from English girls." He pushed me down on the bench, sat beside me, and with the sly smile of a dog about to steal the Sunday joint, put his arm round me. I thought my best bet was to be polite, to talk him out of it, until his free hand dived up my skirt and pulled at the edge of my knickers. In the scuffle that followed, the contents of my handbag scattered in the dust: wallet, mirror, notes for Daisy.

Maya had warned me about Eve teasing, the practice of groping women in the street. "If it happens," she'd advised, "slap the miscreant hard, I mean *really* slap him." She'd demonstrated with a sharp crack on her palm.

"Doesn't that makes things worse?" I'd asked.

"No." She'd cracked her palm again with a stinging sound. "If you give in, they'll hurt you."

When I hit him hard on the side of his face, *Biff!* went crazily through my mind *Biff! Biff! Biff!* as if I were Desperate Dan in *The Dandy*. I swore the worst words I could think, and I had plenty to choose from after nursing in the wards. When the mark of my hand bloomed on his face, I was shocked. He looked towards the street, hesitated, his head wobbling on his neck, and then he hit me back, thud, thud, thud, on my arms and head.

"Don't!" I shouted, "Stop it! I'm having a baby." He raised his fist, and when it came towards my stomach, I grabbed his wrist and shouted, "You bloody bastard! Don't you dare!" He shook me off and landed a punch just below my ribs.

"I know who you are," he sneered. "You are the foreign lady who teaches our Indian girls bad things. We don't want you. Go home!" Then he saw my purse in the dust. He dropped to his knees and scrabbled crab-like towards it.

"Take it." I kicked the purse towards him. He tore the few rupees out of it, ran through the iron gate in the direction of the town, and left me shaking.

- CHAPTER 34 -

It would have been so much better if I'd confided in Anto that night, but I didn't: the habit of keeping hard and potentially shameful things to myself was too ingrained. This is no excuse, but the one or two times in my life I'd confided in my mother had not been a rousing success.

I was bullied once for weeks at a new school in Edinburgh, where my mother was working as a lady companion to a polio victim. A girl called Celia McIntyre, wild red hair and an undershot jaw, had on my second day there pulled my hair and called me a Sassenach pig. She began to ambush me after school and push me off my bike or throw my homework in the bushes. When I finally plucked up the courage to tell my mother, who'd been worrying about my grazed knees and the occasional patch of hair missing, she listened gravely at first, rushed into the bathroom, and turned the taps on hard to muffle the sound, but through the locked door I'd heard her shout, "Oh God! Why does *everything* go wrong for me?" or some such. She'd returned from the bathroom, eyes redrimmed, voice all echoey and sad, and said, "Don't worry, Kit, ignore that pig of a girl."

And I'd said, "It's all right, Mummy, I don't mind," because I had a growing sense of us both being swirled down a plug hole of female powerlessness and rage, and this was the voice that frightened me most. Going, going, gone.

So the lesson learned was that a trouble shared was frequently a trouble prolonged till bedtime and often beyond, and anyway, in later years my mother had recast the whole incident.

"Do you remember that vile girl who hated you? The one who looked like a rugby player? We gave her what for, didn't we?" No mention of "Ignore the pig" or the shouting.

So I lay in the dark that night, eyes open, thinking of that boy: the saliva on his teeth, his skinny Douglas Fairbanks mustache. I was hugging Anto hard. When he'd seen my bruised cheek earlier, I'd sat on a footstool between his legs and he'd bathed my face with warm water.

I knew I should tell him then but instead played the daffy woman.

"Silly me, I took a shortcut through the club garden and had a tumble down the steps and hit a geranium pot. Nothing serious."

And it wasn't, except I had a new fear now that it might have hurt our baby and he might blame me if anything happened to it.

"Poor Kittykutty." He stroked my head in the way I love; it makes me want to butt my head against his hand like a cat. "You should take a rickshaw, I don't want a falling-down wife."

"It's only a ten-minute walk," I protested, but I was still feeling shivery and out of sorts. "I like it."

"Do it for me." He tucked a strand of hair behind my ear. "Your scaredy-cat husband who would die of misery without you."

We laughed and we cuddled, and then he undressed me, and I almost told him as he ran his fingers gently over my breasts and belly, but I kept my eyes wide open instead, over his shoulder checking the exits, the windows, the doors, thinking of the boy, his mocking smile, the line of pimples on his neck.

Over prawns and rice at supper, Anto talked some more about his new job at the hospital, the inspirational boss who had, he said, been pleased with the work Anto had done on their research project. Funds would be provided soon for Anto to travel to the areas of India where doctors were reinstating ayurvedic principles into their work. Dr. Sastry had also read his thesis and thought he should publish it as a book.

"I feel I'm on a journey now," Anto said. "One of striving and of happiness I can say . . ." He closed his eyes and thought. "I can say I feel whole for the first time."

He looked boyish, happy. The extra skin of irony and detachment he'd had to wear in England seemed gone. When he asked me about my day, I told him about Mrs. Nair and her new baby, and all she'd told me during our time together: how she'd given up following the rules of her own caste and burned her sari when she met Gandhi and become politicized.

"Is she a terrifying harridan?"

"Anto!" I said. "Why on earth would you assume that?"

"Because Appan told me about her only recently," he said. "He said he was in court with her and very taken with her sharp brain. She would be a handful if things went wrong," he said, looking troubled. "Sorry for this, but why on earth did she go to the Home? She has plenty of money."

"It's not to do with money. She's left her home, and she hates the thought of hospital. Very simple, really."

"Sorry, Kittykutty, but Appan says she is an angry woman. I'm only thinking of you if things went wrong."

"Well, they didn't." I gave an enormous yawn. "They went well. I must go to bed."

But before I did, I felt so jittery and out of sorts I made him check every single shutter and door and window, my mind flipping back to that rank-smelling hand over my mouth, my skirt being clawed. And now this extra terror, that the boy's punch had harmed our child, and that it was all my fault for taking yet another stupid shortcut.

- CHAPTER 35 -

When I wrote to Daisy and my mother to tell them I was pregnant, I was heartily relieved when my mother, who was still living at Wickam Farm, canceled her proposed trip with the vague explanation that she didn't "do" babies and would "keep out of our hair" until ours was a little older.

Yes, *relief* is the word, but if I'm honest, I was hurt and disappointed too. In some locked corner of myself I must have been looking forward to seeing her.

I worked on at the Home for eight months of my pregnancy and was told I could come back at any time after the baby was born. Dr. A. assured me there would be plenty of willing and experienced hands at the Home who would help with a new baby.

Work was a good thing: like many midwives in their first pregnancy, I found in the first few months plenty to worry about and had to stop myself looking up stray symptoms in old textbooks and take comfort from Anto, who was radiant with happiness and who said I was as strong as an ox and not to worry about a thing.

And he was right—almost. Halfway through my pregnancy I felt as physically strong as I'd ever felt, but the memory of that boy's punch stayed in my mind like a bad bruise that would not fade.

When, at Mangalath, on the veranda, I felt the first cramps of labor, I felt as apprehensive as any woman having her first baby, and mightily relieved when Rema, the family midwife, trained in Madras and wonderfully efficient, came cycling up the drive and walked into my bedroom. She had no idea I was a midwife, and I didn't care. All I wanted was her comfort and guidance, because once my own labor properly began, I might have laughed—had I not been doubled up in agony—that I, the almost-trained professional, felt swept away by forces that I could neither control nor understand. It was the difference, say, between understanding the chemical composition of snow and taking a sleigh ride at breakneck speed down a steep mountain. The sheer force of it shocked me: my own womb clenching and unclenching like a great jaw, and then the joy, the soaring sense of triumph, bigger, better, deeper than anything I had ever experienced, of having put a new human in the room who wasn't there before. Such a very ordinary thing to happen, but for me, my first miracle.

When, at three minutes past two in the morning, my first son, Raffael, was born, after a twelve-hour labor, the midwife part of me checked him over neurotically—two working legs, round little tummy, perfect toes like Jersey new potatoes, a face at first like a furious little tomato—while the mother part was ablaze with happiness. I'd known nothing about this: the helpless love you feel, the vulnerability, the joy and, in a weird way, the strength. If I could do this, I could do anything.

After he was born and we'd moved back to Rose Street again, Anto raced home every night to see him. Raffael was like a little fire burning in the house, and it was a happy time. I took a photograph of him and sent it to Josie, asking if she'd be his godmother, and she wrote back saying what a little corker he was, and she'd be proud to keep him away from damnation.

The only fly in the custard came, six months later, when a telegram arrived at Rose Street saying my mother had booked tickets on the *Strathdene* and would be arriving in Bombay in two months' time.

"So, how do you feel about Mummy finally coming?" Mariamma asked me, with a sugary emphasis on *Mummy*. We were at Mangalath for the weekend, sitting in dappled sunshine, side by side on the summerhouse veranda. I had the telegram in my handbag and was still experiencing its aftershocks.

"Terrified, since you ask," I said. "I don't know what to think." My milk was slowing down and Raffael was on my lap, sucking manfully on his new bottle. When he saw us watching him, he yanked the bottle away, his eyes bulging and affronted.

"Give that young man to me." Mariamma took the bottle from his hand and burped him. "I don't blame you." She put Raffie back on my lap, where he lay watching the sky through his fingers. "Mothers are terrifying—too much power is the problem."

I ran my hand through Raff's soft, thick hair. "It's awful to admit this, but I was almost glad when she couldn't come. It's not that I don't love her, it's just . . . oh God, it's so complicated.

"Damn!" I could feel the slow trickle of Raffael's pee running through my skirt. He didn't wear nappies because Amma believed babies should be trouserless until they learned to potty train themselves. In Raffie's case, to my surprise, it worked about eight times out of ten, and I was learning how he paddled his legs and stretched his arms towards me when he wanted to use the potty.

Mariamma called to Theresa to take him to the house. Theresa, ten last week, was one of a number of his willing slaves. No shortage of them at Mangalath. Amma would spend hours walking him round the garden, showing him the new Leghorn chickens and collecting eggs with him, throwing alfalfa at the donkey, topping up water for Appan's new Tibetan mastiff dog.

As we watched Theresa walk importantly towards the house with Raffael in her arms, I told Mariamma I'd never even held a real live baby until I was eighteen.

"Don't be silly!" She simply wouldn't believe me. "You must have had relatives with babies—sisters, brothers."

"Honest truth," I said. "I was an only child and my mother worked for a living. We traveled a lot."

I'd said almost nothing to Mariamma about my strange childhood because, if I'm honest, it still gave me a queer sick feeling when I thought about the dead-to-me row I'd had with my mother when I'd married Anto. The family would be mortally offended and I didn't want that, plus it only seemed fair to let my mother arrive with a clean slate.

Now I had my own baby, so many of the things that had once driven me mad about my mother—her anxious protectiveness, her hovering, her fudging the truth about so many things—I now understood and felt a sort of anguish about. I should have been kinder.

I changed my damp skirt. Theresa came back with Raffie wearing a strip of cloth worn like a loincloth, both ends tucked into a silver chain clasped around his waist. She put a rug underneath the mango tree and he lay in the shade testing his fat legs for pinginess and stretch. He put a thoughtful toe in his mouth, and took it out again so he could imitate the sounds of one of the birds. *Brrrr brrr, cheep chee.*

He was a sublimely contented child, with a filthy chuckle. He liked nothing better than to be here at Mangalath, handed from lap to lap. On the day he was born Amma looked at him with tears in her eyes and said, *"Entey kochu rajakumaran!"* My little prince. Next Anto had asked Appan to dab gold and honey on his tongue, saying he hoped the baby would inherit his father's brilliant mind, his tenacity, generosity. On the twenty-eighth day, the silver chain was clasped around his waist to tuck the loincloth in.

Happy days, but it was Mariamma I was most grateful to. She was the one who insisted on staying up with me on the first blurry and alarming nights of having a baby of my own to keep alive. She brought me teas and little snacks. When I needed to bathe, Theresa sat with him. When Anto came home, weary often from the hospital, we were free to spend hours lying with him between us, floating in the sweetness of his presence. Nourishing meals arrived, helping hands at every turn. When I thought of my own mother in her isolation, I was ashamed.

"So tell me more about your Mummy." Mariamma threw the ball again, soft but insistent. "What part of India did she hail from?"

I'd shared with her the fact that Ma had been born here in the early days but said almost nothing else. Mixed blood, as I was perfectly aware by now, was not a great calling card in India.

"Well . . ." I dipped a finger in my coconut juice and put it in Raff's mouth. "She's lived for years in England, but I think she went to school in Pondicherry and married my father over here. It's all a bit fuzzy."

"A bit fuzzy," Mariamma crooned, running her fingers through Raffie's thatch and pretending it was his hair we'd been talking about.

"We can question Grandma when she comes," she told him. She smoothed his hair down, kissed the back of his neck.

And this was my dread. I could too easily imagine my mother's cornered looks, the strange replies that could sound so haughty.

"Will you show her around the Moonstone?" Another quick glance.

"Maybe," I said. My mother had agreed to arrive with some new obstetrical equipment for the Home. Nothing big: scissors, forceps, petri dishes to be packed and stored in the hold. "But maybe not. She never liked my being a nurse."

"Even during the war?"

"No."

"Will she mind your work here?"

"Probably."

"She wanted you to be ladylike?"

"The exact words my mother would have chosen," I said. In the silence that followed, I had the small revelation that I had chosen a profession guaranteed to make me least like my mother.

"Do you miss it?" I could feel Mariamma watching me.

"No," I said, "because I'm definitely going back to work soon." I'd decided it was time the week before when I'd made an appointment to see Dr. A. "I'll do two, maybe three shifts a week. They're short-staffed and they have a government inspection coming up. I can take Raffie if I want to, and Kamalam is at home all day and like a second mother to him."

"Oh dear." She could not hide her dismay. "Do Amma and Anto know this?"

"Amma no, not yet," I said. "Anto yes, of course! He's happy about it." Not entirely true, but at least he understood. "He's told me to go ahead."

"And your Mummy when she comes—will she mind?"

"I don't know," I added more truthfully. "We'll have to wait and see."

- CHAPTER 36 -

I started with only two shifts a week. Raffie, who often came with me, enjoyed playing court to a circle of admiring women. Maya was glad to see me, numbers had grown at the clinic, and her husband was angry with her again because she was often home late and his own mother had to come over and cook his rice. Sometimes she looked so weary and crushed, I wondered if he was beating her again. By this standard, Anto was a peach of a husband, except that three days into our new regime, we had a shocking row as sudden as a summer storm.

Anto was lying on the bed, Raffie on his chest, playing the game that Raff loves: "Atishoo, Atishoo, we all fall down." Anto, who still loved to teach me things, was explaining that the song began when people were falling like flies from the plague. Raffie, who hated when people talked to anyone but him, flung his arms around Anto's neck and covered his face in kisses, steering him away from me.

"I love my boy," Anto crooned, "but he's getting spoiled. He needs six brothers and one or two sisters."

"Why not twelve," I said, "enough for a cricket team?"

He held Raffie high above his head and said, "I'm serious, Kit. We're in another phase of our lives now."

He'd explained this to me before: the Hindu belief that a man's life should fall into four distinct phases, the first being Kaumaram, the South Indian word for youth. The next was Brahmacharyam, or celibate student phase—well, Anto had missed that boat—then

Grihasthashramam, the householder stage, in which a man devoted himself to earning a living and having his children, and finally Vanaprastham, the hermit stage, when you left off worldly ties and pleasures and lived as an ascetic sage in the wilds. As a blueprint for life it all sounded intriguingly tidy and purposeful, but from a Western wife's point of view—how could I put this?—claustrophobic.

"So next stop, sackcloth and ashes," I said.

"Don't joke about everything, Kit." He let go of my hand. Raffie had fallen asleep, so he kept his voice low.

"I'm not," I said. It was no surprise to me to know that he wanted lots of children. The Thekkedens saw them as one of life's greatest gifts. I liked that about them and agreed. Up to a point.

When he added, "I want as many as possible," was it wrong of me to suddenly feel like a great big breeding cow? The argument that followed was loud, and when Raffie started to bawl, we continued it in angry whispers in bed.

From me: "Of course I love him, of course I love you—but can't I have any other life at all?"

Him: "You're being dramatic: you have another life now. I don't mind that, but can't you change?"

Me: "Why must I change? For you life is the same now with Raffie here, but better."

Him: "Rmmnnph." The Indian version of *harrumph*. "Don't play games with me, Kit. You're a woman. I can't have our babies."

Me: "I'm not so different from you, or at least, not as much as you'd like to think: I like challenges, I like excitement, I like getting better at things, I like seeing things grow. I'm proud of what we do at the Moonstone."

It was true what I said about the Moonstone. This scruffy, frustrating, life-giving place, with its inadequate facilities and bewildering days, had connected me to India in ways I didn't even understand. I wanted to stay part of it, to watch it grow.

Him, shouting now: "Watching your own children grow, what could be better than that?" And there was more and it hurt us both. What I should have said loud and clear was that I had seen in my mother the fury and the fate of the untrained woman moving from one menial job to another and hating them all.

And he would have said, "But you're not your mother, and I love you, and I won't leave you." I wouldn't have believed him because my sense of men's being abandoners was so deep-rooted. The father who left me, whom I was forbidden to talk or think about, has followed me through life like a bad smell. I've tried my best to ignore him—it makes no sense to miss someone you've never met—but he's there.

I was examining Valli, a village woman who had presented with premature leak of her amniotic fluid, when I heard a tremendous crash in the street outside, as if someone had dropped fifty trays. When the windows trembled, Valli shrieked and disappeared under the sheet.

When I ran into the hall, Jalaja, one of the midwives, yelled, "Ma'am! They're cutting down a tree!"

Outside, I saw Maya shaking her fist at three men stripped to the waist and sitting in the trees branches. She looked white as milk and very frightened. "It's the neem tree; they're cutting its branches. A government department just turned up this morning. No one told us they were coming. They said disease was there and the tree unsafe."

"Do they need to tell us?" The tree, strictly speaking, was on the boundary between our land and the empty building plot next door.

"Very definitely we should know."

I had no strong feelings about the tree losing one or two branches. I enjoyed crunching its pods underfoot because they gave off a refreshing aroma and it was a nice tree to sit under at lunch, but for Maya, this was a catastrophe in the making. The neem, she'd already told me, was a god amongst trees, a shade giver, a maker of creams. Rags soaked in its oils were used as contraceptives. Now, on the verge of tears, she said that the workmen had ignored vital rituals. If the whole tree must go, the axmen must pour ghee over the stump and say, "May you grow with one thousand shoots." Otherwise they would offend the powerful spirits and gods that lived in the tree.

"But what if it's only a branch?" I said stupidly because I was not sure how to comfort her.

"Then you must beg pardon for its injuries," she said. "I have done that now."

As we stood in the blinding light looking up at the tree, my eyes moved to the right, and a strange jangling began in my brain.

A small crowd of curious onlookers had gathered to watch the axmen. Standing apart from them was the boy with the thin mustache. He wasn't looking at the tree, he was looking at me.

I told Maya I was going inside but she didn't hear me. She was praying distractedly, as if something terrible had already happened.

- CHAPTER 37 -

And then my mother arrived. Predictably unpredictable as usual, a day early—blaming a telegram that hadn't arrived—and full of complaints about the appalling service aboard her liner, the *Strathdene*. The food was awful, the staff were rude, her cabin on F deck was next door to a couple who had rowed constantly. She'd hardly slept a wink the whole voyage.

When she showed the bags under her eyes to me, almost as a mark of honor, I thought, Yes . . . yes, once again it all goes wrong for you, and was distressed by my instant meanness.

Her first highly perfumed tentative hug reminded me of a nervous mother burping a new baby, and I can honestly say I felt a big blank nothing.

"Darling, this is perfectly sweet," she said, when she first stepped into our house.

"We like it a lot. You look well, Mummy," I said, the safest thing I could say and the most dishonest. She was as carefully dressed as ever: blue silk suit, feathered hat, stockings, even though the heat was 105 degrees, crocodile shoes polished to a high shine, but I was shocked by how much older she looked and somehow shrunken. Her voice was higher than I remembered it too and lighter, as if it was an effort to talk.

I'd looked forward to showing her Raffie, and when he woke, Anto appeared with him tousled and blinking in his arms.

"Your perakutty," he said. "Mr. Raffael Thekkeden."

My mother, in the middle of telling me about the horrors of the ship, stopped. "My grandson," she agreed. She closed her eyes and held Raffie apart from her as if he were a wet cat. Raffie, who was teething, let out a thin wail and flung his arms towards me.

"Oh! oh! oh!" My mother practically threw him back. "I'm no good with babies," she said.

"Ah," I said. We exchanged a look. Anto rescued us.

"He's always a crotchety old devil after his sleep." He took Raff in his arms and gave him one of the smacking kisses on the tummy that made him laugh. "Give him time."

Because my mother loathed any kind of muddle, we'd had a major spring clean before she arrived. We'd made an anxious inventory of what Anto called Mummy food: prunes and oatmeal for the digestion, which had Babu, who owned the general store, scratching his head; lemons for the early-morning hot water and lemon juice regime she followed strictly; bread from the roaring oven of the old-fashioned baker up the street who had once supplied the Raj. English breakfast tea from a supplier Amma knew in Fort Cochin.

We'd moved from our bedroom into the guest room so she could have the larger bedroom at the front of the house. It was a lovely room now, whitewashed and spare, with the large carved rosewood bed given to us by Amma and a rosewood easy chair with long arms and dainty mother-of-pearl inlays on the headrest that had been in the shed at Mangalath before Amma had had it cleaned up and recaned.

She slept for twelve hours on arrival. I crept around the house, relieved already for the break from her, and for the next two or three days, we danced around each other—polite self-conscious strangers. We carefully avoided bringing up the rows we'd had about Anto and made no mention of the dead-to-me decree or Daisy or my work at the Moonstone.

In the early mornings I fed and played with Raffie, often taking him to the park, where he could be noisy and not annoy my mother. She got up around eleven and sat looking dazed on the chair facing the window, saying gentle, admiring things about the house, the street, the sky, the trees. As I accepted compliments and made bland conversation back, I thought about those nuns who, at mealtimes, must only talk about birds or trees or flowers, to avoid anything controversial.

During the day, she sipped, very daintily, on a lime juice and soda and ate very little. At nighttime, after I'd bathed Raffie and told him a story, she and I drank weak whisky and soda, or a "gin and it" for her, and waited for Anto to come home. This, normally, was the time of day I most looked forward to with him: catching up on each other's day, hearing the gossip from the hospital, telling him about the Moonstone, and hearing about his research. But on those first nights with my mother, I observed him like a stranger. He always washed when he got home and changed his clothes, and I would look at him, shaved, oiled, handsome in his linen trousers and white shirt. His good looks still had the power to take my breath away, but now it was his kindness I marveled at. He angled his chair towards her, he listened to her with sympathy and respect, as if it were a privilege for him to be talking to her, while she chattered to him gaily, as if she'd never said any of the terrible things she had said about him.

Some nights Kamalam would appear, smiling, proud, to present "the perakutty" for a good-night kiss. Often my mother's glance would flicker over Raffie and she'd carry on talking, and I would feel I hated her.

After such a night, lying in bed in the spare room, Anto repeated his instruction to me. "Give her time. This is very shocking to her, being back in India again, and don't forget, you're speaking to her from the grave." He meant it as a joke, but that's how I felt with her—frozen and cold.

My next terror came in the form of an invitation from Amma. She wanted the family to get together for a special celebration lunch to welcome my mother.

When Anto told my mother this, she said, in a small, trapped voice, "How lovely," and then, turning to me as if he weren't there, complained, "But I'd rather hoped to have a few days to lie low. I've been talking to strangers for weeks." And again, I felt that prickle of dislike rising like a thorn in me and I wanted it to go away, but I knew it wouldn't, unless we had it out.

Anto, who had taken a week off from work to welcome her, said there was no rush, whenever she felt like it. The man was behaving like a saint, but it wouldn't last: he had his limits too.

On the morning we left for the Mangalath party, Glory, in spite of another twelve-hour sleep, still looked tired and seemed to have shrunk to half her normal size. For the first time I felt truly sorry for her and a little alarmed. Dressed in a new and very smart black-and-white silk polka dot dress and small hat, she winced in the blinding sunlight as she left our house. Her arm felt twig-like and breakable as I helped her into the car, and she sat gasping for a few moments.

I was enough of an Indian wife by now for a ride in a car—loaned to us by Appan for the day's outing—to be something of a treat for me, and I'd grown to love the drive from Fort Cochin to Mangalath: the rowdy markets, the green paddy fields, the huge sky, the sunlit lakes, on which houses and bridges seem to float. But today I felt carsick and tense about the day ahead.

My mother sat in the back with her eyes closed. I sat beside her with Raffie on my knee. Anto broke the silence.

"I don't think you've been to this part of India before, have you, Mother?" She would like him to call her Glory, but he can't. In his family to call an older person by their Christian name would be unspeakably rude.

"No," she said, in the echoey voice I recognized as a No Trespassing sign. "Further north." When Anto's eyes swam into the rearview mirror, I shook my head slightly.

"It's awfully pretty though." She opened her eyes briefly, the perfect guest again. "Lots of lovely water and birds," as a line of herons flew in a straggling ribbon across the lake, leaving a ruffle of water behind them. Raffie, who watched everything, let out a shriek but turned back quickly to the pattern on my mother's dress. He moved one podgy finger from dot to dot, examining each forensically as if it were a complicated logarithm he must solve.

"Do you mind that?" I asked.

"No." She put her hand on his head and let it stay there for a while.

"This must be strange for you, Mummy," I said.

Less than three miles from the house, I saw her lips moving, her hands grasping the car's leather safety strap.

"It's not very strange," she said. "I'm fine." Then in the silence that followed: "I don't want you to worry about me."

When Mangalath appeared from the red dust of the road, my mother immediately perked up and became someone sociable and fun. I must say it did look lovely. It had rained briefly on our way over and left big fat diamonds winking on the leaves of the flame of the forest trees that lined the drive. There were glints of silver on the lake beyond.

At the house, Amma stood between the gold lions, waiting to greet us.

"It's so good to finally meet you," she said, as she took Glory's hand in hers, and added with her sweetest smile, "I can see where your daughter gets her good looks from."

I saw her cast a shrewd and appraising eye over my mother's clothes and jewelry: that was the way her mind worked, it was the dowry obsession most mothers had here. At the sight of Amma, Raffie let out a longing cry and flung his arms towards her. He buried his face in her shoulder.

"So, what do you think of this rascal?" Amma asked, as we walked towards the house. "Your very first grandchild, Kit tells me."

"Yes," my mother agreed, her heels click-clacking on the path, her voice breathless with the effort to keep up. "My first . . . he's awfully sweet."

Only nine of us for lunch, so Glory would not be swamped, Amma explained as we took our places in the dining room. Appan sat at the head of the table, next to Anto, Mariamma and the rest in their usual places, and there were a couple of elderly aunts whose names I'd forgotten and Ponnamma. I sat next to my mother, who was at her most delightful, exclaiming and smiling at everything. Feeling her sharp bones beside me, I hoped she could cope with all the food, her appetite had been so poor.

In her honor, a magnificent meal was served on very fine bone china plates. The pearly spotted karimeen fish that was a delicacy of the area, a tender mutton stew, soft, fluffy boiled rice with chicken curry, and the usual thoran and sautéed okra, crisp fried pappadams, lime pickle. I'd forgotten to have breakfast and my mouth watered at the sight of it.

Glory had been given a knife and fork, just as I had been given on my first day here. I could feel her stiffen beside me as I ate with my fingers. Below the general bubble of conversation she said, "Don't you find that frightfully messy?"

"I like it now." I added some buttermilk to the rice, crushed a pappadam into it, and popped it into my mouth to demonstrate how elegantly I could do it, and then I laughed at myself. Do we ever stop showing off to our mothers?

Appan pulled up a chair beside us and peered at Glory through his glasses. "We're so happy you're here," he told her with apparent sincerity. "It's like a dream come true."

She gave an embarrassed laugh. "How very kind," she said, very much the Colonel's lady as she began to scatter compliments like cake sprinkles.

"Goodness me, Kit was right, so clever," she murmured in shock when he told her he'd been in Delhi, drafting new government legislation. Appan, an essentially modest man, deflected the compliment.

"It's my son I'm most proud of, working his socks off at the hospital. It's a great joy to have him home again."

This courtly dance continued for a while: the passing of dishes, the tentative questions, the answers, the knitting together of a holey blanket that must, for now, be my mother's vision of her new family. While my mother charmed Appan, Ponnamma swapped places with Mariamma so she could follow their exchange more easily.

She patted my mother on the arm. "Come on," she said, "eat up." She put some of the mutton curry on my mother's plate, spooned a little dhal on the side. "You need feeding up."

As I watched my mother take a little forkful, I felt a piercing sadness. For the first time I could ever recall, she was the center of attention. And maybe she felt it too, because when Ponnamma suddenly blurted out, "Why did you delay your trip here?" she launched into a surprising story.

"Well." She pushed her chair back, took a delicate sip of water. "It's rather a wonderful story, actually: I have a great and dear friend in Oxford. Her name is Daisy. She lives in a very grand but rather run-down house—the war, you know—which she is hopeless at doing up, so I help her sometimes."

That's it, Mother, I thought, still a dab hand at biting the hand that feeds you.

"It's where Anto met Kit," my mother continued. "Anyway . . ."

She wiped the side of her mouth with the napkin, to make sure no stray piece of spinach thoran interfered with her look. "I must tell you what happened there . . ." The thread of excitement in her voice, the long, deliberately held pause reminded me what a good storyteller she had been when I was little. Every eye at the table was now trained on her. Ponnamma's mouth was agape.

"It was shortly before Christmas, dark that night and very rainy—the kind of rain that seems to be poured in buckets not in drops. I was sitting in the sewing room, helping Daisy fix some new curtains for the main room. I love sewing,"—she flung a smile at a mesmerized Appan—"and I was listening to the rain on the window, and suddenly I dropped a pin, and when I kneeled down to pick it up, I saw, through the floorboards, a light shining up at me. A shaft of light." Glory sketched it out delicately in the air.

"From the room below?" Appan was applying his legal brain. "Which room?"

"Ah, well, you see, aren't you on the ball? That's the exact point," said Glory. "There was no room below. Only what we had always assumed was a solid staircase."

She quelled any more questions with her hand. "I called to Daisy," Glory continued in the same thrilling voice. "We got a torch. We went downstairs together."

"Oh my God." Ponnamma clutched her throat. "You were very brave."

Glory ignored this. "Downstairs, on the side of this staircase, we found a small door. When we opened it, there was"—her eyes swept the table—"a room in the house that we didn't know existed. A whole new room."

"What was inside?" Amma asked.

"Well, this is the wonderful thing," Glory continued, her finger in the air. "And the dreadful. Before the war, Daisy's father was a rather good artist. He studied at the Slade, then went to Paris, was taken around all the studios, met all the gang. So . . ." Another long pause. "What we found was a pile of pictures in this very dusty room. They were leaning against a wall. Now, does the name Picasso mean anything to you?" She slid her eyes up at Appan.

"Of course." He was slightly exasperated. "Square ladies with round heads and all such things. One of the most famous artists in the world," he explained to the aunts.

"Well, behind two very ordinary seascapes, we found one of his." The table let out a collective gasp.

"And when we picked it up, the whole thing crumbled in our hands. Heartbreaking—woodlice, wood worm, who knows? As I said, Daisy is not the world's best housekeeper. So I wrapped up all those shards, and I took them to a restorer in Cirencester.

"He looked at them, said, 'Terribly sorry, they're beyond hope.' I begged him to try and save them, but all we could salvage were bits of hands and feet, a skew whiff of a smile, and then tantalizingly the name Picasso, beautifully preserved." She gave a small sigh, then collected herself.

"So how did this situation resolve, and you get here eventually?" Appan the practical wanted to know. My mother looked confused for a moment.

"Oh, I took the chap back to the house, and we found one or two other bits and pieces. Minor artists, nothing special. So we took them to an auction," my mother continued. "Got some money for them, all very exciting,"—my mother's smile was flung about the table like a sunbeam—"but it delayed my trip. Some of the money helped pay for my journey."

"Your friend was kind to give you the money," Ponnamma said. "It was her house. A very good friend to give you the money."

"That's true," my mother replied. "But don't forget, I found the extra room."

In the applause that followed I was in awe of her: her verve, her daring. It was good to see her smiling too and the haggard, hunted lines of her face soften, at least for now.

Was the story true? No idea. Honestly none. She'd never divulged to me the origins of the "little windfall" that had brought her to India, and I hadn't dare ask. And then again, if she was embroidering the truth, I thought Picasso was a mistake—too obvious, too unlikely—but if she wasn't, why hadn't Daisy, who'd reported fully on mother's pneumonia, mentioned a shred of it?

- CHAPTER 38 -

When Anto saw Amma go into the garden after lunch, he followed her down the garden path and towards the potting shed. He knew her well enough to know that lunch with Glory had been an ordeal—this exotic hybrid appearing from nowhere, needing knives and forks, and special conversation. And then the linked thought of how much easier—more fun! more profitable—it would have been with Anu in her place, and Vidya sitting beside him.

"Hello, stranger," she said, when she saw him. She was on her knees planting an orchid.

"Hello, Amma," he said. He sat down on the bench. "Thank you for lunch. I know these things aren't easy for you."

"Did I show it?"

"No, you were kind."

"Kind." She examined the word as she settled the new plant into its bed of bark and soil; a trickle of moisture from her jug colored the gray earth red.

"This one's called lady's slipper," she said at last in a tight voice. "Appan sent it to me from Madras. It came from Mr. Xavier, my specialist grower. He said, 'If anyone can charm flowers from buds, you can, Madam.'"

"Well, it's true." When he touched her hand, he saw her eyes fill with tears. "People bloom here too; it wouldn't happen without you."

She brushed her tears away with a quick efficient gesture.

"What else can I be but polite?" She gave a little gasp. "Life happens to you, you can't control it."

She put away her trowel, and they walked down to the bench facing the water. They watched the sun gild the water with shining bars of light and slowly melt behind the trees in a fiery glow. Across the lake, early evening fires were being lit outside the scattering of huts. The thump of drums came from the Hindu temple, and voices singing evening prayers.

"Just like old times," he said.

"Yes," she said, her face golden with reflected light, "but not really." He wanted her to add something comforting but her expression was both sad and proud.

He knew he confused her now: the jokes, the deep reserve, the uneasy look he gave her before he answered simple questions, as if trying to filter out what would offend her.

Over lunch, he had looked at Glory through Amma's eyes and known what she'd be thinking. A strange kettle of fish that one: so confident, so instantly vivacious, so ever slightly flirtatious. Skinny too—must be ill—and very, what was the word? Slippery about her own past. But where was she from? Why had she stayed away? Where was her family? Underneath Amma's enchanted gaze these questions would have seethed.

"Your father seemed to like her," she said now.

"Yes."

"But men are like babies like that: feed them the sugar of flattery and they bloom too." She smiled to show she didn't care at all.

"Do you mind him being away so much?"

"Of course I think he is working himself to death, but what can I do?"

Anto didn't have an answer.

"But I will tell you one thing," Amma said, breaking the long pause that followed. "He and I agree about one important thing; so, by the way, does her mother. We would like Kit to have more babies and spend less time at work."

A swarm of confused feelings rose up in him at this: How to explain to his mother that this was all he wanted too, without being disloyal to Kit? How to explain to himself the resentment he felt at all these old biddies butting their noses into her reproductive life?

"When did this discussion with her mother take place?" he asked.

"We were alone, after lunch. You and Kit were upstairs with Raffie."

"What did you say?"

"Well . . ." Amma began, innocently bland. "I began by saying, 'Your daughter is a wonderful mother. I hope more are planned.' She said, 'Amen to that. I'd like her to have tons of babies and give up that work she does. I think it's a horrible job.'"

Amma brushed invisible crumbs of dirt from her lap. "She told me she blamed the war for getting her into it. The war changed girls, she said, and not for the better: it got them almost addicted to danger and responsibility. When it ended, she'd begged and begged Kit to stop. Don't look at me like that! You asked me what she said, I'm telling you."

When his mother finished her outburst, with a firm closing of her lips, he felt a moment of dull rage on Kit's behalf: addicted to danger! to responsibility! What insulting claptrap, and what a reduction of her spirit and her bravery and her dedication, of the other nurses too. But he said nothing: the two grandmas were talking, they had found common ground. For everyone's sake, this truce must be preserved, for the time being.

"So you covered a lot of ground." He shifted away from her.

"Not really. It's probably the only thing we have in common." She gave a bitter smile and put her trowel in the pocket of her garden apron. "I'm tired, you know. I'm going to go to bed early."

- CHAPTER 39 -

"Is there anything you'd particularly like to do while you're here, Mummy?" I'd said when she first arrived, thinking there must be an old school, a village, a district she'd want to visit; one that might bring the big blank of her past alive, not just for her, but for me too.

"Not really, darling," came the disappointing answer. "You decide for me, unless there are some amusing people here you'd like me to meet."

When she said this, I could feel myself sinking into the bog of her inertia, her disappointment, the lack of concrete plans I'd dreaded as a child. But then I'd be ashamed of my meanness: the shadows under her eyes were growing and, in the mornings when I opened her bedroom door, she often looked as still and dead as a wax dummy. Then I'd hear her labored breathing, or the long coughing spells that were frightening to listen to. During one of our early days together, Anto took the day off and borrowed the family car from Appan so we could tootle around Fort Cochin. She was perfectly polite about its churches, the monuments, the covered market, the Chinese nets, but when we stopped for a lemonade overlooking the harbor, and when Anto was out of earshot, she said to me, "It is quite a limited little town really, isn't it? And the pong! Why doesn't their new lot do something about it?"

*　　*　　*

After ten days, I couldn't bear these drifting hours any longer, and one afternoon, told her I had to go back to my two shifts a week at the Moonstone.

The house was running smoothly now, and Kamalam would be a willing supplier of tea and toast—the only thing Glory ate in the morning. I'd come home for lunch and in the afternoons we'd be together.

To my surprise, she made no protest. Instead, she stroked my fingers and said, "It's nice being together again, isn't it?" And I wished with all my heart I could say, "Yes, it's nice," and mean it.

On my first day back, there were thirty women waiting outside the clinic, many of them new patients. After clinic, Dr. A. drew me aside to tell me they were dangerously short-staffed and I was to write to the Oxford group to ask for funds for a new trainee midwife and two nurses. I felt discouraged: I wanted to function as a midwife now, not as a cash cow.

I wrote the letter, raced home down the seafront, arrived breathless, only to find my mother peacefully knitting (knitting!) in a patch of sunshine. Raffie was playing with his colored blocks nearby, with Kamalam looking on.

She didn't ask about the Home and I said nothing. Instead she showed me an out-of-date copy of the Army and Navy catalog, which she enjoyed despising.

"Urgh, look at this." Her perfectly buffed fingernail stabbed at a tweed shooting skirt. "You'd have to pay me to wear this."

"You won't get much," I teased her. "Not a big run on tweed since Independence."

"Silly asses," she murmured softly, "kicking us out." I looked at her in silent amazement. Had she completely forgotten who she was, or half was?

"Oh, darling, forgot to tell you." She looked up and frowned. "A funny little lady came while you were out this morning. She wanted to talk to you. She seemed in a bit of a state." She picked up the magazine again.

"Any sort of idea what her name was?"

"Let me think." Her finger stopped.

"Sorry, darling, it's gone . . . . Oh, hang on." I watched a thought form in her head. "I wrote it down." She picked up a scrap of paper and handed it to me.

"Neeta Chacko!" The woman Daisy had revered as a midwife; the woman Daisy said would greet me with open arms—except she'd disappeared into thin air when I'd got there. "Neeta Chacko! How strange. Are you sure?"

"Yes, at least I think so."

"What did you say?"

"I said you were busy. She said she'd come back."

"Any idea where she went to?"

"No, sorry," and then, seeing my expression, she added, "Darling, in India you can't just ask any old Tom, Dick, or Hari in off the street, you must know that by now?"

Neeta Chacko was sitting in the baking sun on a wall in front of a vacant house when I found her. There were two cloth bundles in the dust at her feet. I'd seen a photograph of her at Wickam Farm, but had she not leapt up when she saw me, I wouldn't have recognized her.

"Ma'am, please, I must talk to you," she said, her eyes frantic. "Somewhere quiet, not here."

"Neeta!" I said. "What a surprise!" I'd heard nothing but praise about this woman: her energy, her tact, her competence. It was hard to connect her to the woebegone creature in front of me.

She looked like she needed something to eat. I decided on a modest fish café on the harbor, away from my mother and other nosy ears. Ropes of colored beads covered its dark entrance, and a Bovril advertisement hung on the wall outside.

When we sat down at the wobbly table inside, Neeta, half covering her face with the end of her sari, glanced fearfully at a group of men at the next table drinking beer and eating sambals.

When I tried to wedge a piece of paper under the table leg that was causing the wobble, I saw her toes were scuffed and bleeding.

"Have you walked a long way?" I asked.

"Yes, ma'am, I needed to see you." I ordered chai for us both, and when I asked if she was hungry, she shot me a desperate look, somewhere between shame and desire.

"Yes, ma'am," she whispered.

"Please don't call me ma'am," I said. "My name is Kit, we're colleagues." But she could not meet my eye. She ordered modestly: rice and some lentil thing, and when I ordered two extra dishes, she whispered sorry again in instant gratitude.

"Please don't say sorry," I said. "I'm glad to meet you; Daisy spoke so highly of you. I was disappointed when I came not to meet you." I heard her take a deep breath.

When the men left and the café had emptied, she looked at me over her glass of water, her eyes brimming with tears, and talked about how much she'd loved her time at the Moonstone.

"I felt I was growing every day." She wiped her eyes on her shawl. "I was learning in my profession, feeling part of our new country."

I told her I felt the same. "It's a very special place." And then I had to ask, "Are you ill, Neeta?" thinking this could be the extra cause of distress.

"No, ma'am." She shook her head. "I'm back at my home now, because my family wanted me to leave. My son was badly hurt."

"Where is your home?"

"Near here. Not far," she answered, with a vague flap of her hand. "I don't want to say exactly."

"Is your son better now?"

Neeta looked around the restaurant, then whispered across the table.

"Yes, ma'am."

"So, do you want your job back?"

She backed away from me and shook her head. "No, ma'am. I can't pay the men the money."

"What men?"

"I will tell you in a minute."

Her desolate look brightened for a moment at the approach of two plates of rice with curried goat scattered untidily on top of it. A small boy placed vegetables and chutneys on the table beside them. When she'd eaten ravenously for a while, she wiped her mouth daintily and looked at me.

"My son was beaten by some bad boys. They came to see him last week. They think he knows more than he does because I used to work there. They told him there will be big trouble at the Home soon."

"What boys? What trouble?" The rice I was eating sank like a stone in my stomach. "I don't know what you're talking about."

"They don't want you there. They want their money. When my son said he couldn't pay them, they beat him again. It's not safe."

It took awhile for her words to sink in. "What do you mean, not safe? Are you talking about the Home in general or me in particular?"

"Everything," she whispered.

"So who is paying this money?" I said. "And how much? And why are they bothering your son?"

She shook her head vigorously.

"I don't know. They don't believe him. I can't say any more. They are bad, bad men." She pushed her plate away.

"So, we must tell the police," I said at last.

"They won't care, they're part of it."

I thought for a while. It was hot, very hot inside the café, which had a tin roof. My brains felt fried.

"My father-in-law is a lawyer, a very honorable man," I said at last. "He might be able to help us."

Neeta looked skeptical. "Ma'am, if you say these things, they will close the Home down."

"You must tell me who gives the men the money." I was pleading with her. "I can't keep asking for it if I don't know where it's going."

"I can't say; they will hurt me badly, and if you tell Miss Barker, she'll stop sending the money." Neeta gave a ragged sigh. "She wrote to me, but I knew I must not reply."

She pushed her chair back and raised her eyes to me. A drop of blood fell from her right foot onto the floor.

"So what would you do, Neeta? Help me. Tell me honestly."

"I don't know, ma'am, you must say." A gust of wind, warm and smelling of fish, slammed the café door shut, and Neeta jerked as if she'd been shot. "I can't stay," she said. Scrabbling in one of her stained bags, she pulled out a piece of paper folded into four.

"My address," she said. "Don't show it to anyone, and please don't fix my name to the information I have given you." Her foot made a bloody print on the floor as she stood up.

"You're hurt," I said. "Come back to my house, I'll dress it."

"I can't," she said. "I've got to go home."

I gave her what I had in my purse—only a few rupees left over from paying the bill but enough, I hoped, to buy a little food or get her a rickshaw or bus home.

"One day," she said before we parted, "I pray God will let me do the work I'm trained for."

I wanted to shout, It's not God who bloody well forbids it, but instead said, "I'd back you up if you decided to go to the police. You know where I live now."

She shook her head. "I can't do that. I give my blessings to Miss Daisy Barker and to you." She bowed her head, put the palms of her hands together, and was gone.

*   *   *

Later, much much later, when I tried to piece this conversation together, I was amazed at how I could have been quite so stupid, ignored so many fire bells. Neeta had spelled the dangers out clearly, but in the two blocks it took me to walk home, I had decided to agree with her plan to do nothing. I'm trying to unravel this now. Why did I do that? One thing, but no excuse, was that Neeta's warning made me feel like a foreigner again, over my head and out of my depth in a country in a period of violent change, in a city whose deeper machinations I would probably never understand.

I was also, and maybe this was uppermost in my mind, now part of a family whose honor must be preserved. Any publicity about the Home with my name attached to it would be a social nightmare for them. We were also two weeks short of the government inspection Dr. A. had warned us about, the one that could close the Home down at a moment's notice. No, it doesn't wash, not really. I should have listened. Should have acted.

I was so deep in thought that I jumped when a boy leapt out at me. His skinny arm was festooned with bracelets: crude wooden things shaped like snakes with cheap-looking mirrors for eyes.

"Madam, Madam, stop!" he said. "I love you, thank you, please don't run."

But I was running, down the path, under the banyan tree, and out into the sun, the tarmac burning through the thin leather of my shoes.

I thought about Neeta's surprise appearance on and off all that night and might have mentioned it to Maya the next morning except there was a new crisis brewing at the Home and it involved me. With only two weeks to go before our government inspection, two of the midwives stood up and announced they wanted to go home.

Suleka and Madhavi were both from small villages north of Trivandrum. Madhavi was a small, fierce, wiry woman with wide-set eyes and smallpox scars on her cheeks. Maya said she'd looked unhappy from the start, refusing to dance or to tell the stories of birthing that the other women enjoyed. That morning, during prayers, I caught her looking at me with a hard, blank stare.

During a morning session on birth control, during which we discussed sterilization as one extreme measure, Madhavi stood up in a fury, let forth a fusillade of words in Malayalam, and jabbed her finger at me.

"What is she saying?"

Maya held up her hand to stem the flow. "She is cross."

"I can see that. What did she say? No soft-soaping."

"It's nothing, Kit." Maya blinked at me through her glasses.

"Come on, please." My conversation with Neeta had made me more nervous.

"She thinks," Maya said reluctantly, "you should go back to your own country and sterilize your own women there. She says this teaching is a government plot from your country and you are a spy." Maya's expression was caught halfway between merriment and embarrassment, but for one brief paranoid moment, I wondered whether she wasn't expressing a thought that she'd had too.

"What shall I say?" The other women were staring fixedly at me, one or two muttering in a way which made me feel how quickly the mood could change here.

Maya, keeping a serene smile on her face, muttered to me, "Tell her that's poppycock." She loved this word and used it as often as possible. I took a deep breath and faced the women.

"None of us are spies, that's a horrible thought, and nothing will happen unless we learn to trust each other. Let the men do the fighting." Maya smiled encouragingly. "Also I am married to an Indian man, he is a doctor."

They were still not convinced. Suleka, from Vaikkom, a stout, self-righteous woman, stood up, jabbed her finger at me, and began a shrill rant that went on and on: *squeak squeak*, *rant*, *rant*, with Maya growling back when she could get a word in edgeways.

It was hot. The fan in the reception room had broken, and I felt a sudden primitive urge to strike Suleka round the head and let loose myself. *Ungrateful bloody baggage, what have I ever done to you?* That would have put the cat amongst the pigeons, or am I the pigeon here?

"That mundi. Don't bother with her." Maya's eyes had narrowed into spiteful slits. She walked over to where Suleka was standing, put her face close to the woman, and gave her what sounded like a furious tongue lashing.

"She is life dust," Maya informed me at last. "Not worth talking to."

"Tell me what she said, Maya," I said. "Else I won't know, and my reports will be pointless."

"Nothing to tell. She says she wants money for the days she has wasted here, and money for transport home. She's taking her skinny friend with her, she says she has had a horrible time here also."

So, class dismissed. Five minutes or so later, on our way back to the wards, we giggled nervously when Maya confessed, "I wanted to strike her too. So rude, so ungrateful, plenty more to take her silly place."

"But I can see her point, sort of," I said. "If a group of Indian doctors came to England and talked about sterilization, it might cause a bit of a rumpus."

Maya, like me, was bored with being fair. "She is a rude woman," she repeated. "Please get her sterilized before she has rude children."

- CHAPTER 40 -

Anto felt grumpy when he got home from work. He'd had a long, fruitlessly busy day trying to penetrate layer upon layer of government bureaucracy to get a simple answer about funding for his research. No time for lunch. Kit was late getting home from the Moonstone. When he walked in, his mother-in-law leapt up, gave him a nautical salute, and said in a silly drawl, "Ah, sailor returns." She was sitting in his favorite chair on the veranda.

When Raffie toddled in, gave a reckless gummy smile, and ran into his arms, all Anto wanted to do was to lie on the floor with him and do the pretend wrestling Raffie loved, and smell his sweet skin.

But for Glory, dressed up and lipsticked, this was, as she announced gaily, "the *chottapeg* moment." A gin and it for her, and one for him. He'd tried gin, once at Oxford, hated its taste of old perfume, but she insisted on it: "I don't want to feel like some frightful old lush."

While they were drinking, he looked at her closely. A stunning beauty she must have been in her day, but the prominent cheekbones were growing sharper; her eyes looked bruised.

"How are you feeling, Glory?" She'd insisted on being called by her first name, but he still slipped sometimes and called her Mother. "Did you have a good sleep today?"

"I'm absolutely fine." She moved the ice around with her finger. "I shan't hang around much longer." She dipped her head, took a quick suck of her drink.

"What do you mean?" He was genuinely bewildered.

"I'll get out of your hair. Hotel, go home . . . something."

"Glory," he said gently, "you're not in my hair. You are my mother now too, and always welcome.

"But I'm thinking," he went on quickly, because her chin was puckering violently and she was plucking at her skirt, "you should definitely get your cough checked—an X-ray maybe. No shortage of doctors in our family."

"You're terribly sweet." She took another sip of her drink, recovered quickly, and looked at him grandly. "But you know, when you're old, you expect bits to drop off. So, tell me something funny about your day."

Oh Lord, he thought, the English thing. His tutor used to call them "the Western Orientals." So exhausting sometimes, quenching the laughter, the tears. He understood it only too well, it was part of his own routine now, and while he wracked his brains for a bit of light relief, she rattled on gaily about old people and their ailments and how extraordinarily boring they could be, telling him how Oscar Wilde had only allowed self-pity in the half-hour between three thirty and four. He laughed politely and watched her. She'd come here to die, he knew that: her pallor was growing day by day, and at night there was that gravelly cough. A few nights ago Kit had lain rigidly awake beside him, listening to her gasping and coughing. "I can't go in, can I?" she'd said, her face white in the moonlight. "She wants me to pretend I haven't heard."

And the dying were entitled to their secrets, so pouring another gin, waving the Angostura bitters over the drink just the way she liked, he told her about Arjunan Asan, an insufferable civil servant who'd dropped in to check on their department today and, puffed up with professional pride, told Anto that for the next few weeks he, Arjunan Asan, would be so busy that Anto would only have time to say good morning to him; no other conversation would be tolerated.

"Oh, the pompous prat." This went down a treat with his mother-in-law. "That *ullu ka patta*." She laughed.

Son of an owl. It was the first Indian expression she'd used in front of him, and she looked as surprised as he did. More than surprised. It was Raffie's look when he thought he'd done something very wicked, like being caught with a hand in the sweet tin.

- CHAPTER 41 -

I got home late on the night of the next big drama. I was running across the small *maidan*, the square at the end of our street, panicked at the thought of Mother and Raffie waiting for supper (Anto was away in Bombay), when a man ran up behind me and shouted, "Madam! Stop!" It was Murali from the vegetable shop.

I'd only ever known him as a genial smiling presence waving to me or wrapping my vegetables, but tonight his eyes were bulging with fright, his shirt soaked with sweat, and I had the sudden terrible thought that a bad thing had happened to Raffie and he'd been sent to find me.

Instead he told me, between gulps of air, that his young wife, Kamalakshi, was in very great pain. She was in the seventh month of her pregnancy. She had lost two babies already. "It will break our hearts to lose another."

I knew Kamalakshi only as a pair of dark eyes peering above a veil from a shadowy room at the back of the shop. Whenever she saw me, she backed away, like a beetle disappearing into the cracks.

"Can you get her to the Matha Moonstone?" I said to him. "I work there with the local doctors."

He squeezed his eyes shut to stop the tears falling. "Please, Madam, help me take her there." He clasped his hands together in prayer. "My son has a rickshaw."

In the heartbeat that followed, I thought of dinners going cold, Raffie bellowing for his good-night kiss. I was longing for bed, and a million miles away from being the saint he imagined me to be.

"There's a doctor on duty there tonight, and good nurses. They'll look after you. Try not to worry too much."

He tugged at my sleeve. "Please."

Kamalakshi was lying on a large pile of empty hessian sacks at the back of the storeroom when we found her. She was shaking, crying, holding her stomach. At the back of the room there was a lurid goddess statue, propped up by cans of cooking oil. When I asked if I could look at her, she wailed, but when Murali spoke crossly to her, she stared at him and moaned her assent. A few moments later, I got into the rickshaw with her, and with Murali behind, we sped off to the Home.

When we arrived at the Moonstone and bashed on the door, Parvati, one of the midwives, let us in.

In the surgery, Dr. A., gloved, gowned, brisk, and comfortingly bossy, did the preliminary investigations, removing the loincloth that women here use for their periods. With her hand on Kamalakshi's stomach, she delivered the good news.

"Everything is fine, baby is still there. Find her a bed for the night. This baby is impatient to be born."

Murali said he didn't want his wife to stay overnight, but Dr. A., inflating like a puff adder, said this was not for discussion, it was imperative. Parvati would watch over her, and so would she. Treatment could not be finer.

Murali gave in with the relief of a tired child ordered to bed. His gratitude poured out.

"*Nunni valarey, valarey nunni,*" Thanks, much, much thanks. He insisted I take his rickshaw home, but even so, it was well past midnight when I arrived. Apart from a faint light coming from my mother's room, the house was cloaked in blue darkness. In the distance, I could hear the hoot of a steamship.

When I crept up the stairs and into Raffie's room and stroked his hair, I felt puffs of air coming from his mouth onto my hand, and the simple fact of his being alive seemed in that moment to be the most stupendous gift. I kissed him, adjusted his nightshirt, and he, involved in some lip-smacking dream of his own, barely stirred, except to kick out one fat honey-colored leg.

"I love you, Raffie," I whispered. "I love my boy."

I went out like a light after that, until *meesskweet, misssskweet* . . . Coming up with the greatest reluctance through various levels of sleep, I thought at first I heard birds chirruping and then my name. When I opened my eyes, the predawn light was blue and full of shadows. I heard a jumble of voices in the street and, when I opened my eyes, the rickety sound Raffie makes when he's woken suddenly.

"Miss Kit!" The voice outside was panicked and thin. When I ran to the window, Maya's gray face looked up at me.

"Hurry, Miss Kit, hurry," she said. "The Home is on fire and I can't find Dr. Annakutty." I felt perfectly blank with shock as I buttoned my dress and put on my shoes, as if everything around me would break if I didn't remain perfectly calm. I was calm too when I gave Kamalam instructions about Raffie and my mother's breakfast. During my training at Saint Andrew's, we'd had fire drills aplenty and lots of false alarms, but at the Moonstone, there had been no training and no warnings. I should have thought of that.

Outside on the street, Babu from the grocery shop had arrived, unshaven, groggy with sleep, and in his night lunghi. Maya, crouched near the bushes, was crying and pleading and speaking broken sentences that made no sense. She point-blank refused to get into Babu's rickshaw, so we raced, hand in hand, towards the Home.

The street was shadowy and dark, the sky still full of pin-bright stars. When I caught my heel on a broken pavement and fell headlong, Maya jerked me up roughly. "Hurry, Madam, come."

At the corner of Main and Tower Streets, we came to a skidding halt. It was a terrible shock to see our Home crackling and burning and the sky above it full of a rosy and unstable glow in which black objects floated and swirled.

"Oh my God. Oh my God." Maya wailed and clutched my arm. She'd tried to reassure me on the way that the fire engines would get there before we did.

I felt myself go cold. We'd tried, before the government inspection, to keep patient numbers down, so we could clean and white-wash the wards, but this was our worst nightmare: we had four patients inside: one woman about to deliver, two for observation, and Murali's wife, possibly with a new baby.

At the gate I was stopped by two young policemen with *lathis* in their hands. "Don't go there," said one. "You will burn to death." They weren't exaggerating. From fifty yards away, I could feel the fire's tremendous heat. The flames surged and died and surged again, and when they surged, the small crowd gathered by the gate went "Oooh" and shrank back; one or two of them even laughed as if this were a child's game.

"What are they doing? What are they doing?" I yelled. I could see three or four boys running from the building, putting tables, chairs, a filing cabinet onto a waiting bullock cart. Maya dashed towards them shrieking and came back with her face black with soot.

"Where are the patients?" I yelled to her.

"Two out, two still there," she shouted back. "They're moving them now. Fire has not touched the back ward." She sank to her knees and put her head in her hands.

"Where are the fire engines?" I shouted. "Why aren't they here?"

Maya spat a black cinder into her hand and began to sob. "They were here, they went away. They ran out of water. They said they would come back."

The crowd near the gate was growing. They were watching

smoke pouring from the roof and the porch. When Mr. Namboothiri's lovely yellow and purple sign started to blister and run, someone in the crowd gave a small cheer, and I wanted to punch him.

It was getting lighter now and the flowers, the geraniums we'd planted, stood out in a red haze almost surreally bright in the half-light of dawn. Murali appeared, sobbing with relief. His wife had a three-hour-old baby boy, and they had been rescued. He was taking her home. Then Maya dashed towards me, her big glasses rimmed with soot. She suddenly clapped her hand over her mouth.

"Oh my God, Miss Kit," she said, "there's one more patient in the dispensary room. I don't know if they got her out, and the firemen have gone."

"Do the firemen have the key?"

"I have it here," Maya said. "We must go in."

The policemen on the gate let us through, not eager to come with us. As we walked through the smoke, I saw the main part of the roof collapse in a jumble of wooden struts that stood out like ribs against the predawn light. I heard the murmur of the crowd behind us, as Maya and I covered our faces in our shawls and ran down the path towards the dispensary.

The wind changed as we ran, and when the smoke moved towards us, we started to cough. My legs had turned to liquid and my head was shouting, Don't make me do this! I don't want to die! but I was moving forward. When I looked at Maya she was praying.

"In quickly," Maya shouted, waving the bunch of keys. "Out quickly. We can do it." When we were less than twenty feet from the dispensary door, two local policemen appeared, one tall, one short, faces covered in the black slime that soot and sweat makes. At first they tried to push us back. They snatched the keys from

Maya. Then we all stopped. A baby was crying inside. A high-pitched wail. Maya started to scream and bang on the door.

The dispensary had been flung up as a temporary dwelling—tin roof, cheap door—to house a few patients while necessary repairs had been done to the main house. Its door had swelled in the last monsoon, and now the tall man was having trouble with it, yelling and kicking and shoving the key fruitlessly from side to side.

Maya grabbed the keys back. Now we could hear a woman's voice, a squeal of fear, and a baby shrieking. Maya swore and wrestled and grunted, trying the key this way and that. No luck.

"You try." She handed me the keys. My eyes were streaming, my fingers felt swollen and useless. I tried one key after the other, sobbing, swearing, "Come on, you bastard, do it! Do it."

After a few seconds that felt like a lifetime, I felt the lock swivel, click, give. A gigantic kick from Maya shattered the door and in we went.

The smoke was chokingly thick inside the room. We couldn't see anything at first, we could only blunder in the general direction of a screaming voice, a prolonged coughing fit. The baby had stopped crying. I paused for a moment, hearing the booming crash of the ceiling falling in another part of the building, and after a moment or two of stumbling around, I felt a hand clawing at me. A wild-eyed woman loomed into view, hair loose, face wet with sweat. She was clinging to the bed with one arm, and held the baby in the other. She was shouting over and over in a monotonous wail, "*Ayyoo daivamey . . . Rekshikkaney*," cries for help from God that I was familiar with by now.

The baby was screaming again. Maya wrapped her shawl around its purple face and the tiny body, which now lashed out convulsively.

"Get the baby out," she shouted. "The back, not the front," where the fire was still raging. The policemen, who had hung back, pushed us through the door that led from the back of the dispensary, over a small strip of concrete, and towards the seven-foot wall that bounded our property. Glass and barbed wire had been put on top of the wall after the last break-in.

We stood for a moment, all of us, in the flickering red light. Three women, one postpartum and bent double, two men, and the baby, its mouth a dark red hole of protest.

"We can't do it." I looked up at the wall, the red sky above it, the dark ash spiraling up. "We'll have to run back by the path." I tried to take the baby, but the mother held her like a vise. Maya, shouting ferociously, wrenched the mother's arms apart and flung the baby in mine, a soft, light, shrieking bundle.

"Go first!" she screamed. "Open the gate, take the baby. God bless you."

And then the weight of the baby in my arms. So light, so easily disposed of. I remember closing my eyes and the sensation of running. Quickly speeding through my mind: Anto, Raffie, my mother. Amma. Finally, sitting on the ground, the feeling of grit and earth underneath me, pain flaring in my arm, and bells ringing before the lights went out.

Burns, I knew from my training, don't hurt in the way you might imagine. First-degree burns can hurt like hell: they catch the top layer of nerve endings. The more serious second-degree burns are often less painful, because the damage is greater and the heat seared through the nerve and the sweat glands. Most serious of all: third-degree burns, which can send a patient's body into a state of shock that resembles coma.

The second-degree burns to my arms and lower legs felt like being stung by a thousand bees but were not serious enough to keep me in the General Hospital in Ernakulum for more than a couple of days. A much worse pain for me, as I lay in my room on the third floor, watching my skin turn chalky and white, was the knowledge that I'd been so stupid.

I kept imagining the conversation I might have with Daisy, who would turn herself inside out not to blame me.

"So you were told by Neeta before the fire that funds were definitely being embezzled?"

Yes.

"That the Home had clear enemies?"

Yes.

"That arson, or some kind of attack, had been threatened."

Yes.

"And you decided to do nothing."

Yes. Or was it no, or maybe?

The facts were so shot through with holes and uncertainties that my mind, like a bird trapped in a windowless room, dashed around for excuses. I had definitely dropped hints, tried openings, made tentative suggestions to Dr. A., and asked many times for accounts. But I should have been clearer, braver, less anxious about being the know-all memsahib, and although nobody had been killed, the Home was now a smoldering wreck, and that was partly my fault. I'd behaved like a coward.

On my third day in hospital, it was Glory who, to my horror and amazement, turned up to drive me home. Pale and thin in the blinding sunlight, she was wearing a green silk suit and white crocheted driving gloves, and when I saw her behind the wheel of Appan's car, I thought at first I was hallucinating.

"I didn't know you could do this," I said nervously, as she threaded her way through a street market, hand on horn, shouting *"Kazhutha!"* Donkey! at a careless rickshaw driver.

"Well, there's quite a lot you don't know about me," she said with a pert look. "I did this all the time when I worked in Ooty for Major General Willoughby and his wife." Another employer floating up from the mists of her past. "He loathed driving up hills and rather liked me."

I looked at her in amazement: a pale shadow of herself a few weeks ago, now double-declutching and flipping out her indicator at the crossroads. The mother I thought I'd imagined had flared into life again.

"D'you promise me Anto and Raffie are all right?" I said, when we stopped to let a bullock cart go by. I'd worried about them obsessively in hospital but felt Raffie was too young to visit me. The burns unit was a frightening place.

"Fine and dandy." She was checking her lipstick in the rearview mirror. "Raffie and I played trains yesterday. I think he quite likes his old grandma now."

"Anto?" I gripped the handle on the side of the car.

"He phoned again yesterday, from some godforsaken place. Typical man, never bloody well there when you need him," she added, with a flash of her old bitterness.

She made me rest on the sofa all afternoon, joking I was her "little dolly" again. She played with Raffie and bossed Kamalam, telling her I was tired and to take Raffie for a walk. She went upstairs to find me a decent nightdress to wear. The nighty she brought down, cherished in tissue paper like some holy relic, was Christian Dior. A present from an admirer? Something she'd borrowed and forgotten to take back? Hard to tell. She said she'd never worn it and was keeping it for her funeral.

As I lifted the tissue, the faint musky sweetness of dried lavender floated in the air.

"Wickam," I said, hearing the click of Daisy's secateurs as we stripped the plants and poured the flowers into small muslin bags. I began to cry.

"Whatever's the matter?" my mother asked.

"The Moonstone," I said. "I've got to tell Daisy about it."

"Well, Daisy won't blame you."

"She should."

"That is absolute codswallop," she said. It was strange to feel her arms around me. "How could it possibly be your fault? You didn't do it." The mother tiger again, eyes blazing with indignation.

"I could have done more. I'd heard rumors from the moment I got there."

"Oh, stop that." She adjusted the ribbon on my nightdress and glared at me. "Stop it immediately. There are always rumors. You can't spread panic. Besides, Indians love a drama."

I let it pass. The days were long gone when she could kiss and make it better. "Do you promise nobody died?" I'd asked for the umpteenth time that day.

"Nobody died." My mother said this in a firm voice. She put one hand over her eye, which was never a good sign. "And I actually meant to tell you this: I got a telegram from Daisy this morning. She knows and she says the main thing is you're safe, and you're not to worry about a thing."

"Honestly?"

"Honestly."

"Can I see the telegram?"

She put her cup down and gave me her hurt look. The one I'd dreaded for years. "You never believe a word I say, do you?" she said. "And that's quite upsetting, you know."

I chose my words carefully, knowing the wrong ones would send us both tumbling into a dark and frightening place.

"I believe . . . I think you sometimes tried to make the world seem nicer than it is."

"Oh, really?" Her eyes narrowed. "Can you give me an example of that?"

I thought for a moment. "Well, I seem to remember an incident when we saw a dead rabbit on the road, and when I asked what had happened to it, you said it was having a little sleep on its way to a party. That might be one example."

It felt like a high-board moment, but Glory flung back her head and laughed, the first time I'd seen her do that in a long time.

"I do remember that. Flat as a pancake on the road, and you crying your silly eyes out. We were off to Northumberland: that widower, ex-Navy, who couldn't, in six months, ever quite get the hang of my name. Rude bugger. The car broke down twice. We had to walk the last mile or so with our suitcases."

"I don't remember that bit," I said.

"No," she said quietly. "Of course you don't."

"It wasn't easy for you, Mum," I broke the silence that followed. "I can see that now."

"My fault," she said, almost brusquely. "And please don't call me Mum, it's common."

"Your fault for what?" I said. She was clutching at her pearls, twisting them.

"I was feeble, really."

"Feeble! I'd never call you that!"

"I was." She scratched her head. "I've lived my whole life in a sort of dream. At least you were brave."

Sweat broke out along my hairline and scalp. My mother making me into some sort of martyr felt completely unbearable.

"No."

"Brave enough to make mistakes, I mean, to defy me."

"Well, that." We smiled in a wary way at each other. "I suppose. Not often."

Another long silence fell between us. "Anto wasn't one of my mistakes, Mummy," I said at the end of it. "You do know that, don't you? I love him."

"Oh, love," she said vaguely. She took off her pearls and examined their gold clasp. "We'll see," she said, laying them down. "I can certainly see the attraction. He's very good-looking." Her smile was hard, defiant, her don't-think-you-invented-sex look.

I let it lie. We'd come as far as we could today without hurting each other too badly. Now I hoped she'd go away and have a rest, and I could spend some time with Raffie, whom I could hear upstairs playing with his train with Kamalam, but instead, and to my alarm, she kicked off her shoes and lay beside me.

"One more thing." She sounded breathless again. "You know that story I told at lunch about finding the extra room at Wickam? The one we didn't know about? I don't suppose you believed a word of that either."

"It was a good story," I said, meaning, I'm too tired, don't make me think about it. The clutch of her hand, the frantic look in her eyes signaled more emotion than I could cope with.

"People dream about that," she said. "Don't they? Discovering a marvelous extra room in their house—a place they knew nothing about before, a place that makes everything feel more spacious."

Actually, I'd never heard of this but I let it go. "What was it like? I mean, was there even a hidden basement?" I asked, more out of politeness than anything. "Daisy hadn't mentioned it."

"Well, there is one and it's horrible," she said. "There was a nest of squirrels in the ceiling and their peepee had dripped through the floorboards, so it stank, and all we found at first were heaps of clothes and a dead rat. But here was the thing." She clutched my arm now. "When my eyes had grown accustomed to the light, there were three pictures stacked against the wall. As I said at lunch, Daisy's father was an art student at the Slade before the war. I actually joked to Daisy, 'If there's a Picasso here, all our troubles will be over.' And there it was, suddenly, this tiny canvas, with his signature on the corner. We took it towards the light to check we weren't going mad, and it really did crumble like sawdust in Daisy's hand, and I wanted to scream." Glory shifted on the bed, her sharp hip bone sticking into mine. "I was so livid with Daisy for being so careless. I suppose her mind was on higher things, but what a fool."

"She has an awful lot to think about," I said woodenly. I couldn't bear hearing Daisy described like this.

"Clever women are often very stupid." A favorite theme of my mother's. "It would have paid for *everything*: the roof, the barn, the new fences. And she longs of course to come back to India."

"Wickam felt like the only real home we ever had," I said. "You must have felt it too."

"I know you like her better than me," Glory said suddenly. "I don't blame you; she's better than me."

"Mummy, no!" And then words failed me and we gazed miserably at each other.

"That's not the point. Let me finish what I wanted to say." She hauled herself up on the pillows and clutched my hand again. "Daisy gave me something else that day you might be interested in." She got up from the bed, sat down in a chair, and faced me. "A box of letters." Dramatic pause.

"Love letters, bills, what?" I was sticky hot again and weary of her.

"Not love letters, not bills." Another pause pregnant with meaning. "Letters from your father."

She licked her lips and stared at me. "Enclosing money for you."

"*Money* for *me*?"

"Yes." I could hardly hear her now.

"Ever since you were born, he sent it over, every three months: enough to keep you ticking over. I made Daisy swear never to tell you, so she gave it to me as wages."

My mind went perfectly blank.

"Why couldn't Daisy let me know? And why wages? I don't understand."

"Because your father was a shit." She spat the word out. "Oh, don't look at me like that. He let me down badly, so I sent him away. I told him . . ."

"No, don't tell me! Let me guess . . ." I still felt surprisingly calm. "He was dead to you."

When I tried to get up, pain flared in my hand, and I felt dizzy.

"Why tell me now?" I said to her after an incredulous pause. "What in the hell is the point of that? God, I wish Daisy, at least, had told me, or even showed me the letters!"

"I told her we'd leave if she did, but that's not the point. The point is this," she said in a flat voice. She raised her head and looked at me. "He lives in Ooty. Not far from here. Have you heard of it?"

I had of course. Every one knew about Ootcatamund—snooty Ooty—the butt of many jokes about gin fizzes, polo, brigadiers, retired boxwallahs.

"Are you sure?" I stared at her, feeling nothing: not thrilled, not grateful, not relieved. A big blank nothing. "I don't understand."

"He stayed on. It's a long story, and he stopped sending the money ages ago." I could almost feel her deflating, regretting this already. "And don't expect a fairy tale," Glory continued, voice squeezed. "He'll be old and tired like me. Daisy, who gets the odd note from him, says he doesn't have a bean."

"Well, that's wonderful news." I was angrier than I'd been in a long time. She might have been talking about a distant friend's lost dog. "Anything else I should know? I don't know, a twin I haven't met or something?"

"Not a thing," she said with a defiant look. "And no need to take that tone with me. I'm going to go and have a zizz. I've had enough of today. I just thought you'd want to know," she added in a huffy voice as she left the room, as if I were the one who was being unreasonable.

After she left, I felt so unhinged I wanted to scream. Instead, I sat and stared wide-eyed at the darkness, and then I put a pillow over my head and fell into a strange sleep that was like falling into a deep hole. There were no brilliant dream rooms where I went, just dread, and shock and suspicion, and a sense of swooning shame before my mind shorted out.

The slam of a door woke me up. Anto's footsteps ascended the stairs. When he dashed into our room, I put my good hand over his mouth.

"Have you spoken to my mother?" I couldn't bring myself to tell him about my possible father, in case this proved another version of the dead rabbit story; I couldn't risk the pain.

"Haven't seen her." His words tumbled out. "I wanted to see you first. How is your hand? I'm so sorry I was away. I won't do that again."

"Arm fine." I lifted my bandaged left arm to show him, "And

leg even better. No infection, healed well. Oh Lord." I squeezed my eyes shut, feeling that if I started crying, I would never stop. "Please don't be nice to me. It's not as if I wasn't warned."

He kicked off his shoes, pulled off his dusty shirt, and lay on the bed looking at me. "It's my fault."

"For what?"

"For leaving you alone." He threaded his fingers in my hair. "I don't know what I've been thinking, when I have a wife and child at home."

"No," I said. "That's not right. You have to do your work, but I've been such an idiot, I should have talked to you ages ago. Have you seen the damage?"

He put his hand on his lips to shush me.

"I went on my way here."

"And?"

"It's a mess. There were some locals there, some of them looting. The Home was always going to be controversial after Independence. One way or another, it would have happened. But here's the thing, Kit." He put his hand on the top of my head, and I heard him sigh. "I spoke to Appan. There will be an inquiry, and I think you'll have to give evidence."

"Me?"

"Yes, and the rest of the staff, but you've attracted some attention, naturally."

My mind began racing. "What if they find out I've been delivering babies and I'm not fully qualified?" Anto stared at me, thinking hard.

"I didn't lie to Dr. A.," I said. "We just got so busy. She did say she would write and get me accredited. I've never asked her to show me the papers, and my guess is she's done nothing, because if she'd done something, she would have shown them to me.

"Kittykutty, you're not on trial to me, and the inquiry will be far more concerned with who started the fire."

"I know, but I went ahead without those assurances and that was so stupid. I should have said no."

"Well, you didn't." He stroked my hair. "And if all the unqualified women in India who delivered babies were tried, the jails would overflow."

"But in their eyes, I'm a foreigner. They might make an example of me."

"They might," Anto said calmly. "And if they do, we'll ask Appan for advice. He'll know exactly what to do."

"If he finds out I'm unlicensed, he'll hit the roof."

"Appan is a realist, he'll do what's necessary. Now, stop talking and show me your arm." He unwrapped my bandages and looked closely at the blisters, already crusted and healing. He asked what ointment I was putting on it. Then he applied some more Germolene and bandaged my arm neatly. Looking at his glossy head bent over my arm, I thought, What have I done to deserve you?

A couple of days later, Anto and I, after putting Raffie to bed, were strolling on the waterfront after supper. It had rained fiercely for an hour or two that afternoon, and the sky was misty and gray.

Anchored across the water there was a rusty old cargo ship with Arabic lettering on it. We were trying to imagine what it carried when I blurted out, "Anto, while you were away, my mother told me the oddest thing." I tried for a lightness of tone I didn't feel, because even saying it out loud threatened me. I'm not sure what frightened me most, my longing or my anger, but my family background, whether false or true, seemed so shallow, so threadbare, compared to the clever, dignified, solidly rooted Thekkedens.

When I'd finished talking, he sat down on a bench. I could see him thinking, and I thought, I've put him off me now. I'm not good enough, and never will be—a terrible moment of darkness and insecurity.

At last he said, "Are you angry with Daisy for not telling you?"

"No. I think she knew Glory might leave and never come back, and that would have upset her: Daisy knew I adored her, and the feeling was mutual; she once told me I was the daughter she'd never had."

"Well, I think it was brave of Glory to tell you after all this time," Anto continued.

"Really?"

"Really. She had much to lose and nothing to gain."

"Well, possibly." I wasn't convinced. "And you always stick up for her anyway." It was a feeble joke because I was still shivering and felt in danger.

"Well, I believe in mothers," he said, "even imperfect ones. Don't forget I was without one for many years."

"But yours isn't a nutcase. Don't you think the timing was odd?" I still needed some indignation on my behalf. "I've been nagging her to tell me for years and she waits until the Home burns down."

"Not so odd. She knew you could have died in the fire. Hence the high-speed dash in Appan's car." I'd made him laugh earlier describing the driving gloves, the double-declutching. "I would say it was a moment of truth."

"Not something she has many of." I was still angry. "And that's another thing: how in the hell do I know it's true?"

He gave me a long, considering look, and in it I saw my own hurt and confusion reflected and thought, That's what love looks like.

"What did you feel," he said at last, "when you first heard about even the possibility of him?"

"Nothing," I said. "Not a thing."

He thought for a bit. "I understand that," he said. "That day we arrived at Mangalath, I felt the same. Too much noise, too much attention on me. I thought I wouldn't mind if I never saw them again. I was so used to living without them."

"But at least you knew them."

"Kit." He put his arm around me. "What are you most frightened of?"

"Everything. Really."

"That he'll be an ax murderer, a hopeless drunk, a wog-hating tea planter?"

"All of the above." My laugh was a croak.

"Ooty's not far. We could get there in a day. I'll come, or you can take your mother, if that's what she wants."

I told him there were now more important things to do. A note, signed by Dr. A., had been dropped through our door by a rickshaw boy that morning. "Urgent staff meeting. Moonstone. Two o'clock Thursday," was its brief message, and because I felt well enough— I could move my arm freely, now that a shiny pinkish skin had appeared over the original burn—I badly wanted to go. I felt a survivor's need to talk about what had happened, and I wanted to confirm with Dr. A. that I was officially accredited. If there was to be a government inquiry, I needed to prepare for it.

"And then what?" He was quietly persistent. "The meeting won't take long, and this business with your father will work away at you if you don't act." I told him not to push me. I told him I would have to think about it. I told him not to discuss it with my mother. The whole idea of meeting my father after all this time filled me with a kind of fizzing panic. I needed time to think.

It was a shock seeing the Moonstone again. Everything about it foretold its end. Its splendid purple and yellow sign was a charred mess; the main building, shrouded in tarpaulins, stank of charcoal; the old fish tank we'd converted to keep prem babies in lay smashed and useless, alongside upturned beds and broken petri dishes. Dr. A. held the meeting in the only serviceable room now, a tin hut in the garden where we once stored garden equipment. Maya, myself, and two nurses had been invited.

Dr. A., at her most grand and imperturbable, chaired the meeting from a wonky garden chair. When we were settled, she opened a large leather-bound book with a torn cover and bleached bindings and said in a flat voice, "Fortunately, our account book survived the blaze."

This surprised me, given its illusive nature before.

"So,"—mirthless smile—"let's not waste time on any spilt-milk talk. Nobody died, thanks to quick action by our staff, but we are facing a big crisis." I couldn't tell if she was praying or counting as her lips moved and her fingers slid down a column of figures.

"I estimate," she said at last, "that to restock the Home: chairs, beds, boiler, floor coverings, will alone cost us in the vicinity of"— her eyes went blank as she did some quick sums—"six thousand rupees." She sighed heavily. "Training equipment cost, approximately one thousand rupees. Rebuilding of wards, God knows, I am waiting for quotations from our builder. It won't be cheap."

Maya gave a small groan.

"Replanting garden, five hundred rupees. New sign,"—her voice had sunk to an almost inaudible whisper—"fans, benches. So, actually . . ." She closed the book. "We must face the facts: all our plans, all our hopes are dashed. Work of last five years is over." She looked directly at me and administered the final kick.

"And there were people who didn't like you here," she said.

There was a moment of terrible stillness and calm in the room. Maya took off her glasses and rubbed her eyes. Dr. A. scrutinized the book again, as if the money might be hiding somewhere in its pages. The nurses bowed their heads and sighed. Sweat broke out along my hairline and scalp and down my spine; it was bakingly hot in that shed, and someone's armpits were giving out a fruity pungence.

"The government will not provide this money," she said to me again, "so there is only one solution: we must turn to Miss Daisy Barker and her committee again." I heard Maya murmur her agreement.

I did a quick calculation in my head. Twenty-one thousand rupees to get the Home up and running again. It was roughly three thousand pounds, an awful lot of pots of jam, pickled onions, and jumble sales.

"She hasn't got that much money," I said at last. "She's actually quite poor."

Maya spoke now, in a thin sarcastic voice, one I'd never heard before. "When she was here, I saw a photo album picture of her house and her car. I would like to be poor like that."

"I'm not sure you would." I was stung by her tone. "That house is an elephant around her neck: it leaks, it's freezing cold, there were snowdrifts up to the windows last winter. When you wash in the morning, you break the ice on the water *inside* the house. And the car, by the way, is held together with sticking plaster."

Dr. A. looked at me blankly.

"Won't your new government help at all?" I said. "They gave us a grant."

"No." Dr. A. seemed very sure about this. "They will blame us for the fire."

"Why would they blame us for that?" I asked.

Dr. A. closed her eyes. When she opened them again, she flashed me a warning look. "This for the police to decide, not us. Meeting is over; you can stay behind," she said to me.

The nurses had looked so funereal during the meeting that it surprised me to hear a sudden burst of laughter as they stepped into the flat, bright sunshine, and it seemed to emphasize the sudden gulf between us. In their world suffering, the chaotic nature of life, was accepted as normal, and while I admired their resilience and could see that passivity in these circumstances might be a strength, it infuriated me too. I was also hurt by Maya's flash of hostility; she'd barely met my eye during the meeting.

In the hut, Dr. A. gave me a frowning, considering look.

"I wanted to ask you something," she said. "But not in front of the others. Police found rags in the garden soaked with paraffin. One of the rags had been torn from a dress. The label in the collar of the dress said Tuttles. Is that an English company?"

"Yes, it is."

"Do you have any clothes from there?"

"Yes." I could feel my mouth go dry. "A blue dress. But I didn't do it, you must know that—"

"It doesn't matter what I think," she interrupted me. "And there is more. There was a note left near the bonfire, when it had burned out. It said, 'The Englishwoman is a spy.' Do you have enemies here?"

My head was scrambling. "I don't know. I don't think so," I said, "but you can't possibly believe I did it. Why would I? It makes no sense."

"Police will interview you soon, so you must get your story straight." She put her head in her hand and looked at me, and I saw that lines were being drawn and teams picked, and I was not on hers.

"Could we open the door please?" I asked. The heat was intolerable and I felt light-headed. The hut smelt of coconut oil and female sweat, petrol from the mowing machine.

"No. Others will come; this is private." Sweat trickled down the side of her face. "Is there nothing else you want to say?"

"This may or may not be relevant," I said at last, "but about a year ago, a boy followed me home from the Moonstone. I was taking a shortcut through what was the English Club gardens. He tried to touch me. When I fought him off, he spoke angrily about our work."

Dr. A. remained motionless. Her strangely prominent eyes bulged while she continued to look at me.

"What did he look like?"

I drew a line along my lip. "Thin mustache, about eighteen, I would say. Very skinny."

"What angry thing did he say?" She picked up a pen and began to make notes.

"Oh, the usual. That I was a foreign woman, teaching Indians, no right to be here now, and so forth."

"Why didn't you tell us before?"

"I should have, but I didn't want my husband to know and stop me working here. I thought you might not care, might even . . ." I stopped myself saying, think the same way yourself.

"I do care," she said drily, making more notes in her book. It raced through my mind that I should tell her now about my meeting with Neeta Chacko, but I was in a dilemma: Chacko had pleaded with me, with tears in her eyes, not to reveal her as a source of information. Plus Dr. A. had forbidden me to talk about Chacko again. This could prove a mousetrap with no cheese.

"But there is one more important question to address. When you came here, I was told you were fully qualified English midwife. If you are interviewed, the police will want to see your qualification papers. Do you have them?"

I felt a flush of heat race through my body. "You know I don't, Dr. Annakutty. I am a fully qualified nurse but two deliveries shy of the full midwifery qualifications. I told you that on the first day I was here. You told me that when the time had come, you'd ask the government for full accreditation. I should have asked for that. I didn't. But why, if I didn't have it, did *you* let *me* deliver babies?"

She gave me her basilisk stare. I may as well not have spoken.

"I have no record of it." She opened the leather accounts book and shook her head regretfully. "I took you on in good faith. I'm not saying they will check you, but they might: the gorement now are very fussy about the correct paperwork."

"This is not fair," I said, "and you know it."

"Which is why," she sailed on, "I tried to suggest earlier that money from Daisy Barker would be a better way than trying to get money out of a gorement already squeezed. Do you understand that?"

I did. *Blackmail*: ugly word, ugly feeling.

I was down by the harbor half an hour later, sitting on the seawall by myself, absorbing the shock of all this, when Maya sat down beside me. She placed at her feet the small canvas bag that usually held her lunch tiffin and gave me a sideways conciliatory look as if she wanted to make up.

"What did she say?" she asked. Her eyes darted nervously over my shoulder.

"I think I'm in trouble, Maya," I said. "But I don't really want to talk about it." I wanted to tell her about the scrap of my blue dress they said they'd found and the petrol. I wanted to tell her about the boy in the park, but I didn't know who to trust now or what to say.

"Dr. Annakutty doesn't always put things well into words," she said at last. "But she has no family supporting her, and no children. She's given up everything for this, and she is a fine doctor."

"I know." I was almost too low to speak.

"You should see the home she lives in." Maya peered at me.

"I doubt I will."

"I liked working with you," she added softly. "You were a good nurse. We learned a lot." The past tense saddened me more than I could say.

"So you think it will close too?"

"Yes." Maya scrabbled in her bag. "Sorry." She dabbed her eyes with a handkerchief.

When I thought of what it had cost Maya to work at the Moonstone—the nights spent studying under streetlamps in Madras, the cramped dormitories, the terrible food, the beatings from her husband, her bravery at riding it out—my right foot kicked out in frustration and sent Maya's bag flying. A roll of bandages unfurled and a jar of Germolene cream shattered in the dirt.

"Don't do that," I said. She was kneeling in the dirt, trying to scoop some of the cream onto a shard of glass. "I've got some at home. I'll give you a new jar."

"Don't worry, ma'am." Maya carefully wrapped the piece of glass in her handkerchief. "I can use this too. It's for my aunt. She's hurt her foot."

"I'll bring it tomorrow," I said. "Don't cut yourself."

"I won't be here," she said. "I'm coming next week, for the cleanup." This was something we'd all agreed to do before the meeting broke up.

"What will you do after that?" I asked.

"I don't know." She glanced at me. "Stay home with husband," came the bleak reply. "He doesn't want me to work again. He'll be glad."

As I watched her small, upright figure walk towards the ferry that would take her home, I wanted to scream. I can't presume to understand the thoughts in her head, but I knew they would run along the lines of all this being part of God's plan for her, her punishment even for getting above herself, or for sins committed in a past life.

I admired the stoicism. I hated it too: the meek surrender of all that training and hope and energy. She was a fine midwife; India needed her. Why did it have to be so hard?

- CHAPTER 43 -

On the day of the cleanup, I kissed Raffie good-bye and told Kamalam what to give him for his lunch. I was about to leave for the Moonstone when my mother, after a prolonged cough and an "Oh blast!" said, "Have you thought any more about what I told you?"

"About what?"

"About Ooty?" My mother clung to the veranda railings and took several shuddering breaths. She had dizzy spells now.

"Oh, Glory," I said. "Isn't it all too much?" The very thought of Ooty made me go blank with terror.

"I just thought it might be a nice break for you, darling," she said sunnily. "You've had a perfectly horrid time here recently and it's nice and cool up there."

After work, I took Raffie out in his pram and continued a bitter conversation with her in my head. Oh, a nice break indeed, meeting a father I had never ever seen, who'd been successfully buried by my mother till now. A lovely little hols, tracking him down and filling the black hole of his absence with what? Shock? Embarrassment? Remorse? Or something worse and more damaging: bitter, bilious rage at how he's successfully ignored us for years and years and years?

But another part of me had also leapt into life at the thought of meeting him, and as I walked, I ran a film of him in my head. He was wearing a tweed jacket, tall, distinguished, a kind smile. He was my twin, only older and a man. He was hugging me, saying father things,

My God, my little girl. My darling, after all these years. Crying at the waste of us; hugging Raffie too, the grandson he never knew he had.

When Raffie's bellows interrupted this train of thought, I took him out of his pram and cuddled him. He was teething again and unusually miserable and demanding. Any normal grandfather would hand him right back. That's what I said to myself, trying to make things normal again. I put Raffie on my knee, grateful for the solid reality of his plump little body, now patting me on the lips, then wriggling to be let go, and I thought, This is my life now, and if I met my father and it all went wrong, it would set the cap on one of the worst months of my life. And yet . . . and yet . . .

All these thoughts were spiraling and somersaulting in my head when someone ran up behind me and made me jump.

"Miss Kit. Miss Kit." It was Neeta Chacko, breathless and agitated.

"Please, I beg you to help me. They have caught my boy Pavitran. They have taken him to the police station and beaten him severely there, and now he is in the jail on Tower Road. They came to our house this morning."

"Neeta!" She'd seemed so petrified the last time I saw her, I'd assumed her plan was to scuttle back into hiding. Now she was gray with fear and trembling.

"What did he do?"

"They say he torched the Home. I know he didn't. They are definitely making him a scarecrow."

"A scarecrow?"

"A scapegoat."

She looked on the point of collapse. I led her to a bench and we sat down together. Raffie, worn out with teething problems, fell asleep in his pram.

Neeta resumed her story. "Husband says to leave my son there, but if we do, he will die. He is a harmless boy who loves his animals, his family."

"Who says he did it?"

Neeta shook her head violently; she either couldn't or didn't want to say.

"I know he didn't do it, Miss Kit."

She was crying properly now, and in between gasps and sighs, the whole story tumbled out. She said she knew he didn't do it because the boy had had one of his spells that week, and they always left him very weak.

"What do you mean by spells?" I asked her.

Glancing around her, she said the dread word, "Epilepsy," a condition I knew from Maya was sometimes mistaken here for possession by evil spirits.

"My husband tied him to the bed afterwards. I didn't want him to do this, but he says we must and I obeyed him."

Neeta looked at me then and put both hands together in prayer. "Please help me, Madam. I have no one else to go to, and I need money to get him out of the prison. I'll pay you back. I'll go away again after that."

I looked at her, and then at Raffie, who was stirring again. I opened my bag and collected the few rupees I had there.

"This is all I've got," I said, handing them to her. "I'll ask my husband later, when he comes home. We'll do what we can, but we're not rich people."

She snatched at my handful of notes. "I'm going there now," she said. "If you come with me, it would help. They will see an English-woman and be ashamed of their wickedness."

I doubted this very much, and seeing I was under suspicion, I didn't want to go. But after dropping Raffie off at home, I tagged along with her.

The jail on Tower Street was a twenty-minute walk from our house, a large gray two-storied building with barred windows and crumbling plaster. Looking up from the rubbish-strewn garden in front of it, I saw the glint of eyes peering down at me from behind barred windows. The reception area, a dungeon of a room, was lit by a naked bulb. It was hot and stank of urine.

A large, frowning man was sitting in a kind of cage to the left of the entrance. I saw Neeta disappear into the cage, heard her sobs and pleading. Five minutes or so later she came out again, ashen-faced but with a shaky smile.

"It's done," she said. She patted her empty purse. "It was mistaken identity." Or maybe, she admitted later, his illness frightened them.

I heard footsteps disappear down a dark corridor, the clank of a door, a man shouting. When Pavitran came out, unshaven and blinking, he flung himself at his mother and hugged her hard, mumbling and crying. He was so happy, and so was she. When he looked up I saw he had a swollen eye, and a small cut over his right eye, but otherwise seemed fine. Neeta said he had had another epileptic seizure in jail: his trousers were wet in front and he looked bewildered.

During the interminable paperwork and rubber stamping that followed, the boy looked on placidly like a large, well-trained domestic animal and held his mother's hand. Two hours after we had arrived, we were in the streets again in the merciless flat light of midday. Neeta beamed and told me, "God is good." I was not so sure. She told me never to tell anyone what I had witnessed that morning in the jail.

But I did tell Anto that night about Neeta's son and my worries about Dr. A. and her vague threats to me. It did not go well.

"I don't want you to go back to that place when it opens again," he said. "It's too dangerous. If you won't do it for me, do it for Raffie's sake."

"I don't want to stay away," I said. "I can just see you abandoning your work at the first sign of trouble."

"I'm not talking about me. You're my wife."

He didn't even bother to keep his voice down, as on and on the argument raged, and we were back where we were at Trivandrum during the monsoon, like two angry strangers who had collided in a freak accident.

"Do one thing for me, if not for you," he said, holding my hand when we had both calmed down. "Take a holiday with your mother. Go and see your father. You know that's what you want to do, really, and if you don't, you may regret it forever."

"A holiday!" I said. "Hardly." His words had made me feel instantly tearful, and I didn't want to cry. "It's true I do think about him, a lot." I was childishly grateful for his hand in mine. "But what if it's not true? What if he's not there?"

Anto stroked my hair. "I think it's genuine: Amma told me Glory had hysterics when you were taken to the hospital. She thought you'd died."

"She didn't tell me that."

"Well, she wouldn't, would she?" he said. "She's Glory, but what if she's changed? What if she really wants to do this for you?"

I hadn't properly considered this. I'd thought for so long that my job was to protect her.

- CHAPTER 44 -

September 27, 1950.

I marked the date we left for Ooty in my diary, thinking if we did find him, I'd want to remember it, and then I wrote, "Fat Hope" and underlined it twice, just to keep myself straight.

"So, darling, off we go," my mother said brightly, as we stood on the platform at Mettapalayam waiting for the seven-ten train: the same words she'd spoken with the same upward inflection at the beginning of so many trips, to so many jobs when I was young, as if to light the touch paper on some splendid adventure.

And the usual fudging about any difficulties involved, because Ootacamund turned out to be much farther away from Cochin than Glory had said. It had begun with a bone-crunching, boiling eight-hour drive to Mettupalayam to catch the Nilgiri Blue Mountain train. When we got to the station, Glory, wheezing and pale, sat with her head in her hands in the ladies' waiting room, looking so ill my heart began to thump.

"Are you sure you want to do this?" I asked. "We could just go home."

"Don't be stupid." She gave me one of her famously frosty looks. "We've bought our tickets; we have to go."

Our bright-blue train was tiny and narrow, like a toy train, with uncomfortably upright seats, but as we rose higher and higher, often at an agonizingly slow crawl, my mother seemed to revive. When she began to gasp out facts and figures about the sixteen tunnels we'd pass through, the nineteen bridges we'd cross, I remembered the endless games of I Spy we'd once played to distract me from friends I was leaving behind, or a cat I'd loved, a house, another fading scene.

It was stifling hot in our carriage; if you put your cheek against the window it stuck and burned. When she stopped talking suddenly and fell asleep, the journey took on a nightmarish quality for me: the darkness of the tunnels, the heat, my mother's gargling cough, the screech and cries of the train, lurching views into the steep ravines. Everything was unstable and chaotic and hot as hell.

When we stopped for refreshments at a tiny hillside station, I had to wake her. I felt a clutch of my heart looking down at her; she looked so dangerously breakable, all sharp angles and delicate surfaces. Her hands clasped her handbag for dear life.

On the station platform, almost buried in misty trees, we were served fruitcake and tea by a winsome turbaned man who called out to her, "Hello, Mrs. Shakespeare," which made us laugh. I was hungry enough to eat one of the curries another merchant offered, but Glory begged me not too. "They're riddled with germs."

"I don't think they are, Mamji," I said to her, using my facetious name for her. "I find many Indians are fastidiously clean, far cleaner than the Brits."

Back on the train again, she became more and more silent and more and more fidgety as the train rose higher and higher. She took her purse out of her bag and counted all the coins very slowly. She lit a cigarette and stubbed it out. She strained to look through the window out on the hills where a light rain was falling on a coffee plantation, so green it looked as if it were underwater. She looked at her shoes and examined them from several angles. After the silence had stretched to about an hour, I took her hand.

"All right, Mummy?"

"Fine," she said, in an echo of her brave young voice. "This is rather fun, isn't it?" I thought about this for a while, not daring to speak. Had she really said *fun*?

The train shrieked through another of its sixteen tunnels, and when it came out I said, "So . . . will you tell me more about him before I meet him?" as gently as I could. If there was to be an emotional outburst, I hoped for both our sakes it would be in private.

In the dark tunnel my mother's face flickered, went out. "You'll have to ask him yourself," she said. "It was such a very long time ago."

I could feel my veins go watery with alarm. I should never have come. More tea was served, this time on the train, delicious.

"Orange pekoe," the chai seller told us proudly. "Special from here."

"Your scar has healed nicely, darling," my mother said, looking at my arm. "That was a very nasty do, wasn't it?"

She sipped her tea.

"You know, I've been thinking, and forgive me but"—she placed her cup elegantly on her saucer—"if the subject of your job comes up between you and your father, it might be cleverer to say you don't work."

"Cleverer?"

"Wiser. Better." Her tone implied she was talking to a halfwit.

"Why?"

"Do I really have to spell it out? If he's got any money, he—"

"Oh, Glory! For God's sake, no." I was angry again. "Is that why we're here?"

"Shush." She looked around the carriage. In her world, there were spies everywhere. The old man sleeping opposite did not stir, and our other companions, a peaceful-looking Indian family, carried on handing out oily-looking snacks to each other.

"Don't be ridiculous," she said, "of course that's not why we're here, but there's something else I must say too. Now don't get angry, it has to be said that he will probably be put off by what you do. Birthing native women, it's all very new. I've had to"—she brushed a crumb off her chest—"to like it or lump it, but other people," she finished more firmly, "might see it differently. It will come as a shock to him."

So we start with a lie, I thought bitterly, but did not say it. Another suspicion had grown during her speech. Had she even told him I was coming?

"Absolutely," she said, when I asked her. "All the arrangements have been made, so don't go on about it now, darling." Her lips had started to crumble. "This is not easy for me either, you know."

We were nearly there. I hardly dared talk now, so full up with a feeling I could neither name nor understand. Fear and longing, fury, a kind of breathless anticipation, a homesickness for something I'd never had. Through the carriage window, I saw plumes of mist hugging the trees, peaceful green fields that shimmered and disappeared.

"Look." My mother raised a feeble hand at the church spire that suddenly appeared, an artificial lake, a row of bungalows, all misted in a faint drizzle. "Snooty Ooty," Anto had joked, "frightfully like parts of Surrey."

A uniformed conductor ran through the train. "Ootacamund, Ootacamund. Train stops here."

"Don't rush off." Glory closed her eyes and panted lightly. "I'm a little bit breathless. I hope the old lungs can take this altitude."

- CHAPTER 45 -

The Hotel Victoria was a modest mock-Tudor house at the end of a steep drive. When we got there, I asked for separate rooms and told Glory I'd pay for them out of money I'd earned. An unpleasant dig, I suppose, at her earlier idea of using me as a sort of bargaining chip here, but the truth was I didn't trust myself to share a room with her: we were too vulnerable, too combustible.

My room, small, whitewashed, clean, had a pretty mother-of-pearl chair and a plain white bed. Nothing fancy, we couldn't afford it, and not in what my mother said was the posh part of town.

When the rain stopped, I looked through my window at terraces of shabby little houses, cows, small gardens. The steep hills, the mist around the trees, gave me a strange feeling of vertigo as if I were dangling between one life and another.

There was a Bible, a carafe of water, a copy of the membership rules of the Ooty golf club left by a previous tenant on my bedside table. I put a photo of Anto and Raffie on top of the Bible, stared at them for a while. They at least felt solid and real: not a place that could be changed at whim, neither a destination nor a hope, but a reality like my lungs or my breath.

I could hear my mother next door: the clink of her glass, the trickle of water from a tap, the twang of bedsprings as she sat down. Her cough. I knew her habits so well: the miniature storm of activity in which she laid out her clothes at night: "Hang them quickly before they wrinkle, no matter how tired you are." The splashing of her face, "at least fifteen times, to remove every bit of dirt." The eye mask that never worked in the fight against insomnia. The All-Bran for breakfast, "just a smidgen of milk." Cries of "Gin and it!" at six o'clock.

As I child I had watched these rituals with the deepest fascination: the way she put her earrings on, sliced her bacon, closed her handbag with her beautifully manicured nails. And still she exerted an electrical pull, deeper than words, the circuit fixed during hundreds and thousands of moments shared, habits observed; the kindnesses, cruelties, disappointments added up whether I wanted them to or not.

And tomorrow—my stomach clenched at the very thought of it—I'd meet my father. Or so she said.

"He *said* he'd be here at four," my mother remarked before we went to bed, in the same offhand voice she might use to confirm, let's say, a hair appointment. She was sitting in the visitors' room of the Victoria clutching the key to her room.

"Does that suit you? I've been casing the joint," she said, without waiting for an answer. "I think this will be the best room to meet him in."

This damp parlor on the ground floor had, with its unlit fire and mismatched chairs, all the atmosphere of a dentist's waiting room. I'd imagined we'd be going to his house and said so. I was frightened of making a fool of myself in a public place, but I didn't tell her this.

"Oh, we can't do that, he's married. Didn't I tell you? I'm sure I did," my mother said, as if announcing some minor change of plan.

"No, you didn't, actually. That might have been a helpful little clue for me." I was so angry I could have struck her. The careless way she flung information that I had to snatch and scrabble for, like a refugee with a food parcel.

"Look, Mummy, I think I'm going to turn in early," I said. I didn't trust myself to stay. "I'll have something sent to my room. Big day tomorrow."

"Kit!" A kind of wail. A plea for sympathy and understanding as we looked into each other's eyes. "Don't."

Meaning what? Don't fuss about minor details? Don't hate me? Don't spoil this perfectly ordinary day? A nicer daughter might have amended, *but I love her anyway*, before she turned her lights out, but on that night I hated her: her muddles, her lies, her attempts to be grand, her refusal to ever be straight with me.

Cough cough, clink, clink. Around three p.m. on the next day, I could hear my mother putting her "face" on: the fierce stare in the mirror, then cream, powder, lipstick, scent, several changes of wardrobe, if she had the breath for it now.

My legs felt weak as I put on my stockings, washed my face, combed my hair, buttoned my second-best green dress. From time to time, I stared through the crack in the curtains and saw the hills he'd be driving through now. A solid knot of fear grew in my stomach, and then—hard to describe it since it had never happened to me before—the knot of fear started to uncoil like a living creature, and I only just made it to the sink, where I vomited. No doubt about it, I was terrified, and there was still an hour to wait.

It was cold in the visitors' room by the time I got down. Cold enough for your breath to show, and damp: it had rained off and on all morning. There were not enough logs in the brass bucket to keep the fire burning brightly.

When I walked in, my father, a gaunt, hunched figure, was sitting near the fire. When he saw me, he rose from his chair with a great deal of difficulty. I had imagined him as a much younger man, someone tall and handsome, let's say like Ronald Coleman, with a mustache and mellifluous speaking voice. This man looked old for his sixty-five years—age being the one bit of information my mother had vouchsafed. He was wearing a worn tweed jacket and a too-big shirt that made his throat look shriveled and gizzardy. He had thick white hair, green-brown eyes, same color as mine. So peculiar: my father in the same room as me, both of us staring and trembling a little like dogs about to start a fight.

"Where's Glory?" he asked.

"I don't know," I said, pretty sure she was lying down in her room. "I'm Kit." When I held out my hand, he shook it in an absentminded way and blinked at me several times.

"Is it short for anything?" he said at last.

"Kathryn," I said. "No one calls me that." Thinking, *Surely you know my name!* or was I just referred to as the baby or the child?

"Will she be long?" He glanced towards the door.

"I don't know." When he looked back, there was such longing, such fear in his eyes that I understood in a flash I was not the person he most wanted to see. We sat down on opposite sides of the feebly burning fire. Rain streaked the windowpane. I kept my eyes on my hands, which were folded in my lap, because what I felt most was a flooding sense of shame, as if I had no right to be there.

He patted his top pocket, took out a pipe, and laid it on the arm of the chair. "Is this allowed?"

"I don't know." I sprang up, grateful for an excuse to leave. "I'll ask the landlady. You'll need an ashtray."

"It's all right," he said. "Don't go. I don't need it."

"What's your real name?" I said, when the pipe had returned to his pocket again. "I mean your whole name."

He looked at me warily. "It's William," he said in a quavering voice. "William Villiers. Major Villiers when I was in the regiment."

Kit Villiers. Quite a nice name, all things considered, but I was still in a weird state of shock as I said it to myself. No joy, no relief, still this feeling of profound embarrassment and something like disappointment because he was so obviously not pleased to see me.

"Is Glory ill?" he asked anxiously. "Will she come?"

"I don't know." My voice sounded wooden and strange. "Do you want me to . . . ?" I stood up.

"No, no, no," he said, watery eyes still trained on the door." I was— Only . . . if she wants to."

Which she evidently didn't. My mother had many faults, but unpunctuality wasn't one of them. There were no signs of life from upstairs.

And so we sat there in a trap of her making, the minutes ticking away, the fire gone out by now, until he said, in a small, meek voice, "So, what do you want to know?"

- CHAPTER 46 -

The task suddenly felt enormous. I looked out the window at the gray mist, the trees, and wished I was anywhere but here.

"I am going to have to smoke, you know," he said. "Do you mind?"

I watched him in a kind of stupor fumbling for his pipe, his baccy pouch, his box of matches, all of which he managed to drop and then pick up.

"The thing is," I said, "I don't know anything about you."

He tamped his pipe with one stained finger. "She must have said something?" He actually looked hurt.

"No . . . not really. She told me a couple of weeks ago you'd sent some money to Daisy Barker, that was all."

"No letters?" His finger stopped. "I wrote lots of them."

"To me?"

"Not to you, to *her*." His fingers clutched at the pipe.

"She said there was money in the letters, that's all."

"Well, bless my soul." He squeezed his eyes shut and shook his head. A servant came in with tea. He asked for his black and reached for it with a shaking hand. After another long silence, he said, "I thought she'd told you."

I took a sip of tea. I didn't want to bully him, but I had the sense he was fading fast and I must choose my questions well, before he got too agitated or exhausted to answer them.

"How did you meet her?" I said.

There was a long silence. The teacup rattled in his hand and when he looked at me, his eyes were bright with tears.

"D'you think she'll come down? Today, I mean. It took me ages to get here."

"I have no idea," I said, my own heart starting to pound. I tried again. "Where did you meet her?"

He gathered himself with a shuddering sigh and his eyelids came down, as if he were picturing the whole scene on the back of them. "I was a cavalry officer. Third Regiment," he began. "Family from Somerset. I'd never been out of England before." He stopped talking abruptly and sank a little further down in his chair, his eyes tight shut again.

"Go on," I said. "Please don't go to sleep."

"I'm not asleep." He puffed vigorously on his pipe to prove it. "I'm frightened."

"Of what?"

"Of saying too much. It got me into awful trouble last time."

"Please."

"I had a training accident." Another agonizing silence. "Fell off a horse, broke my leg."

"Look, do you mind if I take notes?" I said. It felt easier to regard him as a case history, rather than face the rising distress (or was it anger?) inside me, or look him in the eyes.

"We met in Bombay. Please could you stop that?" He looked at my pencil. "I want to look at you when I say this."

"It's all right. I'll stop. I understand." I put the pencil down.

"Must we do this all at once?" he suddenly pleaded. "I hardly know you."

"Yes, we must." I felt icy cold. "We leave tomorrow and . . ." I may as well have added, and you're going to die, and I have to go on living. That's what I felt.

"You have to understand how it was then," he mumbled, pulling his jacket around him. "Lots and lots of girls came out from

England, lots of parties, but she was . . . ." His eyes filled with a fresh burst of tears. No words yet.

"Beautiful. What's the word?" He tapped his pipe on the side of his head. "Radiant: very black hair, those cat's eyes full of fun, very warm." He clutched his chin in his hand. "Oh dear, shouldn't bang on like this, but I think of her every day."

"So you met in Bombay?"

"The regiment had its HQ in Poona. There was a ball there. I was halfway up the stairs, and when I looked down and saw her . . ."

He fumbled for his handkerchief. I gave him mine.

"Go on."

"Oh God," he said. "This is why she brought you here."

"I don't know what you mean."

"I loved her," he ended in a gasp. He looked at the door again. "We had, let me see . . ." He counted it on his gnarled old fingers. "Four, five, six months, of complete happiness together. You're very pretty, by the way; you remind me of her. She was working for the Resident, some sort of secretary. When my leg had mended, we rode out together in the morning. Everyone was very keen on her, so it was quite a feather in my cap. Spins on my motorbike. I adored her. She didn't tell you the rest?" He looked at me anxiously.

"*No.*"

His eyes shot open. I hadn't meant to shout, but I was panicked in case he stopped.

"I shouldn't tell you this, but I proposed to her on a beach, north of Bombay. Knew I would never be this happy again. Don't tell my wife that." He gave me an almost waggish look. "No proper ring, so I put a piece of seaweed around her finger and she kissed it." He closed his eyes in a grimacing way.

Don't cry, I thought. I was amazed to hear my mother had ever been this romantic.

"You must have heard the rest," he pleaded. "It's horrible. Awful."

"No! Keep going." I knew I had to ride him hard or he would stop.

His hands fluttered to his face. "If I tell you this, you must swear to God you will never tell my wife."

"I won't say a word." I found it hard not to look incredulous. I didn't even know the bloody woman.

"I hate to think of it," he continued, eyes fixed on the floor. "It makes me sick. Glory was so excited—the dress, the reception, everything, she'd talked of nothing else for months."

"I don't know what you're talking about."

"Our wedding," he all but wailed. "She'd told all her friends at the Residency. She was very popular there, great fun. Women loved her as much as men. We set the date, October seventeenth, Saint George's Cathedral, told my Colonel, got the bans read, and . . ." He'd tailed off. "She was so excited."

"Could you speak up?"

"Sorry," in a squeak. More dab with the handkerchief. "I can't . . . I'm not . . ."

"Then what happened?" Anyone with an ounce of humanity might have stopped there, but I couldn't, knowing I would probably never see him again.

"She turned up at the cathedral before me. Our friends were inside, my chums were there with their ceremonial swords, all ready. The bride runs through them, you know, afterwards. She and I had practiced this together." He stopped again, shrunk into himself, and seemed to have difficulty swallowing.

"Then what?"

"I didn't come." His voice was almost inaudible.

"What do you mean?"

"My Colonel came. She was standing in the vestry and he told her the wedding was off. Another chap in the regiment, who'd had his eye on her, had guessed what I didn't know: that she was a chi chi girl."

"A what?"

"Half-caste. Her father was an English railway worker, mother a local girl. Never guessed. The pale skin, with powder on, was deceptive. The Colonel said that marriage to a native was out of the question. If I did it, other chaps would follow suit, and where would that leave us? I was stupid enough to go along with it. Surely she's told you this. He'd already written to my parents and told them what would happen. He knew they'd agree, and they did."

He looked at me like a whipped dog.

"The worst thing I ever did," he mumbled. He looked up. "You must have known."

"Only bits," I said. "None of this."

"Can I say hello?" he asked. "Please. I want to say I'm sorry."

"I don't know, I doubt it. She's stubborn."

"I know." A wincing smile.

"So, when did you hear about me?" I asked.

"When you were two years old. Daisy wrote. Glory had pneumonia and was in a very bad way."

"Were you horrified?"

William Villiers looked at me. Old, bewildered. He began to weep. "What a waste. What a waste," he said when he could speak. "I'd like to have known you."

"Do you have other children?" I said.

"My wife couldn't have them. Listen." He stared in a dazed way at his watch. "I'd be so grateful to you if you'd go up and see if Glory would come down. I can't stay much longer."

I got up and went to the door. "She's locked us out," I said when it wouldn't budge.

He got up too and tried the handle, said, "How bloody typical," and both of us laughed identically, a sort of mirthless snort.

"She'll be down," I said, knowing with her theatrical flair, it would be in her own sweet time. We returned to the faded chintz chairs, one on either side of the tiny fire.

"Is there anything you want to know about me?" I said at last. "You haven't asked a thing, you know."

"I'm sorry." He blinked and looked at me. "I've worked it out. You're thirty-two years old now, correct?"

"Yes." I put my hands over my eyes.

"Married?"

"Yes. To an Indian doctor. I met him in England during the war. He was a postgraduate student at Oxford." I felt a glow of reflected pride. "He has a good job here."

"Do you love him?"

"Yes." For that moment it felt as simple.

"Children?"

"One. Raffael, seventeen months old."

He thought about all this for a while, sighing and shaking his head. "Was Glory horrified?" he asked at last, gazing down at his battered brogues. "You marrying an Indian?"

"She was. What happened with you can't have helped."

"Any pictures of your nipper?" I showed him one of Raffie lying beside me on a hammock. He was laughing his head off. He'd just stolen my beads, and was wearing them around his neck. William looked at it for a long time.

"What a balls-up," he said at last.

When the door rattled, we both jumped. The servant who unlocked it said, "Madam will come down in one hour," and padded away.

"It's getting dark." He got up creakily from the chair, scattering pipe and matches. "I can't stay that long. I'm sorry, I would like to have asked you more."

I might have reassured him, but the shock of hearing about my mother was followed by a spurt of anger. "Does your wife know you're here?" I said.

"She thinks I'm playing golf."

I shrank from the hangdog look that followed this admission. In some secret, stupid part of myself, I still wanted the Ronald Coleman father, strong, invincible, perhaps in some uniform, not some weed pretending to be on a golf course because he was frightened of his wife.

"Does she know anything about us?"

"No. It would be the death of me if she found out."

"D'you mean she'd kill you?" Hard to keep the contempt out of my voice.

"She's highly strung, older than me. I couldn't do it now," he told the floor.

"Not much more to be said then," I said, hoping to wind things up now.

"No."

I took a mental snapshot of him, trying to strip away the frayed tweeds, the air of defeat, and see him as my mother must have, except there wasn't much left. I noticed his hands, fumbling for the doorknob, were long-fingered, like mine. Before he left the room he turned. "Please try and get her to see me? I could come back tomorrow at two."

I gave him the number of the hotel: Ooty 75. "I can't promise anything," I said. "But if you telephone tonight, I'll let you know."

We didn't kiss. We didn't even shake hands. At the last moment, we seemed to calcify, like Pompeii statues, into stone.

"I was a nurse in the war," I told him quickly, full of an anger I could not name. "In case you're interested."

"A nurse in the war," he repeated. "That must have been grim. A brave girl, then."

"Not really," I said, "not at all. I'm training to be a midwife now."

His expression did not change. "Well done," he said, and there our conversation ended. He was busy looking for the taxi that would shortly take him away.

- CHAPTER 47 -

He phoned again that night but Glory refused to answer. She breakfasted alone and, as our train chuntered back down through the hills, she pretended to be asleep.

When he'd phoned again shortly before we left, I was put in to bat to tell him she was not available, and William (how could I call him my father?) said after a number of wordless sighs and gasps, "I have a message for her, and it is this. She did nothing wrong. She was"—I heard him gasp—"a fine person who was jilted by a weak and wicked man."

But she hadn't asked me a thing, and I, in the midst of my own hurt and confusion, was afraid to broach anything. As the train moved south, what I felt, watching her sleeping beside me, was a complicated mixture of sorrow and hurt.

It was agony to picture her, aged eighteen, innocent and full of hope, standing in the vestry, a bunch of canna lilies in her arms. When the Colonel arrives, she bends her slender neck towards him. She is listening to the news. Oh, it's unbearable to think of her enduring so much pain, and it explains so much: her rootlessness, her prickliness, the important outer armor of good shoes and manicures. "You can always tell a lady by her hands." Her fundamental inability to find a path in life that she could believe in wholeheartedly. She'd never truly felt safe or at home anywhere, and now it was probably too late.

"So what did you think of him?" she said, when the train was approaching Coonor. "He is a perfect shit, isn't he?" Only the second time, as far as I can remember, that she'd sworn in front of me.

"I'm glad I know" was all I could come up with for now. And then, "He was full of regrets. He said you were beautiful, that he was older than you, that he should have known better." She gasped and pulled in her mouth like a person with no teeth. She always hated crying in front of me.

"He wanted to see you."

A tear cut a line through her powder. "Well, he can't," she said, a picture of childlike defiance as she dabbed her eyes. "Can he? He should have thought of that a long time ago." When she fell asleep again, hunched against the window, I imagined the waiting congregation, their shuffles and concerned murmurs, faces craning around to look for her as the minutes ticked by. Had she sped away in a taxi? I wondered. Or been taken to the Colonel's to take her dress off and sit in her underwear on some strange bed wondering about the rest of her life?

When she woke with a cough, I gave her some of her favorite Fox's Glacier Mints from my handbag. In general, she disapproved of eating in public, but now she sucked one quite happily, beside me. In my mind, I saw her in pigtails at the orphanage in Orissa for half-caste girls.

"We didn't do too badly on our own, did we?" she said, after she'd swallowed her sweet discreetly.

"No," I said, "not badly at all." And then, because I meant it, "I'm so sorry about what happened. It was brave of you to let me know." I wanted to hold her hand, but that would have felt false.

"He said . . ." I watched her face anxiously; this felt like inching along a precipice. "He would really like . . ."

"Don't say a thing else. Please. No." She was interrupted by another coughing fit. "I don't want to know," she said when it was finished.

* * *

When our train arrived at Mettapalayam, Anto was standing on the platform waiting. Raffie was in his arms, smiling his reckless three-tooth smile, stretching his podgy arms towards me, giving his grandma a kiss. The kiss seemed to perk my mother up. In the car on the way to Mangalath, where there was a family party, Raffie sat in the back on my mother's lap. She gave him one of her mints and allowed him to rearrange all the things in that normally sacred place, her handbag, even seemed to enjoy it, though she seemed worryingly tired.

Amma came down the path to meet us. She took my mother's hand and led her into the house. "You look dead on your feet, Glory," she said. "Take forty winks before lunch." My mother turned around, shot me a look of wild accusation. "Does she know?" she whispered.

I shook my head. "No." Anto had been primed to tell her we were simply having a little holiday, but Lordy, I was weary of all these secrets.

I was surprised this time how glad I was to be back at Mangalath. Its familiar smells of furniture polish, cardamom, lemongrass felt like another solidly comforting presence. It was not rented, it would not be snatched away but would go on generation after generation being tended to like a demanding but much-loved relative, a little faded maybe, still beautiful.

In the upstairs room that Amma now called "the Glory room," I helped my mother into bed and put the cough mixture Amma gave me on the table beside her. As I straightened her sheet, I heard voices in the rooms below and felt the unfathomable comfort of knowing there were other human creatures around me, and that they would help with sympathy and respect. For this family, hospitality was an opportunity to show love, whatever your private feelings or passing irritations might be. It went beyond good manners or strict codes of conduct, and I appreciated it fully, maybe for the first time.

"She's asleep," I whispered when Anto walked in. He wiped my eyes, and when he put his arms around me, it felt like a transfusion of blood. We looked down at her together. Her face was waxy; her breath came in uneven sips.

"She's dying, isn't she?" I said it out loud for the first time when we were out of earshot.

"We'll take care of her," he said. "It could take months, she's a tough old girl." He was crying too.

"I hope you missed me," I said, when we'd stopped.

"Like mad," he said. "Raffie's not as much fun as you are. We were like two crusty old bachelors."

"I haven't been much fun recently," I said.

"You've had your reasons." He looked guarded.

"Talking of which, any news from the Home while I was away? Did Dr. A. try and contact me?"

"Kittykutty," he said. "Let's think about one thing at a time today. Your mother isn't well. You've just come home. Come here instead."

He led me into a dim and shuttered guest room at the other end of the hall. He locked the door, unbuttoned my blouse, and we lay down on the bed, and it was done at a speed that made us both gasp. A moment of pure animal comfort, deeper than any words he could have said.

"That's the best thing that's happened to me for days," I told him when I was buttoning up my blouse again. I was smelling him, oh delicious! cinnamon and sweat, all of it.

"So how was Ooty?" he asked, propped up on one arm, serious again.

"Necessary," I said at last.

"That sounds bad."

"Not all bad," I said. "I'll tell you all about it when we get to our house. Unless my ma seems too ill to travel. In which case, I'll stay here for a few days."

"Good plan," he said. And then in his Barkis-is-willing voice, to make me laugh: "My life. My old darling." He sighed. "Sorry I have to go back to work. I have a paper to prepare before Wednesday. Dr. Sastry wants funding for a larger program on epidemics."

"It's all right," I whispered, and meant it. "As long as I know you're here."

- CHAPTER 48 -

Lunch felt comfortingly normal: Ponnamma banging on in a loud voice about how it was impossible to make a proper pilau without dribbling saffron-soaked milk over the rice and then slow cooking it, Amma snapping this was plainly nonsense, that she, Amma, had been serving chicken pilaus for years without saffron milk and no one had complained. Raffie was sitting on Mariamma's lap having his toes tickled. Appan, home from trying a homicide case in Bombay that had kept him up for three days and three nights, looked done in.

Amma pushed bowls of salad, date chutney, and pappadams towards me. "Eat up."

When I'd finished, Appan asked me gently, "How is your Mummy faring?"

"Exhausted," I said. "It was a long journey."

Appan blundered on, "But a nice holiday, hey?" Happy shrieks from Raffie interrupted our conversation. Mariamma was counting his toes: "*Onneh, randeh, mooneh, naaleh, unche.*"

When Raffie's head began to droop, I lifted him out of Mariamma's arms and was about to take him upstairs when Amma stopped me. "Walk with me in the garden," she said. "Your Mummy's asleep. Mariamma will take care of Raffie."

We went down the path towards the summerhouse, dry leaves rustling under our feet, a small lizard dashing for safety. "That husband of mine never rests," Amma said as we passed Appan's bent head in his office. "My boys work too hard. By the way, he needs to speak to you later in his office. Do you know why?"

"No." I felt a flicker of anxiety.

"Something to do with your work, I think, he wouldn't say." She picked a dead insect off my blouse. "Sometimes he fusses." Her face was as impassive as a smooth pond.

To the right of us, two farmhands were cutting down a large bunch of small green bananas. They stopped working as we passed, heads bowed in respect. When we stopped at a raised bed of earth behind the summerhouse, Amma pointed to two shriveled orchids, freshly planted in coconut shells.

"Appan brought me two new invalids from Delhi: the brassia and the cymbidium. He'd kept them in his suitcase for two days, completely forgot them. He is so absentminded, but sweet of him to try," she added hastily. Didn't do to criticize husband in front of daughter-in-law. "Orchids aren't like other flowers." Amma prodded the soil gently with her forefinger. "They have both man and woman inside them and make their own babies, and they're all different.

"This one," she turned towards a pink-and-green orchid that trembled like a butterfly at her approach—"I spray twice a day; otherwise, she faints like a lady in a crinoline. This one," she went on, picking up a gorgeous yellow flower stippled with pink, "was shriveled and sad when it first arrived. Now look at it. They all have different natures too. It took me a long time to understand that. This one likes the air, this one lots of feeding and the shade."

"My mother's dying," I said, "and I don't know what to do."

"I know." Amma put down the orchid and looked at me. "I'm sorry for this."

"I'm frightened. I should be used to death after the war and everything, but I'm not."

"Nothing prepares you for this," she said. "But don't be frightened. We'll do everything we can to see Mummy goes quietly."

I squeezed my eyes shut and, when I opened them again, saw a large bumblebee fly into the mouth of the yellow orchid and forage busily there.

"I'm glad you went to Ooty," Amma said.

I took a step back—too raw to discuss it, particularly with Amma, who generally discouraged family holidays that weren't to do with visiting other Thekkedens.

"Why are you glad?" I said.

She looked up at me. "It was my idea. I was watching your Mummy from exactly this place a few weeks ago. She thought she was alone. She was walking like this." Amma mimed someone hugging herself. "I said, 'Come and talk to me.' She was very sad. We had a talk. She said at the end of it, 'How can I make friends with my daughter again?'"

"She did?" I was trying not to sound too amazed.

Amma's head nodded from side to side. "She told me she'd been a hopeless mother. I told her we all felt that sometimes, and that sometimes I came out here and wished I was her."

"Really!"

"Yes. She seems so free. I'm stuck here, very invisible sometimes."

"You, invisible!" I said. "Never. You're home to a lot of people."

Amma made the *tsskkk* sound she made when she was trying to be modest. "So, I asked her for more information about you." Amma prodded the soil around the cymbidium. "Said you never talked about your family or your father or anything like that, and when she told me you knew nothing about him, I was shocked. When she told me he lived in Ooty, I felt worse. Family secrets are horrible." She stopped prodding the plant and gave me a beady look.

"So, tell me. How was it there?"

"Awful," I said. "I've never felt so confused in my life."

"But at least you've seen him. That's a good thing, no?" She was looking at me dubiously.

"I don't know. Was it? She wouldn't see him at all, that was sad."

"Why not?" Amma was shocked.

"I should let her tell her story . . . It explains a lot."

I felt the old sense of shame when I said this, of being slightly substandard goods. Part of a scam.

Amma sighed deeply. Beyond her a heron was dipping his beak into the water.

"I was hard on you when you first came." She didn't say this in a conciliatory way. In fact, having been kind about my mother, she let the same old thread of irritation return to her voice. "There were many things I didn't understand, and I was so nervous about Anto coming home."

"With an English mongrel—I don't blame you." We both smiled uneasily. "Plus our timing was not impeccable."

"He was so like Raffie when he was young," she said, both wistful and aggrieved.

"In what way?"

"He was jolly. He talked to me all the time." She grimaced, then suddenly grabbed my watch.

"Oh, God. You're late for Appan. Run, run, don't upset him, and don't tell him we've had this conversation."

Appan was sitting under his green lamp when I walked in, desk piled with manila folders. His high cheekbones popped out when he smiled at me and put a pair of gold-rimmed spectacles on his nose. "Sit down," he said. "This won't take long."

His sentences began in the usual soft and confiding purr. He was off the following day, he said, to represent a scoundrel in Bangalore who had been embezzling money from his employer. It was a complicated case but the important principle was to marshal what facts you had at your disposal and compress them in the simplest way possible.

"But I have something here," he added, pulling out a folder, "that has caused me a few sleepless nights lately. It concerns you."

I could feel my palms grow clammy and my heart thump. A clock struck slowly at the end of the room.

"Such a noisy thing." Appan waited patiently for the chimes to stop. "I bought it in Hatton Garden years and years ago . . . So." He pushed back his glasses, pulled out a sheet of fresh paper and sighed. "A letter came, while you are away, from my old friend Chief Medical Officer Kunju. He was the one who interviewed Anto when you first got back. He is a bigwig now in the new government, a pompous fellow who is trying to make a name for himself. A stickler for detail also.

"He wants to know . . ." Appan's lips moved silently as his pen moved down the paper. "One: Under whose authority you were working at the Matha Maria Moonstone Home for Expectant Mothers. Two: Who finances the Home? Are you a member of the British government? And he would like, in triplicate, a copy of your nursing certificate and subsequent midwifery certificate.

"Those things you can deal with easily, I'm sure." Appan's pen stayed on the letter while he stared at me. "What follows is more serious: he says that on February seventh of this year, you helped to deliver a baby to a Mrs. Nair. The baby subsequently died, and the woman, who is a fully trained lawyer, a clever one at that, has launched a formal complaint with the government regarding"—Appan squinted to read the exact words—"substandard treatment received at the home. Dr. Kunju wants to know if it is correct that you were the midwife present and thus directly responsible."

"Mrs. Nair? But she and the baby were healthy when they left us. Are you sure it was her?"

"Why would I make it up?" He glared at me.

I could hear a strange shrilling in my ears. "As a member of my family, naturally I can't represent you," Appan's words rolled on, "and it may be nothing more than a warning shot across the bows, but now I have my own concerns. You see, I have been kept in the dark about your real work at the Home." A note of steely authority entered his voice, and for the first time he scowled. "No one actually told me you were a midwife. Not you, not Anto, not Amma. She told me something about missionaries, a charity that you went to see, a nun, a survey you were doing on local midwives. Why has everyone said these things to me if they weren't true?"

I took a deep breath and looked at him. When you married an Indian, I'd been told countless times, you married a whole family, and I was about, it seemed, to disgrace them all.

"Where shall I start?"

"Wherever you like." A flash of anger in his voice.

"I am a fully qualified nurse. I did three years' training at Saint Thomas' Hospital in London. I worked there during the war, and then I studied midwifery at Saint Andrew's, also in London."

"I was told you did charitable works."

"I was told you wouldn't approve. That in your mind it would be a job for a lower-caste woman."

"So are you ashamed of it?"

"Not at all. I'm proud of it. I should have told you that right at the beginning."

He closed his eyes, thought for a while. "I knew about the nursing but not the rest. Does Anto know you're a midwife?"

"Of course."

"This is a most unusual job in our family." He scowled at me. "I've never heard of such a thing. But if you can give me the relevant certificates, that part of the investigation can be rubber-stamped and ended." He began to rub his hair irritably.

"I can't," I said at last, staring down at the desk. "Not exactly. I can give you my nursing certificate, but I'm not a fully qualified midwife and never pretended to be. I had to leave shortly before the end of my training."

"Why?" his voice was sharp as a whip. I closed my eyes and felt my stomach fall away.

"A birth went badly wrong, while I was training . . . I wasn't sure

I could do it again. It happened in London, right at the end of the war, and then my mother got ill and I was called home."

"So no chance to get back on the horse again, metaphorically speaking." A faint smile from him. "Until this chance to practice on Indian babies?"

"That's completely unfair. They were short-staffed at the Moonstone. I was asked to help, and bit by bit my responsibilities increased. Nothing was hidden from Dr. Annakutty, the director of the Home, but it's possible she'll deny it now."

Appan was writing busily. "And so you performed a delivery on Mrs. Nair, in spite of not being fully qualified."

"She asked for me particularly. Dr. Annakutty was in the building at the time."

"Did it not occur to you that Dr. Annakutty knew the dangers of helping such a woman if things should go wrong? A lawyer closely connected to the new government."

"She is a fine and experienced obstetrician."

"And she let you do it." His expression was half-crazed, astounded by my naivety. "Because these facts, twisted, will sound like a classic case of colonial overconfidence."

"Appan," I appealed to him, "what do you think will happen?"

"I can't predict." Appan closed the folder and looked at me. "Too much is changing at the moment, and I'm worried: I've met this woman once or twice in court. She is very sharp. My short-term plan is to telephone an old friend of mine, Suresh Patel, and see if he can represent you. He's a fairly decent lawyer. I must also forbid you to discuss any of this with any other person in this house: not Amma, not your mother, not Mariamma. They don't need to know.

"As for you," his expression softened a little, "we must wait and pray."

- CHAPTER 49 -

I hardly slept for the next two nights thinking of the jail in Cochin—the broken lights, the cracked concrete walls, the stink of pee and Dettol.

If Appan was right and they made an example of me, I would lose everything: my work, my reputation, Anto, Raffie, the honor of the family.

I was also baffled and horrified to think that Mrs. Nair's baby died, when it left us so bonny and thriving and with her so happy. And these clammy, sleepless nights brought me face to face with every bad thing about me: my arrogance, my stupidity, my cowardice in bailing out of the midwifery course with only a month left to go. Why had I done that?

A judge and jury would want clear facts about the Home—figures, account books, official approvals—and mine were shot through with holes and inconsistencies. Straining to remember conversations Daisy and I had had at Wickam Farm, my brain felt too numbed to recall them with any confidence. The Home had been set up in pre-Independence days, a time when proof of Englishness was pretty much all you needed to be a do-gooder in this country and be applauded for it. Now the law would see me as a half-qualified, incompetent busybody, and the fire would further complicate things.

* * *

I poured my heart out to Anto that night. We were back in Fort Cochin, and we sat up late on the veranda and talked long after Raffie had gone to bed. I reminded him that he'd warned me during that awful row in Trivandrum, "Kill one baby and they will kill you."

"Let's hope you weren't right," I said. "But you know, I didn't lie about my qualifications. I thought I'd never have the guts to do another delivery again." Anto tightened his clasp on my hand; he waited awhile in case there was more I wanted to say.

"Do you know something?" He shifted on the swing and sat closer. "You've never really told me what happened that night."

"I don't know if I can."

"You don't have to." After a long silence, he peeled my hands away from my face and looked at me dubiously, not sure he wanted to hear this either. After a few more minutes I started slowly, with a feeling of creeping shame, but then it came out in a rush because it was, I suppose, the confession I needed.

"It was a summer evening, at the end of the war. I was happy as a clam: the last part of our exams were over and I'd done well and I was one month shy of being fully qualified. I had no one apart from Daisy to tell the good news to because, well, you know my mother would hardly be throwing her hat in the air. So, I was cycling over Westminster Bridge with a bottle of gin in my pocket and a cake so I could celebrate with Josie, who was working at Thomas'.

"Josie sneaked me into her room. She'd been on duty for hours. I was pooped too, so we lay on her bed and drank some gin, not a lot, a glass or two, and were just going off to sleep when there was an air raid, and the hospital was full of casualties, and then . . ."

"Kitty, you're shaking." Anto put his arm tighter around me.

"About midnight, there was a pounding on the door. A young girl had been found in a bus shelter on Lambeth Road, just behind the hospital. She'd gone into labor and was petrified, what with the bomb and the fires, so they'd brought her in. No room for her, so they made up a quick bed in the corridor. A friend of Josie's, who knew I was studying midwifery, asked me to help out. All the other nurses were busy; no one questioned it. They just told me to get on with it. It was the war: policemen, firemen were delivering babies. So I did. It was very frightening with the roof shaking and the lights going out, but it was a fairly straightforward delivery, and I was pretty pleased with myself.

"We put the baby—it was a boy—in an air raid helmet because it was still pretty hot, but then I don't know what happened, honestly don't know." I started to sweat and shake just thinking of it. "The baby made this awful sound—it was like a crow or something—and then it began to fit and I didn't know what to do. You know the thing about being a good midwife is being able to react to change very quickly but also to keep calm, and I just didn't.

"I'll never know exactly what I did wrong: maybe I didn't clear his lungs properly, or if I hadn't had the gin, I would have been more alert, but there the baby was, frothing at the mouth, and then it went blue and started choking on its tongue, and the mother was shouting: "Do something! Do something!" She was completely mad with panic. And I didn't, or at least I tried, but not the right thing. I ran to get someone instead of doing the right thing myself. But I didn't know what the right thing was. I got lost in the corridors looking for help. When I came back, it was dead." I had the usual clear memory, as I said this: the mother howling, the baby in the tin helmet in her arms, its lips turning blue.

"Oh, Kittykutty," Anto said when I had finished. "Why didn't you tell me before?" He stroked my hair. "Why are you so sure it was your fault? A congenital heart problem, all kinds of things."

"I couldn't bear to; I felt so disgustingly stupid. I've never properly forgiven myself for going to a party and ending up killing a baby. Don't tell me it wasn't my fault. I was there, and I panicked, and maybe if I hadn't had the gin . . . and I've only just thought of this, but although I'd delivered babies by then, it was always under supervision. I was no good in an emergency—head knowledge but no experience, the very opposite of the midwives we're training. Any one of them would probably have known what to do."

It was all back in my mind now: the wash of green light; the blackout curtain, the smothered cry the girl had made as she'd tried herself to bring the baby back to life.

"And now I've done it again," I told him. "Appan said the lawyer's baby died. It's so hard to believe because it was such a good delivery for us both, but maybe I did do something wrong."

"Kitty." He took both my hands in his. "The first thing to do is to go down and talk to Dr. Annakutty. Thanks to your work, they will have the proper records now."

"No, we don't! That's the point. The records were burned in the fire."

He bit his lip. "Well, Dr. A. is a well-respected woman. She'll vouch for you."

"That's the point." I stared at him. "The last time I spoke to her, she swore she had no idea I wasn't qualified."

"What!" Anto's grip on my hand tightened. "She can't do that."

"You don't know her, Anto, I do. She can be a number one bitch. If it goes to court, she's quite likely to use me as a scapegoat: a baby has died, the mother's a lawyer. I didn't have the right qualifications. I'm her perfect get-out-of-jail card."

"The other nurses?"

"I can't count on them. They're all too new and terrified of her."

"Maya?"

"No, she's a straw in the wind whenever Dr. A.'s around, not that I blame her for that."

"We'll think of something." He was sounding a little desperate himself. "Kitty," he added after a long and thoughtful pause, "going back to what you said earlier. Do you imagine that there is a single nurse or doctor in the world who doesn't feel they have blood on their hands? We're human, we make mistakes. You did the best you could. The alternative that night was what? To say to that girl in labor, 'Sorry, love, can't help: I'm one month shy of my finals, deliver your own baby.' Conscience absolved, girl left screaming. That, in my opinion, would have been the greater sin."

"Ah, sin, Anto," I said, remembering how they'd wrapped the baby in a towel and taken it away. "I wish I were a proper Catholic sometimes, and could empty it all away." Like the rubbish on Monday, I thought.

"It doesn't work like that," he said. "I wish it did."

Then Raffie woke us crying. He was always unsettled when he came home from Mangalath, his favorite place in the world.

Anto ran upstairs and brought him down. Raffie sat on his lap, rubbing his fists in his eyes and looking blearily around.

"Oh, Anto." The two of them seemed suddenly, inexpressibly dear. "What if I do go to jail?"

"You won't," he said, but I saw the strain on his face. "Take your little worry bead and give him a hug." He handed me Raffie. I tried not to squeeze him too hard, as I prayed to a God I wasn't sure I believed in.

CHAPTER 50

When the monsoon came the following week, it was almost a relief to be imprisoned inside the house. But when the rains stopped, I couldn't sit still. I left Raffie with Kamalam, took a taxi to Alleppey and boarded the backwater ferry to Champakulam, Maya's village—the place I'd set out to with such excitement almost two years before.

If it hadn't been for the giant knot in my stomach, it would have been a lovely trip. An earlier shower of rain had left a fine net of diamonds on the hibiscus and palm trees; the rice paddies on either side of our boat were intensely green.

When we arrived at the village, I went to Saint Mary's, the Christian church where we'd done the first midwife class. The streets leading there were puddled and potholed and the whole place looked even scruffier than I remembered it, with debris from the monsoon washed up on its shores.

The church was empty. I sat near a lifelike wooden snake wound around a statue of the Virgin Mary. The snake had a malevolent look, as if to say, I could strike you at any time, and you would never know. I didn't pray to God. I prayed to Dr. A. and to Maya. Please help me. You're my only chance.

An old man was sweeping up leaves outside the church. I showed him the piece of paper with Maya's name and address on it. He put down his brush and pointed very precisely left, then right, in the direction of a scattering of small houses. I thought I'd followed his directions, but the alleyways got narrower and narrower, and one dusty lane hung with washing looked pretty much like another. I was sweating and flustered by the time I got to a bicycle shop and showed my piece of paper again. A man covered in axle grease led me a street away to a flimsy door, which opened when I knocked on it.

If it hadn't been for her familiar gap-toothed smile, I wouldn't have recognized her, she looked so small and squashed.

"Maya," I said, "I'm sorry to bother you at home, but I'm in trouble. I need your help."

"You mustn't stay, ma'am," she said with a panicked glance over my shoulder. "My husband will be back soon; he's at the toddy shop."

But she let me in anyway. I was shocked at how small and squalid the house was when Maya was so meticulous at work. The sitting room, with its broken chair and two stained charpoy beds in the corner, was so low-ceilinged, I could barely stand up. It stank of curry.

"My boy is here," Maya said, looking anxiously at me. The grim-faced boy who used to deliver her to the Home got up from one of the charpoys. There was a large gauze bandage on his left arm. He snarled something to Maya and shot out the back.

"He is shy with visitors," Maya said, looking crushed and ashamed.

"I won't stay long," I assured her, "but Maya, please listen." I told her in a rush about the lawyer, the possible tribunal. I could hear her breathing heavily while I spoke. Twice she went to the door and peered out into the street.

"What can I do?" she asked, when I had finished. It wasn't an offer of help, more a passive acknowledgment that the universe was not designed to give us what we wanted. "I have no job now. Everything has ended for me also."

"Do you miss it, Maya?" I said.

"No." The eyes turned towards me were bruised and weary. "It's too hard. My husband and son don't like it." I heard, out in the street, a shout, the whirr of a bicycle wheel going by. She jumped up and stood at the door, desperate for me to leave.

"Sorry, Miss Kit." I stood up to reassure her.

"Maya," I said, "if there's a tribunal, will you speak up for me?"

"What is a tribunal, ma'am?"

"Three government men will ask us questions about the Home and the work we did there. You won't have to say anything that isn't true." Maya looked dubious.

"Our aim was to make things better, you said that yourself." I didn't like the note of whiney self-justification in my voice, but what could I do? She shook her head, twisted her hands. The boy began calling from the back of the house, a monotonous roar like that of a trapped calf, with a hint of threat in it. A scum of rice had boiled over on the stove and was dripping down the side of the saucepan.

"Sorry, madam." Maya could no longer disguise her panic. "I can't help."

Before she closed the door behind me, she gave a small, sad wave, a wave that felt like the final good-bye to the joyful, practical, funny colleague she'd grown into at the Moonstone. I feared for her, and I feared for myself. I'd lost my first ally.

I went to the library on Lily Street to see if I could find any legal books on the minimum statutory requirements for a midwife in India. I also wanted to check if there was anything in writing about the origins of the Moonstone, hoping it might mention the collaboration with Daisy Barker, the Settlement ladies, and the Indian midwives they'd worked with.

In a mood of increasing despair, I read through back issues of the *Hindu*, in the hope of seeing some stray announcement, but all

I saw in the social columns were memsahibs cutting tapes or open-ing flower shows, long-gone polo and cricket matches, but no news items, nothing. The library, like so many Indian institutions, was in a state of hectic renewal.

Next I plucked up courage to go see Dr. Annakutty. It was three weeks since our last meeting and she already had a new job as a locum at a small government-sponsored clinic on the edge of town. Dr. A., as grand and impersonal as ever, ushered me into a sparsely furnished cubicle on the first floor of a flat-roofed modern-looking hospital. She told me this new job of hers was a logical progres-sion from the Home. In the past, she'd stressed that Indian women liked female midwives because their husbands didn't want another man looking at them. Now she sang a different tune: "We have twenty-five beds here, solely for the women, and we have gorement funding to pay them a little reward when they use our facilities. The doctors here are very kind to the women; they don't want them to be frightened of them. It's important for us to wean ourselves from US and English medicals."

When I told her my problem, she said immediately, "Sorry, can't help. I thought from Miss Barker you were qualified, and we're busy here now." She couldn't wait to get rid of me, and every fiber of every nerve ending in her face and posture said so. Case closed, and there was nothing I could do.

Struggling through the heat on the way home, trying to put the pieces of this puzzle together, I realized that deep, deep down, I didn't blame them particularly. Maya was poor and desperate: why put her life on the line for an Englishwoman who must seem to her to have been already magnificently rewarded by the world?

As for Dr. A., she was ambitious and had already paid a high price for her right to work. Why risk that for a half-qualified for-eigner? I was going to have to face the music alone.

To cheer myself up, I bought sweets from the *barfi* man who was near the beach by the fish market. A twist of brightly colored sweets for Raffie, a sesame ball for me.

I walked the last few blocks home slowly. I put the packets of treats in my left hand and opened the door.

"Anto," I said seeing him there. "You're home early."

"Yes." He was trying to smile.

He had a manila envelope in his hand with a government stamp in the corner. "This came for you," he said. His voice sounded unusually trembly. "I opened it, and they've set the date."

The one relief on the morning of the tribunal was that Glory, who was too ill to travel yet, was still convalescing at Mangalath. With any luck, I thought, she need never know about this, and neither need Amma and the rest of that house.

I woke up with a sense of dread so strong, I could not eat. I took a walk to the Home, where most of the old building had been pulled down and the trees were still blackened. I tried to summon up the good times: the prayers and dancing in the mornings, the gales of laughter as Rosamma had produced the plastic baby from her sari, the cries of the newborns from the ward, but as I stood in the ruined garden, my mood was bleak.

I was about to leave when I heard a sound behind the tin hut, a soft scraping, a murmur of voices. Behind the hibiscus bush I saw two local women sitting on their haunches tending a row of dusty geraniums that had somehow escaped the fire.

One I recognized: she had come into the clinic the victim of violent intercourse that had left her bleeding. I'd stitched her up as tidily and gently as I could during a long and tearful session that had lasted an hour. Nurses had brought her chai and a meal.

Now she looked shy when she saw me and covered her face with the end of her sari. At her feet was a jam jar of water. Her friend had brought a rusty trowel. To the right of the hibiscus they'd erected a tiny shrine with bricks scavenged from the center, a plastic goddess inside. The woman we'd treated sprang to her feet when she saw me, about to run, before her friend stopped her.

"We are here to keep the garden going," the friend announced boldly. "This is a nice place."

That was all, but it meant a lot on a morning full of dread for me.

Eleven a.m.

Anto was pale and we barely spoke as he drove me to the Government Hospital on Fort Street. When we parted, he told me not to worry: whatever happened today, the tribunal would almost certainly only be saber rattling, and I was not alone. I hardly heard a word, I was so nervous. Inside the hospital, I was taken in a clanking lift up to a sterile room on the fourth floor.

Three frowning men looked up as I entered. They sat behind a long table in the middle of the room. The empty chair facing them was mine. A youngish man wearing a turban and a dark Western suit stood up. His eyes were watchful, hard.

"Madam," he said, "today we are convened by the Medical Council of India to inquire into the specific matter of the Matha Maria Moonstone Home for Expectant Mothers and your role in it. My name is Dr. Diwan; these are your other interlocutors. To my right" (a busily scribbling man looked up), "Dr. Vijay Masudi. To my left, Dr. Mohanty. All of us are elected officials of the new Indian government. We have a high level of expertise and experience."

The fluorescent light above my head was so bright, his face became a blur.

Dr. Diwan opened a bulging green file with a fresh piece of paper on top.

"Your first birth name, please."

"Kathryn." Kathryn, my punishment name, only used by my mother or a headmistress, in times of trouble.

"Surname?" The pen scratched on.

"Smallwood." Safer to give my maiden name.

"From what country you are hailing?"

"England."

"Address?"

Wickam Farm seemed the logical choice for this. I could barely remember the other ones.

"Can we see your certification to practice medicine?"

"Here." I tried to smile confidently as I handed it over, but there was a strange wobble in my lip and my mouth was dry. Dr. Diwan took the certificate, read it with forensic concentration, held it up to the light as if it were a dud pound note, passed it to his colleagues, and handed it back to me.

"Midwifery certificate?" Dr. Diwan's expression did not change.

"I don't have one."

He narrowed his eyes, poked his tongue through his cheek.

"You don't have one? How is this possible?" Concerned glances at his colleagues. He went through his papers again.

"You see," he said, scratching his forehead, "I have it here that you've been delivering babies at the Matha Maria Moonstone Home for Expectant Mothers."

"I was."

"Under supervision?"

"Almost always." I heard the rumble of trolley wheels above my head, somebody crying. I took a deep breath. "There were one or two times, when we got very busy, I was the person in charge."

"Dr. Annakutty was the head of your home." Dr. Diwan brandished a letter, in her handwriting. "Was she was aware of your lack of qualifications?" He did not wait for my reply but picked up a letter and read it out loud in a voice that drilled through my eardrums.

"'In November 1948, I was informed by Miss Daisy Barker, one of the trustees of the Settlement, the charitable trust operating from Oxfordshire, that she was sending a high-quality nurse to us. I worked with her in good faith. At no time did I check her qualifications because I was assured that the British Government had done so.'" It was hardly a rousing endorsement.

"So, here we get to the nub of the thing." Dr. Diwan's eyelids drooped. He knotted his fingers and stared at me directly.

"Who runs this charity, and under what authority? We have no proper record of it on our books. We have correct permissions on our books"—he referred to his papers—"for the Dufferin Fund ladies, and a number of Catholic charities from overseas. You're not here."

I kept my voice as steady as I could. "Are you sure there is no record? Our founder, Daisy Barker, worked in India for years before Independence: first in a Bombay orphanage, then setting up this home."

He opened his hands wider. "Miss Smallwood. I can't conjure facts from nowhere. Was this Miss Barker a qualified doctor?"

I stared at him. "No."

"Under whose authority was she here?"

"I don't know."

The three men exchanged incredulous looks. Dr. Masudi shook his head and sucked his teeth.

"Madam," Dr. Diwan said at last, "do you not think it an act of extreme presumption for two Englishwomen to come to our country with no clear understanding of our religions, or proper medical qualifications, and instruct our women in childbirth? How would you feel if the situation was reversed?"

"It wasn't like that." A mouse squeak of desperation in my voice. "Our aim was to work alongside Indian midwives to learn from them too."

"And were the midwives glad for this?" the man on his left rumbled.

"Some were," I said. "Some wanted the old ways."

"Who started the fire?" asked the hitherto silent Dr. Masudi with a penetrating look.

"I don't know," I said, startled by this sudden detour.

"But you were there first." Dr. Masudi cleared his throat noisily.

"Was I? I honestly don't know."

"One of the nurses said you had the key." I saw in his eyes the frozen look of a cat about to pounce. "What was the purpose of the fire?" he asked softly.

"I don't understand the question."

"For money? To cover up false records and end an already hot potato: the death of Mrs. Nair's baby?"

"This is madness." I seemed to be speaking out loud. "It makes no sense."

"Like much of what you've said to us today." Dr. Diwan blew his nose loudly.

"Don't bully me." I was suddenly furious with Dr. Diwan and his frowning friends. "Many women here die horrible deaths because nobody gives a damn about them."

"Watch your tongue, madam," Dr. Diwan almost shouted. "Don't you point your finger at me."

"It was your midwives who told us about women with sticks in their cervix trying to abort babies; about thirteen-year-old girls ripped to pieces in childbirth. I didn't make this up."

I was determined not to cry. "So we tried to discover the best in each other, and now it's gone."

Silence in the room. I've done it now, I thought. They'll lock me up—the madwoman in contempt of court. Instead, Dr. Diwan suddenly looked intensely bored. He licked his finger, rustled through the book. He gave a deep sigh.

"Midwife certificate is not here," he repeated like an automaton, "so don't make any arrangements to leave the country. We know where you live, and we know your husband's family. If you thought you could hide that, you were wrong."

"I won't be leaving. I love this country."

He gave another sniff; he was not impressed.

"All I can repeat is not to leave until we have decided. In the meantime, my strong view is that the Home must be permanently closed."

- CHAPTER 51 -

"You said *what?*" I was sitting on the floor in front of Anto, who was stroking the nape of my neck where the muscles stood out like organ stops.

"I was stupid. I got angry—the stupidest thing possible." I moved his hand to the worst spot. "God knows what will happen now."

"I think they are trying to bully and intimidate you. Some other drama will soon obsess them. A bribe may settle it."

"Anto, I can't believe you said that."

"Your greatest danger is the woman lawyer." He was thinking hard. "If she decides to take you to court, the newspapers will hear about it and then they'll have to do something."

He was right of course. She was highly trained, she was angry and hurt, she could put me in jail, and what kept me awake for the next two nights was the thought that if I put my hand directly into this wasps' nest, I might make everything worse and seal my fate. But if I'd messed this one up, and the baby's death was my fault, maybe my career as a midwife should end; it would be the final proof that I wasn't up to it.

It wasn't hard to track her down, there not being many female law-yers in Fort Cochin. She lived in Quiros Street, a few blocks away from us. Her ground-floor flat, one of three in the house, was so small, the veranda was piled high with cooking pots and suitcases, a cot, and a baby bath.

If she was surprised to see me at the door, she didn't show it. She stood there, very tiny, very poised, very neat, with oiled black hair and in a blue salwar kameeze.

"I'm so sorry, Mrs. Nair," I said. "I've only just heard."

"So you haven't forgotten me?" she asked when she could speak.

"Of course not."

"I'm sorry." She blurted out.

She beckoned me inside a tiny, dimly lit sitting room that looked like an office with a large typewriter on the desk and bookshelves piled high with legal books.

"Sit down, please." She moved a manila folder from the battered sofa. "I'm surprised to see you."

"I came because I heard about your baby. Do you mind talking about him?" I said, very tentatively.

"No," Mrs. Nair said. "And please call me Saraswati." She leaned forward, her brow creased and concentrating. "I wanted to see you," she said faintly at last, "to talk about Sanje."

"He was beautiful," I said, remembering his black hair, his little fists punching the air. "He really was." I watched her anxiously. How much could she take?

"Nobody really knew him but you and my husband," she said. "And now my husband has gone too." Close up, I saw she'd been crying before I came.

"Your husband's gone?" Still feeling my way gingerly, sure the anger would come soon.

"Back to my mother-in-law's house."

"Will he come back?"

"No. Can I tell you the story?" She said this eagerly, hopefully, as if she'd been waiting for me to come.

"Of course."

"Well . . ." She swallowed hard. "We tried for a very long time for this baby. I had my daughter twenty years ago, and then nothing. Everyone was so happy when we got Sanje, but now his family blame me for being too old and for working too hard before the delivery." She shot me a look of wild distress and clutched her handkerchief. "There was so much work since Independence, I did work extra hours, so tell me honestly, was it my fault?"

"That's extremely unlikely," I said as gently as I could. "We have women coming in after working incredible hours in the paddy fields or hauling bricks. Tell me what you think happened."

She took a deep, jagged breath and after a while began. "I was frightened when I came to you, but the Moonstone had a good reputation and I knew English doctors were there." I winced at this. "You were all kind to me and I thought my delivery was good."

"It was," I said. "You were calm, you were . . ." The word *excited* seemed too cruel. "Well prepared, your body strong. You didn't seem in the least tired. Most of the women we see are much more tired; some are very ill-nourished too."

I kept going. "I can see Sanje's head, his beautiful black hair, and you held him in your arms. You said, 'God is good.'" I couldn't go on. There were no words of consolation to cover this loss.

"He died two weeks after I brought him home," she whispered, glancing towards the veranda as if he might just suddenly and miraculously appear. "He was feeding well, all lovely and fine at night when I put him to bed, and then gone." She opened her arms wide. "White like this." She pointed to the tablecloth under the typewriter. "Cold." The word reverberated like a clanging of a bell. "Mother-in-law says it's God's punishment to me."

"Why on earth would God punish you for that?"

"She is a very strict Brahman. When we first met, I tried to follow all the rules for women, but I found them too constricting." She waved a weary arm at the books, the typewriter. She bowed her head, then looked at me directly. "My husband and I were becoming more isolated from religion, both trying to hide it. I loved my job. I loved my freedoms. But I must have done something wrong."

"Nothing," I said, leaning towards her. "Nothing."

I wanted to hold her hand, but I only had words and knew if I chose the wrong ones, they could wound her for the rest of her life. "Babies and small children are always vulnerable," I said. "Particularly in the first few weeks after birth. We don't want them to be, but they are. It's hard to live independently."

"Yes." She was wiping her eyes discreetly, her mouth working violently. "But they don't die like that in your country," she said angrily.

"Yes, they do. It happens many times in our country, to women who are strong and healthy, and to the weak. No one really knows why: it's one of those horrible mysteries."

Beyond her sigh I heard the angelus bell chime from the church. I was going to be late home. A home where my live boy was waiting for me.

"Saraswati," I said urgently, "I'm so, so sorry, but I have to go now. If you like, I'll come back, but I have one important thing to ask you before I go: do you blame me for Sanje dying?"

She lifted her head. "No." She looked absolutely bewildered. "Why?"

"I was told that you may have reported me."

"No!" Even more shocked. "Why would I do that?"

"You said sorry to me when I came in," I said as gently as I could. "Why did you say that?"

"Because I lost our baby," she said. "You were so happy when he was born."

"But forgive me." I was starting to falter. "Last week I had to go before a medical tribunal. I was told before I went that you had something to do with it."

"Me?" She looked horrified.

"That you were unhappy with your treatment at the Home and thought it had led to Sanje's death."

"Who said this?" It was her turn to look flabbergasted.

"I don't know." I believed her instantly; the best actress in the world couldn't have put on that show. "Saraswati," I said, "what happened after you found Sanje in his cot?"

"My husband called a doctor he knew. From the local hospital, an old family friend. It was six thirty in the morning. He examined Sanje, confirmed what we knew. Later, he was the one who told my mother-in-law I'd been working too hard, that my milk was thin. But this man is very traditional, doesn't like me, doesn't approve of working women." Her face darkened when she said this.

"Did he have any idea where you'd delivered the baby?"

"Yes," she said, as we shared the same thought. "He told me not to go there."

Her eyes were wide open now. She stayed like this, thinking, for a while. "So, the Home burned down," she said at last in a faraway voice. "I read about it in the papers. That was a terrible thing."

"It was awful." I felt it in my gut again. "The worst feeling in the world. I think someone put a match to it."

She gave me a sightless look, did some more staring and thinking. She tapped her fingernail on her front tooth. "Don't forget that I am a lawyer," she said at last. "I have a first-class honors degree. If I can help, I will."

Three weeks later, on a wet November afternoon, she turned up on my doorstep—thinner, taller-looking, her hair bobbed and shining, and wearing a raincoat over a chic salwar kameeze. If she hadn't said her name, I wouldn't have recognized her. It was a Friday, and I was packing for Raffie and me to go down to Mangalath and see Glory, who still wasn't well enough to travel.

Saraswati asked if I'd had any news from the tribunal. I told her no, nothing, but that I worried about it constantly.

"We must wait and pray," she said. "Don't forget you have a friend in me now."

We sat on the veranda, drinking tea, and talked for ages.

"There were things I couldn't tell you last time," she said, "but I'm ready to now." Turned out that the husband had another woman in Delhi. "She is ten years younger than I am," she said. "More suitable, more traditional. He'd fallen for her even before Sanje was born. I cried for many days when I heard, but now I've dried my tears and stopped trying to please everyone. I'm ready to work again. I am at your disposal." Her smile wobbled. "It's a good decision. We were never really friends."

I could hear Raffie laughing in the next room, his scampering footsteps. Anto had brought him a new wooden train, and he was obsessed with it, talked to it, put it to bed with him at night. When she saw my anxious look, she shook her head as if to say, Don't worry.

"I have my own flat now," she continued. "I'm earning my own money again." (A sore point for me, this. My last Bank of India statement showed the sum of £21.50 in my account. Soon I'd be completely dependent on Anto.)

"'God Bless the Child That's Got Its Own,'" Saraswati began, putting on a pair of horn-rimmed glasses that made her look about ten years older, "was written by a Negro slave. You may have heard it?"

She didn't wait for my reply but delved inside the large and impressive-looking briefcase she'd brought with her. She put pens and a large notebook on the table, talking all the while. She said that after the shock of her husband's defection had died down, she'd been surprised by a sense of soaring liberation. With no husband and no mother-in-law to placate, no family to impress with her modesty or her cooking, no "rumpy thump," as she quaintly termed it, in the bedroom, she was free to play a proper role in India's Independence now, and why hadn't she thought of this before? The

Matha Maria Moonstone Home for Mothers would be a perfect first project.

"With the tribunal breathing down your neck, I know you are unable to help properly," she said, "but I can make inquiries on that score, and from now on I will call it the MMM to save time, if you don't mind."

"I can help behind the scenes." I felt happier than I had in ages.

"Spot on, then." She handed me an empty notebook and a pencil. "Begin, please, with a full list of everyone who ever worked at the Home: their addresses, and if possible their castes. Include all the trainee midwives. If we are going to get the Home out of the ashes, we must rescue its reputation first."

Addresses for some of the village midwives would be difficult, I told her: some lived in shacks, others were secretive about where they lived, in case their customers had complaints.

"As many as you can, then," she said. "We must rule out nothing and nobody." Raffie wandered in then, his train on a string. He was tired from his play and making the train sounds that went with it. He climbed onto my lap, put his head on my chest, wound my hair round his finger, and murmured sleepily.

"You're a beautiful boy." Saraswati pulled one of his toes gently and watched him fall asleep.

"D'you mind him here?"

"*No*," she said indignantly. "I like it." She kept her hand on his foot. "You know, I've been thinking about it a lot, and it may sound funny, but being in labor with Sanje reminded me of what it felt like to use every ounce of physical and emotional energy in my body. Now I know this energy is there,"—she gazed at me intently through her formidable glasses—"I will dedicate it to the job at hand." It felt like a little speech she had rehearsed for herself and for me, but no less brave for it.

*   *   *

Saraswati would come over almost every morning and was nothing short of magnificent. I thought it might take months for us to get the information we needed. I hadn't reckoned on a whirlwind.

Our first task, she said, was to hire a rickshaw and call on local women so they could write or dictate testimonials about their experience of the Moonstone. The rains had stopped, the air was warmer, drier. I set up a desk at the end of the veranda, the coolest place in the house with its soft sea breezes, and when the testimonials came in, typed them up in triplicate: one for officialdom, one for our files, one for Daisy. It did my battered heart good to read them.

"Husband never let me go to a hospital before, so was very frightened," wrote Bachi from a local slum. "But the ladies at the Home were kind to me and very gentle, I would go again if I could."

"I liked this place: nice food, and very clean" was another typical response, from Parvati.

Not everyone was so rapturous. "They are all government spies there, so good it burned. From a Frend (sic)."

Next, Saraswati had a breakthrough with the Cyclops, the battered old truck Mr. Namboothiri occasionally loaned us. On its first outing since the fire, it belched blue smoke, spluttered, and died, so Saraswati persuaded a cousin, "a mechanical" to look at it. The cousin returned it oiled, tires pumped, surfaces polished, and with a wreath of marigolds and Hanuman, the monkey god, hanging from its rearview mirror. A few days later, he drove us to the village of Nilamperur to see Subadra, one of our first trainees.

Subradra, fatter than ever, yelped with joy at the sight of us. She took us into her hut, plied us with tea and sticky pastries and some livid-pink barfi that reminded me of calamine lotion.

The pride with which Subadra produced her certificate from the Moonstone was touching, and when Saraswati got out her notebook and started to question her, Subadra said, "I've delivered more than twenty babies since the Moonstone training and have definitely changed in my practice. I follow the hygienic wash between the babies, and I use sterile equipment to cut the cord."

The scissors, swabs, needles we'd given her were kept in a jam jar on the shelf and were obviously unused.

"We want you to use them all the time," I told her. "If they get old, we will give you more." She looked at me dubiously as if I might snatch them away. "I like them new," she said.

"So what are you using instead?"

She produced a battered knife, a pair of scissors, a pot of herbs. "But I boil everything in water between women now to keep them sweet and clean." At the end of our visit, Subadra said to us, "It was good, our time with you. We still talk about it. We taught you our ways, but we learned too."

Subadra's words reminded me of the basic goodness in so many of the women we'd met: it lay underneath like an underground river, a kindness deeper than race or nationality. I didn't bother sharing this thought with Saraswati the realist; she might have teased me, and anyway, as Cyclops lurched along the track going home, she was complaining: "Some of these women will go on exactly as they always did, with the rusty knife and with all the ignorance of poverty. They shut their minds." But then she did concede that Subadra was, at least, boiling water now, and very disapproving of another midwife who made girls lie in their own filth for days.

Our truck was passing through a small village where four half-naked boys were washing at the village pump. They ran alongside us, shouting and laughing, jumped on our running board, and waved vigorously through the window.

I saw Saraswati flinch as she looked at them, and then she waved. "Silly boys," she said softly and closed her eyes.

- CHAPTER 52 -

"Don't take this cancer lark too seriously" was mother's breezy message to me, when she broke the news. The doctor had confirmed lung cancer, but she was desperately keen for me to see it as a temporary irritation: another rabbit on the road. But a childlike terror, a darkness was rushing down the track towards me, and I was no good at this game anymore. Don't leave me, I wanted to say to her. Not now. Stay with me. How powerless we all are in the end.

Since Glory was so ill, Amma had suggested I come to Mangalath for a few weeks to be with her, and on my first afternoon back, Glory and I lay on either side of her bed in the cool, restful, high-ceilinged room that she liked so much. We watched a small lizard dart across the ceiling. "Sweet little fellow," she murmured.

Her face was all bones and eyes now and deathly pale. I wanted to hold it in my mind forever. Her teeth looked larger in her head. But there was beauty there, and nobility, and a kind of grace under pressure which I admired, and when my fear subsided, I had odd moments of seeing what was so obvious in the end: I loved her and always would.

"When did you know she was this ill?" I asked Amma one afternoon when my mother was asleep. Amma put a plate of perfectly sliced mango on the bedside table, next to a coffee served in Glory's special cup—the green-and-white Royal Worcestershire.

"We were out in the garden walking," Amma told me in a breathless whisper. "Glory refused the walking stick that made her look like an old granny. I was looking for one of my chickens. When I turned, she was in a heap underneath the flame of the forest tree.

"When she woke up, she said, 'I'm a clumsy clot and a damned nuisance.' Then she said, 'Don't tell Kit.' I said, 'Why not, she is your daughter?'" Amma's eyes widened with shock. "'It's her duty to help and she will be happy to do so.'" Amma touched my hand but I still heard a hint of challenge.

I was aware that Amma was upset. It seemed to me she'd grown fond of Glory in the way of two horses put in field together who will either kick each other to smithereens or eventually sniff and accept each other and become glad of each other's company. I'd eavesdropped on their minor skirmishes on the best way to clean a Persian rug or where scent was best placed (Glory: pulse of your wrist. Amma: folds of your clothes). They appreciated high standards in each other, the many small and unremarked acts it took to create a house of real beauty for other people to carelessly enjoy. One afternoon when we were sitting together, Amma looked at my mother, who was asleep, and said, "Your mother and I are both at the lonely end of life. Children mostly gone, husbands busy or dead. It's easy to think, What am I for?"

I was about to protest but she added quickly, "Don't say anything. I'll always love my little rascal but I don't know him anymore. He's very Western."

My mother hovered between life and death for five days. On the fourth day, when I set her special cup on the bedside table, she opened her eyes and said, "Oh, you angel. Nothing nicer than the smell of coffee in the morning." I watched her take a sip, saw the almost transparent thinness of her hands, the blue-and-white veins that stood out as if in a medical drawing. At nights her cough rattled the house.

"It's nearly nighttime, Ma," I whispered. Through a gap in the shutters the sky was streaked with turquoise and pink stripes; a cockerel was crowing.

She drained her cup, dabbed her lips delicately with a white napkin, and fell back on the pillow. Her breathing, irregular and hoarse, was a tremendous effort now.

"Lie beside me." She patted the empty space beside her. While she slept, I thought of all the ways I'd found to criticize her: for my lack of a father, for the way she'd despised my job, for the constant moving, the advice—that had increasing seemed so trivial—about keeping men happy, or looking smart, or being posh.

I understood better now that the clothes, the right notepaper, the jokes had been her weapons of war in a world which had treated her badly. I could see her life distinct and separate from mine. I pictured the high-spirited misfit she must have been at the orphanage, and later, the glamour-puss at some government ball: coiffed, amusing, a little bit acid, a challenge. Or later still, when life had really left its mark on her, on her own, in a café in London, husbandless, penniless, scanning the Situations Vacant. Me beside her. With no family and no home, no wonder she'd needed, or felt she needed, every mask she could find in order to survive, and I'd despised her for them.

"A rupee for your thoughts, darling," came a faint voice from the pillow. She'd been watching me, as she had for years, anxiously gauging my state of mind.

"Not worth it," I said. Pity was the last thing she would want now. "Only that I . . ." But she was back, as she would put it, in the arms of Morpheus, and while she slept, I wanted her forgiveness.

The next day, she took a turn for the worse: breath labored and harsh; narrow ribs jerking when she coughed; red toenails clenching, unclenching. Conscious, she grimaced, sweated, sometimes roared with pain, or maybe frustration, but my God, she clung on.

At sundown, the family priest, Father Christopher, came and read a prayer.

"Dear God, you love me too much to let me suffer unless it be for my good. Therefore, oh Lord, I trust myself to you; do with me as you please. In sickness and in health, I wish to love you always."

I watched Glory's face while he read this, half expecting a skeptical eye to open and her to say, If this is your idea of God's love, forget it. But she was too ill for quips.

She was never alone. The doctor came with medicines, and we sat beside her hour after hour. Anto, and Mariamma and Amma, and Appan when he was at home, even Ponnamma took her turn, bringing some wobbly sewing with her and saying with the cheerful heartlessness of the old, "How long can she go on for now? Taking her time, isn't she?" Glory enjoyed this sort of tactlessness, laughed about it with me when she had the breath.

Raffie ran in from time to time to show her things: his train, a teddy bear. He told her what he was doing. He wasn't scared, or didn't seem to be. But one day she was coughing fit to bust as we left the room, and he held my hand as we walked downstairs, and he explained to me in his sensible voice, "Grandma Glory is very old now," and glanced at me anxiously, just as she always had, to see if I understood and if I minded.

And then—it was a Sunday morning—she suddenly said, without opening her eyes, "There's no one there," with a note of horror in her voice as if she'd already been to the other side and found it not her cup of tea at all. I missed not being able to laugh about this too.

Around four, I heard the crunch of a car drawing up on the gravel outside, the squeak of brakes. I went to the window, looked out, and froze. It was my father. He was walking slowly towards the house with Amma by his side.

It's all too late, I thought, watching his pottery gait up the path. And you're too old. That's all I felt: not glad, not relieved. I was guarding her now as fiercely as a mother guards a baby, worried that the shock of seeing him might finish her off.

When he came in, he went straight to the bed, put a gnarled hand on her forehead, and gave a queer sound, somewhere between a sob and a groan. It was awful.

"Glory," he said, "it's me. It's William," and then, in the same cracked voice, "I love you, Glory, that's what I've come to say. I love you and I'm so terribly sorry."

His eyes were streaming, so I gave him my handkerchief. Amma turned away from him. I could see she was praying.

"I'll leave you to it," Amma said. She squeezed my hand. "I'll explain later."

When she was gone, I said, "What are you doing here? Please don't do that." He was making a bubbling sound.

"I'm sorry—I'm so sorry," he said, his eyes trained on her. "I couldn't not—you see . . ." His mouth kept opening and shutting without any sound coming out, and when he took her hand, it took all my willpower not to snatch it away. "She wrote to me. She asked me to come. I couldn't let her down again." He sat beside her on the bed and put his head against hers, two shrunken and collapsed puppets almost unbearable to look at.

"She can hear me," he said. "She just squeezed my hand." I looked at him. I looked at her.

Never turn strangers away from the door, lest you turn away angels. It's one of Amma's frequent expressions. Well, he was no angel, God knows, and there had been times since I'd met him that I'd wished him to rot in hell, but even I had to admit that though my mother's eyes were still shut, she had a strange inward look on her face that was different. I saw her fingers bend around his, the tense lines of her face relax into a look of safety, even contentment, as if she'd been returned to a time when his presence meant happiness.

When evening fell, the light through the window deepened

into a purplish black. Pathrose came in "to freshen up water for Mummy" and light the oil lamps that cast a glow. He left a whisky and soda for us both, and some sandwiches, biscuits, and cheese for the English visitor. We ate them in silence but for the pop of the lamp, her breathing between us. And this was strange too, and still painful to write: for the three hours we sat there, we were, for the first and last time, a family, and then it was over.

"Anto," I said, when he walked in at three a.m., "this is my father." William struggled to his feet, crumpled and red-eyed, trying to straighten his spine into what I can only assume was some remnant of military bearing.

Anto smiled at him. "I'm very glad to meet you, sir, but sorry it is under these circumstances. Glory," he knelt down beside her. "It's Anto. I want to see how you are." He turned her thin wrist, took her pulse, rested his hand on her forehead. "I hope you don't mind stepping outside for a moment." His gaze came to rest on William, and then on me. "I need to do a further examination."

I was about to write, "The performance was vintage Anto," but this is the important point. It was not a performance, but a demonstration of everything I valued in my husband now: the kindness, the undramatic goodness, the competence. It would have been against his nature to hurt the feelings of this unexpected guest.

My mother died on the wave of one last spluttering sigh. No death rattle, and absurdly, I was glad about this, she would have hated one. Unladylike! It was over.

Amma and Mariamma came in with water and cloths and clean white burial clothes. They tied her jaw. When we washed her, I was shocked at how thin she'd become, her veins a road map inside her. We dressed her in the Christian Dior nighty she'd been saving, and followed the Nasrani custom of placing her dead body with her face pointing towards the east and her feet towards the west, although Glory, I think, would have preferred it the other way around.

We lit a row of candles beside the carved cot, where I imagined dozens of Thekkedens must have been laid out. It's a funny word to use, but I felt at that moment almost euphoric with relief and gratitude. It was all done so quietly, so kindly, so naturally, with all the dignity that ritual bestows. No high-speed hospital dash, no drama, just this quiet slipping away in a place where she'd been loved.

As for my father, when the shock receded, I was so angry, I could have kicked him. See, she survived, I wanted to tell him. She got over you. She lived her life. We didn't need you. He'd scuttled away soon afterwards.

- CHAPTER 53 -

When it was done, Amma took a pail of hot water into the bath house and spent forty minutes scrubbing herself from head to foot. Hair first, with the coconut oil soap she made herself, then face, nails, legs, arms with a soft brush. She cleaned her teeth with a twig, dressed herself in a clean chatta and mundu, and when she emerged, glowing and oiled, she rattled off a list of instructions to Pathrose on the removal of the bed and mattress and the purification of the house, which would take several days. Father Christopher would come that night to bless the house and sanctify it.

As she walked towards the summerhouse, she was hollow-legged with tiredness. The family had sat with Glory from three thirty until dawn, saying the rosary and singing hymns, drinking endless cups of black coffee and tea. Now the Christian part of her brain muttered prayers for Glory's safe departure; the pagan part rejoiced to be free of the heavy fug of the invalid rooms, the blanket bath, the bedpans until the next time, which would probably be Ponnamma.

"Ten days is a long time to hang on, Glory," she murmured to the deceased. The arrival of the sad old husband had put them all under extra strain.

It was lovely out. An early shower of rain had scattered the path with the scented golden flowers of the champa tree, and death had charged the evening with significance. Tucking a flower in her hair, Amma wondered how many more years she had left. Her eyes misted as she planned her own funeral—sobbing grandchildren, an inconsolable Mariamma and Appan—then the fantasy dissolved into darting concerns about food for Glory's funeral. The traditional meal—vegetables, rice gruel, a buttermilk curry, pappadams—was easy to make, but how many to ask? Who would be staying?

And then she stopped and deliberately emptied her mind. "Take a breath," her father used to tell her when she got too whizzy. "Chew some air."

She looked around her slowly. The garden was always at its most beautiful before the sun set: an intense, luminous underwater that lit up the jagged fringe of palm trees, the flowers, the silver flash of the cove, light that would deepen and fade before darkness descended. Close to the summerhouse, she bent down to the dancing girl orchid, touched its leaves. The sprinkle of purple spots at its tip was as sweet and delicate as the freckles on a child's nose. She was prodding the soil around it, at peace for the first time that day, when she heard a low rasping sound coming from the shed, and then a long drawn-out howl. She picked up a spade, ready to throw it at the pye-dogs who came regularly to scavenge, and, peering through the window, saw William Villiers sitting on the bench, his arms clasped tightly around him. He was rocking and sobbing with the abandon of a child.

She stood frozen for a few moments, spade in her hand. For a man like this to be caught crying would be worse than being seen on the potty. Appan, who'd spent years observing the English with the kind of anxious love a collie feels for its master, had told her once about stiff upper lips, and she'd laughed, thinking it was a phrase he'd made up. She took another step forward, touched the pane of glass with her hand, and listened intently. When the sobs dwindled into a long drawn out "oooohhhhh" of despair, she gave a big sigh, straightened her shoulders, and pushed the door open.

"Mr. Villiers, I'm here also." She put down the spade as if a bit of shed tidying was all she planned to do.

"Oh Lord!" He looked up, dotty-looking in his surprise. His mouth began to work violently, like that of a child determined not to cry. "Oh God." He pulled a spotted handkerchief out of his pocket, buried his face in it. "Sorry," he said in a muffled voice. "Can't go home like this."

She touched his arm. "Don't dash off," she said quietly. "Take your time. We'll be saying prayers for her soul tonight."

"I shouldn't have come," he said. "It's made everything worse."

"It was what Glory wanted," Amma said.

"For herself? For the girl?"

"I don't know."

This was true. During the long night when Glory had raged incoherently about this man, she had told Amma that he should come, that she needed to tell him things, and Amma had indulged her. As for Kit? God knows: she'd played her cards very close to her chest regarding this father of hers.

"Over there was Glory's gin and tonic spot." She pointed at a bench near the water. She picked up his sodden handkerchief and handed it back to him. "She liked looking at the water and the trees."

He stood up, shifting the ripe smell of distress and pipe tobacco towards her.

"Such a shock, you know." He fumbled the handkerchief into his pocket. "Didn't see her for years, decades, and then all this."

"I understand," she said, although the messiness of it appalled her. To give him time to start breathing normally again, she offered to show him her orchid garden.

"These are my invalids." She led him to her row of flowers planted in coconut shells. "My husband brings them from all over India. They take awhile to find their feet. This one," she said, pointing to the orchid tree, glowing against the darkening sky, "is a miracle worker. Stems are used for leprosy, or ulcers, paste from leaves for headaches. You can also eat it as a vegetable.

"And this is my dancing girl," she said at the next plant. "Glory loved her. She was a wreck when she came from Bangalore, now look at her—eight new buds on the stem."

William knelt down obediently with a great cracking of knees and touched the flower. As he did so, his regimental signet ring flashed and fell into the earth. "Damn thing doesn't fit me," he said, as she passed it back. "I'm bound to lose it one day." He shoved it in his pocket and sat back on his heels looking at the garden with a bemused expression. "I never thought she'd come back," he said.

"No way of contacting her?" Amma said with a lemony look. This was going too far.

"I tried. Wrote for years. Never got a reply. Only from her friend, Miss Barker." She heard the clicking in his throat. "Sorry," he wheezed at last. He was at it again, helpless before an unstoppered tide of grief. "Sorry."

She waited until he could talk again. "What would you like to do now?" she said gently.

"I want to go home," he said. "My driver's waiting in the village."

"Will you come back?"

"I don't think so." He looked down at his brogues; they were covered in dust. "There are a few . . . complications."

"I know." Glory had told her about the wife in Ooty. "But not even to see Kit?" She looked at him directly. "Your grandchild?"

"I don't know." There was question in his eyes, and an apology. "Do you think I should?"

"That's for you to decide." She smiled her practiced smile, thinking, What an absolute bloody fool—another phrase that Appan had taught her. Be a man, find out for yourself.

- CHAPTER 54 -

I spent a day at Mangalath with Amma, who was sorting out her linen cupboard and wanted to give me some new sheets and tablecloths, and—hint, hint—some baby clothes that might be useful to me in the future. It was exactly the sort of task Glory would have enjoyed: the folding, the scenting, the doing something undemanding but practical with me. The thought of how, in the last few years, I'd denied her these small pleasures was like a knife in my heart.

Saraswati's arrival later in the day cheered me up, though Amma was clearly annoyed. The Nasrani custom, she reminded me in a tight voice, was to mourn the dead for nine days during which time no one came to the house. "This is not normal."

Well, Saraswati was not normal. With her charming and brilliant smile she apologized to Amma, put a bulging briefcase down on the floor, and as soon as Amma had left the room, exploded with plans.

"I'm twisting the arms of more local businessmen. My sales pitch is straightforward: 'Wake up. See the situation plainly.'" She demonstrated, eyes flashing. "'Too many babies are dying all over India; share the knowledge we have gained in our training centers.' Only one or two have given me some stick. 'Why change old ways?' they say, or, 'Are you a man-hating feminist?' 'Man hater?' I tell them, 'We're here to protect your male babies too, by the way. Your indifference will kill them.'"

Her next rabbit from the hat was a set of plans, donated by an architect she knew. The drawings showed a fifteen-bedroom unit to be built in breeze block with a properly tiled roof and enough room inside for three consulting rooms, a dispensary, a reception area, and a large veranda.

To ensure "no jiggery-pokery" about the Moonstone's ownership of the two acres of land it stands on, she'd also undertaken a search at the local Land Registry office.

She was pretty sure the actual deeds got lost in the fire but also asked me to write to Daisy in case they were at Wickam Farm. The thought of the chaotic attic there made me shudder.

The dark rings under her eyes had grown. When I asked if she was getting enough sleep, she said that with her husband gone and no mother-in-law to please, "I have plenty more hours in the day, and I'm using them."

But the biggest fly in the custard, the one we avoided discussing until the last possible moment, was that we were practically broke. Saraswati estimated that the new home, plus fixtures, fittings, and restocking the pharmacy would cost in the region of one hundred and thirty thousand rupees, the equivalent of ten thousand pounds in English money. An impossible amount, a pipe dream.

Saraswati, busily scribbling the sums down, saw my expression, put her pencil down, and stuck her finger in the air.

"First it was impossible. Then it was difficult. Then it was done," she said, adding, without a glimmer of a smile and with an intensity that frightened me, "It has to work, otherwise I will throw myself on the funeral pyre."

Four months after my mother's funeral, I got a big scare when a khaki-colored official-looking envelope arrived covered in unfamiliar handwriting. Saraswati had told me not to worry too much about the Medical Tribunal, telling me they were months behind with cases and would probably forget me. But in that panicked moment I pictured jail or deportation, or at the very least, a fine we couldn't possibly afford.

It turned out to be a brief note in a large envelope from my father. The spidery hand informed me he was back in Ooty and wanted to give me "one or two things of Glory's that you might like. Nothing precious, mementoes." I was to write back to Box Number 36, the Ootacamund Club.

When I read the letter, anger flared up inside me, and I thought, Stay where you are, you slippery old fraud, with your aliases and your box numbers. I didn't want my phantom father breezing in again and stirring things up.

When Anto read the letter, I watched his expression change from frowning concentration to sympathy.

"Poor old man," he said. "Let him come or at least send whatever it is. This could be the Hope diamond."

"Poor man!" I exclaimed. "The khaki envelope scared me to death, and anyway, what about poor Glory, poor me? He behaved appallingly."

"You asked me what I thought." Anto trained his green eyes on me. "I am saying what I think."

"I'm fed up with you being nicer than me," I said after a while.

"Me too," he said. "It's a burden I bear."

I was pulling his hair. "Gray ones, please!" he said, when he held me close. "When are we going to have another baby?" he whispered.

"Soon," I said, ruffling his hair. "Will you mind if it's a girl?"

"No," he said. He looked hurt, because I get this wrong sometimes and assume things about him that are crude approximations based on what I think I know about Indian men. These are the moments when we make each other foreign and I deeply regret them.

"I'd like one too," I whispered, as he stroked my stomach. "I love my silly old man," and then he looked around like a guilty schoolboy because we were in his mother's house and he was her son too.

"Anto," I teased him, stroking his hair, "how old are you?"

He knew exactly what I meant. "Six years old when I am here," he said.

The next job was to sort through the sea trunk Glory had left in the spare room at Mangalath. As we opened the lid, the rush of something both spicy and sweet came from a half-finished bottle of Shalimar, one of Glory's "little extravagancies" during the grim years, the kind of thing (the Baccarat cut-glass bottle, the little velvet ribbon, her snooty expression as she dabbed it here and there) that had once made her seem, to me, so impossibly glamorous.

Her clothes made a pathetically small pile in the end. Two tweed skirts (Donegal tweed, as she'd been fond of pointing out, donated, or maybe not, from the vicar's wife in Durham), the dull cardigans and liberty bodices worn at Daisy's to stop her "freezing to death." A few light cotton dresses, and underneath them, wrapped carefully in layers of scented tissue, the good clothes: remnants of a life lived for one shining hour, and never again.

Amma and I laid them out on the bed: a slippery green satin dress, a silk suit with a Swan and Edgar label, a shagreen brush and comb set with a chipped handle, lipstick samples, a pair of jodhpurs, an Aertex shirt, a tin of Coty talcum powder with a carefree, brilliantly laughing woman on it, a pair of beautiful gold leather sandals (Charles of Lewes), still in their original box, an invitation for a free facial at the Belle Rose beauty parlor in Chelmsford.

The green satin dress had tiny heart-shaped mother-of-pearl buttons stitched on its waistband. I imagined her wearing it at a garrison party, and the hectic preparations beforehand. Her weapons: the tweezers, the comb, the wax strip. It mattered, really mattered, getting it right.

Inside a faded floral box, I found her wedding veil wrapped in pink tissue. Its brittle fabric was edged with crumbling dried flowers shaped like violets, the final symbol of her humiliation.

I wondered where she'd gone, after the Colonel had driven her away from the church. At what point in this whole horrible shamble had she learned that I was on the way? I ached to find out more, and now I never would.

"Shall I throw these away?"

Amma held out a few faded brown invitations: a pantomime in Braintree, a garden party at Major someone or other's—the name was past reading—house, The Palms, in Malabar Hills, on June seventh, on the occasion of his return to England, a ladies' coffee morning at the Bombay Yacht Club, five days after the canceled wedding.

What a meaty bone of gossip Glory must have thrown to the ladies at the club to gnaw on: "A chichi girl, can you imagine, darling?"

"The poor man had absolutely no idea whatsoever, she does look very pale." I hated them all.

At the bottom of the trunk, there was a book, *The Good Soldier*, by Ford Madox Ford. The inscription on the flyleaf read, "To my darling fiancée Glory, with grateful thanks for her eternal light-heartedness. Love, William."

Bits of me too: a smocked pink romper suit, a rattle shaped like a horse, a letter with a wonky drawing: "When you die Mummy, I will die wiv you." Dramatic child! and finally, right at the very bottom, a picture of me in my nursing uniform, aged nineteen, posing for a photograph on the day I got my certificate. The photo was half-hidden under the lining. It was not her dream for me, and never would be.

My father turned up at Mangalath later that week, unannounced, uninvited, and on the flimsiest of pretexts. He said he'd brought a box of teas from a planter friend, who happened to be driving by, and wanted to give them to Amma, who had been so kind. He'd smartened himself up for this outing: polished brogues, a worn but clean suit, a paisley tie. When he held out the box of teas to Amma, he shot me a quick hangdog look and I could barely look at him. It was Amma who offered him refreshments, a chair, a bed for the night. I would have shown him the door.

After he'd drunk his tea, I asked if he would like to see my mother's things. I don't think I was being deliberately cruel, but my ears buzzed with anger as I took him upstairs. I wanted him to see how little she'd ended up with, that there had been consequences.

Inside the spare room, he looked at her dresses, shoes, and knickknacks in silence for a while. He picked up the jodhpurs.

"I'd promised to teach her to ride," he said. When he started to paw the green dress, I wanted to scream and snatch it from him.

"I've got a lot to do today," I said. He was sniffling again.

He blinked at me like some sort of woodland animal coming out of a hole. "I'm so sorry," he said. "I must let you go on. I've been meaning to ask you, do you have any other children?"

"No, but we will." I was stung by how little interest he'd taken, and wanted the silly old fool to leave.

"But when we do have girls," I said, "we'll send them to the best school we can afford." The words were bursting out of me like hot water from a geyser.

"Good idea," he said. He folded her Aertex shirt, pressed it to his face.

"I want them to have a good job. Something solid and clean. Being defenseless is for the birds."

He looked at me warily. "I thought Glory got rather good jobs. Friends were always very kind and so forth."

"Oh God." That's when I really wanted to strike him. I could feel the blow run like an electrical current through my fingers. But he wasn't listening. The tips of his fingers were running over her green dress, a dreamy expression on his face.

Why did you dump her, if you felt like that? I almost said, but my anger was frightening me, so instead I took a deep breath, said I was tired and wanted to eat. To take a memento if he wanted it. The rest I'd give to charity or chuck away. He winced at that. I wanted him to.

He picked up *The Good Soldier*.

"I'd like this," he said. He was breathing strangely, and I thought for God's sake don't have a heart attack here, and how, if he did, I'd have to tell his wife and cart him out, and all manner of hard thoughts because I didn't want him in my life. Not now. "It was the first present I ever gave her."

"I read what you wrote inside it," I said. "Sweet." I was breathing heavily now too and felt I might at any minute explode with tears.

He touched the dress again. "She wore this at the Willoughby. Turned a lot of heads, I can tell you."

And a fat lot of good that did her.

"'This is the saddest story ever told,'" he said in a faraway voice. "The first line in the book. I only read the thing last year. I gave it to her to impress her. Turns out it wasn't about a soldier at all."

"I know," I said. "It's about betrayal."

In the silence that grew between us, I heard the clink of pots from the kitchen where Pathrose was cooking. He'll be gone soon, I thought, and you won't have to think about him ever again because he doesn't want to know you, not really.

Before he left, he took a small box out of his pocket and said, "I've brought you something."

His shaky fingers struggled with the catch, and then he held up a nondescript gold ring with tiny pearls in it, and a few chips of what looked like garnet. It was dented on one side.

"It was all I could afford on a captain's pay. One of the stones is loose, and one is gone," he said. "I think she bashed it before she sent it back." The hangdog look again. "And this"—he pulled out a silver chain with a milky-colored stone at the end of it, the size of my little thumbnail—"is a moonstone. Common as muck over here, but very pretty."

"They're supposed to be lucky," I said.

"You won't get rich on it." He dropped it into the palm of my hand. "But you might give it to your daughter."

"I'm not sure I can keep them if she sent them back."

"Please have them," he said in a low voice.

Part of me felt like a traitor as I put them in my pocket. I couldn't bring myself to thank him for them. They felt like such paltry gifts, when we could have had a life together.

- CHAPTER 55 -

And then I was arrested. At the time it felt as sudden and jarring as that. I was sitting on the veranda at Rose Street catching up on some paperwork when, out of the corner of my eye, I saw a dusty black car draw up outside the house. Two men got out, cocky, self-assured. It took me a while to see they were wearing policemen's uniforms and had lathis stuck in their belts. They were walking towards my house.

And even then I wasn't too concerned. There had been a spate of robberies in the street, and they were smiling at me in a friendly way, so I assumed they were doing house-to-house inquiries.

The taller policeman took a piece of paper from his pocket. "Your name is Miss Kit Smallwood?"

"Yes." I felt my mouth go dry.

"We are here with a warrant for your arrest. We will take you down to the Cochin Police Station for questioning. We must warn you that anything you say will be taken down and used in evidence. It is advisable to bring a suitcase with you."

"A suitcase!" I was shocked. "Why?"

"You may stay down there."

"I can't! I have a child here." Except by horrible timing he wasn't. On the previous afternoon Raffie, clutching his teddy and a small bag, had walked with me, in a state of high excitement and a few nerves, to stay at his cousin's house a few streets away in Cochin. His first night ever away from me. The cousins had said they'd drop him back this morning, and now I imagined him racing up the front steps, bursting with news about his important adventure, and I wouldn't be there.

Anto was away too: he was giving a paper at a conference in Quilon. It was an important step professionally for him, and the thought of him coming home and finding me gone was horrible too.

"Can't I wait until my husband gets home?" I said. The small policemen leaned close enough for me to see mean dark crevasses from his lip to his chin.

"You have servants here?"

"Yes, two." I'd just seen Kamalam's frightened eyes peering around the door.

"So, let them see to your child, and they can tell your husband where you are," he told me. "There is a room waiting for you." I shuddered thinking of the dark, pee-smelling police station I'd been to with Neeta.

I gave rapid instructions to Kamalam. She must feed Raffie and reassure him I would be back soon. I'd bought his favorite cashew barfi to celebrate his return; she must make sure he got it, and tell him that Mummy loved him. She was not to worry; I would be back soon.

In the back of the car, the small policeman took a pair of handcuffs from his pocket. He locked one around my left wrist and one round his right.

I was driven to a small police substation near the docks and was locked into an interrogation cell—a high-walled room with a small window close to the roof that showed about one square foot of sky. A chair, a potty, a narrow cot, that was it. I listened to their footsteps echoing away; someone in a nearby cell was shouting and crying.

After hours of waiting in the cell, I sat in the chair and fell into a clammy sleep and woke to hear evening sounds outside: the market men putting up their stalls, the shouts of the rickshaw men, and then, suddenly, a policeman appeared in my cell—youngish, with a gap-toothed smile. He was wearing a cheap gold wedding ring and carrying a manila folder. He placed a chair a couple of feet away from me and sat down with an amiable grunt.

"Sorry for all the noise earlier," he said, fixing me with large sad eyes. "We had a man in too much for the toddy. He was calling for his mother."

I tried to smile. I desperately needed him on my side.

"So." The wedding ring flashed as he opened the file.

"My name is Inspector Pillay. You are Miss Kit Smallwood, from the Moonstone Clinic, Fort Cochin?"

"Correct." You blithe bloody idiot, I thought. It was clear from the thickness of the file that they'd had their eye on me for months, maybe from the moment I'd arrived. "And you are married to Dr. Anto Thekkeden." So much for protecting the family name.

"Can I speak to my lawyer?" How corny this sounded; I was in a bad play, one that made my voice tremble and my limbs turn watery.

"Name of the lawyer?" I'd been thinking about this earlier, stubbing my toe on the same door. Saraswati wouldn't do. When I'd asked her, in the early days, whether if the case ever went to court she'd represent me as a lawyer, she'd said it was impossible. "Because they'll call me as a witness, and the law is you cannot be both witness and lawyer." Our only slender hope was that the medical authorities wouldn't want her as a witness because they'd lied about her accusing me and they wouldn't want that can of worms opened. Appan, as my father-in-law, was no good either.

I had a vague memory of Appan mentioning another lawyer who might help, but I'd forgotten his name, and Pillay was saying impatiently, "So you don't seem to have a lawyer, and anyway, that would delay our proceedings tonight, and you have a child to attend to at home?" The sweet smile had turned sour and faintly incredulous. "Isn't that what you think of first?"

No other questions. When he left, I knew it must be dark by

now outside. I heard cell doors slamming, shouting, a subdued whimpering, and then a dead silence. An old woman in a sari came in, she gave me a bowl, some water, a square of cotton to wash myself with.

Don't you dare panic, I told myself. You don't ever, ever, ever have to tell anyone about this. Anto will come soon, Appan's fine legal brain will think of something, and you'll be home soon. You'll bathe Raffie, tuck him into the new "big boy" bed he was so proud of, smell his hair, kiss him *Night night, sleep tight, hope the fleas don't bite*, then a whisky and soda on the veranda with Anto, trying to laugh about what a close shave this had been.

When night fell, the lights went out. A leaking tap in the slop room next door went *drip, drop, flop*. The sounds swelled and magnified and became the nightmare accompaniment to a mood in which I hated myself intensely. I could practically see the lurid headlines already: "Unqualified English Midwife Kills Indian Babies." Anto could lose his job as a result of the fallout. My fault: my laziness, my pride, my condescension, *drip, drop, flop*, and worst of all, I was bringing fear and misery to a child who was too young to understand.

When morning came, the old woman who had strip-searched me appeared. She put a flat bread on the stool, and a small bowl of rice.

When Anto came, two hours later, pale and huge-eyed with shock, I saw him in the visitor's room, a bare space with spittoons in the corner full of sand. When I asked him how Raffie was, he said, "I was hoping they might release you today, so I wouldn't have to tell him." There was a long, tense silence. "I'll tell him tonight."

His expression made me think I had pushed him over the line that separates love and support from complete exasperation, contempt even.

"Are you angry?" I asked him.

"No," he said eventually with the yes-no gesture. "Only with myself."

"It wasn't your fault."

He didn't answer.

"Haven't they said anything?"

"Nothing. Only that it will go to trial. I'm worried they're going to make an example of you." He put his head in his hands.

"Anto," I said, "if it does go to trial, you must tell Amma." I winced with shame at the thought of it. "She'll help with Raffie."

"I can't. I've already spoken to Appan. He doesn't want her to know."

"That makes no sense: she's bound to find out."

The muscle in Anto's jaw was twitching, never a good sign. "He's adamant, but as soon as I leave here, I'm going to talk to him again. And if he won't help, I'm going to borrow Saraswati's law books and work through every precedent for voluntary and involuntary manslaughter, which is what Saraswati says they will charge you with if they charge you at all. She's confident this is just a saber-rattling exercise. The case is so full of holes, it's a farce." His smile didn't make it to his eyes, which were red-rimmed as if he hadn't slept all night.

"How was the conference?" I asked shortly before he left. "Did the paper go well?"

"I didn't give it. I came home when I heard."

"I'm so sorry." He'd spent months writing his paper on the management of epidemics with particular reference to African sleeping sickness. We'd rehearsed it together.

He looked away. "Forget it, but if you do have to stay, I can't just stop work."

We stared at each other.

"Let's wait," I said. "The whole situation might resolve itself quickly," though I knew from Saraswati that the legal system was clogged with cases. "What about Raffie? Should he go to Mangalath?"

"Appan's taking Amma away as soon as possible in case the newspapers get onto it."

"I thought they were strapped for cash at the moment."

"They are. He's not happy about it."

"Will they be bad? The papers, I mean."

"Sticks and stones," he said wearily. "Who cares?"

"Anto, I'm so sorry. I should have listened."

"Don't keep saying that," he said with a twisted smile. "And try not to worry too much. I'm going to talk to Appan again tomorrow. And if it kills me," he repeated, "I'm going to get you out."

- CHAPTER 56 -

He'd lied. The newspapers had pounced on the story with the speed of a dog spying a fillet steak.

"English midwife may be held responsible for new baby deaths" was front-page news in the daily newspaper, the *Malayala Manorama*. The *Hindu* led with a picture of the charred remains of the Moonstone Home. "First arson, now baby slaughter. What next?" was the caption.

When Anto went to work on the following day, his boss, Dr. Sastry, looked grim. The conference organizers were furious that Anto hadn't presented his paper. Their research team would never be asked again. "This won't help matters." Sastry stabbed at his copy of the *Hindu*. "Soon her name will be connected with yours. How many English midwives are there in Fort Cochin?" The same Dr. Sastry who had been so genuinely kind and welcoming was clearly frightened of contagion, and Anto understood why: research grants could be slashed overnight in the new India.

When Anto asked for three days off, Sastry agreed with bad grace, slamming the door behind him. Anto took a taxi and went at breakneck speed to Mangalath, to see Appan. As the car turned into the drive, he saw a pall of black smoke rising above the house, messing up the clear blue sky with cinders and soot.

"I got up early and burned all the newspapers I could find," Appan told him in a furious whisper in his study, where the windows were shut. "If your mother sees them, she will die of shame."

"Those are lies, Appan!" Anto said. "Do I really have to convince you of that? The important thing now is to get her out of jail."

"All I know," his father said, pale with rage, "is that up until recently, I have been systematically lied to about the true facts of your wife's occupation, and I find it hard not to blame you for not controlling her better." Anto said nothing, just stared at his father and shook his head. The final betrayal.

"Are you saying you won't help?" he said at last.

Appan heaved an enormous sigh. "Here are the two possibilities: she could be tried for involuntary manslaughter, which is a serious offense."

"I've looked it up," Anto said, "but it doesn't apply: involuntary manslaughter means you have shown a callous disregard for human life, the same thing you might be charged for if you drove a motorcar while drunk or left someone old with a mad dog."

"So, you're a lawyer now too, are you?" Appan's voice was a slap. "Some midwives are charged with this when things go wrong, but the other possibility is a charge of manslaughter and gross negligence. This could bring up to ten years in jail, if your wife had no license to practice. What was she thinking of?" His eyes bulged with disbelief.

Anto bowed his head.

"So reckless conduct is there too," Appan continued, tapping one hand impatiently on the desk. "And you want me to put my whole career on the line for this? Well, I won't. All I can do is thank God her name is listed in the papers as Smallwood, not Thekkeden."

"Well, what a wonderful relief!" Anto sprang to his feet. "As long as we're all right."

"Who do you think you're talking to?" Anto saw two blue veins bulging in Appan's forehead, the glimpse of back teeth, a sure sign his father was losing his temper, but Anto no longer cared. Let the old bully boy rot in hell.

"I'm talking to you, Appan," Anto said, "and what I have to say is this: my wife is innocent, but you don't give a damn about that, let's just worry about your reputation and the noble Thekkeden name." A drop of his sweat fell on his father's blotting paper.

"Leave my house," Appan said eventually in a quiet voice. "And don't come back if this is how you're going to be. I've spent my whole life in the service of the law. I won't throw it away." He took a handkerchief from the drawer and mopped his face.

"She's innocent. She was asked to help."

"Her innocence was dangerous and naive. How many warnings did you need?"

Anto picked up his coat. "I think we should end this conversation here. I won't come back until she's out."

"Do what you want." Appan shrugged. "Your mother is my main concern now. She's coming away with me to avoid the scandal. If your wife is charged, I'll tell the family she's gone to Madras to do more studying. That way, we won't have to talk about it."

"If that's what you want."

"It's what I want," his father said, his eyes straight ahead.

Anto closed the door behind him and walked away.

- CHAPTER 57 -

I was tried at the High Court of Travancore-Cochin at Ernakulam at eleven o'clock in the morning of Friday, May 5, 1951. The date and the time are engraved on my mind. My crime: manslaughter for gross professional misconduct. Saraswati, who had expected right up until the last moment to be called as a witness, was not called. The sentence: three months at the Women's Correctional Facility, Viyyur, a prison seventy-four miles north of Fort Cochin. The judge said I was lucky to get off so lightly, that gross professional misconduct was a very serious crime.

Six inches of rain fell on the day my case was heard. From the dock, the whoosh of bicycles going through puddles, windows rattling, puddles forming from dozens of sopping umbrellas near the door, steaming bodies—I remember those details but surprisingly little of what was said. The court had a blue ceiling, wicker chairs. Anto sat staring at me, trying to look encouraging, looking desperate; Saraswati Nair beside him, concentrating fiercely, wincing at the shortcomings of the only lawyer we'd been able to find at such short notice, a Mr. Kurup, a cold-eyed man in a badly fitting shiny suit, who mispronounced my name and spoke so fast I could barely understand a word.

Long before the judge—an old foe of Appan's—sentenced me, I had a swooping feeling that I'd started down the path of my own destruction. When the sentence was read out, I felt light-headed: this was happening to someone else.

When Anto came to see me afterwards in my cell, we agreed that he should tell Raffie that night.

"But I'm not going to tell him for how long." He tried to smile. "Saraswati says it could be much shorter than that. She says it's a slap on the wrist." The smile was even less successful this time.

Before he left, I said, "Can you bring Raffie to see me?"

He said, almost curtly, that he'd see what he could do. "It may upset him more." And that was it. I longed for him to touch me, to say something, but this unbelievable thing had left us both stunned and disconnected.

"So, I'd better go home now," he said, even though the guard hadn't asked him to.

"Yes, go." I said. "Give Raffie a kiss from me. Tell him I love him."

He tried to give me strength then: to tell me he was starting to understand the laws of manslaughter as well as any professional lawyer. That a retrial was inevitable, that it might only be a matter of days and weeks before I was set free. I heard these words as if through a thick pane of glass. He was surely talking about someone else.

And then he did kiss me, our arms and heads in a desperate tangle of love and sorrow.

"I'll be back tomorrow," he said.

I was taken in a prison van to Viyyur, a drive of roughly three hours from Fort Cochin, still too shocked to think straight. Before, I'd imagined that Appan with all his powerful friends would pay some fine, pull some string, or that Saraswati with her administrative genius would do something, or even, in my wildest dreams, that Dr. Annakutty would appear and admit that she had asked me to do the deliveries, and we had done them well. Now I felt like the most credulous idiot alive.

I thought about all the unremarkable things I normally did as part of a day's work. Getting up, getting washed, playing with Raffie, then housework, the meals, the study, the letter writing, the walks with Anto, all the seemingly unimportant acts that make up a life. All shut down. The Department for Correction owned me now—my body and my time. A terrible thought.

When we stopped south of Thrissur for petrol, the guard in the van put his hand on the diary I kept from time to time. "What are you writing?"

"Nothing," I said. "A journal." And then, with as winning a smile as I could muster, "You can read it if you like."

For the few seconds his hand hovered over the pages, I almost stopped breathing. Then he sniffed, his face contemptuous, and turned away. Why would an important man like him want to read a stupid diary?

"They may take it away in prison," he warned, when the van had coughed into life and we were moving again. I decided then and there I had to hide it, and hide it carefully. Started on this path of my own destruction, I needed an outlet, and for the time being this would have to be it.

First sight of the prison: worn earth, tired buildings, barbed wire, birds, blue sky, only the tips of trees.

As we drove down its long central road, the guard threw me a few scraps of information. This was mostly a prison for long-term male prisoners locked up for murder, for robbery, for theft. The women's prison was contained in two blocks: F and E in the center of the jail. There were two factory buildings where the women made baskets and clothes for a small wage every week. There was a prison garden.

When the van stopped, I was led down a long corridor into a tiny windowless room lit by one naked bulb. The cell had a charpoy, a thin pillow like a bolster, a gray regulation blanket with Property of Viyyur Prison on it. A bucket in the corner of the room.

An older man wearing stained overalls appeared with a bowl of water and a cloth. He told me to take my clothes off. He turned off the overhead light and locked the door. When I told him a woman should do this, he shook his head as if he didn't understand me. He didn't look at me as he ran his hands over my thighs, my stomach, my breasts, and finally between my legs. It was very mechanical, thank God; in fact, he treated me with some distaste, a contaminating white woman. He took away my dress and my shoes, and gave me a coarse white sari and a white loose blouse to wear. When I asked if I could keep my diary and a pencil, he rustled officiously through its pages, sniffed, and to my surprise, handed it back to me.

He looked at the wall while I was changing, then told me, in a high staccato voice, that I would stay in this cell for one or two nights and then I would be moved. He told me the cell was the regulation size, "with sufficient breathing air." The very idea of there being officially recommended air to breathe made the blood fizz in my veins.

On the next day, a new guard, young and with smallpox scars on his face, came into my cell, handcuffed me, and led me down the corridor and across a square to the women's prison on F block. I stood at the door, blinking and very frightened, as another man drew aside a series of bolts and led me into a large communal cell, about twenty by twenty feet, coir matting on the floor, high, stained walls. A gravy-colored light came from four or five smeared windows set in the roof.

When my eyes adjusted, I saw fifty or so women, some sitting on the floor, one or two vacantly staring, some asleep on thin mattresses on the floor. Most, I found out later, were there for long-term offenses: illegal alcohol making, vagrancy, prostitution, murder. There were three small babies in the room and five girls under ten.

The guard said something about me that I didn't understand but which made some of the women mutter and look suspicious and made me even more nervous about the night ahead.

When he left, a woman with a lopsided gait and her hair cut as short as a GI's, sat down on a mattress opposite me and sneered. I discovered later that this ex-schoolteacher had been one of a group of women rounded up during the riots, taken to the officers' mess, and raped repeatedly. The shame of being raped, and subsequently disowned by her family, had driven her mad. She should never have been there.

As soon as the guard left, the air was full of noise, a parakeet shrieking that shredded the nerves. None of the women spoke English, or if they did, not to me.

It was hot in the room and thick with smells. The madwoman sat staring at me until an older woman with an air of authority touched my arm and led me to a bed on the other side of the room. She held up her finger: Wait! and a few moments later came back with a cup of water for me to drink. She didn't smile when I tried to thank her, but I was grateful nonetheless.

I was hungry, having had almost nothing to eat the day before, but when the gothambu unda, the prison breakfast, a large round dumpling made of wheat—a gritty kind of wheat that smelled old— arrived, I couldn't eat it. I'd imagined, hoped, that after breakfast we'd be given a job to do—factory work, basket weaving—but we all sat for the next two hours, the air soupy and hot. It was impossible to sleep to pass the time, but I lay down on my bed anyway, worried that in this thick fug of perspiring, leaking, coughing bodies, I would catch something and die and never see Anto or Raffie again.

On my third day there, after breakfast of kanji, a kind of rice gruel made from chaakkari, the lowest-quality rice available, we were lined up and made to march across a concrete yard, where we were taken to a room stacked with baskets. A thin woman with a hard, weary face and few teeth gave me a bundle of prickly reeds and machine-gunned instructions to me in Malayalam. I felt as gormless as some of the Moonstone midwives must have felt listening to me. I did my best, but three hours of sitting cross-legged on the floor made my back and hopelessly slow fingers tremble with tiredness. When the toothless one saw my horribly made basket, she held it up and jeered at it and made the other women cackle.

I made baskets for six days, and when, on the seventh, a guard suddenly appeared saying, "Husband is here," I didn't know whether to cheer or weep. I hadn't slept and had a permanent crick in my back. I felt dirty too. When I asked the guard if I could wash myself first, he snapped, "Full female ablutions are on Friday." But then he relented and brought me a basin of water and a small pot of sticky black soap.

Anto was sitting in the visitors' room when I walked in, very pale and still. Raffie was there too—a huge mistake. He leapt at me and covered my face in kisses, then lay on the floor and sobbed so hysterically that the guard warned us he would have to leave if he couldn't stop. Anto knelt down beside him.

"The man says we'll have to go if you cry," he warned. He cradled him in his arms, but the sight of Raffie's brave little face struggling for control broke my heart.

"Mummy smells funny," Raffie said, when he could speak. When he took his thumb from his mouth and touched the ends of my hair, I could feel his heart jumping in his chest.

Anto, watching us, said, "How on earth did we get here?"

"I don't know," I replied. What I wanted to say to Anto was I love you, I miss you, I'll be home soon, but I felt so degraded and ashamed, the words wouldn't come out right. Instead I told him it had been a mistake to bring Raffie, and he hissed in a low voice, "You're not living with him."

Raffie wriggled off my lap and sat on the floor in the gloomy light.

"You're a very good boy, darling," I said. "I'll be home as soon as I can."

When he started to cry again, Anto said I looked pale and had lost weight. He was worried about me. I told him about the basket making, trying to make him smile, then I asked him to bring a Malayalam dictionary the next time he came.

"It won't be for much longer, you do know that?" He cupped my face in his hands.

I looked at him properly for the first time since his arrival. "I'm sorry I told you off about Raffie," I whispered. "Is he sleeping?"

"Not much . . . don't worry . . . not really," he said after a pause. "He misses you."

"Can't Amma have him for a day or two?"

"No. She's . . . Appan's taken her on a holiday."

"Really?" This sounded so unlikely. Amma was as much a fixture at Mangalath as the rocks or the trees, but there was no time to explain, and not much else to say that didn't feel either trivial or freighted with unsaid things. The rhythms of our lives together had changed already: no more laughs, no shared conversations, no tasks to do together, no teasing, just this shared humiliation.

"Saraswati and I are sure we can get you out soon," he said before he left. "I'll tell you more next time." He stared at me intently. "You're not alone," he said. "You're not alone," he repeated. "Do you believe that?"

I nodded numbly. When he hugged me, I wanted to imprint every part of him on me: his chest, his arms, the lemony woody smell of him, but later that night, sleepless and boiling hot in my cot, I felt a desert growing inside me. We had very little money left now after the bad lawyer, and little support, I suspected, inside the prison, so what realistically could he do?

CHAPTER 58

At the end of my second week, I woke to find the ex-schoolteacher with the gray crew cut rhythmically pummeling my face, her yellow teeth bared. It was early morning; I was half-asleep. Two guards, hearing my yells, rushed in and dragged her away, but not before she'd kicked me hard in the head. When I woke next, I was lying in the prison hospital, a large Nissen hut on the edge of the exercise yard. There was a nauseating pain in my temple, and my mouth and right cheek felt bruised.

Coming round was like swimming to the surface of a scummy lake, full of the dirty rubbish in my head. When I looked up, Saraswati Nair staring down became, for a few weird moments, part of my dream, like déjà vu in reverse. Her face was still and unsmiling.

"Is Raffie all right?" I said. My spit tasted of copper.

"Don't worry." She knelt down beside me. "Kamalam and Anto are taking good care of him. Now listen carefully"—Saraswati's glasses were painfully bright—"because I have only ten minutes to talk to you; this is important."

She brought her face close to mine and spoke slowly and distinctly. "There will be a retrial. I have more than one hundred and eighty-three signatures on a petition from Moonstone patients. I am visiting government offices, twisting arms. I am insisting they call me as a witness next time; the trial was a grave miscarriage of justice. Are you listening to me?"

"Thank you, Saraswati," I said feebly, sure she was making it up.

"What kind of talk is thank you?" she said fiercely.

"I shouldn't have done it . . ." I wanted her to stop my head from banging, to take her bright glasses away.

"Listen," she hissed, moving her face an inch or so closer. "You have your husband on the warpath, also the many lion-hearted women in our community, and I am roaring with them. Don't forget this either: you never lied to Dr. Annakutty about your qualifications. She passed you as competent, but don't waste your breath on that, what we need now is money."

"We don't have it," I told her. "Anto spent all our savings on the lawyer, much good he did us. I wish I could have had you, Saraswati."

"I would have blown the case to smithereens," she admitted modestly. "But back to the money: your family is wealthy, let them pay."

"They won't pay."

"Won't pay?" She could hardly contain her frustration.

"Won't bribe—not all Indians are corruptible, you know." Ignoring this sad joke attempt, she jerked back her cuff and looked at the man's wristwatch she wore.

"I have five minutes left, and it's important you understand this is not a good time to be an Englishwoman in prison: that madwoman may strike again." She broke off suddenly. "What's this?" She grabbed my right hand and stared at it in horror. It was crisscrossed with dried blood and small cuts.

"It's the reeds." I felt ashamed, like a child beggar parading her leg irons. "We do basket weaving, for the magnificent sum of one rupee a week."

"Those stupids. What a waste!" Saraswati smacked the side of her head, looked around her. "I'm going to talk to the doctor in charge." She flounced out of the room and came back with a middle-aged man with a set smile, baggy exhausted eyes, and a stethoscope around his neck.

"Dr. Zaheer," she said, "is the chief physician here." They talked over my head for a while, Saraswati translating. "He says the prison

and the hospital are overflowing. He's never known it so busy. They
have a tent in the garden to deal with the extra patients; medical supplies are running out." She broke off for another fusillade of words.

"Show him your hands. I'm asking him if that is a way to treat a
state-registered nurse. Where did you train? Saint Thomas', where
Florence Nightingale worked, am I mistaken? No. One of the fin-
est hospitals in England. Correct?"

"It's certainly . . ."

"Now I'm telling him that you have safely delivered many children." I was shaking my head before she finished.

"Saraswati, stop! Stop! Stop! Please! Tell him exactly why I'm
here." My lip still felt enormous, as if I were talking through an
inner tube. "No false pretenses."

As she jabbered away for a while more, I saw a faint light dawn
in the doctor's tired eyes. He ran his hands over a bristling chin and
talked without drawing breath for several minutes.

"So here's the thing," Saraswati said. "He wants you to understand this facility here once had a very high reputation; he wants it
to be like that again. I told him that was exactly how we felt about
the Moonstone, that we were very proud of it, that we were doing
everything we could to make it work. Sometimes we cut corners,
not because we were stupid or cruel, but because we've had to, and
this time we paid the price. You in particular."

"That's nice," I said wearily, not feeling anything but pain in my
head, my mouth. When I woke up again, she was gone.

It turned out that Dr. Zaheer spoke excellent English.

"Miss Smallwood," he asked me four days later, with the same
slightly unnerving set smile. "Do you have a certificate of nursing
qualifications. Yes or no?"

"Yes, from Saint Thomas', it was just the midwifery I hadn't quite—"

"That's all I need to know." He got out a pad and started to write busily. "I'm signing you off for three days' convalescence; after that I want you to report here every morning at six thirty. We are badly in need of more help with the women's clinic, general gynecological problems, plus several deliveries a month. I will clear it with the governor. Your basket-making days are over." This time the smile made it to his eyes, and I tried to smile, but it hurt too much, and anyway, I saw that if I proved too useful, I could just possibly get stuck in another kind of trap.

CHAPTER 59

Clinic hours at the prison hospital were from eight to twelve in the morning. Nobody stuck to them. Our stream of patients came with every imaginable complaint from boils to stomach upsets to secondary syphilis to broken bones. On my first week there, I treated one woman for vaginal tears that had been the result of a violent rape. Dr. Zaheer told me pointedly that she had been assaulted twice: this time by a prison guard, who had been severely punished, the time before that by a British soldier, on the week before Independence. Whether this was true or not, I had no idea.

Dr. Zaheer, whose mirthless smile looked more like a death's-head grimace every day, said the facility was close to collapse. Our main ward held twenty people comfortably, but we often had twice that number, making it hard to move between the beds.

But I respected this conscientious man, doing his best in difficult conditions. He was nice enough to me—even complimenting me on my stitching of the vaginal tear, an hour-long job—but he made it crystal clear I had no choice about being here, particularly as two local nurses were off sick. He also insisted I speak to the patients in Malayalam. "That's our state language, is it not?" he asked me sarcastically.

After a month I could speak whole sentences without having to think about them, not necessarily phrases you might use in polite society—"Have you tried to strangle yourself before?" "How many men have you lain with?"—but it pleased me to be able to speak more fluently.

The ward nurse, a good-looking, hard-faced woman called Kali, was, I was pretty sure of it, sleeping with Dr. Zaheer, a kind of droit de signeur arrangement that was not uncommon in Indian hospitals—another reason, I imagined, why the Thekkedens found my profession so distasteful.

When I stumbled on them once in the dispensary, they sprang apart, and afterwards, when I didn't understand her instructions, she widened her eyes in fury, like the wicked witch in a panto.

In my third week there, when one of the new prisoners came in almost fully dilated, I was ordered to help a local midwife, Chinna, who came to the hospital whenever she was needed. With no time for formal introductions, we rushed the shrieking woman into a side ward and performed what Sister Tutor would have called a textbook vaginal delivery together. Thanks to the Moonstone, I understood all the words, and we were a good team, and when the baby shot out, Chinna gave me a sort of thumbs-up look which meant "good, competent." That poor baby would spend most of its life in captivity, as the mother was in for the murder of a bullying mother-in-law and was lucky, Dr. Zaheer told me, to avoid being lynched in her village.

By the time I got back to F block, I'd been gone for almost ten hours and I was dizzy with exhaustion. When the guard appeared and told me I had a visitor in the reception area, I felt nothing but frustration.

Anto couldn't hide his shock when he saw me.

"Are you eating?" He grabbed my hand. "You've lost so much weight. What are they giving you to eat?"

I told him that the nursing food was miles better than the ordinary prisoner's diet. That there were dosas in the morning, and fresh fruit, but I was never very hungry in the morning.

"Kit." When Anto ran his thumb gently along my hand, a guard leapt forward; they're always on red alert for "immoral acts" during visiting hours. "Please eat breakfast."

I didn't answer. I was trying to work out whether I should tell him then and there my suspicions about other possible reasons for my paleness. On the days leading up to my sentencing, we'd made love several times with the kind of desperate intensity that reminded me of our early days at Wickam Farm, and now I'd been sick for two mornings in a row and my breasts were tender. I'd put my three-week-late period down to anxiety, hoping this was so. I couldn't think of a worse time or place to celebrate a possible new life. I didn't want to raise his hopes either, so instead, I asked for news of Raffie.

"Sad," said Anto at last. I could see him processing this thought, trying to find a way of answering this without lying to me, which is one thing I'd always loved about him: how he tried to tell me the truth, however hard.

"He misses you."

"Still not sleeping?"

"Not brilliantly." Anto gave a long shuddering sigh.

"Any help from Amma?"

"Not yet." When he looked up, I saw purplish black circles under his eyes. "She's still away with Appan, but don't worry, Saraswati and I are full steam ahead, it won't be long, I promise you that."

"What frightens me now," I said, "is I may have become too useful. They're desperately short of staff."

I blurted this out without thinking, my mind on the pregnancy test I would insist on tomorrow. When I saw the look of anguish in his eyes, I wanted to grab the useless woman I'd become by the shoulders and say, Don't say those things to him! Don't add to the misery of the one person in the world who really needs your support.

A long silence fell between us, Anto with his head resting in his hands.

"How is your work going?" I asked him. An inane question.

"Not bad," he said. "I got my paper in."

"Any news about the promotion?"

He looked up. "Didn't get it."

This was definitely my fault. Before my conviction, Dr. Sastry had said it was a certainty.

"Any point in saying I'm sorry?"

"No, there's always another train."

"You don't need another train, you need another wife."

He tried a grimacing smile. His dark hair flopped over his forehead. I pushed it back.

To fill another silence, I told him I'd helped with two deliveries in the prison hospital.

"Good for your confidence, but do you trust them?" he said.

"Yes . . . no . . . I don't know. Dr. Zaheer is a good man, I don't think he'll twist it. I've asked him if these deliveries can be used for me to get my final certificate."

"But you're still not covered."

"I am. I've insisted they put it in writing that I wasn't the principal midwife. He's told me he'll write to the Royal College of Midwives and get them to rubber-stamp it."

Anto didn't look convinced, and neither was I entirely, but I knew I had to trust Zaheer or go mad with anxiety. Anto opened his mouth to say something else when the bell rang, heart-attack loud; keys were officiously rattled, guards shouted. Visiting hour was over.

"The best thing about being married," he'd once told me, "is you don't have to finish conversations on street corners." Now we did, and when I tried to piece our words together later, they seemed fragile and slippery, and I wished in a way I'd told him about our possible baby, the promise of something new, because when he stood up, I saw I'd aged him. He looked stiff, and there was a sprinkling of gray hairs I hadn't noticed before. He touched the side of my face very gently.

"I love you," he said. "Don't forget that ever." I reminded myself to smile, feeling as empty as the sky.

CHAPTER 60

He'd had enough, Anto decided, as he exited through the prison gates. Two days later, after a quick trip to Mangalath and some detective work with the servants, he arrived, shortly before lunch, at the Crown Hotel in Madras. His father was attending a conference there on the new constitution. At the gate, which was guarded by two uniformed lackeys, he stopped, confused: the hotel—dusky-pink walls, tiled courtyards, blossom-scented garden—was an unusually lavish choice for his normally frugal father.

He was shown to a room overlooking the garden, where he took a bath and dressed himself carefully and slowly for the showdown he knew must follow. At the front desk, the clerk, a smiling, obse-quious fellow in a cherry-red uniform with braided shoulders, said Mr. Thekkeden, "a very great man," was out every day, but he would almost certainly find his mother in the garden, where she usually sat in the afternoon.

When he saw his mother from a distance, his heart clenched. She was sitting under a mimosa tree on a green bench, a small and lonely-looking speck, so deep in thought she didn't look up until he sat down beside her.

"What are you doing here?" She sprang to her feet when she saw him. "What's wrong?"

"Amma," he said, kneeling beside her and taking both of her hands in his, "I need to talk to you."

"Are you sick?"

He'd hoped for a grace period to ease her into this: an exchange of pleasantries, a mental taking of her pulse, but she had led him immediately to the point of no return, and he told her fast, "Amma, we've been lying to you for months and months and months, and I can't do it anymore. Kit's not studying, she's been in Viyyur prison for nearly six weeks now."

Her brown eyes widened. "Is this a joke?"

"No." Telling brought no relief, only the shock of it again.

"For what?"

"Manslaughter. A trumped-up charge, for the delivery of a baby that died." No point in fudging it now. "The full details I can tell you later."

"Oh my God! Don't tell me the details!" Her face wrinkled with disgust. "I knew this would happen."

He looked at her and shook his head. "If you could see your face now, you would know why we lie to you."

She jerked as if he'd slapped her. "Who lies to me?" she almost shouted. "Who else knows?"

"It's been in the papers."

"What papers?"

"You didn't see them, Appan's orders, but I'm telling you now because you're the one person who can really help me with Raffie. He's having a horrible time."

"I knew something was wrong," she said angrily. "I tried to discuss it many times with Appan. I said, 'I think his marriage is on the rocks.' He said, 'How many times must I repeat this: she's away studying. They are a modern couple doing things the modern way,' and now, nice to know everyone was laughing at me."

"My marriage isn't on the rocks," he said, staring vacantly at the terraces of the perfectly manicured garden around him: the orange trees, the mimosa, the rioting bougainvillea, underneath which gardeners had placed, with the precision of artists, dollops of horse manure. "But I need your help." He pushed a mimosa blossom with his foot.

She shielded her face against the sun and stared at him. "Isn't Appan helping?"

"He can't or won't, and this is the point of no return for me, because I'm sick of protecting the family name at all costs."

"Antokutty," she cried, her eyes pleading. "Don't say these things to me. It breaks my heart. I nearly died on the day they sent you away."

"I'm not talking about us, Amma. I'm talking about my wife, my family."

"When you were little, we spent every moment we could together. I've never loved another person as much."

"I'm a grown-up, Ma. I spent a lot of time alone."

"So what can I do now?"

"I need help with Raffie; he's all over the place. I need money for a decent lawyer . . . Oh God, I hate this . . ."

"So give me time!" She put her hand on his arm. "I will think of something. I don't want to lose you again."

- CHAPTER 61 -

When Anto left, Amma went upstairs, locked the bedroom door, and in a moment of pure rage kicked Appan's brown leather suitcase, a present from Hugo Bateman, as hard as she could. Appan had left for a three-day conference, pajamas and papers packed in a small holdall. He'd left this case behind for her to tidy. It will give her something to do, she could almost hear him thinking. She closed the shutter and, hugging herself tightly, paced about the room, crying and shouting.

This was the worst public disgrace the family had ever faced, and what hurt most was that everyone had known but her, as if she were too feebleminded, too conventional, too utterly and completely retarded to be told a thing.

Another source of humiliation was that, freed from family responsibilities and Mangalath, this unexpected holiday with Mathu had, after many years of drought, led to something surprising: they'd started to make love again.

I'm too old, she'd wanted to tell him, on that first night at the Willoughby in Bombay, and it's too late. Nothing but embarrassment at first, but then, her legs softening, her breath quickening, she'd felt something like an ice flow melting inside her. "Don't cry, silly woman," Mathu had said fondly, when she was lying in his arms.

"I'm sorry," she'd said. "I'm happy."

Now she felt duped and stupid and sordid, and during the two sleepless nights that followed, her mind lunged back and forth between disgust at the girl, love for her son, loyalty to Appan, and ice-cold fury at him for making her so stupid, such a nothing in the general scheme of things.

On the third day she sat down on the bed and forced herself to be calm. The time for weeping and wailing had passed. She had made up her mind: she had a plan.

She pulled Appan's suitcase onto the bed and, after forcing the lock with her manicure scissors, tore the clothes from it, flung them on the bed, and fumbled in the pocket of the silk lining for the envelope where she knew he kept his money. Her mood was so savagely vindictive that she was half hoping, as she went methodically through every scrap of paper, to find further evidence of wickedness—a failed business deal, a mistress she didn't know about.

She took a bundle of rupees from the envelope and put in her own pocket. Downstairs, she asked the swanky-looking desk clerk for train times to Cochin that day, wrote the times down carefully, and left a note for Appan on the bed.

"I've taken money from your briefcase. I'm going home to take care of the children. I know about Kit."

Her rage frightened her, and she wondered, as she folded the note carefully, if she would ever be able to forgive him. All the kootchy-coo second-honeymoon stuff was a lie, and she, credulous fool, had lain there as panting and grateful as a starving dog.

She packed the brand-new suitcase she'd been so proud of and then, by force of long habit, folded his clothes and smoothed down the bedspread before closing the door. She was leaving. She was gone.

Calm yourself, woman, Kunjamma Thekkeden warned herself as she walked down the railway platform at nine fifty that morning. Her first trip alone on a train would take all her courage and all her strength. She fell asleep in the women's carriage, with her face pressed against the window, and woke raging at Kit.

"You are a contaminant." She was silently moving her lips as the streets of an unknown town sped by. Everyone knew that nurses had weak morals. Anto, thousands of miles from home, must have been a sitting duck. So fine, sleep with him, be immoral, but don't come home with him, bringing nothing but trouble and distress.

She closed her eyes tightly. What torture to think of all their friends reading their newspapers, gossiping, and giggling about how the mighty Thekkedens had fallen, and in the most sordid and public way possible.

"Are you all right, madam?" the young woman next to her asked when she groaned out loud.

"Perfectly fine, thank you." Amma peered through the window at a rubbish-strewn culvert. "Thank you," she said again just to be clear.

"Perfectly fine." Her words left an acid taste in her mouth. Was this what life was really like, lie upon lie, upon lie? She recalled how she'd walked towards Kit that first day, hand outstretched, smiling, exclaiming; and later, welcoming the unstable Glory into the fold; and sitting in the summerhouse, while the ancient lover soggied up his handkerchief. This suavity, this politeness—look where it had landed her now that the big cat had pounced.

By the time the train had come to its screeching halt, she felt a tremendous weariness creep over her. What Anto was asking of her was not as simple as a change of mind, but a change of beliefs she'd led her life by.

"Why must I do this?" she muttered to herself as, half-dead with tiredness, she pulled down her suitcase. Her plan now was to hail a taxi and go straight to Saraswati Nair's office at the Mother Moonstone Home at Fort Cochin. "If your friends ever need legal advice," Mrs. Nair had said months ago, handing her a business card, "you know where to find me." *Pushy*, Amma had thought at the time, and disrespectful, when she had a first-class legal brain living under her own roof.

It was a surprise to see a stony-faced Anto standing on the platform waiting for her.

"Why are you here?" she said.

"Appan sent me," he said. "The hotel manager told him what train you were on. He phoned my hospital. He's horrified."

A spurt of anger invigorated her. "He has no right to be horrified. He travels all the time."

"He thought you'd left him. He's in an awful state."

"Anto," she said, "I don't care. I have no time to waste. What I want to do now is to go to the place where Kit works. I want to see everything."

When they arrived at the Moonstone, she told him to pick her up in an hour. She needed to talk to Saraswati Nair on her own. A few moments later, she faced the lawyer in her office—a converted Nissen hut under the stump of a charred tree.

"I know about Kit," she said, "I know about the prison, I know about my son. I'm saying this to save your breath, because I have my own questions now."

"Take a seat please, Mrs. Thekkeden," Saraswati said, when Amma's fury had spent itself. "I have a client coming soon, but I am able to talk for"—she consulted her watch—"twenty minutes. Why are you here?"

"I'm here because my family have told me many lies." It grieved her deeply to say this, but it was true now. "I don't trust them anymore."

"But you still care for them?" Saraswati gave her a level look.

"I don't know." Amma took a sharp breath. "They have driven me to the point of madness."

"I understand," Saraswati said with a deep sigh. "But as a professional person and as a friend, I am in a dilemma: I've been told not to tell you anything."

"No line has been crossed," Kunjamma said. "I came to you knowing the truth."

Saraswati snapped the elastic bands on a couple of folders and stared at Kunjamma.

"All right," she said eventually. "But we're going to do this my way because you seem to be on a warpath, and that won't work."

"Are you surprised? This girl has brought nothing but disgrace to our family."

Saraswati snapped the folder shut. "So, I must stop you there. My time is precious, I won't have it wasted. There's too much to do."

Amma pressed her lips together. "Start again." She folded her hands in her lap, trained her eyes on Saraswati. "Sorry . . . please . . ."

"And to go any further," Saraswati continued in the same colorless lawyer voice, "you need to understand some things. Put these on." She handed Kunjamma a pair of galoshes. "Come outside."

They stepped from the hut. "This way."

Outside, a dazzling sun shone mercilessly on the charred beams, the smashed bricks, the soggy mattresses, and the broken fish tank that had once held the premature babies.

"The Moonstone is not at its best at the moment," Saraswati conceded, as they skirted the stump of the neem tree, "but you must imagine it before they burned it down: a beautiful place full of hope.

"Maternity ward was there." She pointed towards burned wire and a sodden sofa. "Reception there. There was the mango tree, but most of all—"she stopped and faced Kunjamma—"it was the people who made it. They were good people. Not just Kit, but the other midwife Maya, the nurses. They were gentle, kind. I'm saying *kind*," Saraswati repeated, angrily. "It's so underrated, particularly by very traditional people."

"When I came here," she continued, as they crunched over some broken floor tiles, "I was full of fear. I had fallen out with my family, who disliked my practicing law. My labor was hard, fourteen hours, but nothing but kindness from Kit. Everything very sweet and clean here. I had a boy, and when she stitched me up afterwards, she was so gentle, I didn't feel a thing."

"She stitched you up!" Kunjamma's hand flew to her mouth.

"If you make that face again, I'll stop. She's a midwife, that's what they do when people bleed: you either take responsibility or you fail to, it's very simple." Saraswati glared.

"I'm sorry. Carry on . . . You're right, that's what they do." Kunjamma made a visible effort to control herself. Her mind tripped back to the awful medical drawings she had seen in Kit's wardrobe: bare women with their bottoms in the air; varicose veins of the vulva.

"So." Saraswati took a shuddering breath. "My baby was born, over there actually." She gestured towards a pile of broken glass and burned timber struts. "And then, a few weeks after that,"—her voice steadied and rose—"he died. It was a cot death. Had nothing to do with the hospital. No infection was there, no injury at all. But this was the single thing that started the witch hunt. They said I would be called as a witness, but I was never called, and this is why I will stay and fight for this place and your daughter-in-law with my last breath, and why your son and I are working around the clock to set her free."

"I'm not a lawyer," Amma said in a low voice. "My husband is."

"Your boy has a good brain, he could probably pass his bar exams now, but he's on his knees with exhaustion. We've been canvassing local women for their support. We have two hundred and sixty-five signatures already on our petition."

Amma sat on a bench and put her head in her hands. "I'm sorry about your son," she said quietly at last. "I had a miscarriage once; it would have been another boy."

She looked down at the ground. That memory had been bur-

ied so successfully—the pain, the total desert of the days that followed—that she had never spoken about it to anyone ever again.

"Well, you're lucky," Saraswati said at last. "You have a live son,
but you will lose him if you cannot accept his wife. He adores her,
and he is in hell right now."

Amma put her hand to her mouth. "I'll talk to him," she mumbled at last.

"Not like this. It won't work."

"No?" Amma looked up, her eyes full of pain and distress.

Saraswati put on her glasses and sighed. "Spout your prejudices
and things will get worse."

"What, then?" Amma was barely audible.

"Come."

Taking Kunjamma's arm, she helped her over a small pile of
charred rubble. To the right of them were the beginnings of a bonfire with a couple of doors and a wooden doll on top.

"Look." Saraswati pointed. Beyond the bonfire, a large rectangle
of earth had been neatly raked and pegged out with lines of string.
"One day this will be our new clinic. We've already painted the sign
to cheer us on. Some local women come every day to pray. They
planted those." She nodded towards a row of marigolds planted
near a fierce plaster goddess brandishing her sword.

"Mrs. Thekkeden?" Saraswati saw her stumble and took her
arm. "Are you tired?"

"Facts I need." Light-headed from lack of food, Amma heard
her own voice slur.

"So facts are these. We treat our village midwives like the lowest of the low. If men did it, it would be seen as the supreme act of
courage."

"Don't point at me," said Kunjamma, "I never treated my midwife like that. She is properly trained, she is clean."

"You're rich, you have influence. A different story for poor women."
Saraswati's voice rose. "Their lives are often destroyed by childbirth."

Kunjamma's eyes floated up in her head. "I am tired," she said. "I need to think, but one thing I would say is, Don't mistake me for a stupid or a cruel woman."

"I don't," Saraswati said softly. "Kit has told me of your kindness to her family, but seriously, would you have the guts to be a midwife? No! Nor would I. Thank God someone does."

Before she left, Kunjamma said she wanted to read the newspaper reports. She opened the *Vantage* first, a local broadsheet. She smoothed it out and read it with her face going from white to red and back to white again.

"They haven't given her our name," she said after a long silence. "That's something, although the gossips will have spread the word by now." She read on. "These are disgusting," she said at last. "Poor Anto."

"Poor Anto!" Saraswati barked incredulously. "What about Kit? Now read these." Saraswati pushed the red file towards her. "This is what the local women said about her. Make up your own mind."

- CHAPTER 62 -

Two days after Anto's visit, Chinna, the midwife, examined me and told me what I already knew: I was pregnant. I was almost sure I remembered the night it had happened, a night of high moon and high heat and desperate last-minute clinging that felt now like a lifetime ago. After Chinna left the cubicle, I lay for a while wondering what this would mean now. Pregnancy in this place was not a get-out-of-jail card: babies were born here and raised here quite routinely. My greatest worry was I'd become indispensable to the crazily overworked Dr. Zaheer, even more so now that my Malayalam had improved. When I warned him that afternoon that I only had six weeks more of my sentence to serve, he'd snapped, "That's not correct. You must talk to the governor."

Panicked, I wrote a letter to the governor asking for confirmation of my release date, but knowing the cumbersome bureaucracy of that prison, did not expect a speedy reply.

A few days later, I was still suffering from morning sickness, and when I felt too ill to work, I asked for an hour off. Dr. Zaheer barked, "Request refused." He still wore the same relentless smile that meant nothing except overwork, but that night I was moved from the women's dormitory into a small cell of my own. A big relief. I longed for sleep with the intensity of a drug fiend, and when it didn't come, or I woke in the small hours, I felt I was in hell and sometimes wept without sound, a clown's crying. It was one thing to lead myself down the path of destruction, quite another to be pregnant here. No one had said a word yet about my release.

The tireder I got, the more frightened I felt, my nerve a frayed cloth that grew thinner every day. Rumors flew around here: about gangs of men and women who'd stockpiled weapons and were ready to riot, about guards who gagged and raped. One night in mid-July, I was escorted back to my cell after work, my feet aching from ten hours on the ward, my head blurry with tiredness. When I walked in, I saw the silhouette of a veiled woman sitting, very still, in the corner of the room. I thought at first it was Govinda, the sweet-faced nurse who sometimes helped me on the wards.

The light in the cell came from a weak bulb high in the ceiling, so it was hard to see, but when I moved closer and saw it wasn't her, I remembered my attacker and froze.

"*Nee endha cheyyanae?* What are you doing?" I said. "Who are you?" The dark shape stood up, laid aside her shawl, and faced me. It was Amma.

She looked so pale, I didn't recognize her at first. Her eyes were staring dark hollows between the folds of her veil. When I looked around the room, I saw that place through her own fastidious eyes—the high, scummy window, the potty, the iron bed, the gray blanket with Viyyur Prison Service on it—and it made me want to die of shame.

"Why are you here?" I said, when the guard had locked the door behind us. Both of us had started to tremble like two small dogs squaring up for a fight, until something more terrifying occurred to me.

"Has there been an accident at home?"

"No, no, no, no." Her expression softened a little. "Nothing's happened," she said. "I'm here because I wanted to see you. You've lost a lot of weight."

"There's been a tummy bug." I backed away from her. "I don't want you to catch it."

"I'm glad to be here."

I didn't believe her of course: I'd seen her immaculately ordered house, the polished floors, the tidy medicine cabinet with labels lined up, even the bloody orchid hospital, for God's sake.

It was only when the light in the cell surged that I saw how much weight she'd lost too. Her skin, once so plump and shiny like a ripe conker, looked as papery as autumn leaves.

"Amma," I said, not even sure I could call her mother now. "I'm so sorry . . . I've made such a mess of things."

She turned away, her lips working violently.

"A big shock . . ." she said eventually. "Everyone knew but me." I heard her gasp. "And when you don't have the facts, your mind goes mad."

"I know."

"You shouldn't have left me in the dark." She wiped her eyes on the corner of her shawl. "You of all people should have let me know. You saw what lies did in your own family? Nothing but pain. But you didn't trust me either."

I thought of Glory then. How I'd clung to her on the night before she died and the lifeboat broke up into little pieces.

"I wasn't sure I could," I said. "I wasn't exactly your dream of a daughter-in-law."

A look of wry amusement passed between us. There it was out, like the head of a boil.

She closed her eyes. "Well . . ."

"And this makes it so much worse."

"That we cannot change, but listen please, we don't have much time." Her face was set and unsmiling. "Anto and Saraswati want me to change overnight. I can't—that would be another lie—but Saraswati showed me the Moonstone. She says if they can raise the money, it will be built again. A long way to go." She sounded resigned and far from happy, and so was I: for me, the whole place felt freighted with failure now.

"Did Appan ask you to come here?" I asked in the silence that followed.

"No." She stared into her lap. "He's not talking to me. I stole money from him to pay the bribe."

"The bribe?"

"How else am I sitting here?"

I was astounded. "Who did you pay?"

"I'm not going to say," she said, pressing her lips together.

"Oh God." The damage was spreading and I was responsible. "Amma, I'm so sorry," I said. She looked so crushed, so old. "I never wanted you to fall out with Appan."

"A shakeup was needed," she said. "He'll be back."

"Have you spoken to Anto?"

"A few nights ago," Amma said tonelessly. "We stayed up late unknotting things between us. He asked me a question: 'Do you remember the parable of the Good Samaritan?' I said of course I did, everyone did."

"'Is it true or is it a lie?' he said.

"'Don't come to me with your clever Downside talk,' I said to him. 'I'm a Christian, I know what it means.'

"'OK,' he said. 'Let me put it another way. Tonight, when you leave me, you see a child bleeding to death beside the road. Do you cross the road, to avoid the mess of it? Do you say to yourself, I'm not qualified, I won't look, or do you see the supreme value of a human life, and do what you can?'

"'I'm not stupid,' I said. I knew where this was leading. 'There are laws, and your wife broke one. Jail was the next step.'

"He was stern with me. 'Listen,' he said, 'I've spent months now looking at the legalities of manslaughter and criminal negligence, and they're muddled and unclear, all lawyers know this. For example, if I was a naval captain on a ship and one of my crew got ill, I could be prosecuted for not doing anything. The law calls this failure to assist. New health system, new country, new laws, we're all at sea,' he said."

Amma raised her eyes and looked at me. She wasn't enjoying this one bit. "He said that you chose to help in a difficult situation, that you might have been foolish in your innocence and optimism, but you were at least brave, and that you paid a high price for it."

"He did?" I could hardly speak.

"He said all this." Her voice was low.

"You don't agree though, do you?"

"I don't know." She looked at me again. "I'm never going to like you doing this."

We smiled the same wry smile. She was, at least, honest.

"Anto says that you'll complete the medical requirement as soon as you get out."

"I'm almost there," I said. "That's the irony. I needed two more supervised deliveries. I should have organized them at the Moonstone, but we were always too busy."

"What next?" She was watching me like a hawk.

"I don't know . . . get my certificate, go back to the Moonstone . . . probably . . . if they'll have me . . . and if the money gets raised to build it again. I don't look forward to it, but I can't seem to let it go. It's not what you want to hear."

"No, it's not." She looked pretty miserable. "It's your life."

We had come to the end of what was possible for now, and hearing the guard's feet again, the rattle of keys, I felt incredible weariness: the heat pressing down on me like a hot, wet blanket, the long night ahead.

"Look, Amma," I said, "I am not in control anymore . . . I try not to make plans."

When she brought her face so close to mine, I thought for one strange moment that she was going to kiss me. Instead, she whispered, "You're wrong. It will happen, and it will be soon. Wait and see."

CHAPTER 63

My knight in shining Amma, I thought unkindly after she'd left and darkness had fallen. She looked too old and frail to have any kind of currency in a place like Viyyur.

But a week later, shortly after breakfast, a package appeared in my cell. Inside it was the blue dress I'd arrived in eight weeks ago, nicely washed and ironed by the prison laundry, a pair of stockings, and my shoes, lying there like messages from another life: both wonderfully familiar and awfully strange.

The guard took me across the F block square to a concrete room with a sign on the door saying Female Ablutions. He gave me a pot of black sticky soap and a strip of cotton fabric to dry myself with. I filled the copper bucket, and I washed my body from head to toe.

My heart was crashing in my chest as I dressed, combed my hair, and later, as I walked into Dr. Zaheer's cramped office on the side of the main ward.

This is a trick, I thought, listening to the piping birds in the tree outside. It won't happen, I told myself, gazing at the prison walls, the brilliant blue skies beyond.

But then Dr. Zaheer, in his grimy lab coat, with bruised eyes, said to me in his I'm-speaking-to-you-from-the-grave voice, "You're leaving today. Not my choice." No smiling now. He had the look of a man betrayed.

There were, he said, a couple of important strings attached: I was to come back to the hospital and work two days a week at the clinic for the next six months. Part of this arrangement involved helping the resident midwife.

"If I do that," I said, "could I please be officially supervised? I'd like to get my final qualifications."

I watched his eyes flicker thoughtfully while I waited for this penny to drop, then he said in a barking voice, "Prisoner rehabilitation is at the heart of what we do. We have a prison library here. I will order any books. You can be our first midwife graduate."

When I saw Anto waiting for me outside the prison walls, I could not speak at first. When I got in the car, we clung to each other.

"Stop it!" Anto said, wiping his tears with his sleeve. "We're bloody idiots! You're free."

And then I told him about our new baby, and we started again sobbing and laughing and clutching each other for dear life.

"Actually, I'm not quite free," I said. As we drove away, I told him the agreement I'd made with Doctor Zaheer.

"Do you mind?" He glanced at me and grabbed my hand.

"No," I said, and then to show off my Malayalam, "*Athu nalla kachavadam tannae.* It seems like a fair exchange." Which in a queer sort of way it did.

It took a while for things to feel right again. On my first morning home, the beautifully sliced ripe Alphonso mango laid out on my breakfast plate, the cup of freshly brewed coffee looked as if they had arrived from another planet. There was a note from Anto: "Morning, wife. I hope you slept well."

The house had rearranged itself in my absence. Raffie kept asking if he could sleep in Kamalam's bed. We let him for a while in order to avoid the explosion of tears detonated on the first night at the thought of going back to his old room.

At the end of my first week back, I sat with him on the veranda, where he was playing listlessly, jumping in and out of a cardboard box. When I tried to join in, he stood in front of the box and folded his arms like a sentry. "I only play this with Kamalam," he said.

"Give him time," Anto said, when I told him later. Anto, who was wearing glasses for the first time, had lost weight and was starting to look like Appan. In my absence, our bedroom had been converted into an untidy study covered in papers and legal books. I wanted him to take those bad memories away but didn't dare ask until I felt less of a stranger here.

I knew everything would start to get better when I slept, but I'd been running on adrenaline for so long, my motor wouldn't stop, and one night when I woke and felt Anto's hand on my head, I yelled so loud, I woke Raffie up. "I'm sorry," I said, "I'm sorry . . ."

Then, one night when Anto came home from work, he put me to bed. When he took off his new wire glasses, I was aware again of the beauty of his eyes, how they opened up in a seam of tortoise-shell and green. He needed a new haircut; his hair was soft and silky when I touched it. He brought me fresh lemon juice in a tall glass. He asked me if I would like to go with him and spend a few days at Mangalath. Not yet, I told him, not ready to face the relatives. Their displeasure, their polite smiles. Not yet.

I didn't want to see anyone for a while, but Saraswati came anyway. Said she'd hired a special rickshaw to take me down to the Moonstone. It was a huge shock to see it again: the soil all churned up, the foundations dug in, but nothing, apart from that, but broken glass and charred beams. Saraswati took my arm to help me over a pile of broken bricks. She wanted to show me the new Durga statue in the one patch of vegetation that had survived. This Durga, huge and pink, had been paid for out of donations by the ever-generous Mr. Namboothiri, the paint manufacturer. She was sitting on a lion, and to me seemed a fanciful waste of what little money we had left.

"Do you know what she stands for?"

"No." I closed my eyes and thought, Here we go.

"She has three eyes," Saraswati said, with the gusto of someone describing a marvelous friend.

"Her left eye is for the moon, or desire; the right eye, the sun, stands for action; the central eye is knowledge. And the lion," Saraswati ended with a flourish, "determination. Willpower."

"I had some of that once," I joked.

"You still do," said Saraswati. "Shock will go and you'll be back. The three weapons in Durga's hands are a thunderbolt, a sword, and—your mother-in-law's favorite—a lotus in bud but not fully bloomed. That symbolizes certainty of success but not finality." While she was talking, I saw two huge rats move over the ground.

"I need some of your strength," I told her.

"Give it time," she said.

Mariamma came next, unannounced and unexpected, with a bag of fresh pastries in her hand. She stood at the door, framed in sunlight, motionless for a moment, as if taking the temperature of the room before walking in, and then came towards me and, sinking to her knees, put her arms around me.

"Welcome home, sister," she said. "I'm so happy to see you."

She stayed for lunch and in the afternoon washed and braided my hair: the beautiful smell of coconut oil. When I told her I was expecting a baby, her eyes filled with tears, and she hugged me. "You're the first person to know," I said, "and don't tell anyone else, it's too early." As a midwife, I was extra superstitious about that.

"I'm so happy for Raffie too." She dabbed at her eyes. "He was miserable when you were gone."

We caught up with the family gossip, what Mariamma calls

vayadi, literally, flapping mouth. Theresa, she said, had graduated top of her class and was becoming a right little madam. Ponnamma was growing more and more nutty. Recently she had bellowed across the table at Amma, "Do you miss sex, daughter? I do!" which had caused Appan to choke on his thoran. "You know what she's like," Mariamma continued, enjoying my laughter. "She says, 'Now I am old, I never apologize for being a nuisance, I *am a nuisance!*'"

I wanted to ask her about Appan and whether he was angry, but I couldn't find the words yet and was grateful to Mariamma for keeping things light.

That night there was a flamboyant sunset—peach and vermilion flames in the sky—and I sat in the courtyard (I never used the veranda anymore) and watched it dumbfounded, thinking of all the things I'd taken for granted. When Anto came home, I made him a gin and tonic the way he likes it, with a slice of lime.

After Kamalam bathed Raffie, he came and of his own accord sat on my knee. His skin was warm, his hair damp. He said, "You were a bad girl, Mummy, for being away for so long."

He slept in my arms.

Mariamma came again a couple of days later. She slipped her feet out of her slippers, sat next to me, and we chatted about normal things.

She was up to her neck in preparations for the festival of Onam, the biggest feast of the year in South India and at Mangalath. I'd enjoyed it last year, but this year, with forty-four close relatives invited, I wanted to run for the hills.

"Oh my God, look at all these things I must do now." Mariamma, indignant and happy, pulled the master list from her handbag. "Banana leaves, chickens, fifty coconuts, rice, pearl fish, yogurt, lentils. New cricket and Ping-Pong bats for the children, new pillowcases, new glasses. Such a carry-on."

Raffie, who was sucking his thumb while leaning against my knee, was already excited about Onam. When Anto got home from work, they burbled on about playing cricket with his cousins, dressing up as tigers, the usual family boat race.

"Do you think you can make it?" Anto asked me gently.

"Not sure," I said. "I'll think about it, but you must go," I added, manufacturing a smile when I was still frightened of every knock on the door.

"Do you know why we celebrate Onam every year?" Anto asked. Raffie was sitting on his knee now. "It marks the ancient King Mahabali's return from Patala, the underworld. The story goes that he loved Cochin so much, he had to come back."

Raffie took his thumb out of his mouth, "I'm going to be a tiger!" He barred his milk teeth.

"Noooo!" Anto shrank back in mock terror, then put him back on his knee. "But do you really know why we're going to Mangalath?"

"Sweets," shouted Raffie. "Cricket?"

"Harvest, home, family ties." Anto flicked his eyes towards me.

"Here endeth the lesson," I said, and even to me my voice sounded bitchy. I walked out of the room and sat on a bench in the courtyard, trying not to cry.

"Appan and Amma had a wee ding-dong about the Onam food last week." Mariamma was back again with more Mangalath snippets. "As you know, the veggie dish is traditional, but Appan wants to offer chicken and prawn dishes as well. "'Come on, woman!'" Mariamma's voice deepened. "'Times change. Guests don't want to eat food like cattle.'"

"Amma got very huffy," Mariamma continued in the same semi-delighted whisper. "'*Mundan!* Idiot,' she said quite audibly. Appan rushed out out of his study. 'Sorry, did you say something?' Amma smiled like this," Mariamma mimicked her rictus smile, "and said,

'No, husband, nothing at all.' She said she would be going into the garden and might be gone for some time."

Mariamma took a bite of her pastry, still chuckling. After a silence I said, "It's been kind of you to come every day like this."

"You are my sister." She brushed the crumbs from her skirt. "I missed you badly while you were away. I thought about you every single day; my heart was breaking."

She got down on her knees and clasped both her hands around my knees.

"Come back for the feast. Please. Appan and Amma really want it."

"They do?" I could hardly hide my surprise. "I thought it would be less awkward if I stayed here."

Before she'd left me that night, Amma had stabbed her finger in my direction and said, with her fiercest look, "You must never tell anyone about this!" meaning the bribe, meaning her intervention. Since my release, I'd imagined I'd become her guilty secret.

"No!" Mariamma said vigorously, big brown eyes trained on mine. "They want you home."

Mariamma dropped a parcel into my lap. "You may wear it, if you decide to come," she wheedled, her head on one side.

Later, I opened the parcel. Inside was a brand-new beautiful white-and-gold sari. The perfect symbol of a spotless Indian wife. I gazed at it, not knowing whether to laugh or cry.

- CHAPTER 64 -

In the end I went, reluctantly, and mostly to please Anto, secretly dreading the ten days of enforced jollity ahead. After a few tries, and some help from Kamalam, I managed to put on the new sari Mariamma had so thoughtfully provided, feeling inside that sack-cloth and ashes might be more the ticket.

Mangalath was in its party clothes when we arrived: the sky almost artificially blue, the courtyard covered in the *pookalum*: a giant, brilliantly colored carpet of roses and marigolds, orchids and lotus blossoms, bursting with color and light—the everyday miracles I was still too battered to appreciate.

When he saw all the flowers, Raffie shouted, "Zippity-doo-dah!" his favorite new word. He struggled to get out of the car and raced towards the house.

"Are you all right?" Anto touched my hand.

"Fine," I said, taking a deep breath. "The jailbird returns."

"Stop it." He tucked a strand of my hair behind my ears. "Half of them won't know, the other half will, in great Anglophile tradition, never mention it again, so stick with me, kid. You look beautiful, by the way. Really beautiful. How do you feel?"

"Physically fine," I said. In the past few weeks I'd felt that mid-term-pregnancy energy starting to flow into my bones, my hair, my skin, which had lost its pallor. "Mentally, a bit like the wrong sort of prodigal daughter."

"You'll be fine," he whispered. "It's our baby's first trip here."

Walking towards the house, I saw Amma, standing where she'd
been on the first day I met her, between the gold lions, wearing an
almost identical white-and-gold sari. My heart began to thump.
Given all that we knew about each other now, it felt presumptuous
to be wearing the same uniform. She took both my hands in hers,
looked at me for several fraught seconds, and then talked over my
head to Anto, as she probably always would.

"I'm very glad you came," she said. "We were worried you
wouldn't." As we walked up the petal-strewn path towards the
house, she rested her hand on the small of my back.

"Should I speak to Appan before joining in?" I said. A trip to the
headmaster's study felt like the least I could do.

"Only if he wants to speak to you," she whispered quickly. An
army of small children were racing down the steps to claim their
youngest cousin. "And don't worry too much. He's forgiven me for
taking the money. A beautiful bunch of orchids came today." She
squeezed my arm. "We did what was necessary; it's over now," she
added firmly.

Anto was right: no one, on that first day, said a word about prison,
although I held myself in readiness and felt stiff with nervous tension at the end of it, and very much aware of Appan: elegant, gracious, commanding, circulating, checking drinks, patting children's
heads, roaring with laughter at jokes. When he saw me, he dipped
his head in my direction and said, "Welcome."

But on our fourth day there, I got up in the middle of night,
jangled and unhappy and unable to sleep. Not wanting to wake
Anto, I walked downstairs barefoot and went into the family prayer
room, where a candle burning in a rose-colored glass jar shed a
dim warm light over the Virgin Mary. When my eyes had adjusted,
I saw a man huddled in the corner of the room praying. He was
wearing loose pajamas and was barefoot.

"Appan." I started to back away. "I'm so sorry . . . I . . ."

"Kit." He looked at me. "Are you all right?"

"I didn't mean to disturb you; I'm going back to bed."

"Don't go." He hauled himself onto the pew with some difficulty. "I've been thinking about you all day."

"You have?" I sat tensely at the end of the pew, waiting for the recitation of my sins I was sure would follow. He was staring at me.

"You were brave to come back like this. I mean to Mangalath with the whole tribe here." I watched the candle flame flicker.

I told him it had been Anto's idea.

"And do you always do everything your husband wants?"

"In this instance, yes. He's been amazing."

I heard a sad snort. "In what way?" He shifted on the pew, making it creak like a ship's bows.

"Loyal," I said at last. "Kind. I feel like the truest version of myself with him."

I saw his head bow. "I let him down," he muttered. He glanced at me quickly. "Do you think he will ever forgive me?"

It was quiet enough in the chapel to hear the faint sizzle of the candle burning, his bare feet brushing against stone.

"He loves his family," I stalled, reluctant to talk for Anto. "And," I went on after a long pause, "I think we all get it wrong differently. Look at me."

He gave me a strained, considering look, the look I imagined had terrorized many prisoners in the dock.

"You erred on the side of wanting to help," he said at last. "Amma has explained your work to me, the good things your patients said about you. She says that you're going to finish your qualification. When you do, I'm going to send some money to the Home. A penance maybe."

"A penance!" I gaped at him and shook my head. "I wasn't even sure I could come back here."

"You were punished harshly," he said. "I knew that all along, and all I'm giving is a few rupees, too late, probably. If I'd been another kind of lawyer, I would have got you off, but I couldn't. I've lived my whole life with certain rules and I found I couldn't break them, so what I've decided to do is donate the same money as the bribe, and then we must never talk about it again."

He shivered as if he had reached the end of some long ordeal, and then he looked up at the window.

"This is a creepy time of night, no?" He wrapped his shawl around himself. "The veils are at their thinnest. I can almost imagine King Mahabali, creeping back from the underworld."

It took awhile for his words to sink in. I was still experiencing a kind of flooding relief.

"What a discovery the world must have been," Appan murmured. I followed his gaze towards the window. The candle had gone out but a soft streak of light was brightening the stained-glass window; I could hear the clucking of birds.

"Thank you for talking to me," I said. "I was so frightened of coming back."

"Families are frightening. They mean too much. You look tired, daughter. You need rest."

"I am," I said. "I'm going to go upstairs now and get some sleep."

I slept for twelve hours straight. It was like a tight hat coming off my head. And later, when night was falling and the prawns and the chickens were sending out tantalizing messages from the kitchen, forty-three members of the Thekkeden family played cricket on the lawn behind the house. I could hear Raffie's excited voice breaking through the hubble-bubble of sound. The game lasted until it was too dark to see, and then the batsmen played with Davy lamps on their heads, with fireflies flitting in the dark, shouts and laughter. Appan (two whiskies to the wind) was an erratic fielder, his Tibetan mastiff barking and leaping for stray balls. Mariamma ran stoutly between the trees. Anto bowled athletically, doing his Sunil Gavaskar impersonation. I stayed on the dark fringes of the fielding, where the lawn dissolved into darkening trees, and beyond I saw birds skimming down across the silver backwater.

When it got too dark to play, Amma, proud and mocking, stood framed in light on the veranda watching us. She rang the bell.

"Dinner everyone. Don't let it get cold!"

After dinner, the youngest cousins got into their nightclothes and lay in piles on charpoys on the veranda. Boxes of old cinema film were unpacked. Mariamma, bossy older sister, told Anto to help put the screen up: "Not there! There, higher! No, lower than that." It was time, she said, in a bad attempt at a Barnum and Bailey accent, for "The Thekkeden Motion Picture Showee."

The film began with a few babies toddling drunkenly onto the screen, herded by a jolly-looking mother, who waved at the camera.

"That's me," shouted Ponnamma, who had drunk more than her fair share of ginger wine and whom I had avoided all day. "What a minx I was!"

Then Appan, mustached and dapper in his plus fours, and Amma, his radiant bride, on a honeymoon holiday in Madras.

"Don't you dare go to sleep." Mariamma shook Raffie awake. "Wait for your Daddy."

Raffie's hair was still damp from his bath. He put my arm around him.

Anto, who'd disappeared into the kitchen for drinks, came back and sat beside me. He was barefoot and carrying a bowl of golden banana chips. He handed me a weak whisky and soda.

A few seconds later, a jerky black-and-white image of him bloomed into life on the screen. He was about fifteen, messing around and doing pretend cricket shots for the camera. In the next shot he was wearing the same tweed jacket I'd met him in, the one with leather patches on the elbows, and he looked so young and sweet and skinny and undefended, my heart leapt with sorrow for him. Behind him was the ocean liner that would shortly take him away from all this, and the whole of the wild sea ahead.

There were wolf whistles, catcalls. Ponnamma pinched him. "Handsome devil!"

"Spiffing suit, what, Uncle Anto?" Thaddeus, one of the younger cousins, said. "The Playboy of the Western World."

I was thinking as I joined in the laughter what a lot he had made of his life: how resilient he'd been, and brave. I felt the blaze of the new baby inside me. I'd started to talk to it now, to feel sure of its heart beating. I made up my mind to tell Amma tomorrow, which of course meant everyone—assuming Mariamma hadn't already. "In the strictest confidence of course!"

Appan, staring at the screen, groaned and sank down in his chair. Amma patted his hand. And then, to my surprise, there was me. I hadn't been aware of being filmed at the time. Me in the blue dress, smiling and shaking Amma's hand, looking scared out of my wits, as well I might, faced with the great roiling mass of contradictions, horrors, and wonders ahead.

After the film, Mariamma and I helped to push sleepy children upstairs. One of the toddlers was spark out, draped like a shawl over Mariamma's shoulder. Raffie said he wanted to sleep in the cousins' room; otherwise he would dream about black spiders.

It was late by the time we'd left the cousins in a murmuring bundle in the spare room. Anto said, "Let's go for a walk in the garden."

We went down the steps towards the summerhouse and sat on a bench overlooking the water. The air was warm on my face. It was spicy and sweet from the flowers. I told him about my conversation with Appan, and as I watched his face change and grow hopeful as he absorbed the news, I felt the pure flame of my love for him again.

The water, lightly touched with gold from an almost full moon, grew black and crinkly towards the distant shore. From the temple across the lake, where Onam was in full swing, we could hear the pulsing of drums, the sound echoed and added to in villages for miles around. The priests had lit a bonfire. Its flames made a million sparks in the sky, in all-night celebration for the crops that didn't fail.

ACKNOWLEDGMENTS

First I must thank Rema Tharakan for her constant stream of emails and her advice and encouragement with this book. Rema and her husband, Anthony, were fantastic hosts and guides during my research trip to Kerala.

Midwife Rachel Walker and her obstetrician husband, Dr. David Walker, gave generous guidance on midwifery matters, as did Jane Ash, Dr. Suhas Choudhari, Joan Liburn, and Gabrielle Allen from Guys and St. Thomas' Charity. Any mistakes are mine.

I'm indebted to numerous books on Indian history, Nasrani customs and climate, particularly Diane Smith's fascinating, *Birthing with Dignity*, and Alexander Frater's *Chasing the Monsoon*. Emma Jolly, from Genealogic, dug out some fascinating facts.

Special thanks to Delia and Caroline for their inspiration and support and for my book club friends for making me laugh and opening my eyes to a wide range of books.

Many thanks to my editor, Heather Lazare, for all her help and to Clare Alexander for being simply the best.

Finally, more thanks than I can express to Richard for his advice, his generosity, and good humor during many readings of this book.

MONSOON SUMMER

Julia Gregson

This reading group guide for *Monsoon Summer* includes an introduction, discussion questions, and a Q&A with author Julia Gregson. The suggested questions are intended to help your reading group find new and interesting angles and topics for your discussion. We hope that these ideas will enrich your conversation and increase your enjoyment of the book.

INTRODUCTION

Nurse and midwife Kit Smallwood survived the Blitz in London only to find herself at loose ends after the war ended. Thrown together on a project with the captivating Anto Thekkeden, she follows her heart . . . straight into marriage. Before she knows it, she's on a ship for India to meet her husband's family and, later, to a job educating Indian midwives.

Once in the stunningly beautiful, oppressively hot, and bewilderingly confusing homeland of her husband, Kit takes up her work, much to the chagrin of the Thekkeden family. Fulfilled by her work, but uncertain of her place in society, Kit must overcome the challenges posed by her decision. When disaster strikes the Moonstone Maternity Home not once, but twice, even Kit's faith in herself is tested. It's only by going back—into her family history, into her in-laws' past, into her own failings—that Kit can move forward.

TOPICS & QUESTIONS FOR DISCUSSION

1. When *Monsoon Summer* opens, we're given a portrait of a crumbling British estate, Wickam Farm. In Part Two, we are introduced to Mangalath, Anto's family home. What do the descriptions of the decorative lions at each place tell us about the family fortunes involved? At Wickam Farm, "The crunchy fur of a lion skin beneath our feet. The severed heads of foxes, deer, a tiger, staring coldly down," and at Mangalath, "At the end of the drive, two large gold lions glowered from gateposts, their paws resting on shields." How does each estate mean "home" to the characters?

2. Although *Monsoon Summer* begins in the aftermath of World War II, the political strife in India is of a much different nature. Why do you think Julia Gregson chose to open the novel in the more familiar setting? Did you learn anything about World War II from the book? What about Indian Independence?

3. Kit and Anto's marriage is not always as idyllic as the lovers imagined in bed at Wickam Farm. At what points were you most worried about the state of Kit and Anto's marriage? When did you feel most secure? Do you think that your opinion differed from that of the characters, if you were to ask them?

4. The book explores the many midwifery superstitions and traditions local midwives taught Kit. When the midwives and the staff at the Moonstone are discussing how to ease labor, Kartyani describes how she "would open all her cupboards and doors" to open things up for the mother. What other old wives' tales have you heard about easing childbirth pains or ensuring a healthy baby, perhaps handed down from mother to mother?

5. Traditional garb is very important to the characters in *Monsoon Summer*. Reflect on the different ways traditional Indian dress is used: to signify home to Anto, as welcoming by Mariamma, a return to wifeliness when Kit is released from prison. Why do you think dress is so symbolic, and do you think that Western modes of dress carry the same significance to people in Europe and America?

6. In the last pages of the novel, we find out a secret that Glory has been carrying about her own past. How did this revelation change your perception of her, if it did? How do you think that experience shaped who she became as a mother, as an Indian woman, as a woman living in the U.K.?

7. The birth of Mrs. Nair's baby gives Kit back the confidence she'd lost during the war with the baby in the tin helmet. Have you ever lost the ability to perform a task out of nerves, even briefly? What helped you gain back the confidence to perform the task again?

8. In India's caste system, to be a midwife is considered to be a lowly job, an unclean profession. How was Kit prepared or unprepared to confront prejudice about her job in India? Do you think you'd have continued to do the work after finding out the truth, or would you have given up the job for the sake of family harmony?

9. Anto's intended, Vidya, never appears in person, so Kit never meets her. Did you feel anything for her, the daughter of a prominent Indian family, who'd expected her marriage to already be taken care of? What would you feel about Kit if you were in Vidya's shoes? How does Kit seem to feel about her?

10. Why do you think that Julia Gregson chose to make the Thekkedens a Catholic family in India? How does the Hindu influence of the region play out with their family's religion? Does religion have any place in Kit and Anto's home?

11. *Monsoon Summer* begins one year after India has achieved Independence from British colonial control. Did *Monsoon Summer*

change your ideas about post-colonial India ? Were the relations between British and Indian characters what you expected of the time period? How were they different? How do you think the story would have been different if it had been set before Independence?

12. Kit is physically assaulted in India. Why do you think Kit chose not to tell her husband about the assault in the garden? Do you agree with her decision not to? Or would you have told him and enlisted his help? How do you think the story of how she lost her virginity, and her mother's reaction, might have influenced her?

13. Anto and Kit have one of the most intense experiences of their married lives during Kit's first monsoon. What significance does the coming of the monsoon rain have for Kit? For Anto? For you, as a reader? Why do you think Julia Gregson chose to name the book after the rain?

14. Between her father's British heritage and her mother's origin and insecurities, Kit herself contains a lot of British-Indian history within her person. How does Kit's experience of India differ from her mother's? How do you think Kit's children, also of mixed heritage like their maternal grandmother, will experience racial tensions in India as they grow up?

15. Motherhood is explored across generations and cultures in *Monsoon Summer*. Kit seems to accept as fact Glory's need to steal small items from her employers. Why do you think keeping up appearances is so important to Kit's mother? How does motherhood get played out by the various characters in the novel: Kit, Glory, Amma, Mariamma. Which of these representations of motherhood felt most authentic to you? Why?

READ MORE FROM JULIA GREGSON

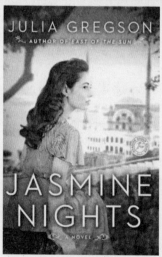